Will Love

Conquer All?

Book 1 of the
Mountains and Valleys of Life

Risel Buhler

Copyright © 2014 by Risel Buhler
First Edition – July 2014

ISBN
978-1-4602-4236-0 (Hardcover)
978-1-4602-4237-7 (Paperback)
978-1-4602-4241-4 (eBook)

All rights reserved.

No part of this publication may be reproduced in any form, or by any means, electronic or mechanical, including photocopying, recording, or any information browsing, storage, or retrieval system, without permission in writing from the publisher.

Produced by:

FriesenPress
Suite 300 – 852 Fort Street
Victoria, BC, Canada V8W 1H8

www.friesenpress.com

Distributed to the trade by The Ingram Book Company

The *Mountains and Valleys of Life* series

Book 1 - Will Love Conquer All?
Book 2 - Better Now than Never

I dedicate my books in memory of my husband. If it weren't for his love and encouragement, I would not have written my books.

When this picture was taken I told him this is where I would start my first book. Our time together was too short but I thank God for the time we did have.

Chapter 1

THE OCEAN WAS RELATIVELY CALM and yet there was a continuous roar. Dawn couldn't imagine what it might be like standing here during a storm. She observed wave upon wave splash up against a huge rock that jutted out of the ocean. Even thought the day was reasonable warm, Dawn rubbed her arms to rid herself of the chill that permeated her body. She stood staring at the beautiful sea green color of the ocean until a wave washed over her feet. As the water retreated it left behind a variety of shell. Some were complete while others were shattered, just like her life. As the ocean lapped at her feet, she bent down and picked up several of the shells. She was amazed at the beauty of them. Then as the sea gulls screamed up above, she tossed the shell back into the ocean.

Dawn continued walking along the beach, letting the sand squish through her toes, before returning to sit on one of many logs that lay along the edge of the shore. She wiped the sand from her feet before slipping on her shoes. She then watched the man that was allegedly her husband, as he stood staring blankly out to sea. Dawn absorbed the warmth of the sun, while trying to rid her of the chill of loneliness that continued to engulf her, ever since leaving the hospital. It was like she was dropped from another planet into a total foreign place.

The doctor had told her that she had been in an accident. She had apparently had a severe concussion and been unconscious for days. She was assured that her memory would return, but as of yet, she could not remember the accident, her family, or who she was. She had been shown pictures and documents, which she reluctantly accepted as fact that Bill Spencer was her husband and that they had a son and daughter.

Dawn quickly cupped her hands around her head, as a sharp pain shot through her brain. She was thankful that the pains lasted only for a few seconds, but they usually left her with a slight headache. She gently touched the gash on the side of her head, where the stitches had been, a couple of weeks prior. Her hair was bristly around the wound as they began to grow back. She was grateful for her long hair, which for most part covered the scar.

Dawn jumped up quickly, when Bill unexpectedly laid his hand on her shoulder.

"Are you all right?" He asked, grabbing her arm to prevent her from falling between the logs, which she had her feet resting on.

For a second her vision blurred and she gave her head a quick shake to get her eyes to focus, before answering. "Y-yes thank you, I must have just gotten a bit too much sun." She said slowly, not wanting to let on what was happening in her head.

When she looked up their eyes met, his eyes were as blue as the sky, yet there was a sadness there that even his smile did not erase. She knew it was because of her. Dawn quickly turned away so he could not see the tears that filled her eyes. Bill was a good-looking man, with just a touch of gray at his temples. He was 45 years old, and stood 5 ft.11 inches and weighted about 190 lb. He had broad shoulders with a muscular body and yet for a man his size, there was a gentleness about him.

Dawn held onto Bill's arm, as he assisted her through the maze of logs. Why couldn't she remember? The doctor's words rang in her ears. *"Just give it time and your memory should return."* How long yet? How could she have forgotten a man like Bill? Were they really happy together? Why did he seem like a stranger, when they had been married for over 20 years? Her mind was full of questions.

Will Love Conquer All?

Bill gently put his arm around her, as they walked up the path, to the parking lot. "Would you like to go into Tofino for a coffee and something to eat?" Bill asked.

"That sounds good to me." Dawn replied. She had a feeling of contentment and safety, every time Bill had his arm around her.

"Are you glad that your doctor suggested we take a holiday?" Bill asked as he turned the key in the ignition.

Dawn looked around at the scenery before answering. "Yes, and I am glad you chose this place." "It is so peaceful." Then after laying her hand on his, she added. "I couldn't ask for better company either." Bill just acknowledged her comment with a smile.

Tofino is a small town located on the west central part of Vancouver Island.

It's a place where many tourists come to spend time at the beach or go whale watching.

When they arrived, Bill found a place to park near the docks. He then went around the car to open the door for her. "There is a gift store over there," Bill said pointing to it. Through the window, Dawn could see several pieces of native art work. Would you like to go in to look around?" He asked. "You always tried to drag me into those places, or I would go have a coffee while you would check them out." He said squeezing her hand.

We must have been happy together, Dawn thought as they walked towards the store. Once inside Dawn was attracted to a particular piece of native art. "I've seen this piece before." She said, examining one of the soap stone sculptures.

Bill looked at her with hopes that perhaps her memory was starting to return, so their life could go back to the way it was before the accident.

After spending some time in the store, Dawn turned to Bill. He was obviously getting bored. She smiles up at him saying. "Let's go get your coffee. We don't want you going into caffeine withdrawal."

"Good idea." Bill said glad to get out of there. They walked over to the near by cafe, where Bill ordered them each a coffee and muffin, which they took to one of the outside tables. Here they sat in silence eating, while watching the boats and floatplanes come and go.

"Wouldn't it be nice," Dawn said slowly as if thinking aloud. "To live along the ocean." "Well back a bit, a--and up a bit where the water couldn't get at us." She said dreamily. "Oh! But then." She said suddenly, looking at Bill. "You don't like to be near the water, do you?"

Bill looked at Dawn at which point she realized, this was the second time she had referred to the past. "It will come back." Bill said at her questioning glance. "I'm sure of it." He added, before taking another sip of his coffee.

Dawn looked away suddenly. Was that tears she saw in his eyes? Dawn felt a sudden stab in her heart. She couldn't stand to see him hurting. I must have loved him a lot to have feelings like this, she thought to herself.

Bill and Dawn watched the people get off and on the boats. They came to the conclusion, that many of these people were probably living along the shore and this was how they came to do there shopping. When their coffee cups were empty, Dawn got them refilled. They discussed the idea of going whale watching, but then mutually decided against it. Instead they would start back and stay the night at Port Alberni.

When they passed Long Beach, Dawn looked out across the ocean. There was something about it that was calming and yet frightening. Much like she felt inside. They drove in silence, as the road twisted and turned around the edge of lakes and up and down the sides of the mountain. Dawn began to feel slightly carsick. She opened the window for a bit of fresh air. Bill looked at her and then began to slow down. He patted her hand, acknowledging that he understood her situation. He remembered how on there last trip through here, she told him to slow down or she was going to be sick.

When arriving at Port Alberni, they immediately looked for a motel. These were the times Dawn dreaded the most. She knew Bill was her husband, but he still felt like a stranger although she was beginning to really like him. Bill always made sure they had two beds in the room. He never tried to force himself on her, other than giving her an occasional kiss on the forehead.

"We will wait until you are ready." He had told her. But she knew he had hoped for their love to be complete again.

Most places were booked as it was still tourist season, but they did find one Motel that had one room available. It had a kitchenette, with a couch and television in the first room. The bathroom was small, with the usual white towels. Near the sink was a basket, that held an array of shampoos and lotions nestled in a white washcloth. When Dawn entered the bedroom, she was shocked to see only one double bed. When Bill touched her shoulder to explain, he felt her muscles tense and saw the color drained from her face.

"I did not plan this to happen." Bill said sharply. "I'll sleep on the couch."

Bill was hurt and angry. It was not like he picked this place intentionally. However, he did long to hold her and yet he knew he had to give her all the time she needed. *Why did this have to happen?* He was frustrated. Even with Dawn near, he still felt so alone. They used to discuss everything they did. He wondered if their lives would ever be the same again. "I'll go get our suitcases." Bill snapped. Dawn stood there feeling numb, as she watched him go to the car.

She knew how patient Bill had been with her and could only imagine how difficult it was for him. She felt an ache in her heart and wondered why he affected her like this?

Bill handed Dawn her suitcase when he returned , at which time she excused herself to go have a shower. Right now she needed to be alone and have a place where she could go to cry and no one would see her.

The water felt good as she let it wash over her. There were several bruises still visible on her body, from the accident, but they were slowly beginning to fade. Dawn covered her eyes with her hands as she began to cry. No one understood how afraid and lonely she felt. There were times she would like to have just run away and hide from life itself. Slowly Dawn began to pull herself together. Feeling sorry for herself was not going to help. Besides she wasn't the only one hurting. Dawn came to the conclusion that she had to try harder. She would give in to Bill's needs, if he asked her to. After all, she could not refute the fact that she enjoyed the time Bill and her spent together. She began to think of how safe and good it felt to be near him.

When she finally came out of the bathroom she felt drained but a bit more refreshed.

"I thought you might have drowned in there." Bill said sternly.

"I'm sorry I took so long." Dawn said, as Bill brushed past her on his way to the bathroom. Dawn sat on the edge of the bed, trying to over come the strangeness of being Bill's wife. Perhaps tonight they could sleep in the same bed. After all it wasn't fair to him to have to sleep on the couch. She was also afraid that if this continued she could lose him and something told her she didn't want that. Dawn went to the other room, where a small coffee maker sat on the table. She picked up one of the packages of coffee and after opening it placed it into the coffee maker then added the water. She then sat on the couch staring blankly at the television. She looked up when Bill came out of the bathroom.

"Bill," Dawn said slowly. "Come sit with me, I think we should talk."

"About what?" Bill said abruptly.

"Please." Dawn said getting up and taking his hand to lead him to the couch.

Bill followed, but hesitated from sitting down. He was finding it harder to be close to her, without taking her in his arms. Anger seemed to be his way of protecting himself from the hurt he felt.

Dawn put her hands on Bill's bare shoulders. Then putting

slight pressure on them, indicating that he should sit down. Their eyes met briefly. When he felt her hands on him, it took all his resistance to not grab and kiss her as he used to do. When he sat down, she sat next to him.

Dawn began slowly. "I- I don't know how to explain to you how I feel Bill." "For some reason, I feel that we were deeply in love." It was then, that Dawn saw Bill clinch his teeth.

"We were," Bill said gruffly, before returning to his silence. Right now he could not look at her.

Dawn hesitated, feeling extremely nervous. She looked down fidgeting nervously with the rings on her hand.

Bill waited, wondering what she was about to say next.

"I still can't remember anything." She said frustrated. "But it's a feeling I have with in me, when you touch me. I don't want to lose you." She said now looking into his blue eyes. "I don't want you to sleep on the couch, it's not fair to you. After all we are married---may- maybe I should try to act like it."

Bill took Dawn's hand and kissed it. Then slowly he put his arm around her, drawing her against him. For a moment they sat looking deep into each other's eyes. He wrapped his arms around Dawn, kissing her hard on the lips. Dawn's first reaction was to resist, but she soon relaxed, and began to return his affection. She clung to him never wanting this to end. After Bill slowly released her, Dawn laid her head on his bare shoulder. Bill kissed her on the forehead, and then let his arm linger around her, while they sat silently watching television. Dawn again felt engulfed in the safety of his arms. It was as if nothing could harm her there.

For the first time since the accident, Bill's hope was renewed. Dawn would love him again and truly, everything would be all right. He would do everything he possible could, to get back to normality, but it was extremely difficult to be patient.

Dawn got them each a coffee, then returned to Bill's side. Even though she enjoying being near him, she still felt uneasy about sleeping next to him. Dawn decided to go to bed while

Bill finished watching the news.

She excused herself and went into the bedroom where she knelt by the bed. God had been faithful. Somehow, even though see never remembered her family, God still remained a vital part of her life. She thanked God for never abandoning her and pleaded for him to restore her memory. She asked God for help to once again be a wife to Bill and Mother to their children. Dawn then took off her housecoat and slipped under the covers, before turning onto her right side to face the wall. She closed her eyes, still fearful of facing Bill, when he came to bed.

Bill looked at her when he came into the room, at which time her breathing became shallow, as if it would help her to hide. Bill went to the other side of the bed, and took off his trousers. He knelt beside the bed, asking God to give him patients with his wife, and for God to show him how to help Dawn to regain her memory. He needed her more then he realized and so did their children. When Bill slipped under the covers, he laid on his back. He placed his hands under his head, staring up at the ceiling, wanting desperately to hold his wife.

Dawn felt rather uncomfortable as she felt Bill's elbow close to her head. She could feel the heat radiate from his body. Why did she feel like she was doing something wrong? After all the man that lay next to her was her husband. It was as if she was committing adultery.

Dawn didn't know how long she lay there, but soon she heard Bill's breathing change. Once she felt that he was asleep, she let herself drifted off into a light sleep. She was suddenly awakened when Bill turned and placed his arm around her waist. Her muscles became tensed at his touch. Then slowly she relaxed. She felt so comfortable and safe in his arms that she slowly snuggled up against him. Dawn had to admit that she liked laying here like this. Then as Bill slipped his other arm under Dawn's pillow, she went back to sleep.

***

Dawn awoke the next morning to the smell of coffee. Did Bill know what she had done last night? Why did she feel like a teenager that had done something wrong?

"Good morning sleepy head." Bill said cheerfully, when Dawn came into the other room. "Did you have a good sleep?" He asked, kissing her on the forehead. "How about a cup of coffee before we pack up? Then we can go for a good hearty breakfast." Bill said unusually cheerfully.

"Your sure in a good mood this morning," Dawn said. Bill just smiled and winked at her. Dawn blushed and looked away. Did he know that she had snuggled up to him last night? Just the thought of it made her embarrassed.

After breakfast they left Port Alberni, driving again in silence until they came to a park along the side of the road. They had past it on their way to Tofino, but decided to stop on their way back.

"Do you feel up to taking a walk?" Bill asked, looking for a parking spot.

"It would be nice to get some exercise," Dawn said. After getting out of the car, she stood in amazement staring at the massive size of the trees. They were beautiful. The air was so nice and fresh. Bill and Dawn began to walk hand in hand along the trail. A few drops of water were still filtering through the branches, from the evening shower. They stopped to read every informational sign along the trail. Then as they arrived at a small cool clear stream, Dawn turned to Bill.

"Wouldn't it be nice to have a place like this? Just to get away from everything once and a while," Dawn said.

"You wouldn't see much sun in here, with these huge tree." Bill told her. They continued on with their walk, only to find themselves right back to the same spot they had been before.

"I can see how one could get lost in the bush." Dawn said. After that, they were more careful to follow the route signs. They continued to walk hand in hand enjoying God's beautiful creation and thankful that there were places that man had not yet destroyed.

Time past much to quickly and soon they were back to where they started. Once back on the road, neither one of them spoke for several minutes. They were both deep in their own thoughts, when Bill suddenly said.

"Dawn, tonight I have something special in mind for us to do."

Dawn glanced at Bill, who looked much happier today, which intern made her feel better. "Are you going to tell me what you have planned?" Dawn asked. But Bill did not elaborate.

"You will just have to wait," Bill said smiling.

They drove on in silence until they reached Victoria. Bill first found a motel and booked a room for the night. Dawn waited in the car, wondering what Bill was up to. They spent the rest of the day wandering through museums and a variety of shops, before going to a very nice restaurant for supper. When they finished eating, Bill kept looking at his watch as if he had an appointment to keep. Then when he decided the time was right, he paid for their meal and lead Dawn back to the car. Bill drove off seemingly knowing exactly where he was going.

It was just getting dusk when they found a place to park near the Victoria parliament buildings. They walked hand in hand to a street where several horses with buggies stood, waiting for someone to hire them, for a tour around the area.

"Your carriage awaits." Bill said, helping Dawn into the buggy, before climbing in beside her.

The driver immediately handed them a blanket. "The night air gets cool so cover up if you like." She said, slowly guiding the horses away from the curb.

Bill took the blanket and laid it on their lap, letting it hang over their legs. When Bill put his arm around Dawn, she snuggled up to him, absorbing the warmth of his body.

"So this is what you had planned this evening." Dawn said.

Just as their buggy passed in front of parliament building, the entire circumference of the building came alive with lights. "Oh Bill," Dawn said. "Isn't it beautiful."

Will Love Conquer All?

Their driver started to go through her usual talk, telling them about the area and the history of the buildings. But at that moment, Bill and Dawn were just enjoying being with each other.

Bill leaned over and whispered to Dawn, not wanting to disturb the driver as she chatted on. "Dawn, I feel like I'm dating again. I love you so very much," he said.

Dawn tilted her head towards Bill. He kissed her gently on the lips. "I feel I love you too Bill," Dawn said.

Bill held her close as they sat in silence listening to the clip clop of the horses hooves on the pavement, while their driver continued on with the tour.

The half hour passed much to quickly. When they got out of the buggy they walked hand in hand to the railing on the edge of the sidewalk, that over looked the water. They stood watching the water lap at the sides of the ship, that sat tied up at the dock. The reflection from the lights on the parliament building glistened on the water around it. Neither Bill nor Dawn wanted this night to end. Bill turned Dawn to face him and they stood looking at each other. Bill slowly bent over and kissed her hard on the lips. Dawn eagerly returned Bill's kiss enjoying this magical moment. He slowly released her, then hand in hand walked silently, along the shore, before returning to their car.

"Thank-you Bill for a night I will always remember." Dawn said, as she placed her hand on Bill's leg while driving back to their motel.

"I hoped you would like it," he said, taking her hand in his and kissing it. When they got into their room, Dawn noticed Bill had once again made sure they had the two beds in their room.

Bill had so wanted to have her snuggle up to him again and to love her, but he was afraid it was still to soon for Dawn. He wanted her to be sure that she was ready.

"Please God." Bill prayed. "Give me patients and restore her memory."

After Dawn got ready for bed, she knelt by her bed to pray.

She then sat on her bed waiting for Bill. Dawn was thankful to God for giving her a gentle and loving husband, and that they both had God to turn to, in times of problems. If only she could be more at ease with Bill in the evenings. Dawn wished she could over come the feeling of doing something wrong, when she was in the bedroom with him. After all, she supposedly had been married to Bill for the past 22 years and they did have a family. She thought of the night before, when she snuggled up to him. She wanted that comfortable feeling again, even though it made her feel guilty, which she knew she had to overcome.

Bill was just about to crawl under the covers when Dawn said softly "Bill, why don't you come over here with me?"

Bill hesitated, remembering her body against his the night before. He very much wanting to hold her and love her. Bill walked over and sat on the edge of her bed. He took her in his arms and kissed her on the lips. "I love you very much Dawn," Bill said.

"We've had a romantic evening and I would love to lay with you, and hold and love you, but I'm afraid you may hate me in the morning. Maybe we better take it slow, but if you still feel like this tomorrow night, I may join you then." Bill said softly. Then cupping her head in his hands, he kissed her. Bill saw her flinch when he touched the wound on her head. "Are you having pains in your head again?" Bill asked suddenly, his voice now full of concern.

"N-no." Dawn said slowly. She remembered the pain she had at Long Beach, but that hadn't lasted long. Dawn was thankful that the headaches she had in the hospital, had not returned. Those made her head feel like it would burst, and at the same time made her feel very nauseous. Try as she might she could not remember her former life with this wonderful man. Bill kissed her gently on the lips then returned to his bed. They turned facing each other, then reached out and held hands. Dawn knew he was probably right, but she was still somewhat disappointed.

" I love you Bill." She whispered. "I may not remember our

former love, but I do know I love you now."

Bill squeezed her hand while he lay there looking at her.

Dawn was glad for the darkness, so Bill couldn't see her blush. She was even more positive, that he knew she had snuggled up to him, when she thought he had been sleeping. She could still feel his bare chest against her, while his strong arm held her close. She remembered his feet touching hers, which made her smile and she snuggled into her blanket and dreamily drifted into a deep sleep.

Suddenly Dawn started screaming while holding her head and crying. Bill jumped up, quickly going to her side. He tried to calm her, while asking her what was wrong. He finally just held her tight, while she wept on his shoulder for several minutes as he continued to console her.

When Dawn realized where she was, she began to calm down. She finally came to the conclusion that she had just had a bad dream, but it left her with a massive headache. The nauseous feeling also returned.

"Are you all right?" Bill asked.

Slowly and thoughtfully Dawn said. "I heard a big bang, and then a bright flash in my head. It just scared me."

Bill said nothing, but was sure it had something to do with the accident. "Do you feel better now?" Bill asked, stroking her hair.

"Yes." She said thankful for the darkness, so Bill could not see her wince from the pain in her head. She reached for a Kleenex on the nightstand. "Would you please get me a drink of water?" She asked. When Bill went for her water, Dawn quickly took a couple of her headache pills from her purse. She didn't want to burden him with her problems. Quickly she put the pills in her mouth before Bill came with the glass of water, which she gulped down, swallowing her pills.

Dawn squeezed Bill's hand, apologized for waking him. She laid her head on the pillow, but the pounding in her head only brought tears to her eyes. Dawn turned on her side, so Bill would not see her tears as she tried to bare the pain.

Bill pulled the blanket up over Dawn's shoulders, as she felt cold, when he touched her. He then sat on the side of her bed, for several minutes, before slowly crawling under the covers with Dawn. He put his arm around her, holding her close, wishing he could somehow help her.

Dawn snuggled up to him now thankful for the warmth of his body, as she was now shivering, from a chill that rippled through her body. She needed the feeling of safety right now. If only the pain in her head would subside. It was some time before Dawn drifted into an uneasy sleep. It was full of a mixture of strange dreams, and an occasional moan of pain.

Dawn awoke with Bills arm still firmly holding on to her. He released her when he realized that she was awake.

Bill did not sleep much that night, because he was worried about Dawn. He wondered if her moans were from dreams, or was she having headaches again. Bill said nothing, but just watched her every move. He was trying to see if there was any indication that she was still getting her migraine headaches. He wanted so much to help her but he wasn't sure how.

Dawn had a very restless night. Her head still ached, and she thought perhaps a hot shower might help her to relax. She also knew she had to eat something before taking another pill or her stomach would hurt as much or more than her head. Dawn let the warm water flow over her head and neck, trying to wash away the pain. But it didn't seem to help. She was thankful it wasn't quite as bad as last night. Another pill should get rid of it she thought, stepping out of the shower. But when she reached for the towel, she suddenly got extremely dizzy and almost blacked out. Dawn quickly grab onto a nearby rail. She fell back with a thud against the wall, sending her shampoo and conditioned bottles crashing to the floor. At the same time, her other hand caught her cosmetic bag sending it flying, scattering it's contents. The next thing she knew, Bill was knocking at the door asking if she was all right, but Dawn didn't answer. She

Will Love Conquer All?

was to busy shaking her head and blinked her eyes, trying to get things back in focus.

Bill suddenly kicked in the door, breaking the door trim, only to see Dawn leaning against the wall. Her complexion matched the white towel that she held in her hand. Bill grabbed her naked body and pulled her close to him. "What's wrong?" Bill demanded.

Dawn slowly regained her composure, when she felt Bill's bare chest against her. "I-I-I am fine now." She said. She was now more embarrassed then ever that he was seeing her like this. "I-I just slipped on the wet floor," she said.

Bill slowly released her looking at her body, but Dawn pushed him away from her. He noticed a few bruises still marking her body, and he suddenly realized how much weight she lost over the past two months. How he longed to take her in his arms and love her.

Dawn quickly wrapped herself in the towel, her color going from white to red as Bill let his hand brush her thighs, as he lowered his hands.

"It's all right Honey. Remember I have seen all of you before. You are beautiful." Bill said, bending down to kiss her on the neck.

Dawn firmly pushed him out the room and closed the door she wondered what was going to happen next.

She felt extremely embarrassed, and just wanted to go away and hide. Perhaps if she had something to eat, or a cup of coffee it would make her feel better. But then she thought of having to face Bill after him seeing her like this. She got dressed slowly, not wanting to look at him when she came out of the bathroom. Only he met her with a frown on his face. He was determined to find out if she was all right.

She knew he was concerned about what happened, but she was unsure whether he had believed her explanation. Bill bent down and kissed her on the forehead before going to the bathroom. Dawn gathered her things together while Bill got ready.

"I'm sorry I slept so late this morning." Dawn said apologizing, while Bill checked the bathroom door, before putting his things in his bag. "You are probably hungry, and I could use a good breakfast myself." She said, talking to over come her nervousness. Bill took their bags to the car before they walked over to the restaurant.

They ordered their breakfast then sat drinking their coffee, discussing whether they should spend another day of sight seeing in Victoria. But after Bill looked at Dawn he decided it might be best to start back to the mainland. Dawn knew she couldn't handle walking around all day, because her head was pounding again, so she was just as glad for his decision.

Dawn reached into her purse that lay on her lap under the table. She quickly took two pills from the bottle, hiding them in her hand. After a few bites of food she tried to slip them in her mouth without Bill noticing, but instead, one slipped from her hand falling onto the table. Dawn quickly picked it up and put it into her mouth then, taking a drink of water she swallowed them. She looked up at Bill, hoping that he had not noticed, but he sat looking at her with a frown on his face. Dawn knew he was angry. "Why can't you tell me the truth? Do you plan on hiding everything from me?" He demanded.

Tears filled her eyes. "It's just a slight headache." Dawn said feeling guilty for not being totally truthful, as her head ached something awful. "We were having such a wonderful time, and I didn't want you to worry about me." They ate their breakfast in silence, but Dawn was relieved when it was time to go.

She was also thankful that the wait to board the ferry was short because of the tense silence.

The last two days were so glorious, why did it have to end like this? Dawn did not like having Bill angry with her, as the tension between them seemed to make her head ache even worse. How she longed to lay her aching head on Bill's shoulder. When they were on the ferry she decided to lay back and relax, perhaps then it would go away. It was a two-hour trip and

Will Love Conquer All?

Dawn hoped she could enjoy most of it. Bill sat staring out the window, while Dawn laid her head back in her seat and closed her eyes. After a half hour the pain thankfully began to subside. Dawn felt like getting some fresh air, but when Dawn glanced over at Bill, she could tell by his face, that he was still angry with her. Dawn laid her hand on his, but he did not look at her until she started to speak.

"Let's go for a stroll out on the deck." Dawn said, standing up. Bill studied her eyes before slowly, following her outside. They both took a deep breath when they stepped out on the deck. Bill and Dawn walked to the front of the ferry, where the sun shone down on them, while the wind whipped at their clothes and hair.

"How is your headache now?" Bill asked, looking directly at her.

"It's practically gone." Dawn said turning to Bill. "I'm sorry I didn't tell you, but we were having such a good time. I didn't think it was anything to worry about."

Bill took her hand in his. "I want you to tell me when you get a headache like that again." He said firmly. "Especially since it hasn't been very long since your concussion. I don't want anything to happen to you Dawn. Do you understand?"

Dawn could see the concern in his eyes. She squeezed his hand. "I'm sorry Bill. I will tell you next time, but I really don't think it's anything to worry about," she said.

Bill kissed her on the forehead. "Just promise me you will tell me and I'll decide if I should worry or not." He said stroking her hair.

"Ok," Dawn said. "I promise." But secretly she still didn't feel that there was anything to worry about.

"When we get back," Bill said. "I think we best go see the doctor, to be sure everything is fine."

Dawn just nodded in agreement, even if she didn't feel she had to. She dislikes going to see the doctor.

But she was not about to get into an argument with Bill. He had his mind made up and she was sure she wouldn't be able to change it.

The rest of their trip on the ferry was delightful. Bill and Dawn sat on a bench, discussing the different colors in some areas of the water, as they watched several boats pass by. They sat watching the sea gulls follow along side, looking for food. To soon the announcement came across the intercom, to go to their cars. Bill took Dawn's hand as they went back inside, then back down the stairs to their car. Dawn wished this holiday would never have to come to an end. She was nervous about settling into the normal routine of wife and Mother.

Bill decided they would go as far as Kelowna and there check into a Motel. They traveled in silence wondering what life had in store for them. When they entered their motel room, Dawn was relieved to see the two beds. Bill made no move to join Dawn which hurt, as she wondered if he was still angry with her?

The next morning they got up early and had their breakfast. Before leaving the area Bill decided to stop at a fruit stand and purchased some fresh fruit. Bill was determined to get back for Dawn to have a check up. He had to be reassured that she was all right. He felt Dawn had not been telling him everything that was happening to her, so that he wouldn't worry. Until Bill had the reassurance from the doctor, he would not feel comfortable. They had come this far, and he wasn't about to lose her now! If he ignored the headaches she was having, and something happen to her, he would never forgive himself. Bill was also nervous about moving Dawn into a strange area, hoping it wouldn't hinder her from getting her memory back.

Dawn handed Bill some fruit while he drove through the mountain in silence. She was dreading going back to the hospital, afraid they would keep her in again. She wondered where Bill and her would be living, and how it would affect her family if she never regained her memory. She was just starting to adjust to Bill, but what about their children. Could she handle the times, when Bill and their children would talk about the past leaving her out, because she could not join in on their memories.

Will Love Conquer All?

Dawn felt a sadness cover her like a cloud, but when Bill suddenly placed his hand on hers, it made her once again feel the love pass from him to her through his touch.

Chapter 2

BILL AND DAWN SLEPT LATER then usual the next morning. Then after breakfast, Bill drove to the doctor's office. There he had quite a lengthy discussion with the doctor's receptionist, before she finally consented to let him talk to the doctor. Bill only talked to Doctor Rogers briefly in the hall, but it was enough for Doctor Rogers to tell his receptionist to make an appointment for him to see Dawn the next day at the hospital.

Bill had some business to attend to, so they spent the rest of the afternoon in Calgary. After supper they left the city and drove an hour north, to a place Bill wanted to show Dawn.

Dawn was nervous and sat fidgeting with her rings, while wondering what was facing her next. She knew Bill had bought a place for them to live, when she was in the hospital. They had apparently sold their place up north and had been traveling and living in their RV for the past year. But with Dawn's present situation, the doctor suggested a more stable environment, for her to recuperate.

After turning off the main road and into a driveway, Bill stopped the car and turned to face Dawn. He reached over and laid his hand on hers and gave it a squeeze. "I hope you like this place." He said nervously. "When you were in the hospital, I went for a drive to think about our future." That is when I came across that FOR SALE sign," Bill said pointing to the sign, which now had SOLD across it. "I had lots of time, so I decided to turn in. Instantly, I had a feeling that this place was right for us." Bill let go of Dawn's hand, and started to drive down the lane. He hoped he had made the right decision.

On either side of the road, there was tall wild grass, which looked very scruffy, while up ahead was a large stand of poplar and spruce trees. They drove slowly through the treed area, avoiding a deer that bounded across their path. The road then descended to the valley below. There in the distance stretching high into the sky, the sun was slowly sliding behind the Rocky Mountains. Then she saw the old country style home, sheltered on three sides by very large spruce trees. A few hundred yards to the right was a barn that was somewhat, neglected.

Bill drove up to the house and stopped the car. He sat looking out the window no longer sure he had done the right thing. "It does need some work but it was similar to what we used to talk about." He said. Bill looked at Dawn hoping for some sign of approval. "I'm sorry I didn't discuss this with you before I bought it. We've always talked things over with each other before doing things like this, but it just felt right." Bill said nervously, as he got out of the car then walked around and open the door for Dawn. They walked slowly towards the house. Bill watched Dawn. He was looking for some sign that she approved of his decision. He followed her, as she walked slowly around the house.

There was a porch that wrapped around two and a half sides of the house. Dawn walked along the porch then stopped on the west side. Here two wicker chairs sat, still in good shape but in need of some white paint. The railing around the porch needed a few new boards, but other wise it was not too bad. At the back of the house there was an opening in the railing. Dawn walked over to it then stepped down onto a wood walkway that crossed the lawn, to the outhouse nestled in the spruce trees. The lawn around the house had apparently not been looked after for some time.

Dawn took a deep breath, inhaling the aroma coming from the spruce trees. "It definitely needed some work but it does have a lot of potential." Dawn said thoughtfully. "It is so peaceful and quiet out here she said watching as squirrel scurried across her path. Bill walked over to Dawn and gave her a hug "I hoped you would like it. Apparently the elderly couple that lived here had passed on. Their children decided to sell this quarter section of land to settle the estate. Let's go have a look at the inside." Bill said taking Dawn's hand, as they walked around to the front door.

Bill unlocked the door then lead Dawn into a large country kitchen, which was now full of ladders and tools. The remodeling process was already under way. The linoleum on the floor was well worn from years of use. The cupboards were the old style that went up to the ceiling and were in desperate need of paint. There was one window near the front door facing north, with a row of old style windows, which looked out towards the west. Dawn walked over to the west windows and noticed a metal gate almost hidden by weeds and grass at the edge of the Spruce trees.

It probably used to go to the barnyard, she thought to herself. It had obviously not been used for several years.

Dawn walked through the door that led to the living room. There was a window facing west, and two facing the south. There was a door leading out onto the back porch, the other lead into the master bedroom. The polished hardwood floor in the living room, extended on into the bedroom. The living room floor was in excellent shape. Just as if this room had been hardly used.

In the bedroom, there was a well-worn rug with several inches of hardwood flooring around it. The window faced east in this room, with a large walk in closet off to the left.

Bill took Dawn's hand and led her back through the kitchen. There to the right of the front door, he led her through an archway. Immediately to the right was a stairway that went upstairs, while straight ahead was a combination bathroom and utility room.

Will Love Conquer All?

Bill looked around the room. Dawn could hear the excitement in his voice, when he spoke. "With a bit of remodeling and perhaps a few antique fixtures, I thought we could make a proper bathroom out of this. Over by the stairway, we could make a separate room for the washer and dryer. I know it needs work, but it has so much potential. Come lets go up stairs." Bill said excitedly. He then led her back to the stairs. Dawn went up first. The steps were no longer flat, but were now indented from years of continuous wear. When Dawn got to the top she stepped into a large bedroom with two windows facing west and one window facing north. Dawn walked over to a west window and looked out. There through the spruce trees, Dawn saw the most beautiful sunset she had ever seen. The sky was ablaze with a yellow, pink and gray, and blue as the sun slowly slid behind the Mountains.

Dawn excitedly turned to look at Bill. "Can we use this room for the master bedroom?" She pleaded.

Bill laughed. He was glad to see that Dawn finally saw what he had, in this old house. "Yes," Bill said. "If that is what you want, this will be our bedroom." It was the first time Dawn had said anything since they entered the house. He was a bit concerned at her lack of reaction, but not any more.

"It needs some tender loving care. But it would be fun and a challenge to fix it up and perhaps find a few antique furnishings." Dawn said.

"We'll stay in town for a while. But we can't forget about your doctor's appointment in Calgary tomorrow afternoon. If you feel up to it, first thing in the morning, we should pick out some new floor covering for the kitchen and bedrooms."

"The painters and carpet layers can get at it this week, if we can decide on what we want," Bill said.

Dawn looked around the room. "What if we paint all the walls off white with natural wood trimmings? Then if we decide later to add a splash of color, we can put up some wall paper borders." Dawn said, turning to see what Bill's reaction was.

Bill smiled and nodded in agreement. Dawn walked through the house one more time. This time, she began to imagine all the things they could add or change to make it a real cozy country home.

"Can we plan a few special changes in the bathroom to make it more appealing?" Dawn asked.

"If that's what you want we will see what we can do." Bill said.

Dawn flung her arms around Bill's neck. "You are the best!" She said.

"I was afraid at that you didn't approve, because you were so quiet." Bill said wrapping his arms around her.

Dawn looked at Bill. "No it's not that. I-well, it's just that it feels like maybe I have been here before?" She said thoughtfully.

Bill smiled releasing his hold on her. "Maybe this is the place of our dreams, Only the stream you used to talk about, you may have to just pretend there is one."

"Other than in the spring, there may be some run off from the hill." Bill said giving Dawn's hand a squeeze.

After Dawn finished exploring the house, Bill locked the door behind them. They walked around outside for a while but it was now getting dark.

They looked up at the hill covered with a mixture of poplar and spruce trees. Bill told Dawn what he liked, was how well the building site was sheltered from the north wind.

They walked over to the metal gate that Dawn had seen from the kitchen window. Bill pulled out the grass and weeds, so he could open the gate. The old worn path was still visible through the high grass that led to a barn. Dawn looked towards the southwest, where the mountains loomed high in the distance. Why couldn't she get over the feeling of been here before? It must be as Bill said. They had apparently talked about a place like this, so it may be just hidden somewhere in her subconscious.

Dawn turned her attention back to Bill. "Maybe, if the barn isn't to bad, I could make a work shop out of it. Later on, perhaps we could get a few cows and even a horse or two. What do you think about that?" He asked looking at Dawn.

"That's up to you." Dawn said, clinging to Bill's arm affectionately, as they wandered around the yard. Dawn listened to Bill, talk about things he would like to do here in the future. It was plain to see his excitement. She was happy for him especially after all he must have gone through since her accident.

Bill looked at Dawn, "I'm sorry, you must be getting tired and tomorrow will be a long day. I don't want you getting another headache." He said putting his arm around her.

Dawn smiled as she looked into Bill's eyes. "I'm fine, really I am. It's just nice to see you so happy."

When Bill took her in his arms and kissed her, she put her arms around his neck and clung to him, returning his embrace. Bill slowly released her. "When we move in here, there is a lady in town, who will come to help you do what ever you need done." Bill said cupping Dawn's face in his hands as he looked deep into her eyes. "I hope we can make this our dream home." He added.

"I'm sure it will be, it is a great place. I only wish I could remember what we had before. It must be very frustrating for you to---." Dawn said only to be cut short by Bill.

"I am confident that it will be as it was again. Love conquers all, remember that." He said putting his arm around her, as they began to walk back to the car.

Neither one of them spoke on the way back to town they. They stop briefly to purchased a few groceries before going to their motel.

Bill had made prior arrangements to stay at the motel in town while their house was being renovated. Their room was similar to the one they stayed in at Port Alberni, with the kitchenette, couch, television and a very small table with two chairs. The only difference was that this one had two beds. Bill put the groceries in the cupboard, while Dawn made some coffee.

"It's been a long day, we better get to bed early." Bill said, putting the milk into the small refrigerator. Dawn was looking very tired and Bill had already begun to recognize the warning

Book 1 of the **Mountains and Valleys of Life**

signs that lead up to her headaches.

Dawn picked up her suitcase and placed it on her bed. "I'm going to have a shower, by then the coffee should be ready." She said. Everyday to Dawn was new. No old memories, only things that may be real or perhaps a dream. She had no way of telling the difference from a dream or reality.

Dawn took what she needed into the bathroom. After getting undressed she turned on the shower. She stepped into the tub and let the water run over her head and down her body, she suddenly felt very tired. Dawn grabbed for her shampoo bottle just as a sharp pain shot through her head. She instantly dropped the bottle into the tub and grabbed her head, shouting "Ouch!!" Much louder than she had realized. In a few seconds the pain past, leaving only a dull ache, which she hoped would also leave.

"Are you all right?" Bill called suddenly from the other side of the door.

"I'm fine." Dawn replied, holding her head. "I just dropped the shampoo bottle on my toe." She wasn't being totally untruthful, as the shampoo bottle did land on her toe. She picked it up and began to wash her hair. She decided to have a quick shower instead of lingering under the water as she had first planned. She did not want Bill coming to her rescue again. After she brushed her teeth, she wrapped the towel around her hair and slipped into her nightgown and housecoat. She was happy to feel somewhat refreshed. Dawn decided to make coffee before brushing her hair.

Bill filled two cups with coffee when, she came into the room. He looked directly into her eyes when he handed it to her. "It's hot, so be careful." He said.

"Thanks." Dawn said looking away. If he knew she was not totally truthful with him, he would be extremely angry with her. Besides the pain was gone now so why should she worry him.

They sat in silence watching television, while enjoying their coffee. When Dawn emptied her cup, she took it to the sink and washed and dried it, before placing it back into the cupboard.

"I think I'll call it a day." Dawn said removing the towel from her head to let her blonde hair fall down around her shoulders.

Bill watched her leave the room. His body ached thinking about the times he held and loved her. Oh, if she only knew how much he wanted to make love to her.

Bill jumped to his feet and shut off the TV. He decided to take a shower to help take his mind away from what he was thinking. He would wait until they got into their own home, at which time their love for each other would over come all barriers.

Dawn was just getting into her bed after saying her prayers, when Bill came out of the bathroom. She looked at his broad shoulders and muscular arms, as he knelt down by his bed to pray. Neither one had made a move to sleep together, since that night in Victoria. Part of Dawn ached to be held like he had done before. Then there was a part of her that still felt very uneasy. She was afraid that Bill would not feel the same as she did, because she could not remember what they had before. Dawn could feel herself blush when she thought of him seeing her naked in the bathroom. She remembered his hand gently caressing her. Love Conquers All, he had told her. She was sure, that she loved him now, and apparently the old her did too. What else mattered? She said to herself before closing her eyes, remembering how she felt, when Bill held her in his arms and that was all that mattered.

Chapter 3

The afternoon was rainy and cool when Bill and Dawn drove up to the Hospital.

They had made a quick stop that morning to try to pick out some floor coverings. There were three different ones that they both liked, but as time would not permit, they decided to make their choice later.

That morning Dawn received a phone call to come in earlier for an X- ray before she saw her doctor. She was also informed that the doctor wanted her to under go a couple of different tests, so they could rule out any unforeseeable problems. What upset her the most was when they told her that she would have to spend the night in the hospital.

Dawn felt as gloomy as the weather, when she settled down in her hospital bed.

Bill took her hand firmly in his. Then looking into her eyes, he said sternly. "I want you to be truthful with the doctor, and tell him everything that has been happening to you. Including dropping the shampoo bottle on your toe."

Dawn looked away, not wanting Bill to see the tears that began to fill her eyes.

"I mean it, no half truths," Bill said sternly. Bill's grip became gentler, as he bent over to kiss her on the forehead. "I'll be back in the morning." He said squeezing her hand gently. Bill turned and walked towards the door.

Her eyes followed him, then giving her a wave, he was gone

leaving her feeling all alone and scared. Dawn suddenly felt the same terror engulf her, as when she had realized her memory had been wiped out.

It was 7 o'clock in the evening before the doctor made his rounds. Doctor Rogers pulled a chair up beside Dawn's bed, while his nurse stood at the foot end.

The look on her Doctor's face was very stern, as he began. "I understand you are having some bad headaches yet. Bill also feels you are not totally telling him everything that has been happening either. Is that true?"

Dawn spoke slowly, her voice cracking. "It's hard enough for him. I don't feel right putting more of my problems on him."

Doctor Rogers patted her hand. "He's a strong man, he'll do fine but it may be easier on him if you were truthful."

"This way, he wonders if you are actually having a problem, or is it just his imagination. After all, it is you that we want to help, so spill it. What has truthfully been happening?" He asked.

Dawn looked down at her hands while fidgeting with her rings. "W--well." She started slowly. "Occasionally I do get sharp pains in my head. Thankfully it usually doesn't last long, but it does leave a dull ache for a while. A couple of times my vision became blurred, but that only lasted for a few seconds."

Doctor Rogers was silent for a moment before continuing. "Have you had any severe headaches, or any memory returning?"

"I have had a few headaches that may last for hours, but not as bad as the ones I had in the hospital. As for memory returning, no not really." She continued on slowly. "There were a couple of things I had said when we were at the coast, but I don't know if you would call it remembering."

"Like what?" Doctor Rogers said interrupting her.

"Well, there was an item in the gift store that I said I had liked before and I made a comment about Bill not liking water, a-and--." She said trailing off deep in thought.

"Well, what else?" The doctor asked breaking into her thoughts.

"This place that Bill bought i-it's like I've been there before." She said trying hard to remember why.

"You and Bill have never been there together?" Asked Doctor Rogers.

"No, Bill figures it may be because it is much like what we used to talk about. He bought it when he had gone for a drive, while I was in the hospital." Dawn said.

"Well." Doctor Rogers said standing up. "I can't see anything seriously wrong, but I do want to do a brain scan in the morning. Perhaps it will tell us why you are still getting these headaches. I'll talk to you before you leave tomorrow." He said, patting her hand when he got up to leaving the room.

Dawn lay back recalling the past few days, it was so relaxing and different. As Bill had said, it was just like they were dating.

Her mind drifted back to their new home. She tried desperately to remember why it was so familiar. But she soon drifted off into a restless sleep.

Dawn suddenly started screaming and crying, which got the quick attention of the nurses and her doctor. They tried talking to her, but not until she felt the prick of a needle in her arm, did she begin to relax as the drug she was given took effect. Dawn was still sobbing into her pillow when she heard Doctor Rogers calling her name. Her whole body was still trembling when she turned to look at him. The fear she felt inside now showed on her face.

"There was a flash of light in my head and then terrible pain." Dawn said. "So many strangers and people scurrying all around me." Dawn glanced around the room at the three nurses and her doctor. She continued to tremble from the chill that now ran through her body.

The doctor took her hand. "Dawn do you know where you are now and how you got here?" He asked

"Ye-s." She said slowly. "I am in the hospital, and Bill brought me in." She said, wondering if she was right.

"That's right." Her doctor confirmed. "What you experienced

was probably just flash backs from the accident. You should relax and sleep now." Doctor Rogers said.

* * *

The next thing Dawn knew, a nurse was waking her up.

"Time to wake up Mrs. Spencer, you are to go for your scan in 20 minutes."

Dawn opened her eyes sleepily. Mrs. Spencer was that her name? It seemed unfamiliar to her as every one just called her Dawn. "What time is it?" Dawn asked yawning.

"It is 6:40 so you have 20 minutes before we take you down stairs." The nurse told her.

Dawn lay there a few more minutes before slowly getting up to go to the bathroom.

She splashed water in her face to wake herself up, then brushing her teeth and hair. When she came out of the bathroom the nurse appeared from around the corner with a wheel chair.

"Time to take a ride." Her nurse told her with a smile.

Dawn slowly slipped into the chair. She tried to relax, while the nurse wheeled her into the elevator. Dawn hated the nauseating smell of hospitals. It did not take her long to go through the multitude of tests. At 8 a.m. she was again back in her room.

Dawn's breakfast tray was waiting for her when she got back. She lifted the lid to find one slice of dry toast, a boiled egg, a bowl of cream of wheat, with a glass of milk, and a cup of warm coffee. "YUK." She said, finding a small container of honey, which she spread on her toast. She cut the boiled egg in half and scooped the egg out of its shell. Sprinkling on a bit of salt and pepper from the small packets she found under her plate. Dawn did manage to eat her egg and cold hard toast. Then washed it down with a half cup of warm coffee. Dawn always said you had to be awful hungry to eat hospital food, because it was never good.

Bill arrived about 10:45 with Dr. Rogers following him. "Have you two been talking about me behind my back again?"

She asked, when they walked into the room.

"Can I leave now?" She asked anxiously.

"Don't like the accommodations, or is it the food?" Dr. Rogers said smiling.

"Both," Dawn said taking hold of Bill's arm. "Its better where he is." She said smiling up at Bill, who gently put his hand over hers.

"That's a good sign." Dr. Roger said as he continued. "We have found no new problems when, we looked over your tests. Your headaches and blurred vision should pass as your brain continues to heal."

Bill glanced suddenly at Dawn. She had never mention anything to him about blurred vision.

Doctor Rogers continued, "You must remember you had a very severe concussion. There may be some things you may never remember, but I believe most of your memory will still come back. As for yesterday evening's occurrence, it is just flash backs from the accident.

But that to should pass with time. I have a good feeling that this will sort itself out soon." He said walking towards the door.

Before leaving, he turned and said. "If you have a problem, be sure to contact me. I do recommend a few more weeks of rest and no bumps to the head and by the way, make an appointment for two weeks from now. We will see how your headaches are then." He said, after which he left the room.

Bill followed the Doctor out of the room while Dawn got dressed.

"Excuse me Doctor." Bill called.

Doctor Rogers stopped, waiting until Bill caught up to him.

"What happened last night?" Bill asked, his face now showing the stress he had been under.

Doctor Rogers put his hand on Bill's shoulder. "She'll be fine, don't worry so much, or you will be my next patient. Dawn woke up last night, crying and screaming. I had to give her a sedative to calm her down."

Will Love Conquer All?

Bill interrupted, "A bright light in her head and then a headache?"

"Something like that," Dr. Rogers replied. "It's flash backs from the accident, it should pass with time. She may have headaches for a while and the blurred vision could be pressure on a nerve, but as everything continues to heal, it should go away. She also commented about a few things she had said on your holiday, which makes me sure, that her memory will return." The doctor patted Bill's shoulder and said. "I would like to see her in a couple of weeks, be sure to make the appointment." At that, Doctor Rogers was off to his next patient.

Bill went back to Dawn's room. He sat in the chair, waiting until she was ready.

He was deep in thought when Dawn tapped him on the shoulder.

"I'm ready." Dawn said.

Bill looked up at her, the strain of everything showed in his face. He slowly stood up and took Dawn in his arms. Holding her tight against him. "I missed you," he said.

Dawn laid her head on his broad chest, putting her arms around him. "It feels so good to be in your arms. Don't ever let me go." She whispered.

"I would like that to, but I am afraid we would never be able to leave the hospital this way." Bill said teasing her as he kissed her on the forehead.

Dawn gave him a big squeeze. "Your just my big teddy bear." She said.

Bill pushed her back holding her at arms length, while looking at her.

"Did I say something wrong?" Dawn asked quickly.

"No," Bill said softly, "You said something right, someday you will understand." With that he kissed her passionately. Then as he released her and went to pick up her bag, he said, "I'm sure you could use a good meal about now? I know I could."

As they left the hospital, Dawn looked at Bill. She wondered what Bill meant by that comment.

After dinner Bill took Dawn shopping. She purchased a blouse with a charcoal color blazer and slacks, as well as a forest green dress with gold buttons that ran down the front. Dawn was looking at a plain nightgown and housecoat, when suddenly a sheer one caught her eye. It looked very elegant, with a mixture of pale pastel colors, but it was very short with a knee length housecoat to match. With the persuasion of the clerk, Dawn decided to purchase it. She would put it away until Bill and her were more comfortable with each other. Dawn concluded her shopping, by purchasing a pair of casual shoes.

With shopping completed, they drove back in silence to the small town near their new home. Both were deep in their own thoughts. Just before getting to the motel Bill finally broke the silence.

"It will be a while before we can move into the house. The painters are there now and we should decide on the floor covering tomorrow so they can put it in as soon as the painting is completed." Bill said.

"That sounds great, I bought a magazine that has a few pictures and ideas in it that we may use in our bathroom and utility room." She said excitedly.

When they reached the motel Bill and Dawn each took a few packages in, and set them on the bed.

"Show me what you bought." Bill said propping himself up on one arm, as he lay on Dawn's bed.

Dawn pulled out her new clothes and shoes. But Bill caught site of a package that got him curious. Dawn tried to divert his attention to her blouse, while at the same time moving the package containing her nightgown out of sight. Bill noticed Dawn's attempt to hide the package. "Is there nothing more exciting than that?" Bill asked with a twinkle in his eye. Bill leaned over and pick up the package that Dawn was desperately trying to hide. He then emptied its contents onto the bed. Dawn's face went crimson with embarrassment.

Bill picked up the short nightgown and held it up to Dawn while admiring it. "Will you model this for me?" He asked.

"Maybe some day." Dawn said, grabbing it from his hand, and quickly shoved it back into the bag.

"Why not now?" Bill said, turning her to face him. Bill smiled as he stuck his finger through the handle of the package, then dangling it on his finger.

"We'll keep this for our house warming." He said, dropping the package back on the bed. He reached over and pulled her down to him. He kissed her first gently, then with more passion.

Dawn returned his kisses while clinging to him, but he suddenly stopped, then looked at her for a moment.

Slowly Bill released her as he again picked up the package and handed it to Dawn. "Our house-warming gift to each other." Bill said, winking at her as he walked out of the room with out saying another word.

Dawn's knees felt weak so she quickly sat down on the edge of the bed. She felt shaken by Bill's latest kiss. She loved him very much, and yet tears filled her eyes. There were things they once had that Bill could not share with her, because of her lack of memory. *Pull yourself together*, Dawn said to herself as she got up to put her packages away.

It had been a long day so they decided to turn in early. Even though they each had their own bed, Dawn always made sure that she was in the bed before Bill.

It was to embarrassing to change in front of him. Once in bed, they would reach over to each other and briefly hold hands. It was not long before they both would drift off into a peaceful sleep.

Chapter 4

Dawn got up early the next morning, and got dressed, while Bill slept peacefully. She was tempted to give Bill a kiss on his cheek, but she didn't want to wake him. Dawn picked up her magazines and went to the couch, where she sat looking out the window. She watched the sun as it began to peek through the trees. She noticed the leaves were just beginning to show their autumn colors, which meant winter would soon be here. The thought of winter sent a chill through her. She did not like the bitter cold weather. But for today it was shaping up to be a beautiful day.

She slowly paged through her magazine, marking some pages by folding over the corners, when she saw something that she liked. This morning they were to go out to the house for one more look, before choosing a floor covering. When she heard Bill was getting up, Dawn laid her magazine down, and started to make breakfast.

"Breakfast smells good." Bill said kissing her on the cheek.

"Have a seat." Dawn said. "I decided to try my hand at cooking this morning. I didn't know if I even knew how to cook."

"You always made good meals." Bill said, smiling up at her.

Dawn put some hash brown potatoes, with bacon and eggs, on a couple of plates.

She then placed one in front of Bill and the other for herself, before putting a plate full of toast between them. When Dawn sat across from Bill, he took her hand in his then bowed his head and give thanks to God for their food.

"I hope the eggs are hard like you like them." Dawn said looking across the table at Bill.

"Everything is just right. It's good to have some of your cooking again." Bill said taking another bite. They ate in silence, then Bill said. "I think we should go out to the house first thing, so we can make up our mind on the floor coverings. We can take the samples with us, but we must decide what to do in the bathroom."

Dawn showed Bill the pictures in the magazine of a pedestal sink and old cast tub on legs. Dawn knew Bill liked a large shower, so she showed him a picture of one that would fit in fairly well with everything else.

Together they cleared off the table, and washed the dishes, all the while excitedly discussing their new home.

***

When they drove into their yard, Dawn looked at a freshly painted house, but that same feeling of being here before crept over her. The grass had now been cut around the house and trees. It was even neatly trimmed under the fence. They got out of the car and walked around the house. Dawn wondered how they had managed to do so much, in such a short time. The deck and railing had been fixed and some parts were replaced, as was the fancy trimming on the outside edge of the house. Even the outhouse had taken on a fresh coat of paint. Dawn walked over to it and opened the door. She was surprised to see that even the inside had been redone, right down to a new toilet paper holder with a fresh roll of toilet paper. Dawn suddenly started to laugh.

"What is so funny?" Bill asked, opening the door wider to see what she was laughing at. Bill put his arm around her waist. Dawn pointed to a wooden box that sat in a corner. Someone had taken the time to cut up tissue paper to make it look like the apple and orange wrappers from by gone years. While above the seat hung an old calendar, which read in large print 1952. They both stood there laughing when someone come up behind them.

"I see you like my added touch." He said. "I thought you might enjoy that."

Bill turned to face the man. "Dawn this is Joe. Joe, I would like you to meet my wife Dawn. He is our miracle worker." Bill told Dawn.

Joe held out his hand to Dawn, "Nice to meet you, but miracle worker I'm not."

Dawn shook his hand saying. " Pleased to meet you. You picked the right year for a calendar, as that is the year Bill was born. It couldn't have been easy to find a calendar in that good a shape for the year."

"I can not lie, I found it in the house," Joe said.

Bill glanced at Dawn as he closed the out house door. He was surprised that she remembered the year he was born.

"Watch the paint outside and in, because it may still be wet." Joe said, when they entered the house through the back door. The walls were all painted with a primer that now covered any patched holes and cracks that had been in the walls. The floor in the living room and bedroom had been sanded and then carefully covered as not to get any paint on them. The kitchen floor was now bare, as the old linoleum was now gone. It to had been sanded and ready for the new floor covering. A box of new hinges and handles sat on the counter, waiting to be put on when the cupboards when finished. The staircase trimming had been replaced, but not much else had been done to the stairs. Bill and Joe discussed whether to replace the stairs, because they were worn from years of use. But they were still very sturdy.

Dawn looked at the stairs, thinking of the years of use they got, from someone going up and down them. Dawn slipped her arm under Bill's. "Let's not change the stairs, but just sand them a bit, as they have there own identity." Bill put his hand over Dawn's.

"You heard the lady." Bill said after a moment of thought.

"That means less work for me to." Joe said glad to not have to replace the entire staircase.

Bill and Dawn then brought Joe into the discussion of how to remodel the bathroom and utility room. Neither room would be large, but as long as they served the purpose.

"Well," Joe said. "Now that the staircase problem is solved, it means we can get at this room quicker!"

Bill and Dawn finally came to a decision on floor coverings. The living room and back bedroom would remain hardwood, with a partial rug in the bedroom. Where as they would just replace the old wall rug in the bedroom upstairs and put new linoleum through the kitchen and bathroom.

Once they had decided on that, they spent the rest of the day and part of the next ordering the items needed. After notifying the gas and phone companies of the appropriate changes, Bill called the power company and asked if they would install a yard light for them.

After that, Bill spent his time helping where he could, but as the men did not feel there was much Dawn could do at this stage, she spent her time exploring their new property.

Bill was getting anxious to get everything done as soon as possible, so during lunch, Bill suggested they go to Calgary, to see if they could find the items they wanted. Dawn was excited by the idea of shopping for their new home, but first they had to stop at the motel to clean up and picked up a few things to take along.

* * *

When they set out on their trip, Bill wondered how to approach the subject of their children. Dawn had never talked or asked about them, even though she had met them briefly in the hospital. He wondered how much she remembered of those first few days, or if she even remembered that her children were there to see her at all. They drove in silence for some time, while Bill tried to figure out what to say. It was difficult, as he did not want her to feel guilty about it.

"Dawn," Bill said, then hesitating for a moment.

Dawn became tense at the sudden change in his voice. Had she done something wrong?

Bill continued. "We have to talk about our children. I talked to them yesterday and we thought perhaps we would try to get together for thanksgiving. They have wanted to come to see you, but decided to wait until you felt comfortable with me first."

Tears began to run Dawn's face as she began to cry. Bill slowed down looking for a safe place to stop. He reached out to Dawn, and pulled her to him, holding her while she wept on his shoulder. Bill stroked her hair, apologized for upsetting her and yet telling her it was something that he had to do.

Bill handed Dawn a couple of Kleenex's as she slowly regained her composer.

Wiping the tears from her eyes and embarrassed for crying, she was angry with herself for not being strong.

"I"m fine." She said slowly. "I seem to remember a couple of young people visiting me in the hospital, but it's just a blur. I just don't know anyone."

"They must hate me by now, for not getting in touch with them, but I just would not know what to say." Dawn felt drained as she turned and looked out the side window. They sat in silence for several minutes. "Will you tell me some thing's about our family?" Dawn asked.

Bill slowly released her, then started the car and pulled back onto the highway.

"Well, we had three children." Bill started slowly, not sure how to tell her everything with out unsettling her more.

"Had?" Dawn interrupted. "You mean have?"

"No -- I mean had." Bill continued.

Dawn sat in silence, as she listened intently to what Bill was about to say.

"There were 2 boys and 1 girl. Darcy is the oldest and is 21 years old. He is doing long haul Trucking, going U.S. and

Canada. "Stephen," Bill hesitated. "He would be 19 now, but he was killed in a car accident."

Dawn gasped, covering her mouth with her hand at the terrible thought of Bill losing a son in an accident, and now going though all this with her.

Bill continued. "He was 16 just a few months short of his 17th birthday." He glanced at Dawn, who was now looking very pale, but he continued. "Then there is our daughter, Lisa who is 18 and is going to college this year, in Edmonton. They both miss you very much, especially Lisa." Bill said. Bill drove in silence thanking God for once again giving him the strength and wisdom of dealing with another difficult moment.

Dawn sat staring at the road ahead taking in everything that Bill had just told her.

It lay heavy on her heart at the thought of losing a son in an accident. How fragile life is. It can so easily and quickly be taken away, and it can never be turned back. Yet Bill seemed so strong in everything he had gone through in the past years. She felt guilty not being able to console him in his hurt, but she remembered nothing of what he had just told her. She was just getting to know Bill and now two more people needed her. It felt strange and yet good to actually be needed by someone. At times she felt so alone and empty, perhaps this was why. Dawn was more then ever determined to get her memory back, even if it took another bang to the head.

Which she admitted to herself, may be more detrimental.

Bill was somewhat startled as Dawn said.

"Why don't we plan on having thanksgiving at our new home. We can try to bring our family back together, even if it may be strange at first, but I am sure we will soon get over it." Slowly Dawn asked. "Where was our sons accident?'

"Up north in the Peace River area." Bill replied. "We used to live up there."

Dawn began to wonder if that was where she should start. Perhaps if she went back there, it would trigger something in her memory.

"Would it be possible to go up there?" Dawn asked.

"Not right now." Bill replied. "I was not going to tell you all this now, but I had promised Darcy months ago, that I would drive his truck for a couple of weeks. He needed a break. The plan was for you and I to go together, but it does not appear to be such a good plan now. If you needed to go to a Doctor in the U.S., the cost would be outrageous. Plus you would never get your proper rest while sleeping in the truck."

Dawn looked at Bill. The strain was showing more all the time on him, which made her heart ache.

"When do you have to leave?" Dawn asked sadly, beginning to feel the stress of everything, but trying her best not to show it.

"In a couple of weeks in fact, just after your next Doctors appointment. I want to be sure you are all right first. If you do not feel you can handle it by yourself, I will call Darcy. I do want you to meet Marie." He said. "She is the one that will help you around the house if you need it." "She is also willing for you to stay with her while I'm away, or her with you. She knows the situation, and seems very nice." Bill said.

Dawn felt like the weight of the world was sitting on her shoulders. She could never tell him not to go, even if she would like to have. Darcy was counting on him, and she felt she had disappointed her family enough. Bill had made all the arrangements already, so there would be no problem for her to stay by herself. After all she felt fine.

"You have to go and I understand." Dawn said putting her hand on his leg. "You could use a break from everything and really I'm feeling fine, but I am missing you already." She said sadly.

"Me too." Bill said putting his hand on hers and giving it a squeeze. He took a deep breath, before adding. "It's a relief to have told you everything and to know you understand. I didn't know for sure, if you could handle this so soon after the accident."

"I don't want you worrying about me." Dawn said. "I'll be just fine. You just see that your careful and come back to me."

The rest of the trip was on a more cheerful note, as they talked about the things the hoped to find for their home.

They went to a couple of antique shops, as well as places that handled bathroom fixtures. It seemed unbelievable that in a short time they found a old cast bathtub, sink, shower, as well as a beautiful wash stand with a basin and matching water pitcher. Then as added pieces they found a framed mirror and shelves. Both places they bought the items from, promised to ship everything the following day.

They decided to spend the night in Calgary and then finish their shopping, the following day. As they both felt relaxed and were becoming more comfortable with each other, they chose a motel with a pool. Only now they had to go shopping for some swimsuits, before going for supper.

They spent the evening in the hot tub and swimming pool, and at 10 o'clock they left the pool to return to their room. Bill was feeling like he had finally gotten his wife back. They had talked about their future, and Dawn listened to every word Bill said, when he talked about their past.

When they got back to their room, Dawn took a shower. When Bill went for his shower, Dawn made them coffee. She handed Bill his coffee before he sat on his bed to watch television. Before she joined him, she washed out their swimsuits and hung them on the shower curtain rod to dry. She then sat on her bed to relax with her coffee, while watching Bill fidget with the remote, trying to find a station he liked.

"Dawn, have you thought of what kind of bed we should get in our bedroom?" He asked.

Dawn hesitated, noticing he had said bed, not beds. She had enjoyed the times he held her, but she had avoided thinking about them always sleeping together. She knew it would, sooner or later come up, but the thought of them buying a bed left her nervous. "You decide." She said taking another drink of her coffee.

"Dawn we have to start acting like a married couple. I did sleep with you when I felt you needed me. Was that so bad? I still need you Dawn." Bill added. "When we got married, we were together the first night. I can't see why it should be different now? We do love each other, don't we?" Bill added

Dawn knew Bill was getting frustrated with her. She too had mixed feelings. She enjoyed being near him, but she felt -- well embarrassed, as her mind drifted back to the time Bill saw her naked.

Bill went and sat beside her on her bed. He grabbed her arms firmly, pulling her to him. "Do you love me?"

"You know I do." She said looking into his eyes. "You're hurting my arms." She said pulling away from him.

"I'm sorry Dawn, but it's hard for me not to make love to you." He said, going back to his bed. "We'll be putting only one bed in our room." He said firmly.

Dawn felt shaken by Bill's outburst. She thought back to the time she asked him if he wanted to use one bed, but he told her to wait until she was sure she was ready. She knew he wanted their life like it was before. She too would do anything for that, but she had no control over it. She was afraid of losing him and as Bill turned off the television she quietly turned and sobbed into her pillow.

The next morning Bill was his usual self. When they left the restaurant, Bill turned to Dawn. "Well, let's see what we can find for bedroom furniture." He said, putting his arm around her, as they walked to the car.

They went to several stores, but ending up at another antique shop, where they found a beautiful old bedroom suite in immaculate condition. It consisted of bed, chest of drawers and a dresser with a round mirror and a stool that slid under the dresser. It was medium brown, with some fancy blonde inlay designs. Dawn rubbed her hand along the smooth shinny wood, before making eye contact with Bill, who stood watching her.

He nodded his head, and she nodded back, both knowing this was the one. They looked around and found some beautiful old light fixtures, and a couple of old lanterns. They also came across a roll top desk that was in fairly good shape, which they decide to put in their room. When Bill and the salesman came to an agreement on price, they discussed how soon it could be shipped. It would arrive a day later than their other order. But that was fine, as they figured by then their bedroom would be ready. They did take the light fixtures and lanterns with them instead, of having them shipped.

After lunch they headed back home, deciding to possibly find some of the other furniture they needed locally. Bill told Dawn they still had a few things in storage.

Upon returning home Bill made a couple of phone calls. When he got off the phone, he seemed quite pleased. The day had left both Bill and Dawn feeling a bit overwhelmed and Bill decided they should both have a rest. Not till now did Dawn realized how tired she really was.

Both Bill and Dawn felt rejuvenated after their rest. It was a beautiful evening so they decided to walk to the nearest restaurant and have a light lunch before calling it a day.

That night, Bill said nothing about their sleeping arrangement when they got ready for bed. He took her in his arms and gave her a long loving kiss, that sent her heart racing, while she clung to him. He smiled at her and then returned to his bed leaving Dawn somewhat disappointed. She was beginning to feel more comfortable with Bill, and was now positive, that if Bill wanted her in the way he said, she would gladly accept his love.

Dawn lay there for some time wondering how their life would be, once they moved into their home. But then sadness engulfed her, as she thought of Bill going away for two weeks. She lay there wondering how she would ever manage without him.

CHAPTER 5

BILL LEFT EARLY IN THE morning, to help Joe at the house. He told Dawn that he wouldn't be home before 5 o'clock that afternoon, so Dawn figured it would be a perfect time to check out the town. She went into several stores hoping to find a suitable couch for their living room. What she would like to have had was an antique couch, but so far she had found nothing she liked. After checking out the one furniture store, Dawn decided to go for a walk. It gave her a chance to see what the town was like. She spent about an hour, just walking when she came across someone moving out of a small older home. It was then that a garage sale sign attached to a tree caught her attention. She slowly walked around looking at a few of the items outside when a middle age gentlemen, came out of the house.

"See anything you want? Most of this stuff will probable have to go to the dump if no one wants it," he said gruffly.

"Do you have anything in the house that you'll be selling?" Dawn asked.

"Yup," he said. "Go on in and have a look around."

Dawn slowly scanned the items in the house. She was not that impressed with anything in there and was about to turn to leave when she got a glimpse of something in the back corner. She made her way through boxes, lamps and misc. items and there to her amazement was what she thought would be perfect in their house. Both rocker and couch were a dark solid wood with brown leather on the seats and backrest.

"Is this for sale?" Dawn asked, pointing to the couch and rocker.

"Everything's always for sale at the right price, lady. It makes into a bed too," the owner added.

"May I open it to see what it looks like?" Dawn asked.

"Go ahead. It's hardly been used." The man said.

After checking it over, Dawn was pleased to see that it was in very good condition. There was a bit of wear on the leather and wood arms, but it wasn't that bad, for it's age. She sat on the couch and then the rocker, and found both amazingly comfortable. Dawn opened it to check out the bed. It looked as if it was never used, just as the man had said.

She could just picture Bill sitting in the big rocker, looking at his paper, after a hard days work.

"How much do you want for this set?" Dawn asked quickly, not wanting to sound to excited, or he may just up the price.

"Fifty bucks." Came the reply from around the corner.

"Is that for the couch and chair?" She stammered, thinking he must have made a mistake, for she expected to pay much more.

"E-e-up, take it or leave it." He said. "Not a penny less."

Dawn paid the man, and then asked if she could use his phone to call her husband to come and pick it up. She dialed the number, hoping to reach Bill or Joe, at the house. She let it ring at least ten times and was just about to hang up when Bill answered.

"Hello." Bill said, breathing heavy.

"Bill." Dawn replied. "Is that you?"

"Yes, are you ok?" Bill asked, now wondering what happened, for Dawn to be calling him.

"I'm great." Dawn said excitedly.

"You're lucky to have caught us near the phone. What's up?" Bill asked.

"I found a couch and rocker and I need a truck to pick it up." Dawn turned to the gentlemen to ask what his address was then she passed it on to Bill. "Joe would probably know how to find it." Dawn said. "I'll tell you more when you get here."

"Give us 20 minutes to a half hour," Bill said before hanging up the phone.

Dawn wondered around, checking what else may catch her eye. It was about a half hour later that Bill and Joe arrived, Dawn was a bit nervous, wondering what Bill would say. Especially since she bought the couch without discussing it with him first, like he said they used to do. After all she thought, it was not that expensive and Bill had bought their place without discussing it with her. She was being foolish to think that way she said scolding herself. She watched Bill and Joe, check out first the chair, then the couch before loading it. Dawn was quite pleased with her purchase, when both men seemed to think it was quite all right.

"We still have another hours work." Bill told her before offering her a ride back to the motel.

Dawn declined, saying that she really didn't mind walking.

On her way home, Dawn decided to buy some ready cooked chicken and fries for supper. But it was two hours later when Bill finally walked in the door.

"I'm sorry I'm so late." Bill said. "But there were so many things I had to do."

He kissed Dawn on the forehead, on his way to get cleaned up for supper.

Dawn warmed up their food and had it sitting on the table when Bill sat down.

"I'm sorry about supper, but it is hard to have the fries and chicken fresh after you warm it up." Dawn said.

"It'll be fine," Bill replied. "Now tell me about your day and how you came upon your find? Joe and I checked it over and everything seems in real good shape, what did it cost?" Bill asked.

Dawn told Bill of how she had gone for a walk, and happened upon this garage sale. Bill raised his eyebrows when she told him how little she paid for it. After they finished their supper,

Dawn cleared the table and washed the dishes, while Bill sat drinking his coffee. Dawn had wondered how Bill's day was, but he had not volunteered to tell her. However he did seemed to be in a very good mood. Dawn notice Bill looking at his watch several times as if he had an appointment to keep.

It was almost time for the sun to set, when Bill came and grabbed Dawn around the waist. "Would you like to go check out our place?" He asked holding her close.

Dawn smiled up at him, her hands resting on his shoulders. When Dawn saw that mischievous twinkle in his eyes, she knew he was up to something.

"Let me comb my hair and get my purse." Dawn said.

Bill looked at her still holding her tight. "Na, you don't need to do anything. You're beautiful the way you are." Bill said kissing her gently. Dawn felt very lucky to have Bill as her husband. He took Dawn's hand and led her out to the car. Neither one spoke a word as Bill drove out into the country.

The sun was just setting as they drove through the trees. Bill stopped the car before descending into the valley below. The sunset was breath taking as it slowly disappeared behind the mountain leaving the sky, coloured with crimson, blue and gray. Bill slowly drove down the hill, where the freshly painted white house was now a sharp contrast to the green grass and trees.

The porch light was on when Bill led Dawn to the front door. While Bill unlocked and opened the front door, Dawn wondered if the items that they bought, had arrived yet.

Dawn was about to walk in, when Bill turned and swooped her up in his arms.

He carried her into the house, setting her down, in their now beautifully renovated kitchen. Dawn gasped as she looked around.

"How?" She said turning to Bill in surprise. "How did this get done so fast?"

Bill smiled "I told you Joe was our miracle worker." He said.

Dawn walked over to the cupboards, rubbing her hand across

the white doors then the Black hinges and knobs. She ran her hand across the new granite counter top.

The walls were off white with oak trim around the doors and windows, just as she has wanted. A beautiful old cook stove that sat near the south wall had been polished to a shine. Dawn was in amazement at how beautiful it all looked.

"The old stove is hooked up, if you ever want to use it." Bill told her. "But as you can see there is also the electric one there." He pointed.

When Dawn stepped into the living room, she stepped onto a highly polished floor. A couple of beautiful mats now lay in front of the polished couch and chair she had just purchased that afternoon. One of the old lanterns they bought hung near the back door. When Bill turned on the light switch, the crystals on the old chandelier sent a rainbow of colors dancing around the room. Dawn went into the back bedroom. Here again the smell of paint was strong and the oak trim made it look so rich, but it was empty except for the new partial rug that lay on the wood floor.

Bill led Dawn back through the kitchen and into the bathroom. She gasped in surprise as everything was done just as she had imagined it. She went first to the pedestal sink with chrome taps, and hanging above was the framed mirror. She moved over to the wash stand that stood near the sink, running her fingers over the blue design on the glass bowl and water pitcher that sat on it. She turned and walked to the shower stall that sat in the corner. Lastly there was the old cast tub with gleaming chrome fixtures.

Dawn went next to the laundry room, where a new washer and dryer sat, and tucked in under the staircase was a cupboard.

Bill then lead her back to the stairs, where he switched on the light that lit up the staircase to the bedroom. The walls were again off white with the oak railing attached by black holders. The indentations still showing on the stairway, but instead of covered with paint now sported an oak stain. Bill took her hand

and led her up to the bedroom. He then wrapped his arm around her. "Dawn, welcome to our room," he said.

Dawn was speechless as she walked on the soft-carpeted floor towards their new bedroom suite. It looked perfect in this room. The roll top desk sat near the north window and it was as if everything here had always meant to be together.

"All you have to do is find curtains and bedding, I thought I would leave that to you." Bill said.

"Oh Bill," Dawn said giving him a big hug as tears filled her eyes. "It's better than I could ever have imagined!" Dawn wandered around the room opening drawers touching the top of the dresser, just letting it all soak in. After a few minutes he took her hand and led her back down the stairs and outside, to the two wicker chairs that now sported a new coat of white paint. The weather was unusually warm for this time of year, as they walked around the outside of their new home. Bill had a couple of black carriage lanterns installed on the west and south walls of the house that dimly lit up the porch. Dawn looked up just as a star fell from the sky.

"Make a wish." Dawn said quickly, as it disappeared behind the trees.

"I did." Bill said taking her in his arms, looking longingly into her eyes.

They held each other for some time before Bill released her. Putting his arm around her they went back into the house. Dawn made one quick tour through the house, shutting off all the lights behind her. After leaving the house, Bill locked the door behind them. He took Dawn's hand in his as they walked back to their car.

"Tomorrow we move in." Bill said on their drive to town. He was silent for a moment. "Dawn, do you think you can still drive?" He asked.

She had not driven since the accident. "I suppose I can." She said. "Why do you ask?"

"Well, when I'm gone, you'll need a vehicle to get around."

He replied.

"Gone?" she asked momentarily surprised.

"I mean when I go to drive Darcy's truck." He said putting his hand over hers. "You know I would never leave you."

* * *

The next day they began moving into their new home. Little by little Bill brought their things out of storage and there were boxes strewn everywhere.

Dawn looked first for the dishes and pots and pans then, after washing them, she placed them into the cupboard. Bill then brought in a beautiful round oak games table with four matching chairs, which would have to do until they purchased a kitchen set. After which it would graduate to the living room. There was also a cedar chest which Bill told Dawn, her parents had bought for her, when she was about fifteen.

Dawn walked over to the cedar chest touching it slightly, as Bill and Joe carried it into the living room. She had never asked about her or Bill's family. For now Bill was all she needed. She told herself she would go through the cedar chest when they were all settled in. Dawn was about to unpack more boxes, when Bill interrupted her.

"What would you say to taking a drive into town, to purchase some bedding for the bed?"

Dawn felt guilty spending so much money, especially having no idea what their financial status was. Dawn's first purchase was a pair of queen size pillows, and a beautiful embroidery duvet, which came with matching sheets and queen size pillowcases. That would have to do for now. She was actually pleased with her purchase when she left the store. They went out for lunch before returning home to resume unpacking.

Dawn and Bill were exhausted and anxious to try out their new bathroom that evening.

Dawn lay soaking her tired body in a tub full of warm water, all the while admiring her new tub and surroundings. She couldn't imagine that her former life could have been any better than this. She would like to have relaxed longer in her bath, but she knew Bill was waiting to have his shower. After slipping on her old pyjamas and housecoat, she went to the kitchen to make a fresh pot of coffee while waiting for Bill.

It was a while before Bill came down from the bedroom, where he'd been resting. He looked around very pleased with the way the bathroom turned out. He stepped into his new shower, letting the water wash over his aching muscles. If only he would not have to leave Dawn so soon after moving into their home.

When Bill came out of the bathroom wearing a clean pair of pants and T-shirt he noticed Dawn was still wearing her old pyjamas and housecoat. "No! No!" he said tugging on her housecoat. "Please?" he pleaded, looking longingly at her.

Dawn knew what he meant, but had hoped he had forgotten. Dawn went back up stairs and fumbling through her drawer to find her new nightgown and housecoat. *Why did I buy this*, she said to herself, when she slipped it on. For some reason she actually felt different when she looked in the mirror. The soft layers of shear material made a swishing sound when she twirled around. At least the housecoat would cover enough, that she would still not be embarrassed.

Bill stood up when Dawn walked into the kitchen. Her eyes seemed to sparkle when she looked at him. She never looked more beautiful, he thought to himself. Dawn joined Bill at the table but he could not take his eyes off of her.

"It's a warm evening. Why don't we sit outside, with our coffee and watch the sunset." Dawn said.

On their way outside Bill reached for a blanket that hung over a chair. "Just in case you get cold." He said.

"Let's go sit on the grass where we can see the stars later, seeing as you already have a blanket." Dawn said to Bill.

It was refreshing to get outside in the fresh air, because the house was quite warm and the smell of paint lingered everywhere. Bill spread the blanket on the grass. He took Dawn's hand in his, as they sat in silence, watching the western sky, as God painted his masterpiece of brilliant colors in the evening sunset. They sat drinking their coffee until the last of the sunset faded into darkness. But soon God's handy work appeared again. This time it was millions of stars twinkling above them. Bill lay back on the blanket, pulling Dawn down beside him. "This is the way to watch the stars." He said.

While Dawn lay on Bill's arm, they tried to find the different constellations. "A shooting star!" Dawn said pointing up, as it shot through the night sky. "Did you make another wish?" She asked.

As Bill turned to face Dawn, he laid his hand on her waist then gently he leaned over and gave her a kiss. With each kiss came more passion, which Dawn returned. She could feel Bill's heart beat faster and at the same time, she was sure he felt hers do the same. She no longer resisted his love as the stars seemed to twinkle their approval from up above. They lay under the stars for sometime holding each other, before Bill realized how cool the air had gotten. He gently took Dawn's hand and helped her to her feet. Then wrapping the blanket around her shoulders, he gave her a hug. Bill put his arm around her as they walked together into their home. Bill locked the front door and shut off the lights while Dawn got ready for bed.

That evening, they both knelt down beside their bed thanking God for everything he had done for them. Especially for giving them a new start in life.

Dawn open the bed and slipped under the covers. She waited until Bill got into bed then gently pulled the covers over him. Dawn laid her head on his bare shoulder then placed her hand on his chest.

"This truly is our bed." She said softly, as he placed his hand over hers. "I love you." She said.

"I love you too." Bill replied.

They lay there for sometime, just enjoying being together, but soon they drifted off into a peaceful and restful sleep.

Chapter 6

Now that Bill and Dawn had settled into their new home, Dawn spent as much time as possible exploring the area. Soon it would be Saturday and Bill would be leaving for 2 weeks. She was not looking forward to him going, even though she knew she could manage by herself. It was the feeling of loneliness that haunted her.

Marie had been a big help to Dawn. They soon began confiding in each other and it was not long before they became very good friends.

The two weeks that lead up to Dawn's doctor's appointment seemed to have disappeared like the wind. Bill and Dawn left early in the morning as Bill had a few things of his own to do, before going on the truck. The first thing he had to do was renew his US medical at a walk-in clinic. He said it was quicker than waiting to get an appointment with a new doctor. Besides he had been at this clinic once before. When he'd completed his medical and had gotten his card, he waved it in front of Dawn. "I have a clean bill of health, now it is your turn." Bill said with a big grin on his face.

There was still 2 hours left before Dawn's appointment, so they went clothes shopping for Bill, which they concluded by going out for lunch.

They arrived at the office of Doctor Rogers at 1 p.m. As soon as Dawn arrived, she was whisked off to x-ray. They waited for almost an hour, before getting to talk to her doctor.

"Everything shows fine." Doctor Rogers said. "Have you regained any of your memory?" He asked.

Dawn shook her head. "Nothing." She replied.

"We must be patient. Some times it takes longer then we hoped." He said, patting her on the hand.

Doctor Rogers called Bill over to talk to him in private. "Has any of her memory returned at all?" He asked Bill.

"Nothing lately." Bill said. "Is there a possibility, she may never get it back?" Bill asked.

"Yes, that is always a possibility but I feel it is still to early to say that." Doctor Rogers said as he placed his hand on Bill's shoulder.

"How is everything else?" Dr. Rogers asked, looking at Bill.

"Great now." Bill said with a gleam in his eye, which pretty well answered his question.

"That helps." Doctor Rogers said, smiling as he walked away.

Bill went back to Dawn. "Are you ready to go?" He asked.

Dawn was looking very unhappy. She sort of expected her Doctor to give her a specific time as to when her memory would return. As if by some miracle he would say something like, next week, or next month, but then she knew his guess was as good as hers. Dawn looked up at Bill. "What did you and Doctor Roger's talk about?" She asked.

"Oh, men things." Bill said teasing her.

"You men." She said, picking up her purse, and then holding on to Bill's arm, as they left the doctors office.

On their drive home, Dawn sat close to Bill. She laid her head on his shoulder. "I'm going to miss you when you leave." She said sadly.

"Me too." He said putting his arm around her. "I promise to phone you every chance I get." He added.

When they got home they sat outside on their wicker chairs drinking coffee and enjoying their time together.

"Let's call it an early night." Bill said taking her hand and led her into the house.

Will Love Conquer All?

Dawn slipped into her nightgown and walked over to the west window. She stood looking out at the stars, feeling very lonely. Bill came from behind her and wrapped his arms around her. She would miss him terribly when he left. It took all her willpower not to turn and beg him not to go.

Bill gentle caressed her thighs. "Are you all right?" He asked kissing her neck.

Dawn turned to face him. "Yes Bill, as long as you are with me."

They held each other for several minutes, cherishing every moment, as if it could be their last. When Dawn knelt by her bed that night, she asked God to protect Bill and help her to overcome the depression that now began to engulf her. She pleaded with God to restore her memory.

She just felt she couldn't go on, not feeling like she was part of her family.

Bill also asked for protection over both of them and their family especially during their time of separation. He questioned God as to why he had not restored Dawn's memory, but did thank him for the love they once again shared.

When they slipped under the covers Bill took Dawn in his arms and kissed her passionately. How he wished he could make everything right for her. How Bill wished that he would not have to leave her so soon, but he had made a promise to their son, and felt he should keep it.

Dawn clung to Bill, returning his kiss, cherishing there moments together. They loved each other and right now, that was all that mattered.

They slept later than usual, only to wake up to a cloudy morning. Dawn rubber her eyes and yawned when she opened her eyes. She had her back to Bill with his strong arm lying across her waist. When she gently caressed his arm, Bill pulled her firmly against his body. She clung to his arm, the feeling of ecstasy passing through her body. How thankful she was for a loving husband like Bill, but tomorrow he would be leaving and she would not have his arms to hold her for two weeks. She tightened her hold on his arm, not wanting to let him go.

Bill released her and looked at his watch. "Oh! I didn't realize it was this late." He said. "There are several things I have to do here, to ensure that everything will be looked after when I'm gone."

"Don't worry about me." Dawn said getting up. "I'll go have a shower then start breakfast. You just rest for a while." She said before bending over to kiss him on the cheek.

By the time Bill came down for breakfast, the clouds had rolled away and the sun was shining through the trees. Dawn watched two squirrels chasing each other through the branches. Then leaping from tree to tree and in turn disturbed a couple of birds that were perched on the branch. She watched as the birds landed on the railing outside the window, chirping at the squirrels angrily, for disturbing them.

It was 10:30 when Dawn cleared off the breakfast dishes. Bill looked outside when they heard a vehicle drive in.

"Looks like we have our first visitor." Bill said going to the door. When Bill opened the door, he looks surprised and not in a good way. He stood there briefly then quickly went out to meet their visitor. The two men stood talking for sometime, but Dawn could not hear what was being said. By the facial feature these two men didn't seem too happy. What Dawn found strange, was that Bill had not greeted this man with a handshake as he usually would. Several minutes passed before they came into the house. Anger showed all over Bill's face, even if he did his best to hide it with a smile when he introduced Dawn to their visitor.

"Dawn this is our neighbour Nick." He said rather curtly. "His parents were the previous owners. He lives just west of here a couple of miles." Bill added.

Dawn walked over to Nick offering him her hand. "Nice to meet you Nick." Dawn said. "Its good to see you again, a-a--I mean to meet you!" He said giving Dawn's hand an extra squeeze. Nick looked at her in a way that made Dawn somewhat uncomfortable.

When Dawn gave Bill a quick glance, she could see he was angry. "Can I offer you a cup of coffee?" Dawn asked Nick who was still holding her hand.

Bill put his arm firmly around Dawn shoulder and pulled her towards him, at which time Nick released her hand. Nick took a quick look at Bill, his facial features now showed the same dislike.

"No, perhaps another time." He said trying his best to mask his anger, while handing Dawn his business card. "I just thought I would leave my number with you, in case you ever needed something. Just being neighbourly." He said looking angrily at Bill.

"Thanks but I don't believe that will be necessary" Bill said, still holding Dawn possessively.

Nick looked at Dawn then nodded his head before putting his hat back on and walking out the door.

Dawn turned suddenly to face Bill, who was obviously very angry. "Bill what has gotten into you? Nick just came over to be neighbourly and extend a hand of friendship. Is that so bad? I have never seen you like this." She said sharply. "I think you owe him an apology for your attitude."

She said going back to her dishes. "Do you two know each other and what did he mean by saying, nice seeing you again?" Dawn asked.

"Bill ignored the last part of her question. "We met a couple of times years ago and I just never liked him." Bill said.

"Did you know this was his parents place?" Dawn asked.

"No." Bill said angrily stomping out of the house, leaving Dawn wondering what was going on.

When Bill came in an hour later he had calmed down. Giving her a hug and kiss on the forehead, he apologized. Dawn did not feel this was the right time to ask any more questions.

"Let's go for a drive. I want to be sure that you can still handle a vehicle. I should have done this before." Bill said.

"If I drove before, I can't see why I shouldn't be able to do it now." Dawn said.

They had a light lunch then left for town to do some grocery shopping.

"I'll let you drive, while I take the passenger seat." Bill said holding the driver door open for her. Bill closed the door as Dawn settled in behind the steering wheel it felt somewhat familiar. She had not driven since before the accident, but she felt confident she could do it.

"Ready to go?" Bill asked sliding in, then closing his door behind him.

Dawn drove slowly at first, but after a couple of miles, she found she quite enjoyed it. Bill was quiet all the way to town, which gave Dawn time to wonder why Bill and Nick had such a dislike for each other.

"I'm sure of one thing." Bill said to Dawn, when they arrived at the grocery store "You can still drive. I'm going to fill the car with gas, then come back and wait for you to finish your shopping." Bill said sliding in behind the steering wheel.

Dawn already knew how much Bill disliked shopping. He had told her that he would rather sit in the car, which he was patiently doing, when she came out with a cart full of groceries.

Bill helped Dawn put the groceries into the car. "Dawn, I want your opinion on buying a truck." He said getting into the car then driving towards the truck lot. "I want to know what you think of that one?" Bill said pointing to a dark green 1 ton dual wheel truck.

"Is it new?" Dawn asked.

"No." Bill said. "It's three years old, but it has low mileage and in excellent condition." "I thought we could trade off the old brown truck, unless the fellow at the storage place still wants to buy it. We would be better off to sell it out right."

The first time Dawn saw the brown truck, was when Bill used it to move their things from the storage place to their home. At that time Bill mentioned he had hoped to get a newer one, even though his was still in reasonably good condition, for it's age.

"It's up to you." Dawn said. "If you feel you can afford it."

"The fellow at the storage place had offered me a good dollar for the old one and it may be the right time to sell it." Bill added.

Bill went to talk to the salesmen then motioned for Dawn to come join him.

"Let's take it for a drive." Bill said opening the door for her. They drove through town and out into the country. Dawn was surprised how smooth the ride was. She thought it would have been much rougher, but it was almost as good as their car.

"I want you to drive it back and see what you think of it. There will probably be times that you will have to drive it too." Bill told her.

Dawn was nervous at first, but once she got the feel of it, she quite enjoyed driving it. "It's great." Dawn said, driving into the lot." "I thought it would be a lot different, but it isn't to bad."

Bill talked to the salesman for a while before returning to the car. "I decided to take it, if the other fellow will buy ours." Bill said.

When it came to shopping for trucks it was totally different then grocery shopping, she thought to herself. But Dawn was happy for Bill, when she saw the pleasure it brought him. "Take me home so I can put my groceries away. Then you can go back and do your wheeling and dealing." Dawn said.

Bill agreed, then talked all the way home about the different features that the new truck had. But as soon as they drove into the yard, he suddenly became very silent.

"Is something wrong?" Dawn asked looking at him.

"Nothing is wrong." Bill snapped, changing from cheerful to angry in just a few minutes.

"Bill, did I say or do something to upset you?" She asked.

Bill looked at Dawn, and seeing the hurt in her eyes, he instantly became angry with himself.

"No." He said, curtly. "I'm angry at myself."

"Why don't you tell me what's going on?" She asked.

Bill reached over and gave her hand a squeeze. "It's ok I'll get over it." He said trying to be more cheerful.

They took the groceries into the house and set them on the table. Dawn faced Bill and said. "You go get your new truck. That should cheer you up." Dawn watched Bill walk over to his brown truck and waved to him as he drove off.

Dawn put the groceries away wondering all the while what could have caused the friction between these two men. They obviously had met and had a mutual dislike for each other. She was about to throw some papers into the garbage, when she noticed Nick's card. She picked it up and read the name Nick Helmsley and his address and phone number. She had laid it on the cupboard, after he gave it to her, but Bill must have thrown it away. She tapped the card on her hand pondering the whole scene that morning. She then placed the card in the back of her address book, which lay by the phone. She was sure Bill had no intention of telling her anything more about the whole event. She wondered if she should ask Nick if the opportunity ever arose.

Dawn was putting the last of her groceries away when the phone rang. "Hello," Dawn answered, wondering who would be calling them.

"Hi Dawn." Marie said cheerfully. "Guess What?" She continued with out Dawn saying another word. "A friend of mine is going up north for a few days. I had mentioned to him, that I had a friend who would like to make a trip up there. He offered to take us along to keep him company. Isn't that great?"

Dawn hesitated, She was unprepared for this, especially going without Bill but Marie continued.

"Bill will be gone for two weeks and it not good for you to be alone all that time."

After all it is only for a few days. Please say yes." Marie pleaded. "I would love to go, but I won't go alone."

Dawn laughed at Marie's excitement. "Have you got a crush on this friend of yours?" Dawn asked.

Marie laughed, "I guess I am acting like a school girl, but I do like him." She said.

"His wife died a couple of years ago and we have become friends."

"I would have to talk to Bill first." Dawn said thoughtfully. "I had hoped to go with him, but he seems to be holding back and not wanting to go. When would your friend be going?" Dawn asked.

"He's leaving Monday morning and we would be back Wednesday night, it'll be a quick trip." Marie said, her voice full of excitement at the possibility of Dawn accepting the offer.

"I'll talk it over with Bill this evening and let you know tomorrow." Dawn said.

"Thanks Dawn. I guess I should be thinking more of the reason you should go, then my wanting to." Marie said, now feeling bad for thinking of mainly, herself.

"Marie you need a good man and I hope he is the right one for you." Dawn said. They laughed and joked with each other for sometime before saying goodbye.

When Dawn sat at the table a deep sadness seemed to cover her. She had lost a son in a car accident, that she could not remember. She felt very strongly that she had to go back to try to pick up the pieces of her life. Bill couldn't go now and it was obvious, that he did not want take that trip north. But after everything that had happened lately she couldn't blame him for not wanting to relive those days. He would just say, some day we will make that trip. It must be hard for him and their children, she thought. First losing a son and brother and now a wife and Mother who could not remember them.

"No." Dawn said out loud, her eyes began to fill with tears. "I will not let Bill see me upset. I need some fresh air." She said heading for the door.

Dawn walked around the house before deciding to explore the treed area to the north of the house. She followed the trail, which lead her into the bush, where she took a deep breath, inhaling the smell of the trees. It was so peaceful here. She stopped to watch the birds flutter in the trees while others sat singing happily on the branches above.

The leaves shimmered and rustled in the sun, as a light breeze made its way through the trees. It was then Dawn decided to get a bird feeder. That way she could watch the birds, while she had her morning coffee. She turned back, determined to do more exploring of the area at a later date. Dawn loved the out doors. It made her feel free, like the creatures that scurried through the trees. When she got to the edge of the bush, Dawn saw Bill drive into the yard with his new truck.

She ran to meet him, but upon arrival, she could see the two wrinkles that ran across his forehead were deeper then usual. She had come to know that meant he was not totally happy about something, even if the new truck seemed to give him some pleasure.

"Where have you been?" Bill asked, when she got close enough for him to put his arm around her shoulder.

"I went for a walk." She said cheerfully, feeling the warmth and strength of his arm around her.

"You be careful. I don't think it's a good idea for you to go walking out there in the bush alone, there are wild animals around." He said, his voice full of concern.

"I will be fine. The only wild animals I saw were birds and squirrels." She said.

Bill's voice took on a serious tone as she turned her to face him. "Dawn, I am not joking. I heard today, that there was a mountain lion spotted west of here. Promise me you will stay out of the bush and stay near the house." Gripping her shoulders, the creases on his brow grew deeper as his eyes opened wide. "Dawn do you understand what I said?"

Dawn knew he meant business. "Yes I promise." She replied.

Bill took her in his arms and gave her a big hug. "I just don't want something happening to you again." He said gently.

Dawn pushed back from Bill and looked up into his blue eyes

and said. "Will you promise me the same thing? Will you be extra careful on the road?" She asked.

"I am always careful, you know that." He said, changing the subject. "Now, what do you think of our new truck?" He asked.

"Looks good to me." She said laughing at his excitement.

Bill opened the hood to show her the motor.

"Why do men always open the hood and look at the motor? What can you see besides a motor?" Dawn asked.

Bill just laughed and closed the hood. He put his arm around her, while walking towards the house.

After having a late supper, they cleaned up the dishes before relaxing in their living room. They had spent very little time in this room, but now that the windows were draped with new curtains, this room felt warm and cozy.

Bill ran his hands on the smooth wooden arms of his rocking chair.

"You know, this chair is quite comfortable but what it needs is a foot stool." Bill remarked.

Dawn smiled as she looked at Bill. "I'll see if I can find something for you."

She said. The whole day had been very stressful for him, but now as he sat in his chair, he was finally beginning to relax. She wondered how to approach him about going with Marie and her friend, up north to the Peace Country.

"What have you planned to keep yourself busy with, when I'm gone?" Bill asked. "I sure hate leaving you alone so soon after moving in here." Picking up a magazine he continued. "Can Marie come and stay with you for awhile?"

Dawn felt this was the perfect time to approach Bill about the trip. Laying her magazine on the couch beside her, she said.

"Marie called this afternoon, when you were in town. She's got a friend who asked her to go up north with him. He apparently has to go for a short business trip and asked her to go along, to keep him company. But--," Dawn continued slowly. "She didn't feel comfortable going alone, so she asked me. Well

— more like begged me to come along." Dawn chuckled as she continued, "I think Marie has a crush on this guy. Apparently his wife passed away a couple of years ago and I think she is actually falling in love."

Bill laughed at the thought of Marie in love. She was in her early thirties and had never been married, even though she was a good-looking woman. When she got excited, she could act as giddy as a schoolgirl.

She'd been a lot of help and a very good friend to Dawn in the short time they had known her. The wrinkles on Bill's brow once again became more pronounced. Dawn knew he was not all that impressed.

"When and how long?" Bill asked.

"We would be leaving early Monday morning and be back late Wednesday evening." She said. "I really would prefer to go with you." She said slowly. "I do feel I need to go up there sooner or later. It doesn't give me much time but one day maybe enough to jog my memory. I have to try something." She said sadly. There was silence for several minutes. "This way I wouldn't be alone for the full two weeks." She added.

"I don't like it." Bill said, doing his best to discourage her. "What do you know about this friend of Marie's?"

"I don't know who he is." Dawn said. "But I know Marie well enough in this short time, that she wouldn't go with him, if he didn't have the same Christian values she has."

Bill could not argue that point. Marie had stood by Dawn and did her best to help her in any way she could. He had to admit she was competent, and would see that Dawn would be all right and yet he felt uneasy. Slowly he agreed, but made sure she knew, that he was not totally happy with it.

"I'll call you Monday before you leave and again Thursday morning, so I know you got back safely." He said. "I'll give you the company number as well as Darcy's cell number. Just in case you have to get hold of us. I should be back two weeks from Sunday, if all goes well." He continued. "Darcy will be gone on holidays so in case you can't reach him, I will give you Lisa's number to."

They both sat in silence staring at their magazines and yet not seeing what was in front of them. Bill was thinking about Nick. He should have checked around before he bought this property. At least he was able to tell Nick about Dawn's accident and memory loss, before he got to the house. Otherwise he would have to explain to Dawn who Nick was. Bill was positive that Dawn did not remember Nick and he preferred to leave it that way. He now understood why Dawn felt she had been here before, which left him concerned.

Dawn also was thinking of the strange way Bill and Nick treated each other.

Why had Bill suddenly gone out to talk to Nick, when he obviously had known who he was. What had they talked about? Dawn was just about to ask Bill but decided against it. This was their last evening together before he left and she did not want to spoil it.

"Did you want to ask me something?" Bill asked.

"No." Dawn said. "But I would like to thank you for being a wonderful and supportive husband." She said gently.

"It takes a good woman to make a good man." He said, with a chuckle.

Dawn threw her magazine at him.

Then on a serious note, Bill said. "You know, I think we should get a dog. It would be company for you when I'm gone and may warn you if any animals did come around."

"Are you trying to scare me?" She asked.

"No, Just caution you. I want you to stay near the house and I mean it." Bill said. "A dog may be a good idea."

Dawn went over to kneel beside him. She took his hand in hers.

"Don't worry about me. I promise I'll be careful although it may be a good idea to get a dog, if we can find a good one. I'll check into it on Thursday, when I get back. I also promise not to wander into the bush and if I have a problem, I'm sure Marie would stay here with me." She kissed his hand before standing up. "Perhaps we should go to bed. After all it has been a long enough day and you should have a good sleep before you leave tomorrow." She said.

Bill agreed laying his magazine down, to follow Dawn to their bedroom. It amazed Dawn how cozy the atmosphere in their bedroom was once the curtains were hung.

Bill looked at her. "What are you thinking?" He said curiously.

"Oh-, just how glad I am that we chose this for our bedroom and how lucky I am to have you for my husband." She said.

"Now don't you wish you wouldn't have wasted all that time, using two beds."

He said jokingly, as he walked over to her and gently rubbed her arms, before letting his hands rest on her thighs.

"Oh Bill, I wish you wouldn't have to go." She said hugging him as she laid her head on his bare chest.

"Just think of how good it will be when I get back. I wish I wouldn't have to leave you either. You know that." He said holding her.

After getting ready for bed, they knelt down and held hands as they asked God for protection over each other and wisdom in dealing with what ever may come their way in the future.

Bill got into bed first. Then Dawn walked over and gently tucked him in, kissing him on the forehead.

"You are spoiling me." Bill said. "Who is going to tuck me in on the road?"

"No one." Dawn said laughing. "That is for me to do for my Teddy Bear."

Bill looked at Dawn sadly. "Did you know that you used to call me your Teddy Bear?" He said holding her tight after she climbed into bed.

"I love you." Dawn said. "You are gentle, loving and cuddly. I can see why I would have called you that."

Bill held her tight. "I love you too and don't ever forget it. I will never let you go. We have been through so much, but our love has always been there to get us through."

As they snuggled up close to each other, they were both dreading the two-week separation.

Chapter 7

Dawn woke up early the next morning with a slight headache. She decided to let Bill sleep until she had breakfast ready. While making herself some coffee and toast to take with her headache pills, she put a few last minute things into Bill's duffel bag. She then wrote a note to Bill.

To my precious Teddy Bear who I love very much
I will be waiting at the door for your return so, I can
Once again hold you in my arms. Hugs and kisses.
Your loving wife

She placed the note in with Bill's razor and toothbrush, where he would be sure to find it. When she heard Bill rustling around upstairs, she began to make Bill's favourite breakfast, which was bacon, eggs, hash browns with toast and coffee.

"Mmm breakfast smells good. I'm Hungry." Bill said sitting at the table.

"Good." she said pouring Bill a cup of coffee. Dawn placed a full plate of food in front of him. She then put a dish consisting of one egg and a slice of toast on the table for her.

Bill glanced up at Dawn. His eyes showed some concern. "Aren't you hungry this morning, or are you not you feeling well?" He asked.

"No, I'm fine." "I'm just missing you all ready." She said forcing a smile.

Bill sat studying her face and then bowed his head, to thank God for the food.

They ate in silence watching a couple of birds hoping along the railing outside.

"I was thinking of getting a bird feeder." Dawn said. "I enjoy watching the birds in the morning and it may attract a few different kinds."

"You do that." Bill said, still watching her.

After breakfast, Bill checked to make sure he had everything he needed.

"Have you got your wallet?" Dawn asked, wanting to be sure he didn't leave it behind. Bill had left his wallet on the dresser a number of times, after changing into clean jeans.

Bill reached to his back pocket. "Yes I have it." He said. "I think I have everything I need."

Bill then gave Dawn all the phone numbers, of their children and also the number of the company that Darcy worked for. After telling her how to reach him if need arose, Bill called Darcy to tell him that he was on his way. When he was about to say goodbye, he covered the receiver with his hand. "Dawn would you like to talk to our son?" He asked.

Dawn hesitated when she saw the pleading look in Bill's eyes she slowly took the phone from Bill's hand.

"Hello Darcy." She said slowly.

"Mom is that you? It's good to hear your voice! How are you doing?"

Darcy asked somewhat surprised.

"I'm fine. Did you Father tell you, that we're planning on having thanksgiving here?" Dawn said nervously.

"No, but that sounds great. Are you sure you're going to be all right when Dad is gone?" Darcy asked

"I'll be fine." She said, before asking about his vacation. Darcy told her that he was going to some beach near Vancouver. Dawn then wished him a good and safe holiday, before handing the phone back to Bill.

Bill was now ready to go. Bill looked deep into Dawn's brown eyes as he held her, in his arms. "You wait. By thanksgiving, you'll probably have your memory back. If not, our love for each other will get us through anything." Bill told her. They held each other without saying anything for quite sometime. When Bill reluctantly released her, he saw tears in her eyes. They stared at each other for a moment before Bill embraced her.

Dawn knew she would miss Bill terribly. She clung to him dreading the moment he would let her go. Then the moment she dreaded arrived. When he released her, he walked over to his bags.

The morning air was cool, as they walked towards the truck, each carrying a bag. Bill put the bags into his truck and then with one quick kiss, he climbed in and waved as he drove out of the yard. Dawn stood watching until the truck was totally out of sight.

When she walked back to the house it was like she was carrying the weight of the world on her shoulders.

She had no idea how she was going to get through the next two weeks.

She set to work cleaning the house and doing laundry, to keep herself from thinking about Bill's leaving. When she finally looked at the time it was 1 o'clock. She made herself a sandwich and a cup of tea and then sat watching the birds flutter around the trees, only to land on the railing. She must get a bird feeder and some birdseed the next time she went to town, she told herself. Dawn put a CD in and sat listening to the words of the song, while sipping her tea. It talked of God's mercy and love and how he prayed for everyone, which included her, while hanging on the cross.

Tears filled her eyes. God knew her and he knew what had happened to her.

Dawn thought of all the things Jesus had gone through while on earth which included dying on the cross for her.

She felt ashamed of feeling sorry for herself. Dawn bowed her head and said.

"Thank you Jesus, for your forgiveness and mercy. It is all in your time." She said now feeling better.

Just then the phone rang making her jump. "Hello? Oh Marie!" Dawn said. "I'm sorry for not calling you. I got busy after Bill left to take my mind off of his leaving, and totally forgot."

"I understand." Marie said sympathetically. "I suppose that means you aren't going to go?" She said, her voice full of disappointment.

"No." Dawn replied. "I'll come along if the offer is still open?"

"Yippy!!" Marie shouted.

Dawn almost dropped the phone at Marie's out burst, before laughing at Marie's giddiness.

"Oh, I'm sorry." Marie said apologizing "I thought all my hopes were dashed when you didn't call me back. "By the way," Marie continued. "What if I come and get you tomorrow morning, so we can go to church together? After that we can go out for lunch?"

"That sounds great, but I'll meet you in town, that way you don't have to drive all the way out here." Dawn told her.

"Ok, I'll wait for you at 10:45 just outside the church. Then you won't have to go in alone, and I can introduce you to a few people." Marie said.

Dawn felt bad for not remembering to call Marie back. Poor Marie, she must have been biting her nails in anticipation.

She suddenly realized that her headache had disappeared. Perhaps I should get busy and not think of my problems so much. Then maybe I wouldn't get all these annoying headaches, she thought.

Dawn went outside to cut the lawn around the house. That should take up most of the afternoon, she said to herself. Bill had bought a garden shed for the lawn mower and all the gardening tools, which he sat it in the northeast corner of the lawn. Dawn opened the door to take out the lawn mower. She was thankful that it started after the second pull of the rope. While she mowed the lawn, she kept singing and thinking of the words to the song she had listened to. After a while she stopped in the shade, for a break. She wiped the perspiration from her brow then looked up the driveway. For a brief moment she thought she saw some movement across the road. Dawn stood there trying to see what it could be, but finally decided it was just the wind blowing some twigs and tumbleweed across the road.

By the time she finished cutting the lawn, and trimming under the trees and around the house, two and a half hours had passed.

I'm glad that's finished, Dawn said to herself, while taking a cold drink of water. Now that her headache had returned, she decided to try out their new shower. Maybe it would help her to relax so that it would ease off. Too much sun she said to herself. Next time she would be sure to wear a hat, when she worked out in the yard.

That evening Dawn went to bed early, totally exhausted from her days work. She stroked the pillow where Bill, just a few hours ago, laid his head. "Oh Bill." She said sadly. "I miss you." Dawn lay there asking God to send his guardian angel to protect Bill on the road and to bring him back safely to her. She also asked God to fill the emptiness and remove the terrible loneliness she felt inside. Then slowly she drifted off to sleep. Suddenly she was jolted awake by what she presumed was a noise, coming from outside. She quickly sat up, listening for several moments for any sound, as she wondered what had woke her. But everything was silent, except for the chirping of the crickets.

I must have had one of my dreams, she thought lying back down to hug Bill's pillow. The scent of Bill's hair still lingered there. All Dawn could think about was Bill and it was some sometime before she fell asleep again.

***

The next morning, Dawn was awake early. She had gotten dressed and was making her breakfast when the phone rang.

"Hi Dawn. How are you this morning? Did you have a good

sleep?" Bill asked.

"It's good to hear your voice Bill. I miss you terribly." She said.

"Well that's a good sign." He said teasing her. "That way you won't forget about me. What did you do, to occupy yourself yesterday?" He asked.

Dawn proceeded to tell him what she had done. She also told him she was going to meet Marie at church, after which they were going out for lunch.

"Don't you go over doing things and be sure you get your rest?" Bill said. "I'm now on my way to Pennsylvania for a load of machinery. If I ever do this again, I'm taking you with me." Bill told her.

"That sounds like a plan." Dawn said looking at her watch and realizing she didn't have a lot of time before she was to meet Marie. "I better go Bill, so I am not late for church. I do miss you and love you very much."

"Me to. I'll call you in the morning, if all goes well. Look after yourself!" Bill told her.

"I will." She said hanging up the phone. How she wished she could have talked longer but she did not want to be late.

Dawn quickly ate her breakfast, and then washed her dishes. She had only fifteen minutes to spare.

When Dawn drove into the churchyard, she could see that Marie was already waiting for her.

"I hope I didn't keep you waiting?" Dawn said to her friend.

"No, I just got here myself." Marie said as they walked into the church together.

Marie introduced Dawn to the pastor and a few other people, but by the time they sat down, Dawn could not remember the names of the people she had been introduced to. Dawn listened as the pastor gave his sermon, which she felt he prepared just for her. She listened to the verse, all things work for good for them that love the Lord, but wondered what good had come out of her being in the accident. Then the verse, God will not give us more than we can bare and she began to think about Bill and all he had gone through, before and since her accident.

After the service Marie and Dawn went to a quiet restaurant for lunch. They sat there talking, when Marie looked past Dawn and smiled at someone who was approaching their table. Dawn did not turn around to see who it was. She was shocked to see that it was the same man that had come to their house. Marie moved over to the next chair as she began to introduce her to Nick. He was now sitting right across from Dawn.

"We have met." Nick said smiling as he reached out to shake Dawn's hand.

"Yes. Nick stopped in before Bill left." Dawn replied, somewhat uneasy.

"That's great." Marie said cheerfully. "He's the friend we'll be going with tomorrow."

"Oh! I didn't know." Dawn said in surprises.

Nick also raised his eyebrows in somewhat of a surprise. Marie had told him about this friend of hers, but not until now, did it all fit together. Nick chuckled to himself. Bill would be furious, if he knew it was Nick that she would be going with.

He wondered if Dawn would tell him.

"By the way." Nick said. "Did you say that Bill went somewhere?"

"Yes." Marie said. "He's gone for two weeks, driving his sons truck."

"The fool." Nick muttered softly, as his dislike for Bill, once again showed on his face.

Dawn looked at him, as anger began to weld up inside her. How dare he, call her husband a fool. Again she wondered what had happened in the past, to make Bill and Nick dislike each other so much.

Marie chatted on happily, not noticing that anything was wrong. "The four of us will have to get together, when Bill gets back." She said.

Dawn was quick to reply. "I don't think that's a good idea, because Bill and Nick apparently disliked each other." Instantly she wished she would not have said anything.

"Oh!!" Marie said in surprise turning to face Nick. "Did you know Bill before?" Marie asked.

"We've met." He said casually as he looked from Marie to Dawn.

"They probably had a argument over some girl." Marie said, jokingly.

Marie and Dawn laughed, but when Dawn glanced at Nick, she felt a sudden chill. Nick was not laughing. But instead she saw the sadness in his eyes. Dawn wondered if Marie's comment had hit a nerve. What happened, she wondered.

Were they both in love with the same girl, or was her imagination working overtime.

Nick suddenly said he had to go. He told Dawn that he would pick her up at eight the next morning.

"We have to get a early start, because it is a long drive." He smiled and gave Marie's arm a light tap then nodding his head when he looked at Dawn, before leaving.

Marie had not noticed the things Dawn had, because of sitting beside Nick. "Isn't he great?" Marie said happily. "Wouldn't it be something if Bill and Nick were in love with the same girl at one time. What a story that would make." She said excitedly.

Dawn didn't like the thought of Bill loving someone else. It tugged at her heart.

"If you would have seen how angry Bill was after Nick left, I'm not totally sure that's it. The two men do have a definite dislike for each other and Bill wouldn't tell me why." Dawn said.

"The plot thickens." Marie said. Her imagination was now running away with her.

"Bill would be furious, if he knew Nick was your friend that we will be going with." Dawn said.

Marie quickly looked at her friend. "You aren't thinking about backing out, are you?" She asked soberly.

"No, I have to find out if there's something up there, that will jog my memory." I don't want to live like this. I have to try something." Dawn said determined to do anything to get her memory back.

"I'm sorry." Marie said, sympathetically reaching out and laying her hand on Dawn's. "I'll do all I can to help. You know that."

"I know." Dawn said. "I don't know what I would do without you. You have been a great friend."

Marie now feeling guilty for her motives of getting Dawn to come along said.

"I'm sorry Dawn, I've been thinking more about myself and my wishes, when I know how important this trip can be for you. It must be difficult for you, especially with Bill gone for these two weeks."

Dawn quickly changed the subject. "Ah, but you have to get your man." She said.

Then they both laughed, which lifted the tension.

They sat chatting for sometime after they finished their lunch and were surprised at how the time went by.

"I really must be getting home." Dawn said. "I have a few things I have to do before morning."

"That reminds me, I better get some packing done too. One thing about Nick, he is punctual and does not like to be kept waiting." Marie said.

"I'll remember that." Dawn said paying her bill before going their separate ways.

CHAPTER 8

THE NEXT MORNING, DAWN AWOKE to the ringing of the phone. She glanced at the clock by her bed. It was 6 a.m. and time she got up. It was a good thing the phone woke her, she thought when picking up the receiver.

"Wake up sleepy head. "Bill said cheerfully.

"Oh Bill, it's good to hear your voice." She said.

"Is everything OK?" He asked.

"Yes, It's just that I miss you so much." She said, rubbing her eyes.

"That's good. Are you still going north with Marie?" He asked, hoping she had changed her mind.

"Yes I am. I feel I have to Bill." She said. "Besides Marie is all excited, how could I disappoint her."

"Dawn, when you get up north, you can contact our friends, Lyle and Sharon Neufeld. You and Sharon were good friends and I'm sure she would be a help to you. They don't know about your accident and memory loss, but if you need anything contact them. Ok?" Bill wished he had made more of an attempt to go north with her. But there were so many memories there and right now he didn't want that on top of everything else.

"I will." "Marie has become a good friend too. She'll be looking out for me, you can count on that." Dawn said.

"I hope this friend of hers is a decent guy. I wish I knew who he was. I should have checked him out before agreeing to this." Bill said.

Dawn quickly changed the subject, not wanting Bill to ask any more questions.

She didn't want to lie to him. "Where are you now?" She asked in a cheerier note.

"I'll be crossing the border into North Dakota this morning. The weather sure is hot, here in Saskatchewan, for this time of year. Thank goodness for air conditioners." He said.

"I better get ready Bill. We're leaving around 8 this morning and I have a few things to pack yet. I'll be waiting for your call on Thursday morning at which time I will tell you all about my trip."

"You be careful on the road, I love you." Dawn said, wishing she could just tell him to turn around and come home.

"I love you too." Bill replied. "I'll talk to you Thursday morning then."

After hanging up the phone, Dawn was relieved that Bill had not asked any more questions about Marie's friend. How would she explain to Bill, that Marie's friend was Nick. He would have forbidden her to go, if he had known.

Dawn quickly had her shower and got dressed. Then in between scurrying around and putting the last few items in her suitcase, she made herself some coffee and toast. When she looked at the clock, she noticed that she only had 15 minutes before Nick arrived. She didn't have much time to eat her breakfast. She was deep in thought as she stared out the window watching the birds.

She was startled by the knock on the door, which made her spill some of her coffee on the table.

When Dawn looked out the window, she saw Nick's blue truck parked outside.

He's early she said to herself opening the door then invited him in.

"I didn't hear you drive in." She said surprised to see him already.

"Sorry, I'm a bit early." He said apologizing. Dawn motioned

Will Love Conquer All?

for him to take a seat.

"Finish your coffee." He said, looking at the half cup of coffee sitting on the table.

"Would you like some?" She asked.

"Sure, we have a few minutes yet." He said looking around the room. "You sure spruced this place up. Do you mind if I have a look around?" He asked.

"Go ahead." Dawn said, wiping up her spilt coffee, before pouring a cup of coffee for Nick.

Nick made a quick tour through the house. "You sure have done a lot to this place. I see you put the master bedroom upstairs. That used to be my bedroom, when I was a kid." He said.

Dawn almost spilt her coffee again. The thought of Nick in the room that her and Bill now called theirs, disturbed her.

"Are you all right?" Nick asked, noticing her hand shaking.

"I'm fine." She said quickly changing the subject. "Have you and Marie known each other long?" Dawn asked

"Oh, about 5 years." He said smiling, as he thought of Marie and her cheerful disposition. "She is a breath of fresh air." He added.

Dawn got up and placed her empty cup in the sink. She poured out the rest of the coffee and washing up the few dishes, while Nick gulped down the last of his coffee.

Then handing Dawn his cup he looked at his watch and said. "We best go, as it is 8 on the button. These all your bags?" He said, picking them up and heading out to his truck.

"Yes." She said taking one look around to be sure she had not forgotten anything.

She picked up her purse and walked outside and locked the door behind her.

Nick put Dawn's bags in the camper shell on the back of his truck before opening the door for her. Then taking a quick glance around the yard, he walked to the driver's side and slid in behind the steering wheel.

Book 1 of the **Mountains and Valleys of Life**

They were almost to the treed area when Nick suddenly slammed on the brakes. Dawn reached for the dash to prevent hitting it. Nick made no apology, but backed up, all the while scanning the bush with his eyes. He stopped and got out to check something on the moist ground beside the truck. Dawn could see he was angry when he got back in. He quietly muttered the words. "That stupid fool."

Dawn was now getting upset with him. Who was he calling a fool?

"When is Bill getting back?" Nick asked angrily.

"In 2 weeks." She said, looking away from him.

Once again they were on their way. Nick was almost to town when he was finally calm enough to speak to Dawn. "Did Bill mention anything to you about a cougar in these parts?" He asked. His knuckles now white as he angrily gripped the steering wheel.

"Y-yes," She said slowly. "He told me not to go wandering, out in the bush anymore, but to stay near the house. Apparently there was talk of one west of here."

"How nice of him." Nick said sarcastically. "Well those were cougar tracks back there and I don't think you should stay there alone, while Bill's gone."

"I'll be fine." She said defiantly. "Bill did say we should get a dog though, just in case some animal did come around. He didn't want to leave right now, but he made a promise and I felt he should keep it." She was very defensive when it came to Bill. Why blame Bill for some old cougar that happened to be running around. She was no fool and had enough sense to be cautious.

They drove the rest of the way in silence. Marie was ready and excited when they got there. She greeted them cheerfully but immediately noticed the friction between her friends.

"What's up? You look like you just had a argument. What happened?" She asked.

"I don't appreciate my husband being called a fool." She said angrily looking at Nick.

Nick looked directly at Dawn. "Any man who leaves his wife at home alone, in a strange area with a cougar around, in my opinion is a fool!" He said angrily.

"Keep your opinions to yourself." She said curtly.

Dawn turned to Marie while trying to calm down. "Nick thinks." *Dawn said emphasizing the word thinks.* "That he found cougar tracks in our driveway."

"That's it. You're staying with me until Bill gets back." Marie said. "It really isn't safe for you out there alone. Especially now that there is proof that the cougar has been around your place."

Nick looked at Dawn with an odd smirk. He had Marie on his side now. He patted Marie on the shoulder while winking at Dawn. "I think that is a good idea." He said.

All Dawn said, was that she would think about it. At the present time she still planned to stay in her own home.

"Are you ready to go?" Nick asked Marie taking her suitcase then placing it in the back with the others. Nick opened the door and waited while Marie slid in the center. When Nick closed the door their eyes met briefly, which left Dawn feeling very uncomfortable. She told herself she must have been mistaken and put it out of her mind.

When Nick started the truck, he said. "Well we're off then, if everyone's ready?"

The day was a mixture of rain, cloud and sun. It was like the saying in Alberta. If you don't like the weather, wait a minute it will change and that's what it seemed to do throughout the day.

Marie was determined that everyone would enjoy the trip and for the most part, she was successful in doing so. The morning argument was over. No one brought up the topic of the cougar, nor was Bill's name mentioned. Nick and Dawn avoided talking to each other as much as possible, but Marie chatted almost non-stop. She tried her best to include everyone in her conversation. Marie asked Dawn if there was anyone in the area that would be able to give her the information that she was looking for? Dawn told them of Lyle and Sharon, but was careful not to say that Bill had mentioned them to her that morning.

They stopped at Whitecourt for lunch and then drove non-stop the rest of the way.

Nick had booked three single rooms at the main motel in Peace River. He told Marie he had done it, just in case Dawn wanted to be by herself. He was sure she would need time to reflect on everything she may learn. He also knew Marie meant well, but privacy was not what Dawn would get, with her constant chattering.

After taking their suitcases to their individual rooms, Dawn was thankful to whoever had the foresight to book her a room for herself.

They went to a different restaurant than the one at their motel for supper, but when they were about to leave, a lady quickly came over to Dawn and excitedly gave her a hug.

"Dawn you look great. When did you get into town?" She asked excitedly.

She was speechless and somewhat taken back by the suddenness of what happened.

Marie could see the surprise and confusion in Dawn's face. She quickly introduced herself and Nick to the lady that Marie presumed to be Dawn's old friend.

"Hi." Marie said as she stretched out her hand to this now excited lady. She did her best to divert the attention away from Dawn. A man who Marie presumed was the ladies husband came over to join them.

"I'm Marie a friend of Bill and Dawn's, and this is a friend of mine Nick Helmsley." They shook hands and the Lady introduced herself as Sharon Neufeld and her husband Lyle.

Dawn now over the initial shock and grateful for Marie's sudden intervention, realized these were the people Bill had told her about. "Bill told me to contact you when we got here." Dawn said when Sharon turned her attention back to Dawn.

Sharon found her comment rather strange. Hadn't she

planned on looking them up, after coming all this way? "Where is Bill?" Sharon asked.

"He promised Darcy to drive his truck for a while. He'll be gone for a couple of weeks." Dawn said. At that point Dawn noticed Nick had taken Lyle aside to talk to him.

"Where are you living now?" Lyle asked, returning to talk to Dawn while Marie and Sharon struck up their own conversation.

"Bill bought a quarter section of land north of Calgary about a month ago."

"We had some remodeling done to the existing older house and we both love it there." Dawn said catching a glimpse of Nick out of the corner of her eye.

"Where did you say Bill was now?" Lyle asked.

"He's driving for our son Darcy for a couple of weeks. Right now, he is on his way to Pennsylvania." She said.

Dawn saw Sharon quickly cover her mouth and gasp in horror while looking over at her. Dawn realized that Marie had probably told Sharon all about her accident and memory loss. She presumed Nick had already told Lyle, which deflected an awkward situation for Dawn.

Sharon came over to Dawn and gave her another hug, while tears rolled down her cheeks. "I'm so sorry Dawn I did not know." She said. "How long are you going to be in town?" Sharon asked.

"We are leaving Wednesday morning, after Nick finishes his business here." Dawn said. "I want to see a few things before we go back." I would appreciate it if you could tell me all you can about our sons accident." She said.

Sharon looked at Lyle, then at Dawn. "Are you sure this is a good idea?" She asked before inquiring as to where they were staying.

Dawn told her, and they made arrangements to meet at the restaurant in their motel at 10 o'clock the next morning. Then at one o'clock they would meet up with Nick at the restaurant when he finished with his meetings.

Dawn did not sleep much that night. She was very restless and sat watching television until two in the morning. She finally shut off the television and tried to sleep, but it was some time before she drifted off. She was wide-awake by 7 o'clock so she had her shower and got dressed. I might as well go for coffee instead of sitting here, she thought to herself.

Dawn was sitting drinking her coffee and looking out the window when Nick walked over to join her.

"Didn't sleep much, I gather." He said looking at the darkness around her eyes.

"Something like that" She said staring into her cup.

"That's understandable." He said.

"I want to thank you and Marie both for deflecting an awful situation last night." Dawn said.

"Glad to help. I hope you find what you are looking for. I'll help in any way I can." Nick said. "I have a meeting this morning for a couple of hours, but this afternoon, Marie and I are all yours."

"Thanks." Dawn said. "I do want to see where we lived, where our son was killed and anything else that may jog my memory."

"Is that wise?" Nick said wondering if she was really doing the right thing.

"I have to Nick." She said looking at him. "I just have to try something!" She said sadly.

Nick looked at her, wishing he could hold her in his arm to comfort her and tell her that everything would be ok. He again found himself becoming angry with Bill. He should be here, he thought to himself, instead of trucking off to the U.S. Nick ordered his breakfast, then tried to encourage Dawn to eat something, but she said coffee was all she wanted.

"I'll eat something later." She said.

They sat in silence while Nick ate his breakfast, but several times he'd glance over at her.

Each time she just stared out the window. When he drank the last of his coffee he said. "I have to go now, but I will see you

Will Love Conquer All?

at lunch."

Dawn only acknowledge him with a slight smile, leaving Nick with a feeling of concern and helplessness. Had he done the right thing in allowing her to come with them?

Soon after Nick left, Marie arrived. I'm sorry I slept so long." She said, looking at Dawn's pale complexion. "Are you feeling all right Dawn?" She asked.

"Yes I'm fine. I just didn't sleep very much last night. Thanks for the help at the restaurant last night. Your a great friend." Dawn said.

Marie ordered coffee while looking at the menu. She asked Dawn if she had eaten anything, but Dawn insisted that coffee was all she wanted. She would eat later. After Marie finished her breakfast, they decided to go for a walk to see what the town was like. To Dawn's disappointment nothing seemed familiar to her at all. She began to wonder if this trip would accomplish anything.

Sharon arrived at the Motel only moments after Marie and Dawn. She was in somewhat of a dither as she began to apologize to Dawn. She explained that something unexpected had come up at work so she had to be back in two hours.

"Don't worry about it. Nick said he would be free this afternoon and was willing to drive us around. Would you tell me a few things about the years we lived here? Especially about Stephen's accident." Dawn asked.

Sharon first told Dawn how they had met, then went on to tell her what she remembered about the day of the accident. How the police had come to inform Dawn of the accident, then tried to contact Bill and Darcy who were on their way to Edmonton.

Dawn and Marie sat listening to the details intently. When Sharon finished, Dawn asked if she would mind taking them to the scene of the accident. She also wanted to go to the place they used to live. Sharon wasn't sure Dawn was doing the right thing, but Dawn insisted that was what she had to do. Sharon then agreed to take her and Marie to both places.

They drove a few miles west of town, when Sharon pulled into a driveway.

"It was in this area, but the exact spot I'm not sure of." Sharon said.

Dawn sat silently for a moment studying the area. All she saw was a straight stretch of highway with a few houses nearby, but nothing unusual. After a few minutes, Dawn asked Sharon if she could take her to where they lived.

Marie and Sharon chatted to each other on the way, while Dawn sat in silence taking in the scenery. She tried real hard to remember something. Soon Sharon turned into a driveway that lead through some trees and into a large opening. Dawn looked at the house and garage that was surrounded by a couple acres of lawn. There appeared to be no one home, when Sharon stopped in front of the house. Sharon went to the door, but came back to inform Dawn, that no one was home. Dawn got out of the car and spent a few moments wandering around the yard. It was a very peaceful setting and she decided to ask Bill why they had moved from here. She was very disappointed that she could not see the inside of the house, but perhaps the people that lived here would be home later.

Time was going by and Dawn knew Sharon would have to be getting back, plus she too was beginning to develop a slight headache. Once they returned to the motel, Dawn gave Sharon a hug and thanked her for all her help.

"I hope the next time we meet, it will be under better circumstances." Dawn said.

"I hope so too." Sharon said returning Dawn's hug.

Dawn excused herself, telling Marie that she would meet her and Nick later for lunch, leaving Marie and Sharon standing there, watching her go into the motel.

Sharon and Marie talked for several moments, both sharing their concern about Dawn's appearance. "It was been nice meeting you. Keep an eye on Dawn, she looks awful pale."

Will Love Conquer All?

Sharon said.

"I will." Marie replied, before saying goodbye to Sharon.

Dawn unlocked the door to her room, thankful to be alone for a while. She glanced at herself in the mirror. Her complexion was pale with dark circles under her eyes. No wonder everyone asked her if she was all right, she thought to herself. Dawn took the washcloth and ran some hot water over it. After squeezing out the excess water, Dawn slowly wiped it across her face. It felt refreshing, so she did it all over again, only this time she held the warm cloth on her face for some time. Dawn took out her make up and did her best to cover the dark circles around her eyes and at the same time, help put color in her cheeks.

When she stood back and looked at herself in the mirror, she was somewhat pleased at the transformation. Dawn laid down to rest while recalling all Sharon had told her. She lost all track of time. Then suddenly she heard a gentle knock on the door.

"I come to get you for lunch." Nick said when she answered the door. He was glad to see she again had some color back in her face.

Dawn glanced at her watch while picking up her purse. It was 1:30. Dawn and Nick walked together to the restaurant where Marie was waiting. Dawn sat across from Marie. She winked at her when Nick placed his arm around Marie's shoulder. Marie then kicked Dawn under the table and the two of them did their best to control their laughter. Dawn was thrilled for Marie and hoped Nick would someday tell Marie how he felt about her.

Nick and Marie ordered a meal but Dawn ordered only a bowl of soup. Marie urged her to eat more, but Dawn refused. She didn't really feel like eating anything, but she knew she must eat something before taking the pills for her headache.

Dawn ate her soup in silence, thankful that Nick and Marie were occupied in their own conversation. It also gave her the opportunity to take her pills without them noticing.

Marie suddenly turned to Dawn and apologized for leaving her out of their conversation.

"Where would you like to go next?" Nick asked, picking up the check and refusing to allow either of them to pay any portion of it.

"I would like to go to the grave site." Dawn said thoughtfully. "Sharon explained where Steven was buried, to the best of her recollection. I think I could find it." Dawn said. "I would also like to see the inside of the house where we used to live too." She added, while looking at Nick.

Nick went to pay the cashier while Marie and Dawn walked out to the truck.

Marie turned to her friend while they waited for Nick. "Dawn, are you feeling all right?"

She demanded. "You aren't fooling me with all that make up."

"It's just so much to take in and I'm doing my best to make myself remember, but it just won't come back, but I am learning something about my past." She said.

"I really would like to have a bit of a rest after we get back from the grave site. That is if you don't mind being alone with Nick for awhile?" Dawn said teasing Marie.

"Oh, that may be real difficult." Marie said at which time they both started to laugh.

Nick watched them, as he walked towards them. He was glad to see that everything was not total somber for Dawn, thanks to Marie. "Can I get in on the joke?" Nick asked when arriving at Marie's side.

Marie looked from him to Dawn "It's private." She said and they laughed even more.

They became silent when they neared the graveyard. Nick parked the truck and walked over to open the door for Dawn and Marie. He took Marie's hand as they followed Dawn, as she walked in the direction of where Sharon told Dawn to look. It wasn't long before they found what they were looking for. Tears filled Dawn's eyes when she read the name on the gravestone.

Stephen William Spencer

June 1980 - Sept 1996

This was Bill and her son, she thought as her heart began to ache for Bill.

Dawn reached into her pocket for a Kleenex to wipe the tears that ran down her face.

It had really not meant much to her, until she stood by the grave of their son.

Marie made a move to go to her friend, but Nick gently held her back.

"Leave her for a few minutes. It may help her to remember." Nick said.

Marie wiped a tear from her eye. She wished there was something she could do to help Dawn through her struggles. Tears fell on the gravestone, when Dawn bent over and ran her fingers across the name.

Marie looked at Nick when he released her arm and nodded his head, indicating that it may be time for Marie to join Dawn. She quickly went to the side of her friend. They hugged each other and wept.

Marie stroked Dawn's hair. "I'm sorry Dawn, but I'm sure God will make everything ok for you again." Marie said. Dawn slowly gathered her composure. They began to walk back to the truck with Nick following slightly behind.

Nick opened the door for them, then walked around and got in. He felt somewhat uncomfortable, as they sat in silence for several minutes. Marie softly said to Nick. "Dawn would like to go back to her room and rest."

Nick took a quick glance at Dawn before starting the truck. When they arrived at the motel, Nick said to Marie. "I have something I have to do and you can come with me. But first I'll see Dawn gets to her room."

Nick walked around to open the door for Dawn. He went with Dawn to her room. He wanted to make sure that she was all right. He took the key from her hand and unlocked the door.

Dawn thanked him, but before she could close the door, he grabbed her arm gently but firmly. "Dawn, are you sure you'll be ok here alone?" He asked.

Dawn was surprised at his concern. Then as their eyes met, she again saw that look in his eyes. This time there was no mistaking it for only concern. "I'm fine really." She quickly said trying her best to keep her voice calm. "You and Marie go and enjoy yourselves."

Nick slowly released her arm while studying her face. He finally nodded his head, accepting the fact that she would be all right, as he closed the door.

Dawn was confused and rather uncomfortable. She could not understand his sudden concern for her. He hardly knew her and yet, there was no mistaking the look in his eyes. It was definitely more than concern.

Dawn's head was pounding something awful. She no longer concerned herself with Nick or anything else for that matter. Wherever she touched her head it hurt. She suddenly felt sick to her stomach, which sent her running to the bathroom. Vomiting was not a thing she did often but it made her head hurt worse, if that was possible. She decided to have a shower. It may not get rid of her headache, but the water running over her head, helped her to relax a bit which relieved some pressure. She stayed in the shower for quite a while wishing it would wash away all her problems.

After getting dressed, Dawn looked in the mirror at her pale complexion. She did her best to bring it back to some normality with the help of her make up kit.

Dawn crawled into bed, and then snuggled into the blankets, feeling suddenly very cold. She covered her eyes to keep the light out of her still throbbing head. She lost all track of time when she heard a knock on the door and Marie's voice. Dawn couldn't bring herself to get up. It took all her will power to fight the pain in her head. She wished Marie would go away as every knock made it feel like someone was hammering on her head. Just go away, she said to herself. Thankfully the knocking stopped, but soon she heard a click when someone unlocked her door. Nick and Marie rushed to Dawn's side when they saw her lying in bed. Dawn could hear the anger in Nick's voice, but right now nothing mattered to her.

"Why didn't you tell us you weren't feeling good?" He snapped. It was not that he was angry with Dawn, but extremely worried about her.

"Nick!!" Marie scolded, as she felt Dawn's cold forehead. "What has gotten into you?" She said sitting on the side of Dawn's bed. "It's one of those headaches again right?" Marie said softly. Dawn's answer was yes but it was so quiet that Marie barely heard her. Marie turned to look at Nick. He stood beside Dawn, not knowing what to do next. "We better take her to the hospital, they may be able to give her something for the pain." Marie told Nick.

Dawn didn't refuse to go, nor did she turn down Nick's help, as he put his arm around her tightly, while helping her out of bed. She laid her head on his shoulder for support as they walked out to the truck. Dawn didn't even realize, Nick's grip on her tightened as he held her closer to him.

Nick wanted to hold Dawn in his arms and kiss away her pain. He was suddenly shocked at himself, when he realized the feelings that he still had for her. He thought he had gotten over her years ago. He told himself what he felt was empathy for her, just as he would for anyone in her situation. Marie opened the door, letting Dawn go in first. After Marie slid in, she told Dawn to rest her head on her shoulder.

Nick slowly drove to the hospital wondering why Dawn had to come back into his life? He was free but she was not.

Then there was Marie. Dear Marie. He was beginning to think that he was falling for her. Just being near Dawn, totally confused him.

Dawn covered her eyes to keep the light out and with every bump it seemed to worsen the pain. Dawn bit her lip trying to fight back the tears, which she was determined not to give in to.

Nick stopped the truck by the emergency door, he then went

around to help Dawn out.

Just as they entered the hospital, Dawn felt a sudden chill come over her. She stopped abruptly feeling very shaky and week.

"What is it?" Nick said feeling her whole body begin to tremble.

Dawn reached for Marie's hand. "They brought him her." She said suddenly grabbing her head with both hands, as a sharp pain shot through her head. Then she collapsed in Nick's arms.

***

Dawn slowly opened her eyes but everything was blurred. She rubbed her eyes trying to get them to focus. Where was she? Nick and Marie quickly came to her bedside, when they saw she was coming around. Her headache was almost gone now. Her vision began to clear and when she looked around, she realized she was once again in a hospital.

"You gave us quite a scare." Marie said, brushing a strand of hair from Dawn's face.

Nick gave Dawn's hand a squeeze. "Is your headache better?" He asked, trying to read her facial expression. But he couldn't.

"Yes." Dawn said. "I'm sorry for bothering you guys."

"No bother. We're just glad your ok." Nick said putting his arm now around Marie.

Just then the Doctor walked in. "We would like to keep you overnight, just for observation." He said.

Dawn quickly sat up in her bed. "No!! I am fine." She said.

"I think you should stay." Nick said firmly.

"No, I am fine. Really." She said again.

"Well." The doctor said slowly looking at her friends. "We'll keep her for another three hours to be sure nothing else stirs up. If everything is fine at that time, she can go." Dawn did agreed to that.

Dawn then told Nick and Marie to go and enjoy them selves as she had taken up enough of their time. When Marie was satisfied that Dawn was actually feeling better, she suggested to Nick, that they go for a walk along the dike.

Dawn smiled while watching Marie link arms with Nick at which time he placed his hand on hers.

"You two go on." Dawn said. Marie was again her bubbly self. She winked at Dawn when they left for their walk.

Dawn laid back and stared out the window at the occasional cluster of billowing clouds that floated by. Her mind went back to just before she past out. What was it that gave her that terrible feeling, when she entered the hospital? She closed her eyes and tried to focus on the moment she entered the hospital. Her first vision was of the grave and then another vision popped into her head. A body draped with a blanket lying on a stretcher. All she remembered was his brown hair showing from under the sheet and his work boots on the other end. "Stephen." She said quietly trying to remember more, but the vision disappeared. Dawn covered her eyes with her hand trying to hide that terrible vision. A deep sadness came over her and reluctantly she tried to remember all that she had seen and heard. She again felt very tired. Partially from little sleep the night before and also the medication she had been given earlier was still taking effect.

Dawn had no idea how long she had slept. But she woke up when a nurse came in to take her blood pressure and temperature. "What time is it?" Dawn asked.

"It's 7 o'clock." The nurse said, putting the cuff on Dawn's arm. Then squeezing that rubber ball at the end of the hose, until Dawn was sure that her arm would blow up. When the nurse finished, she asked Dawn about her headache. Dawn told her it was much better now.

To Dawn's relief, she was informed that she could go home. She was hoping Marie would bring her purse in. Her hair looked terrible and needed a brushing and she also needed something to put color back into her face. She had just drawn the curtain back, when Nick walked into the room.

"Where's Marie?" Dawn asked.

"She's resting at the Motel." Nick said. Laying Dawn's purse on the bed.

"Is she all right?" Dawn asked wondering why Nick had come alone.

"Yes she is fine. She just thought she would wait for you there." He said offering his arm to Dawn, which she ignored. "Give me a moment" Dawn said opening her purse. She brushed her hair, while thanking him for bringing it in. He didn't say anything, until she was done.

"How's the headache, truthfully?" He asked.

"I'm fine now." She said avoiding his eyes. "It's practically gone."

"Good." He said starting the truck. "I talked to the people that live on your old place." "They said it was fine, if you wanted to come up and look around, and—"

Dawn looked at him. "And what?" She asked.

"Well." He started slowly. "Apparently the car your son was in, is still sitting out back in the bush."

"I want to see it." Dawn said quickly.

"I don't think it's a good idea." Nick said. "But, I will take you to see the house."

Dawn was determined to see the car with or without Nick. She decided not to say anything until after she saw the inside of the house. When they walked up to the front door a young couple greeted her warmly. They were quite willing for her to wander freely through the house alone. Allowing her to spend as much time as she needed while they talked to Nick. Dawn was sure she would remember something here, as she slowly went from room to room. She felt like she was in a dream world. Everything seemed vaguely familiar, but so did their new home. If only she could say, "Yes, I remember that." It was all very disappointing for her. When they were about to leave she asked the people about the car. They looked at Nick and then back at Dawn before telling her where it was.

Nick was not happy as he drove her to the back part of the

acreage. They walked in a few hundred yards to an opening. Nick touched Dawn's arm gently, then pointed to a black car that sat almost hidden in the trees.

She slowly walked over and stood quietly looking at it, before walking around it.

She took in every detail. First she looked at the driver's side, which obviously had been torn apart by the Jaws of Life, to get at the victim. The driver's bucket seat was bent way back. The steering wheel had been bent almost in half, which obviously must have caused massive internal injuries. The rear window was the only one intact.

Dawn closed her eyes as once again the vision of the body in the hospital haunted her. It must be Stephen she said to herself as she laid her head on the car and wept.

Nick went over and put his arms around her. He held her close, allowing her to weep on his shoulder.

After a few minutes Nick handed her a couple of Kleenex. Dawn slowly began to get control of her emotions when Nick guided her back to the truck. "Let's go." He said.

Dawn had regained her composure by the time they got into the truck. She saw Nick wiped tears from his eyes, when he thought she wasn't looking.

Nick looked straight ahead with his hand resting on his steering wheel. "I didn't think this was a good idea," he said.

"No," Dawn said. "I'm glad we came. It makes a couple of things fit together."

"Do you remember any of this?" Nick asked.

"There are a couple of flash backs, which is more than I had before." She said.

They drove back to town in silence. Marie was waiting for them at the restaurant.

She looked at Dawn then at Nick. "Did you see it all?" She asked. He nodded as they joined Marie at the table. They each had a coffee but Dawn decide to order a muffin, because she hadn't eaten much all day.

Marie changed the subject by telling Dawn about their day. She did her best to cheer Dawn up. It had been a long trying day for all of them and after Dawn had finished her coffee and muffin, she decided to turn in. But not before they set a time to meet for breakfast. Nick told them he hoped to leave no later then 9:30.

* * *

The next morning Dawn again was up early. After showering and doing her hair, she realized she was actually hungry. She had everything ready to go before she went to the restaurant. She had finished her first cup of coffee when Nick and Marie came in.

"Your up early." Marie said looking at Dawn who appeared to look well rested.

"Yes." Dawn said. "I'm actually hungry this morning."

"Well then lets order." Nick said, as he and Marie joined Dawn.

They ate a hardy breakfast, while talking and laughing at Marie's jokes. It wasn't long before Nick interrupted by putting his arm around Marie. "I'm going to have to interrupt, as it's 9:35, and high time that we were on our way." He said.

Marie leaned against Nick. "It's a shame our time is up, but I guess we better start back. After all, it is a long drive." She said.

Nick again refused to take any money for their meal, so while he went to pay Dawn and Marie checked out of their rooms. When they met Nick back at the truck, he took their suitcases and placed them in the back, while Marie and Dawn got into the truck.

Their drive home was uneventful. Marie and Nick chatted most of the way occasionally bringing Dawn into their conversation as to not leave her out. Dawn didn't mind though. She had a lot to think about. How she wished Bill would be home when she got there.

They decided to have supper together when they got back. Dawn's stipulation was that this time, she was paying the bill, to which Nick and Marie grudgingly agreed.

"Have you decided to stay with me until they catch the cougar?" Marie asked Dawn.

"Oh!" Dawn said. "I totally forgot about it. It's probably moved on by now and besides, Bill's going to phone first thing in the morning. I don't want to miss his call."

"We'll talk about it tomorrow then." Nick said, looking directly at Dawn.

Dawn quickly looked away to avoid his glance. "Well Dawn, you know your welcome to stay with me." Marie said.

"Thanks and I do appreciate it." Dawn said smiling at Marie.

Nick set Marie's suitcase inside the door of her home then gave her a hug. He returned to his truck where Dawn sat nervously waiting. Neither one of them spoke when he drove Dawn home. Dawn knew Nick was looking carefully for any sign of the cougar, when they drove down her driveway. Dawn didn't wait for Nick to open her door, but went straight to the house and unlocked the door, while he got her suitcase. The house felt cold and empty so Dawn turned up the heat. Nick came into the kitchen and sat her suitcases near the door. "I'm going to check around the house before I leave." Nick said heading back out the door. Nick walked around the house checking the ground for any signs of animal tracks. When Nick returned, he said.

"You better tell Bill about the cougar. I'll check to see if any one has seen or got him yet. I'll talk to you tomorrow but I would feel better if you considered staying with Marie."

"I'll think about it." Dawn said avoiding his gaze. "I would like to thank you for all your help. I really do appreciate it." Dawn said.

Dawn looked at him as the tone of his voice changed from anger to tenderness.

"Do you still have my number, if you need me?" He asked walking to the door. Dawn nodded that she did. "I'll talk to you tomorrow then." He said closing the door behind him.

Dawn watched him walk to his truck and drive off leaving

her alone, to gather her thoughts and reflect on what she had seen and heard the previous day.

Chapter 9

When Dawn looked at her clock the next morning it was already 10 o'clock.

My goodness, I must have been exhausted to sleep this late, she said to herself. Dawn laid there for a few more minutes, listening to the wind blowing outside. Fall was definitely here she thought, as she got up and slipped on her old but warm housecoat. The temperature was cooler this morning, which made a nice warm bath sound good. She was just about to step into her tub, when the phone rang. Dawn quickly put her housecoat back on and ran to the phone.

"Hello." Dawn said a bit out of breath.

"Hi, where did I get you from?" Bill asked.

"I was just about to have my bath. It's sure good to hear your voice again."

"How is everything going?" Dawn asked.

"Everything's going good. I should be unloading tomorrow and hope to pick up my next load later tomorrow afternoon, or Friday morning. How was your trip up north? Did everything go all right?" Bill asked.

"Everything went fine. I'll tell you about it when you get back."

"What was Marie's friend like?" Bill asked.

Dawn had hoped to avoid telling him, that Nick was Marie's friend.

"Oh, he was ok and quite helpful. Marie talked a mile a minute, but was fun to be around." Dawn quickly changed the subject. "Marie wanted me to stay with her until you got back, but"---

"Why, what's wrong? Are you all right?" Bill asked interrupting her.

"I'm fine." It's just that Nick thought he saw cougar tracks in our drive away." Dawn knew instantly after mentioning Nick's name that she should have rephrased it.

Bill went silent for a moment. "I don't want that guy hanging around there, understand. If that cat does come around, you be sure you call fish and wild life. If you don't feel safe there, please go stay with Marie until I get back. Which may be what you should do anyways. You be careful, and don't go wandering away from the house."

Dawn could tell by Bills voice that he was now very concerned and feared for her safety.

"I'll call you tomorrow and if you aren't there I'll call Marie's."

"Do you have her number?" Dawn asked.

"Yes, I think so, but give it to me again, just to be sure." Dawn gave him, Marie's number, at which time he told her that he had to go. How he wished that he was home and had not left Dawn, with that cougar lurking around. Not only that, he was wondering why Nick had been there. "You be careful and look after yourself." He said.

"I will, and you do the same." She told him. "I love and miss you, very much Bill."

"I love you too, and thanks for the note. I'll talk to you soon." He said hanging up the phone.

After warming up the water, Dawn climbed into her bath. She laid back and closed her eyes, trying to relax, but the past few days, were indelibly engraved in her mind. When her water began to cool off, she suddenly felt hungry.

Dawn sat up and looked around at the newly decorated bathroom. It felt like she was in a dream. Nothing seemed real to her and even her friends and husband were still strangers. Dawn was lonely even though she had a family and friends.

Will Love Conquer All?

After getting dressed she brushed her hair. The scar on her head was less predominant as her hair grew longer. "Time heals all wounds." She said to herself, while going into the kitchen, to make herself something to eat.

The sun was shining through the trees as she sat eating her breakfast, which was now more like brunch. She watched the birds fluttering in the trees, which reminded her of the bird feeder she had still not bought. Dawn reached for a piece of paper and began to make a list of what she needed from town. She put some clothes into the washer then refilled her coffee cup and went out on the porch, to sit on one of the wicker chairs. She was enjoying the warmth of the sun when she heard a dog barking and the clip clop of horse's hooves. Gradually through the trees she saw a horse and rider, with a dog running along side. She wondered who it could be, but upon coming closer, she could tell that it was Nick.

Dawn got up when he approached the house. The dog found Dawn immediately and was all over her before Nick got off his horse. When Dawn bent down to pet the dog, it licked her face while wagging its tail vigorously.

"Did you have a good sleep after your trip?" Nick asked.

"Yes, I must have been exhausted, for as late as I slept this morning." She said as the dog nuzzled her hand for more attention.

"This is a beautiful dog." Dawn said patting it on the head.

"I got her for you. She should let you know if you have some unwanted company. By the way, did you talk to Bill about staying with Marie?" He asked.

"Yes" Dawn replied. "But if the cougar hasn't been sighted around here, it may have moved on. I would like to find out first." She said not backing down.

Nick shrugged his shoulders while tying his horse to the fence. She was a very independent woman and determined to have her way. The dog ran around the house only to start barking briskly. Nick and Dawn went to see what she found and then stood laughing as they watched a couple of squirrels in the tree taunting her.

When Dawn knelt down to pet the dog, it jumped up on her and knocked her off balance as she fell down on the grass. Dawn sat on the grass stroking the dog's thick coat of fur, while it laid its head on her leg. It was obvious that the dog had taken a liking to Dawn.

"Well." Nick said joining them on the grass. "It looks like the two of you should get along fine."

"What's her name?" Dawn asked.

"Everyone just calls her Pup." Nick replied sitting down on the grass to ruffle Pups hair with his hand, before continuing. "She's the last of a litter of pups my neighbour had. They got rid of the rest except for her and as they have three other dogs already, they were anxious to find a home for her. She seems to be well trained but I would advise that you keep her outside, as she is a farm dog, not a house dog."

They sat in silence for some time, when Dawn noticed Nick looking around.

"You must miss this place. After all, you did grow up here." She said.

"I do at times." He said, turning to look at Dawn. "There are a lot of memories here but we must move on."

Dawn looked down at Pup to avoid the look in Nick's eyes. They continued to talk for sometime, when Dawn suddenly jumped to her feet, the color draining from her face.

"Are you all right?" Nick asked quickly, wondering what was wrong now.

"Y-yes." She said slowly looking directly into Nick's eyes.

Nick got up, but noticed Dawn was still studying his face.

"It's your birthday." Dawn said slowly.

Nick wondered what she was talking about. His birthday was not until next Spring.

Dawn stood there looking around as if seeing everything for the first time.

She walked to the front of the house with Nick following her. But he still had no idea what she was talking about.

Dawn pointed to the spot they had just been sitting. "We were sitting there talking and then--." She hesitated taking a few steps along the driveway. "We went for a drive." It was like she was she was in a daze.

Dawn turned suddenly and looked into Nick's eyes and said. "That's when we kissed." Dawn now understood why he had looked at her that way. Only now it was a cold icy stare. She knew she had hurt him and she quickly turned away. "We were friends weren't we?" Dawn said with her back to him.

"Yes, until Bill came along." He said his voice full of bitterness.

"I'm sorry Nick, but you can't blame Bill." She said, walking over to sit on her wicker chair. Nick leaned on the railing watching her as she continued. "You and I saw very little of each other, but I always liked you. Then after that day we started to write each other." She said as she began to remember her past. "Then I met Bill. He was always there for me." She said looking down as the events flooded back to her."Even though we were friends and wrote to each other, it wasn't the same as being together. Then she said softly. "Bill and I fell in love and got married. Later on I heard you also got married." She said looking up at him. "Now I understand why you and Bill dislike each other so much. It's because of me." Dawn said tears filling her eyes.

Nick stood looking down at the floor, his face like stone. Neither one spoke for several moments.

Dawn wiped the tears from her eyes. Bill must not have known whose place this was or he would never have bought it, she thought to herself. That was why he was so angry when Nick first showed up. They had met a couple of times before at some family functions. Marie never knew how right she was, when she joked about Nick and Bill and a girl. Dawn would never have expected that the girl might have been her.

Dawn softly said to Nick. "I'm really sorry Nick. I never meant to hurt you, it just happened, I did liked you a lot but

I never knew how you felt until that day. But I just fell in love with Bill. He really is a great guy as I hope you will someday see and you also fell in love with the woman you married, didn't you?" Dawn asked.

The look on Nicks face suddenly softened as he thought of his now deceased wife. "Yes." He said. "I did love her."

"I'm sorry that you had to be separated at such a young age, but I do wish you all the happiness again."

Nick went over and sat on the wicker chair beside her. He took her hand gently in his and kissed it. "Dawn I did love you, and I will always love you." He said, still holding her hand. "It hurt deeply when you married Bill. It took a while but I knew I had to move on. As I said, we can't dwell on the past. I do miss my wife a lot and it is hard. Then you moved here." Nick said. He hesitated briefly then adding. "A place where you and I should have been together, but it turns out to be not me but another man. I thought things were getting better, but this is like opening up old wounds. You did clear up one thing for me. I guess I should have made more of an effort to go see you." He said. "Long distance relationships can have their drawbacks and we were young."

"What about Marie, Nick? Do you love her?" Dawn asked.

Nick let go of Dawn's hand. "I think so, but it's not the same." He said looking down at his hands.

"If you do, don't loose her. She's a great person." Dawn said. Pup came over to nuzzle her head under Dawn's hand, looking for more attention. Dawn sat scratching her behind the ears while they sat in a strained silence.

The silence was suddenly shattered by a gunshot that rang out in the distance.

Pups hair bristled and her muscles tensed, as she was now on the alert and barking furiously. Nick jumped to his feet, and quickly ran to untie his horse before leaping up into the saddle.

"You better stay inside." He told Dawn. He told Pup to stay as he galloped off, with the dust flying from beneath the horse's hoofs.

Dawn stood watching for several minutes. She felt the quiver of Pups muscles as she stood there growling at the sound of another rifle shot. Dawn bent down and patted Pup on the head. "It's ok girl." Dawn said. "It's ok." Pup licked Dawn's hand as she walked towards the door. Pup stood just outside the door as if guarding her new friend.

Dawn finished her laundry and did a bit of house cleaning, all the while hoping that Nick would be all right. She also hoped that Nick and Marie could make a life together and wished him all the happiness in the world. Dawn felt suddenly very lonesome for Bill. She prayed that God would keep him safe and wished he could have come home sooner.

Dawn looked around the house going from room to room. Everything looked different now. She began remembering the kitchen as it was before. That was the room they were in mostly, when her and her parents came to visit.

She made herself a cup of tea, then went into the living room and opened her cedar chest. It was full of miscellaneous things, but Dawn went through it little by little remembering the past. Towels, crochet items and potholders given to her by her Grandmother. A small skirt and blouse she wore as a small child. Her and Bill's wedding picture and even her wedding dress that she fondled gentle as she examined it. There were several pictures of their children, as well as her and Bill's parents. Then going through an old album, she came across pictures of Nick and his parents. Dawn looked at the pictures of her children and tears filled her eyes. She sat down studying the pictures, as other parts of her memory slowly began to return.

When Dawn got to the bottom of the cedar chest, she found a little blue box.

She carefully opened it to find, two bundles of letters and cards. The first bundle were letters and cards she had gotten from Bill before they were married. She smiled as she read through them. Dawn then held them against her heart, as she thought of her dear husband. She then gently put them back into place. She picked up the second bundle and looked at the return address. Instantly she knew theses were the letters she received from Nick. Dawn began to read through them. In Nick's letters he would tell about what he had been doing and then he would ask about her.

In one specific letter he told her that he loved her and hoped they could get together soon. The following letters were always signed off with, *Love Nick*.

Dawn decided not to put his letters back. Instead she would destroy them, so no one would ever see them.

She took the letters into the kitchen and got out some matches. Then taking each letter individually, she lit it and placed it into the old cook stove. She had burnt all but three when the phone rang. It startled her and she dropped the remaining letters on the floor, then quickly scooped them up and threw them into the fire, before answering the phone.

It was Marie. "Hi, Dawn" Marie said cheerfully. "I was wondering if you were coming into town tomorrow and if so, how about going out for lunch?"

"That does sound great." Dawn said. "I made a list this morning of things that I need, so I'll meet you and then do my shopping later."

"What have you been up to today?" Marie asked.

"Oh not much. I was just going through my cedar chest and I now have a mess to clean up." Dawn replied.

"Find anything interesting." Marie asked. Dawn hesitated. Marie finally asked if everything was all right.

"Yes." Dawn replied. "Just a lot of memories to catch up on."

Marie found Dawn very distant. It was like she was thinking of something else and not totally on their conversation. "What's happening girl? Are you trying to tell me you are starting to remember things?" She asked.

"Yes, sort of." Dawn said.

"That's great." Marie said. "Do you want to talk about it?"

Will Love Conquer All?

"We'll talk later." Dawn said.

"Is that a dog I hear?" Marie asked as Pup started barking. Dawn glanced out just as Nick was driving in.

"Yes, Nick brought her over this morning." She said motioning to Nick for him to come in.

"We're going out for supper tonight." Marie said excitedly. "He called me this afternoon and said he had something to ask me. Do you think it is what I think it is?" Marie said hopefully.

"I wouldn't be a bit surprised." Dawn said, laughing with her friend. Dawn turned to see Nick reading a letter. She gasped. She thought she had burnt all of them.

"I have to go." She said abruptly. "I will see you tomorrow," Dawn said quickly hanging up the phone.

Nick's face was white as he handed her the letter. One must have slid under the stove when she dropped them. Dawn glanced down to see the words *I love you*. Of all the letters it had to be this one, she said to herself.

"So you kept these all this time?" Nick said.

Dawn could hear the hurt in his voice. She took the letter and threw it into the smoldering embers and watched as it slowly started to glow and them burst into flames. "I'm sorry you had to find that. I thought I got rid of all of them. I didn't want to cause any trouble so I thought it would be best to destroy them. I didn't want Bill to ever see them." She said.

"Why did you keep them?" He said grabbing her by the shoulders and looking into her eyes.

"I don't know I guess, just a memory from the past," she said.

Nick's grip tightened on Dawn's shoulders and she winced in pain as he bent over to kiss her hard on the lips. Dawn stood there in momentary shock, before pushing him away. Nick quickly released her. "I'm sorry, I shouldn't have done that." He said.

"I think you better go." Dawn said. "And please don't ever do that again."

Nick, now forgetting what he came for, said. "I'm sorry."

Book 1 of the *Mountains and Valleys of Life*

Then he turned and went out to his truck and drove off.

Dawn ran up stairs and dropped on the bed and wept. "Oh Bill, I need you." She cried. "Please come home." After a few moments, she wiped her tears way and wondered how she could ever face Nick again. Why did he have to find that letter? Why had she not destroyed them years ago?

Dawn went back into the living room, where she continued to sort through the last remaining items, before carefully putting everything back into the cedar chest. She kept out Bill and her wedding picture. Dawn touched the picture of Bill gently as she looked at how much they had aged. She decided to leave their picture out. When she closed the lid, she placed the picture on top of the chest. "Oh Bill," she said. Her heart ached, for him.

It was 7:30 before Dawn realized that she had not eaten supper. The cup of tea she had made earlier, still sat half full on the living room table. She picked it up and went into the kitchen to make something to eat.

While eating her sandwich, she suddenly thought of Pup. What would she give Pup to eat. She had no dog food to give her. When Dawn opened the door Pup greeted her, by licking her hand. There to her surprise was a dish half full of dog food, with a big bag sitting beside the door. Nick must have brought it this afternoon. That had to be why he came over. Dawn could still feel his grip on her shoulders when he kissed her. She shook her head trying to forget that moment. Dawn patted Pup then set the bag of dog food inside the house. Dawn found an old bowl and filled it with water and placed it beside Pups food, then watched her lap it up.

"You were thirsty weren't you girl." She said patting her head, before going back into the house. Dawn turned the radio on and sat watching the last of the sunset slip away, while sipping her tea. Her thoughts went to her children, especially after going through the photo albums. Little by little things were flooding back. There were some things that were not clear to her yet, but she knew her memory was coming back. The accident, or even the events leading up to it, she still could not remember. What she did remember was waking up in pain in the hospital and the terrible headaches, and not recognizing the people around her.

Then the fear she felt when she was told that, the man who held her hand was her husband. And the two young people, who stood nearby were her children. It was a feeling she would now never forget. A chill ran through her body as she relived those days. She remembered feeling like she was being lied to, that someone must have done something terrible to her and these people were not telling her the truth. With the pictures and documents they showed her, it surely had to be true. She gradually accepted what they told her.

She began to think of her daughter and son and what it must be like for them. Their Mother was alive and yet did not know or contact them in all this time. It must feel like their Mother had died, she thought to herself. She was grateful to them for giving this time to her and Bill so they could first get to know each other before they gradually try to fit in. Dawn smiled as she remembered how Lisa and Darcy were always teasing each other. But the sadness wiped away the smile as she thought of the son they lost. For some reason his accident was not yet totally clear. It was like a dream. She didn't know which was truth or perhaps a movie she had seen, or was it that she didn't want to remember.

Dawn's thoughts turned to Lisa. She began to wonder how she was doing with her schooling in Edmonton. Dawn went over to her phone directory and looked up Lisa's number. She felt a bit nervous as she dialed her number. It rang several times before Lisa answered.

"Hello?" Lisa said, somewhat out of breath when she answered the phone.

"I'm sorry." Dawn said. "Did I get you at a bad time?"

"No it's ok, I was just----" Lisa hesitated. "Mom is that you?" She asked.

"Is everything all right? Dad said he told you to phone if you needed anything."

Lisa said, wondering what happened now.

"I'm fine, I was just thinking about you and wondered how you were doing?" Dawn said.

"Everything's going great. My marks are good and I met someone. I was thinking of bringing him down on thanksgiving to meet everyone." Lisa said excitedly. "I really think you would like him. Where is Dad at now?" Lisa asked.

"He's probably in Pennsylvania by now." Dawn replied.

"Why didn't you go with him, this trip?" Lisa asked, knowing her parents had always done things together. You barely see one without the other. Lisa suddenly realized after talking for some time that it was like old times. Her Mother had asked things that Lisa now realized she would not have known unless--. "Mom!" Lisa said suddenly.

"You got your memory back, haven't you? When and how?" She asked.

"Well how isn't important, but things started to come back slowly this morning."

"There are still a few things that aren't clear. I still can't remember the accident."

Lisa hesitated a moment before asking. "Does Dad know?"

"No this all happened after I talked to him this morning. I better let you go and by all means bring your friend on thanksgiving. We would like to meet him. I love you and take care of yourself." Dawn said.

"I love you too Mom. It's good to have you back. I have missed you." Lisa said tearfully, when they said goodbye.

Dawn decided to go to bed and read for a while, but just as she was about to shut the radio off, the news came on. Dawn listened as she heard.

"*Two shots were fired at the cougar which has been sighted several times in the areas west of town. Unfortunately, there is now a wounded cougar on the loose. This makes it even more dangerous for the people living in that area. If you have reason to believe he is in your area, call fish and wildlife or the R.C.M.P."*

For the first time since she had heard about the cougar, she feared being alone.

She started up stairs, then stopped, turned and went to the door and opened it. Pup stood up wagging her tail as Dawn gently coaxed her to come into the house. Nick had told her to leave her outside, but tonight she didn't feel comfortable in doing so. Dawn then closed the curtains. Pup laid down on the mat by the door, watching Dawn disappear up the stairs.

Dawn read late into the night before shutting off the light and going to sleep.

She was jolted awake from Pups barking. Then there was that continuous growl. Dawn got up and took the flashlight from her nightstand, but decided not to turn it on, as the light from the full moon seemed to be enough to light her way. But just in case, she decided to take it with her.

Dawn slowly crept down the stairs. When she stroked Pups fur, she felt Pups whole body quiver. Dawn slowly went to the window by the door and at the same time tried to calm Pup down, by stroking her. But still the continuous growl emerged from her throat. Dawn moved the curtain ever so slightly. What she saw made her blood run cold. A huge cougar was just inches from the door, eating what remained of Pups food. There seemed to be a large dark spot on its side, and it limped badly as it moved. The wounded cougar, she thought as an icy chill ran through her body. She quietly crept upstairs. Her hands shaking as she took the phone book, and began fumbling through the pages trying to find the number for fish and wildlife. Her whole body was trembling when she dialed the number, only to get a recording. She looked at her clock, which now showed 5 a.m. Dawn found the R.C.M.P. number and quickly dialed it.

A low voice answered at the other end. *"R.C.M.P. How may I help you?"*

By now Dawn's heart was beating hard and fast and she could feel it in her throat as she said softly. "This is Dawn Spencer and

I'm calling because I could not reach fish and wildlife. I think the wounded cougar is just outside my front door." She said her voice quivering.

"I'm sorry, could you repeat that. I couldn't hear you." He said.

"This is Dawn Spencer, and I live 10 miles west of town, at the old Helmsley Place." She said. "There is a cougar at my front door. I think it's the wounded one."

"Is your husband home Mam?" He asked.

"I'm alone with my dog." Dawn said

"Where is the dog now?" He asked

"She's inside by the door growling." Dawn said nervously.

"If you can." The officer said. *"Get the dog away from the door and try to keep her quiet, as not to rile the cougar."* *"Do you have a close neighbour?"* He asked.

"Yes Nick Helmsley." Dawn said softly.

"I know him." The officer said. *"You try to get your dog away from the door and we'll have someone there as soon as possible."*

Dawn hung up the phone and was shaking like a leaf when she crept back down the stairs.

Pup was now standing at the bottom of the stairs, her hair bristling as low rumbles came from her throat. Dawn took hold of her collar and held it firmly, patting Pups head and rubbed her hand along her back and side trying to calm her down. Dawn slowly coaxed Pup to go up the stairs, as she continued to pet her. Dawn sat on the floor firmly holding onto Pups collar, talking to her softly, when suddenly there was a bang on the door. Dawn heard the sound of glass shattering when the big cat jumped up on the door, breaking one of the small panes of glass. Dawn clamped her hand around Pups mouth, trying to keep her from barking, while still holding tightly onto Pups collar. It took all the strength to hold her back, but Dawn knew she had to. Dawn had fears of the big cat crashing through the door or window.

Dawn and Pup sat there for what seemed like an eternity. Suddenly she jumped when she heard two rifle shots. Pup bolted from her hand and ran down the stairs barking frantically. Dawn sat silently rubbing the burn on her hand, which she got when Pups bolted, ripping the collar from her hand. Then she heard someone knocking on her door, and calling her name. She slowly went downstairs, her legs feeling very weak under her. When she looked out the window, she saw Nick standing there. She opened the door, trying to avoid the glass that littered the floor. Nick was almost bowled over when he stepped into the house with gun in hand, as Pup bolted passed him, barking wildly.

"Are you ok?" He asked Dawn, switching on the light.

Dawn was still too frightened to answer, other than nodding her head.

"The cougar is dead. It's all over." Nick said looking at Dawn's pale complexion.

Dawn hung onto the door for support.

"Are you all right Mam?" The police officer asked when he entered the house to see the broken glass on the floor.

Dawn felt suddenly very dizzy. "I--I think I better sit down." She said. Nick and the Police officer quickly went to Dawn and assisted her to a chair by the table.

Dawn put her arms on the table then rested her head on them, she knew she couldn't speak or she would start to cry. She sat there for several moments not able to stop shaking.

Nick put his hand gently on her shoulder. "It's all over Dawn."

"It can't hurt you." Nick said, before walking to the door with the police officer. They talked for some time, but Dawn was not listening to anything that was being said.

The officer returned to rest his hand on Dawns shoulder. "Mrs. Spencer. I'll talk to you tomorrow. Everything's fine now. Try to get some rest." He said.

Dawn did not acknowledge that she heard him, but just wanted everyone to go away. The officer left, closing the door behind him. Nick sat his gun behind the door and went to make some coffee. When it was done he set a cup beside Dawn, who had not moved. Nick sat across from her holding his cup. "Drink some coffee, it may help." He said.

Dawn slowly lifted her head. Her face was still as white as a sheet. Nick would like to have held her in his arms to comfort her, but after what he had done earlier he felt he better not. They sat for some time in total silence. Dawn looked at her watch. It was just 6 o'clock. Only and hour had past since she made the call, but it felt like a lot more. Soon it would be morning, she thought. Things never seem as bad in the daylight.

Dawns hands were still shaking so she used two hands to hold her cup.

"I've never been so afraid in all my life." Dawn said.

"You did fine." Nick said. "What made you bring Pup into the house last night?" He asked.

"I heard the news, about the wounded cougar on the radio. I just couldn't see leaving her out there alone." Dawn said

"Good thing you did or that cat could have killed her." Nick said, sipping his coffee.

"Thanks for coming Nick. When I heard glass breaking, I was afraid it may break the door in, or come through the window" Dawn said.

"Why didn't you phone me right away, when you saw the cat?" Nick asked.

Dawn hesitated. "I--I decided to do like they said on the radio. I phoned fish and wildlife, but there was just an answering machine, so I called the R.C.M.P." She said.

Nick got up to refill Dawn and his coffee. "Dawn I'm really sorry about this afternoon. I shouldn't have done that. I want us to still be friends and be able to face each other when we meet." Nick said continuing. "I can't tell you that I don't have strong feelings for you Dawn.

That would be a lie, but you have Bill and I have to except that. I have to get on with my life and this evening I asked Marie to marry me and she said yes." Then as their eyes met, he said. "You will always have a special part in my heart. You gave me quite a scare tonight." He said.

Dawn's eyes filled with tears. "I'm so happy for you and Marie. I want us to be friends too. I only wish somehow that you and Bill would get to know each other and be friends. You're both very special people." Dawn said.

"That may not be so easy." Nick said going over to stand beside Dawn.

"How about a hug." He asked.

Dawn hesitated, but then slowly stood up. She was grateful to Nick for all his help, but he was nothing more then a friend to her.

Nick however felt very different as he held her in his arms. There was something different that stirred in his heart as he held her for several minutes. "Now you go back to bed. I have a few things to clean up out side." Nick said, kissing Dawn on the forehead when he released her. "It's a good thing Bill and Marie aren't here. They may get the wrong idea." Nick said backing away from her.

"This is just between you and me Nick. No one else." Dawn replied.

Nick agreed. "Go get some sleep." He said on his way out the door.

Dawn swept up the glass that lay shattered on the floor. She then taped a piece of plastic over the spot that just a few moments ago held a pane of glass. Dawn was thankful that it was only a very small pane of glass that the cougar had broken with its paw. Dawn suddenly realized she was still in her flannel pyjamas. Thankfully she had not been wearing her skimpy nightgown. She said to herself as she climbed under the covers. She hadn't realized until she got back to her bedroom, that she didn't even have her housecoat on when Nick hugged her. Dawn's head was beginning to throb from all the excitement. She was extremely tired and it didn't take her long to fall asleep.

Dawn woke up in a cold sweat, and shaking like a leaf. "Oh Bill." She cried, sobbing into her pillow. "I need you." Dawn's headache seemed to be getting worse. She went downstairs to have a shower. She tried her best to relax while standing there letting the hot water run over her head and down her body. After getting dressed Dawn combed her hair then headed to the kitchen.

She made herself a slice of toast, which she ate, then washed down her headache pills with a bit of juice. Dawn had just gone back to her bedroom when she realized she was to meet Marie for lunch. When she looked at her watch, it was already 11:30. She was just about to give Marie a call to let her know that she would be a bit late, when the phone rang.

"Hi how are you this morning?" Marie asked. I heard you had some excitement there last night. It was even on the news." Marie said.

"Excitement like that, I can do without." Dawn told her.

"I was wondering if you still felt like going out for lunch? If not I'll understand." Marie said.

"Yes, I am still planning to meet you. I was just about to call you to let you know that I would be a bit late. If that's all right?" Dawn said. "I sort of overslept. Then after taking an extra long shower, I found myself running a bit late." Dawn told her friend.

"That's great, because I have to talk to you." Marie said.

Dawn had a good idea that Marie wanted to tell her about her engagement to Nick. He had already told her about it, so she would have to act surprised when Marie told her. It would spoil it for Marie, if she knew Nick had already told her. It could also lead to questions of what else they had talked about. Nick and Dawn both felt that what just happened, was best never spoken of again.

Dawn was about to leave, when she realized she had not fed Pup. She scooped up some food from the bag, but before opening the door, she peered out the window to be sure the cougar was gone. She knew it would be, but she had to check anyhow. Pup ran over to her when she poured the food into the empty dish. After filling the other bowl with water Dawn locked the door behind her. There was not a sign left to indicate that the cougar had ever been there. Nick had covered the blood on the driveway, where the cougar died. Dawn was very grateful to him for his thoughtfulness, but it was best that he didn't come over as often.

Marie was waiting for her, when she came into the restaurant. When Dawn sat down to order her coffee, she knew Marie was obviously dying to tell her all about her engagement.

Marie placed her left hand on Dawn's, to show off her beautiful diamond ring.

Dawn eagerly congratulated her, while admired the ring. "When are you planning to have the wedding?" Dawn asked.

"Oh sometime in the spring." Marie said all excited "He has to tell his children first. I do hope that we can all get along. He has a son and daughter and it'll be difficult for all of us at first. Can you imagine me as the step Mother!" Marie said.

"What about a Mother." Dawn said, at which Marie laughed just at the thought of it.

"I hadn't thought of that I guess. First of all, I have to fit in to his family." Marie said. "But it would be nice I suppose." she said in a daze.

The waitress came over to take their order, before Marie excitedly told Dawn all about her evening. "Oh!" Marie said. "Here I have been talking about myself when your whole evening was, -- say somewhat frightening. I was actually hoping you would spend a few nights with me, until they got the cougar. That way we could have discussed wedding plans. But now that's spoiled because they got it." She said.

"We can still get together to do that. I really do appreciate the offer though." Dawn said.

"You mentioned yesterday on the phone, that you were starting to remember some things. Did you remember why Bill and Nick dislike each other so much?" Marie asked.

Dawn hesitated. "Perhaps you should ask Nick. He'll probably tell you."

Dawn said. Dawn figured it was best coming from him, then

he could tell her as little or much as he felt comfortable with.

Marie was disappointed, that Dawn did not say more. "Was I right about them and a girl?" She asked. Dawn nodded as Marie's continued. "So the plot thickens after all. This could even be a movie." Marie said chuckling.

Dawn smiled. "It isn't that interesting. You just have an over imaginative imagination." She said to Marie quickly changing the topic, to Marie's impending marriage. While eating their lunch, Marie told Dawn some of her plans.

They just finished their lunch and were about to leave, when the police officer that had come out that morning, came over to their table.

"Excuse me ladies." He said before turning to talk to Dawn. "Do you feel up to giving me a brief statement of what happened this morning?" He asked. Dawn nodded her head as he sat down beside her. "Everything fine now?" He asked.

"Yes, I'm fine thank-you. It just isn't much fun thinking about it." She said.

"Yes, I can imagine it was frightening." He said, taking out his pen and note pad.

"Just tell me briefly what happened and that should be the end of it." He said.

Dawn slowly went over everything in her mind, telling him what she remembered. The police officer took a few notes then apologized for disturbing them and left.

"Oh. It must have been terrifying! I think I would have died from fright. See I told you, that you should have stayed at my place." Marie said.

"Maybe so," Dawn answered. "At least now it's over, and we know that the cougar is gone. I can now have the freedom to walk around my yard without wondering if it's watching me," Dawn said

Marie looked at her friend. "What do you want to bet that you'll still be looking over your shoulder?" Marie replied.

"Ah, wait until after you're married and Nick moves you out

to the farm." Dawn said.

"Well. I guess not being used to the country life, I probably will do that at first, but I'll have to get used to it." Marie said slowly as they got up to leave.

The first thing Dawn shopped for was a bird feeder and some birdseed. She also bought a windowpane to replace the one the cougar had broken. With instructions and the materials she had bought, she was sure she could fix it herself. She wasn't looking forward to the evening alone. She couldn't wait until Bill called her. She felt very lonely and needed his arms to hold her, and this time she would remember the way things were before. She missed their evenings together, when they would discuss things. What would Bill's reaction be when she told him that her memory was coming back? "Oh Bill, I wish you were here." Dawn said, while driving home.

Chapter 10

Bill sat alone eating his supper. It was a change to get back on the road again, but it wasn't the same without Dawn. He didn't like the idea of leaving her home alone, especially with a cougar lurking nearby. Then there was Nick. He should have insisted that Dawn stay with Marie, or even if Marie had stayed with Dawn, while he was gone. He was still upset for buying the place without checking out who lived there previously. Why had he not remembered that Nick lived somewhere in that area. He did not like him hanging around his wife. He would put a stop to that, when he got home. It was at least a relief to have known that Dawn was again in love with him. He wished that he had taken her with him. The biggest problem was her health. It was still unstable and if she needed to go to a hospital in the U.S., the medical bill would have been phenomenal. It was best for her to be near the doctor that knew her situation.

Well at least the truck was loaded and he was heading home. Bill enjoyed driving truck, but this trip wasn't as enjoyable as he had originally hoped. Most of his life, he had spent farming and driving truck. But after moving back south, they had decided to take a bit of time just for themselves.

Bill found he enjoyed working with wood. He had made some country furniture as well as other smaller items. He had surprised himself at what he could do.

Bill looked at his watch. It was 7 p.m. With the 2-hour time difference it would be 5 p.m. at home. He decided to eat supper and have a shower before calling Dawn.

While Bill sat drinking his coffee, his mind wandered back over the years he and Dawn had spent together. They had always been very close to each other, not like his brother and sister's. They all seemed to live very separate lives from their partners. He saw very little of his siblings since his parents died.

Another truck driver sat in the next booth. It wasn't long before he and Bill struck up a conversation. They started talking about the companies they drove for, then the topic turned to their families. Bill listened as the other driver told him about his wife's affair with a mutual friend of theirs and how she told him she was leaving, the last time he was home. Bill listened, but in so doing, his thoughts went to Nick. Did he have an ulterior motive for dropping in to visit Dawn? Bill suddenly excused himself, saying that he had a call to make. He walked slowly back to his truck, deciding to use the cell phone, instead of the public phone by his table.

Bill dialed his home number. He let it ring for quite some time and was about to hang up, when Dawn, somewhat out of breath finally said hello.

"Where did I get you from?" Bill asked.

"Outside," Dawn said. "I was just about to put up my new bird feeder." She told him.

"How's everything there?" Bill asked. He longed to be with her and have her snuggle up to him. It would be good to get home.

"Oh Bill, I miss you and wish you were here." She said as her voice began to quiver.

"What's wrong?" Bill asked suddenly.

Dawn proceeded to tell him of the prior evenings events. How she had brought the dog into the house, for fear of the cougar showing up, after listening to the news and how her worst fears were realized.

Bill listened intently to all she had to say before asking. "Where did you get the dog?"

"Oh, Nick brought her over. She's a beautiful dog and great company. You'll love her. I'm sure she'll make an excellent watchdog. He got her from someone he knew." Dawn added.

Bill was silent for a moment. Nick was over at their place way too much lately. He now began to have fears of what Nick's motives were. His thoughts went back to the trucker he had just talked to and how his wife had left him, for a so-called friend.

"Bill. Are you still there?" Dawn asked.

"Yes I am still here." He said in a deeper voice, as the anger built up inside off him.

"What's wrong?" She asked noticing the tone in his voice.

"Nothing." He said trying not to bring out the anger he felt. He had left Dawn alone in a situation that could lead to all kinds of complication. He had no one else to blame but himself.

"Bill I do have some great news to tell you." Dawn said excitedly. "I—

"Dawn!" Bill said interrupting her. "I thought I told you to stay away from Nick. I don't want him there and I also don't want you excepting anything from him either." Bill said angrily.

Shocked by Bill's outburst she slowly said. "He only brought the dog over for company and protection for me. We had talked about getting a dog, if you remember. I never called him, when the cougar showed up. It was the police that had called him. He just happened to be the closest neighbour." She said trying to defend herself.

"Just stay away from him." He snapped. "I just don't want him on our property."

Dawn was hurt and it showed in her voice. "You sound like you don't trust me Bill." She said.

Bill knew suddenly he had said too much. He was just angry for not being there for her. It was Nick that was helping her, instead of him. He should be grateful, but why did it have to be him.

"I'm sorry." Bill said. "It's not you that I'm mad at I'm angry at myself for not being there when you needed me. I'm sorry."

He said.

Dawn didn't answer, but bit her lip while fighting back tears. She had so longed to hear his voice, and tell him that her memory was beginning to return, but now it seemed so insignificant. She felt a stab of pain in her heart at the thought of Bill believing that she would be unfaithful to him.

"I love you Dawn." He said, trying to make amends. He then changed the subject by asking. "What was it that you were going to tell me?"

"It's not that important. I'll tell you some other time. Lisa said to say hi to You, when I talked to you again." She said soberly. "I better let you go." Dawn said, needing desperately to be alone with her feelings. "It costs a lot of money talking on the cell phone. I do love you and I miss you." She said, before hanging up the phone.

Bill slowly put the phone back. He blew it, and there was nothing he could do or say from here, to show Dawn how sorry he was. Bill suddenly remembered something Dawn had said. She had apparently talked to Lisa and what was the good news she was about to tell him, before he interrupted her? It was the fact that she had talked to Lisa that made him even more curious. Bill quickly picked up the phone and dialed his home number.

He let it ring for some time but there was no answer. Had Dawn regained her memory? Well perhaps she was putting up her bird feeder or had he actually hurt her deeper then he realized. How could he be such a fool, he said to himself as he hung up. He knew deep down he could trust Dawn and it was Satan that had put the doubts into his mind. Could he end up driving her away from him, just when he regained her trust and love?

Bill climbed into the sleeper on his truck. "Oh God," he cried. "Don't let me lose her. Forgive me for being so stupid and jealous of another man. When I know it was all my fault, for not trusting you to look after everything." Bill prayed. Bill lay there for some time before going to have a shower. After Bill returned to his truck, he didn't sleep very well. He got up early the next morning, had his breakfast then checked over his truck and load. His mind wandered back to the day of Dawn's accident. He had taken a trip to Vancouver for Darcy, and had just returned to the yard when Darcy ran to meet him. His face was pale and his voice quivered. "Dad. Mom was in an accident and is unconscious in the hospital!" Darcy had said. Bill could still feel the shock he felt at that moment. His first thoughts were, first my son and now my wife, please God not her too. He was terribly hurt, when Dawn didn't know him, when she regained consciousness. They had somehow got through that and their love for each other had been strong enough to survive. His only hope was that he had not undone that by one stupid phone call.

Dawn had never asked about the accident and the doctor felt that in all likelihood she would never remember the time prior to, or the accident itself. Bill had never brought it up either, but he knew he would have to do it soon. He thought it best to wait, just in case she did remember. If not he would at least give her time to know and trust him. Bill's whole world was in turmoil and more than ever he wished he were home. Bill decided to wait until evening before calling Dawn again. Right now he had to make some miles.

The sky was clouding over quickly and a few drops of rain began to fall when Bill filled out his logbook. He was glad to be heading home. The weather didn't help Bill's mood.

He listened to the C.B radio as the truckers talked about the wind and heavy rain they had just come through. They were warning other drivers to be cautious when heading west.

Just what I need to slow me down, Bill said to himself. Bill had only traveled 10 miles when the wind picked up and large drops of rain began to hit the windshield. He looked back at his load thankful that it wasn't a load he had to tarp. Especially when he saw the torn and flopping tarp, on the truck he had just met. He hoped that it would not take him to long to get through the worst of the storm. The rain soon turned into a real torrential down pour. Even at full speed, the windshield wipers could not do the job. It was a good thing that the traffic was light. Bill geared down, reducing his speed according to the road conditions.

The truck traffic was still moving, but one by one the cars were pulling over wherever they could, to wait out the storm.

"How far does this storm go?" Came a voice across the C.B.

"You got another 30 miles of this but the wind is strong almost through out the entire state of Pennsylvania." Said another eastbound truck driver.

Bill knew he was not going to make very good time. His only hope was that nothing else would slow him down. The wind was getting stronger and Bill's knuckles were white, as his grip tightened on the steering wheel. With the push of the side wind and straining to see the road through the torrential down pour, it took all his concentration. He was watching for cars that had pulled off to the side where it was unsafe and at the same time, trying to keep the truck steady in the wind. He no longer had time to think about things back home. Suddenly a voice came across the CB radio.

"How about the west bound machinery hauler. There's a car coming up fast behind you and is just looking for an accident to happen."

Bill looked in his rear view mirror, where he saw a flicker of light. He took the C.B mike in his hand and said. "I hope he's not stupid enough to pass, because there's a truck coming from the front." Bill said. Bill quickly dropped the mike. He grabbed the steering wheel with two hands, when he saw the car pull along side. Bill knew the car was not going to get by before the on coming truck reached him.

He slowed slightly moving over to the right as far as he could. The truck driver behind Bill warned the on coming truck of what he was up against. The car made no movement to slow down but kept on going. Oblivious to the fact that he was putting other peoples lives in danger. They did their best to make room for him and at the same time keep the trucks on the road.

Bill could feel the shoulder of the road, beginning to give way under the wheels.

He fought to pull the truck back onto the road and at the same time, trying not to hit the car between him and jeopardize the life of the truck driver, going the opposite direction.

"Hang in there, Buddy." Came a voice across the C.B.

It took all the strength Bill could muster, to keep the truck from being sucked in by the soft shoulder. Bill's forehead was covered with perspiration when he got his rig back on the driving lane. He was very angry, when he reached for the C.B. mike. Shaking from fear he said. "That fool is going to kill somebody!" He then thought about the driver. "How about that east bound truck. Are you ok?" He asked.

After a slight hesitation, came the reply. "Yea, but that shoulder sure is soft. I thought for a moment it was game over." He said.

"Yea, that was to close for comfort." Bill replied.

"I just called the police to be on the look out for that idiot. I hope they get him before he kills someone." Came the voice of the driver behind Bill.

'Thanks for the warning." Bill said, his muscles aching from the tension of pulling on the steering wheel, as well as bracing himself, to what he feared the outcome may be. Bill wondered how Darcy, who was not as experienced a driver as himself, would have made out in this situation. *"Thank-you God."* Bill whispered.

That's all we would need is another accident in our family he thought to himself.

Bill had no time to dwell on that, as his concentration quickly returned to the road conditions ahead. He still had several miles to go to get through the storm. The C.B. was once again quiet as everyone concentrated on their driving. With the heavy rain and wind, it made it almost impossible to see. Bill decided if he got to a rest area before the storm let up, he would pull in and wait it out.

After 40 miles the rain began to let up and the wind died down slightly, relieving much of the strain. Once again a voice came on the C.B. "West bound, you have a couple of bears (which is a name used on radio's meaning, police) ahead of you about 10 miles, with a four wheeler in the ditch. There's only one lane open, so slow down."

"What do you want to bet it's our boy?" Came the voice from the driver following Bill.

"It wouldn't surprise me." Bill answered.

By the time Bill got to the accident sight, the rain was very light, but the wind was still blowing. There was a line up of cars but they were still moving slowly. When Bill got closer, he could see two cars and a jackknifed semi trailer in the ditch. That could have been me he thought. There were two cars in the ditch and yes one of them was the red car.

"Wouldn't you know it?" Came the voice of the driver following Bill. "That idiots car has very little damage compared to the other guy. I hope they throw the book at him." He said.

"Yea, and he'll probably be out of jail tomorrow and driving the same way until he finally kills someone." Bill said.

Slowly the traffic was let by and apparently, they heard later, there had been no serious injuries. Bill was thinking how fragile life really was. Once something happens you cannot turn the time back. It's so easy to mess things up, but not so easy to undo.

The rest of the day was uneventful, and as far as Bill was concerned, that was fine with him. What Bill really wanted to do was to talk to Dawn. He needed to hear her voice and for her to say she forgave him. He was glad when it was finally time to shut it down for the day. The truck stop looked mighty inviting.

The strain of the day was catching up to him. He was hungry and tired. He decided to have supper before calling Dawn. After that, he would be only too happy to crawl into the sleeper for a well, deserved rest.

Bill was relieved when he found a place to park and the truck

Book 1 of the *Mountains and Valleys of Life*

that was following him parked right along side. Bill was surprised to see that it was a truck from the same company that Darcy was working for.

The driver, who was about Bill's age, came over to talk to him.

"Hello, I'm Ted." He said reaching out to shake Bill hand.

"Nice to meet you. I'm Bill. How about joining me for supper?" Bill said.

Ted was only too happy to talk to someone that drove for the same company and especially when you are so far from home.

They walked together to the restaurant. After washing up, they sat down at the table and ordered coffee. They talked about the weather and the stupid driving habit of some people before ordering their meals. The topic then went from talking about the trucking industry to their personal lives, like where they lived and their families.

"Didn't I hear that your wife was in an accident?" Ted asked.

"Yes." said Bill. But she's coming along fine now. She lost her memory, because of a blow to her head and it still hasn't returned."

"That must be hard to live with." Ted said.

"Yes it has been tough, but we are hopeful that it will return soon." Bill said.

Bill's mind drifted back to what Dawn was going to tell him, but then Ted asked if he planned to drive steady. Bill told him he was only doing this while Darcy took a two week holiday. When Bill looked at his watch, he realized that it was already later than he thought. He excused himself, telling Ted that he had a couple of calls to make.

Bill was deep in thought, as he snapped his jacket shut while walking back to his truck. It sure would be nice to be home in his warm bed, he thought as he climbed into the truck. He started the truck, to warm it up before dialing his home number. The phone rang once, twice, then six, seven times and yet no answer. Bill hung up the phone. He was concerned and disappointed, when he was unable to reach Dawn. He missed hearing her voice and his arms ached to hold her. He looked at his watch. It would be almost 9 o'clock at home. Where could she be? Perhaps, she had gone to Marie's, he thought looking up her number, then dialling it.

"Hello, this is Bill." He said. "I was wondering if Dawn happened to be there?"

"N-no why, is there a problem?" Marie asked.

"No, not really. I just wanted to ask her something, and I wasn't able to reach her at home." He told her.

"I'm sure she's fine. She's probably outside, or in the shower and didn't hear the phone," Marie said. "Give me your phone number in case I have to reach you."

Bill gave Marie the number before saying goodbye.

He took off his boots and climbed into the sleeper. He'd rest for 15 minutes to a half hour and call Dawn again. Bill was physically and mentally exhausted. The day had been very strenuous and Bill was only too happy to relax and close his eyes. Soon he drifted off to sleep.

* * *

Bill awoke to find the sunlight drifting through the window. He sat up on the edge of the bed and looked at his watch and was surprised to see that it was already 7 o'clock in the morning. He didn't want to phone Dawn to early, so he decided to wait until after he ate his breakfast. He slipped on his boots and combed his hair, before heading to the restaurant. Ted was not anywhere around. He too had probably slept in. That was fine with Bill because he wanted to make up for the poor day he had yesterday. Bill ate his breakfast, while listening to the other drivers talk about the problems they were having with their dispatchers, or the company they worked for. Nothing has changed Bill thought to himself, as he gulped down the last of his coffee. Bill left a tip on the table for the waitress, then after paying his bill, he went out to his truck.

He checked his load and made sure everything on the truck was fine, then climbed into the cab. Bill called home again, but still there was no answer. He was getting concerned. All kinds of things went through his mind, like imagining that Dawn may have gone somewhere with Nick. It instantly made him angry for allowing such thoughts to penetrate his mind. Jealously and his imagination, would only get him into more trouble. That was the problem the last time he talked to Dawn, he said to himself.

Bill decided to call Lisa before she left for school. "Hi Lisa." Bill said. "This is Dad, how are you? Have you talked to your Mother lately?" He asked.

"Yes, she phoned a couple of days ago. Isn't it great that she's starting to get her memory back." Lisa said.

Bill was silent, and somewhat surprised, even if he had suspected it.

"Dad are you still there?" She asked.

"Y-yes." Bill said hesitantly.

Lisa was surprised that her Father did not know. "Didn't she tell you?" She asked.

"Well." Bill said. "She started to tell me something, but I was mad about something else and she didn't mention it again. I haven't been able to get a hold of her on the phone since." Bill said. "Did she mention anything about going somewhere to you?" Bill asked.

"No." Lisa said, wondering what her parents had argued about.

"I'll call her again later. I'm probably calling when she's outside, or busy doing something and she just didn't hear the phone." Bill said, changing the subject.

"How is school?"

"Oh. It's ok. My marks are still good." She said. "How are things on the road?" Lisa asked.

"The same. I had a close call yesterday, with a stupid driver." He said. "Some guys shouldn't even have a license." Bill added.

"You better be careful." Lisa said. "There has been enough accidents in this family already."

"I'll be careful." "I have to get going, so take care of yourself." Bill said.

"I love you Dad." Lisa told him.

"I love you too." Bill replied before saying goodbye. He was wondering where Dawn could be.

Bill had just filled out his logbook and was about to leave, when Ted knocked on his door unexpectedly, making him jump.

"Sorry about that." Ted said. "I didn't mean to scare you, but have you had breakfast yet?'

"Yes." Bill said. "I was just about to leave. I was hoping to make better time today, than I did yesterday." "The weather put me a bit behind schedule. I guess I sort of slept in this morning to." Ted said. "You have a good trip then and we may see you around the shop sometime." Ted said, waving as he walked toward the restaurant.

Bill was determined to make better time today. He whispered a prayer for Dawn and his family.

He asked God to look after them wherever they were. He also prayed for a safe trip for himself. There was nothing he could do now to try to reach Dawn. He would try later in the afternoon or that evening. His goal now was to make some miles and get home as soon as he possibly could.

Chapter 11

Dawn sat looking at the phone with tears streaming down her face. She could not believe that Bill did not trust her. Nick had been a big help to her, but she knew it was best if he did not come over, when she was alone. Even thought there would never be anything but friendship between them. Dawn decided to get out of the house and go for a walk, to clear her head. She loved Bill very much and would never be unfaithful to him. Her whole life revolved around Bill and her family. She wished there was something she could do to show Bill how much she cared for him.

Pup greeted Dawn the moment she stepped outside the door. Dawn wiped away her tears then bent down to scratch Pup behind her ears. "Lets go for a walk girl." Dawn said. Pup walked beside Dawn, looking up occasionally for approval to run ahead. Dawn waved her hand for her to go. Off she ran barking at a squirrel that scurried up the tree. It then angrily chattered at Pup for disturbing him. Dawn was grateful to Nick for giving Pup to her. Pup had become a wonderful companion and was becoming very protective over Dawn in the short time she had her. Dawn walked for some time along the outside edge of the bush. She shied away from taking the trails through the trees even though she knew the cougar was gone.

She sat on a stump looking back at their yard. It felt so new and strange to call this home. It was as if she was on a holiday and this was all temporary. Bill had worked hard to get their new home ready before he left. He had gone along with her ideas and had bought her so many nice things. If only there was something she could do for him, she said to herself.

Just then a couple of deer appear at the edge of the tree line, only to be frightened off by Pup, when she started barking. Dawn yelled at Pup just as she was about to set off on the chase. She wished Bill was here to enjoy the outdoors with her, but his recent jealousy bothered her. This was their home now and whether Bill liked it or not, Nick was their neighbour. After Nick and Marie's marriage, Dawn would still be friends with Marie and it would be difficult if Bill and Nick did not resolve their differences. Dawn had chosen Bill years ago and nothing would change the love she felt for him.

Dawn lost all track of time, until Pup started pawing on her leg. She suddenly realized it was getting dark and she was quite a distance from the house. She did feel somewhat safe with Pup, who now remained close beside her, as they walked quickly back home. Dawn occasionally glancing towards the bush. With the on slot of darkness, everything seemed frightening. The lengthening shadows were now reaching out to her, as a breeze rustled through the leaves. There were a multitude of sounds. The crickets were chirping the crocking of frogs, then a timely hoot of an owl hidden deep in the bush.

She jumped when a squirrel scurried through the under brush nearby, then quickly disappeared up the tree.

It was the distant howl of what she hoped was only a coyote that sent chills up her spine. She was glad when she finally approached the barn. Here the yard light began to give her some sense of security.

Dawn suddenly stopped between the house and barn. She remembered Bill and Joe talking about converting the old barn into a workshop someday. She turned and walked over to the barn. She pushed hard on the edge of the large door, it grudgingly began to slide on the rail above. Dawn saw nothing but darkness. She reached in and carefully slid her hand along the side of the wall, hoping to find a light switch. Just when she thought she felt the switch, something hit her leg. Dawn jumped back and let out a screech and in doing so, almost tripped over Pup. Her heart was pounding when she looked down. There sat Pup looking up at her with those big brown eyes. She then realized it had only been Pups tail that hit her leg. She took a deep breath to calm her racing heart. Dawn reached down to stroke Pups head, before looking for the light switch.

Once she found the switch, she gave it a flick and was glad that the lights did work. Even though they weren't very bright, it was enough to light up most of the barn. She looked around thinking of all the work it would take to get this place the way she would want it. Dawn noticed the ladder that led up to the hayloft. It was too dark to climb up there now. She would have to wait until daylight, but she was determined to begin working on it in the morning. Dawn turned off the lights and closed the door. While walking towards the house, she began laying out the plans of what she needed to do.

For the first time, Dawn felt she had a cause to work towards. She needed something to do instead of sitting around and feeling sorry for herself, she decided to start working on it early the next morning.

There was lot of work to be done before Bill returned. Dawn knew, she would need some help with the painting, and repairs and Joe was her only hope. She would have to call him to see if he had time to do it for her.

* * *

Dawn was up at the break of day, determined to get a start on her new project.

When she came down the stairs, Pup stood up wagging her tail, waiting for Dawn to open the door and let her outside. Since the cougar incident, Dawn kept Pup in at night then first thing in the morning she would let her out. Pup would always lie on the mat by the door when she came in and there she stayed until she was let out in the morning.

Dawn had a quick cup of coffee and a slice of toast. Then placing one of Bill's caps on her head, she set off for the challenge of cleaning up the barn. Dawn slid the barn door open and looked inside. It looked different in the daylight. She was pleasantly surprised, to find it did not look as ominous a task as she first thought. There was a cement floor that went from the front, right through to the back door, which look to be in reasonable good condition. On both sides of that were the stalls, which consisted of plank flooring, that was raised about 6 inches above the cement. Several planks were missing and others needed to be replaced, but that could be done when they removed the stalls and mangers.

Everything was covered with a thick layer of dust. There was a pile of old bales stacked in one corner and when she looked around, she could see that the floor in spots may need a bit of scraping.

Dawn looked up at the ceiling to check for holes or broken boards, in the loft above. It looked fine, except for one small spot that was covered with plywood. Dawn aimed for the ladder that led to the hayloft. She cautiously climbed up, just enough to see what was up there. There were a few old bales, in a pile near the side door, but the rest was mainly loose straw scattered throughout.

Dawn went back down to search the area. She soon found an old pitchfork and shovel lying outside. They were in poor condition but still usable. She also found a broom in reasonable condition, standing in the corner of the barn.

Dawn was glad that she had brought a pair of Bill's gloves with her, as the fork handle was full of splinters. She took the fork and broom to the ladder and pushed them up ahead of her, as she climbing up into the loft. Dawn then unlatched the small door on the side of the loft and found it swung open with ease. Then checking to see that Pup was out of the way, she began to throw out the dozen or so bales, after which she proceeded to scrape the straw together and pitched it out. Time seemed to go by quickly as she finished up, by carefully sweeping out the loft as clean as she could. She leaned against the door, to get some fresh air and watched the dust particles being sucked outside. She then surveyed the results of her labour. It would do for now she thought, turning to look down at the mess she had made outside. Dawn dropped the fork and broom on the pile of straw below, then closed and latched the loft door. She would have to get something to haul the straw away but she would solve that problem later. It was at least out of the barn, she said to herself, while climbing down the ladder.

"A set of stairs would be much nicer than using the ladder." Dawn said to Pup, who sat waiting for her, at the base of the ladder. Dawn looked at her watch when she leaned against the barn door. She was surprised to see that it was already 2 o'clock in the afternoon. "Way past lunch time." She said to Pup as she slowly picked up the broom and fork, setting them inside against the wall.

Dawn walked slowly to the house, feeling itchy and suddenly very tired. She gave Pup some food and water then decided to have a shower before lunch, to get rid of the itchy feeling. She placed her dirty clothes in the washing machine then climbed into the shower, to wash her hair and scrub the dust that covered her body. This job was not going to be as simple as she first thought. The loft was the easy part, the rest would be much more exhausting. She hoped Joe would have time to do some renovations and painting for her. She would call this evening, when she was sure he would be at home. After showering Dawn felt to tired to make something to eat. She took a banana and went straight upstairs to rest. It was 4:30 in the afternoon when she woke up she was angry at herself for wasting valuable time. She knew if she wanted to have the barn ready for Bill's return, she had to get back to work. Her body ached all over, as she picked up her cap and gloves, and once again headed back out to the barn. She worked much slower now. She took out the old bales, piling them beside the barn, only to have several of them break open just as she got near the door.

When that happened, she would take the fork and throw them on the pile she had already started. After the bales were out, she began scrapping and shovelling the rest of the straw and dirt onto the same pile. Dawn tried to pace herself, working slowly but steady the rest of the afternoon. She was feeling exhausted, but made herself keep at it, or she would not get it done in time. One more day and the lower part would be cleaned out, she said to herself.

Dawn realized it was getting late when shadows began to fill the barn. She had just decided to call it a day, when she heard a noise outside. She froze to the spot, when she realized Pup was nowhere in sight. Surely Pup would have barked if something or someone came around, Dawn thought. Just then Pup came into the barn waging her tail. Dawn bent over and scratched Pup behind her ears. "So there you are. I thought you left me." Dawn said.

"She wouldn't do that." Nick said. Dawn jump back in fright, falling into the pile of straw. Nick went over to her and offered Dawn his hand, pulling her to her feet. "What in the world are you doing?" Nick asked angrily.

"What does it look like? I'm cleaning the barn." She replied.

"I can see that, but why?" He asked. Totally confused to what possessed her to take on such a large task.

"I must look a mess. I wasn't expecting company." She said brushing the straw from her clothes.

"You look like a farmers wife." Nick said, laughing at her while picking some straw out of her hair.

"I didn't hear you drive in and Pup didn't even bark." She said, looking at Pup as if scolding her.

"I rode my horse over." Nick said. "Marie phoned. She was in a panic because no one has been able to reach you."

"Bill called her, wondering where you were, because he couldn't get you on the phone. He was getting a bit upset, not knowing what happened to you."

"As you can see I am fine." Dawn said leaning against the wall. She suddenly felt very weak and tired.

Pup came up beside her and began to whimper, sensing something wasn't right.

Nick looked at Pup and then at Dawn. "Are you all right?" He asked.

"I'm just feeling a bit tired." She said walking outside slowly.

When Dawn started to walk back to the house, while Nick closed the barn door. He put his arm around Dawn, assisting her on the way back to the house. She didn't object, as she felt weaker than she first realized. However she did feel a bit uncomfortable having him helping her again.

Once in the house she sat on the chair, thankful to be able to just relax.

"Have you eaten anything today?" Nick asked.

"A bit." She said.

"Don't you have enough sense to know, if you work, you have to eat to keep up your strength?" He said, scolded her.

Nick cut up an apple that lay on the cupboard. "Eat this it should help you feel a bit better." Nick said. Dawn ate it while Nick sat watching her.

"Do you have any canned soup?" Nick asked going to the cupboard.

"In the lower left, on the bottom." She said. "Why?"

"You go have your shower and I'll make some soup. Then I want an explanation as to what you think you were trying to pull off." Nick said pointing to the bathroom, for her to do as he said.

Dawn did not feel to comfortable with her situation, but she felt to itchy and tired to argue with him.

Dawn stayed in the shower for a long time, trying to wash all the dirt from her hair and the chaff off her skin. Nick was right the apple did seem to help, but she was not about to let Nick take charge of her. She must regain control of her situation.

Will Love Conquer All?

"You look better." Nick said pouring her a bowl of soup, then placing a glass of milk beside it.

"I don't like milk." Dawn said pushing it away.

"I don't care. You'll drink it or I won't leave until you do. You need to get your strength back. Here are some sandwiches." He said placing them in the center of the table.

"Now sit down and eat." He said firmly.

So much for her regaining control, she thought, bowing her head to give thanks for the food. Nick was quiet until she was done praying. " I hope you don't mind me joining you. I haven't eaten yet either. I'm not a cook, but I have learned how to make sandwiches and soup from a can." He said.

"It's very good, thank you." She said looking tired and pale.

Nick pushed the glass of milk back towards Dawn. She had a feeling he would do as he said, so between bites she did manage to get it down. When they were done eating, Nick asked, "Now what is this barn cleaning fit, all about?"

Dawn got up and started to clear the table.

"Leave it and sit down." Nick demanded. "I want an explanation?"

Dawn turned to Nick, frustrated that he was taking control of her life. "Look Nick." She said. "I do appreciate the help, but I don't like you acting like your my husband." She said.

"Well, I should have been." He said with a grin on his face.

"That's not funny." She said angrily.

"I'm sorry, but I am concerned about you. It hasn't been that long since your accident. I'm sure if Bill were here, he wouldn't be too happy with you, knowing you're not looking after yourself. Then being out there alone doing all that work, anything can happen. Now sit and tell me what you think you are trying to do!" He demanded.

Dawn sat down explaining to Nick what she wanted to do with the barn.

Nick leaned back in his chair with his arms folded across his chest, listening to Dawn's plans. When she finished, Nick sat silently for a moment looking at her.

"Bill doesn't know how lucky he is to have a wife like you." He said. "But," he added. "You should have the good sense to know that you cannot do all of that alone."

"I thought I would give Joe a call tonight to see if he would do some fixing and painting for me." She said.

Nick was silent as he thought for a moment. "I believe there are still a few days before Bill gets home, so let me see if I can help. I'll call Marie, I'm sure she'll stay with you for tonight and I'll take no argument from you.

We don't need you back in the hospital when Bill gets home." He said.

Dawn got up to clear the dishes from the table.

"Are you going to be ok until we get back?" Nick asked looking at Dawn's pale face.

"I'm fine, but I do get tired of everyone thinking I'm an invalid! Marie is probably busy. I don't want to be a bother. This was my decision to do this work and I don't feel right to have to impose on everyone else." She said rather frustrated.

"Marie would love to stay with you. You know that and don't try to be so blamed independent." Nick said going to the door. "We wouldn't help if we didn't want to. Besides this will give you and Marie some time to talk about, whatever women talk about. I'll be back." He said closing the door behind him when he left.

Dawn watched him walk to the barn, where his horse had been tied. It was now dark when she watched Nick get on his horse and ride off.

Dawn washed the dishes then made herself some coffee. The evening was warm, so she decided to drink her coffee outside. Dawn took a deep breath of fresh air as she sat out on the porch. The sky above was clear and full of millions of stars, while the almost full moon shone brightly through the spruce trees. Dawn felt her heart beat faster as she remembered the night her and Bill laid under the blanket of stars. She felt warm inside as she

Will Love Conquer All?

dreamed of Bill holding her in his arms.

Pup got up suddenly when she heard the sound of the p.. ringing. Dawn didn't hear it at first, but did wonder what ha gotten Pups attention. She listened, then soon realized it was the phone, but by the time she got there, whoever it was had hung up. Dawn wondered if it was Bill and hoped he would call back. She dearly wanted to hear his voice again.

She felt a slight headache coming on, so decided to lie down for a while. Her body ached all over. While lying on her bed, she thought of all the work she must do, to get the barn to where she wanted it, before Bill got home. The moon shone brightly through her window, lighting up her bedroom. Shortly after, Pup started barking at the sound of a vehicle driving into the yard. But by now her head ached and she felt too exhausted to get up. She heard someone at the door and then Marie calling her name.

"I'm upstairs Dawn called back." She saw a beam of light from below, when Marie switched on a light.

Marie quickly ran upstairs. "Is everything ok?" She asked switching on the bedroom light.

The moment the light hit Dawn's eyes, a shot of pain ripped through her head. Dawn winced and quickly covered her eyes with a small cushion.

"It's just a headache." Dawn said, as if it was just a normal everyday occurrence. "Would you please shut off the light?" Dawn asked.

"Can I get you one of your pills or have you taken one?" Marie asked switching off the light.

"They're on the shelf, above the sink, in the bathroom." Dawn said.

Marie quickly went back down stairs, returning with the bottle of pills and a glass of water. Dawn took two tablets, downing them with a gulp. "I'll be fine." Dawn said, giving the bottle back to Marie, who stood there with a worried look on her face.

"I'll be back up later." Marie said. "I'm really concerned about your headaches, Dawn."

Marie went back downstairs. Dawn could hear Nick and Marie talking, but she couldn't make out what they were saying. Right now her main focus was on the throb in her head. Soon she heard the front door open and close and the sound of a vehicle, as Nick drove out of the yard.

Marie came back upstairs to sit on a stool near Dawn's bed. "You have everyone worried about you girl." Marie said.

Taking the cushion away from her eyes, Dawn said. "I'm sorry, but I'm just trying to get on with my life. I can't just sit around and do nothing or I'll go crazy."

"Nick told me what you want to do with the barn and I think it's great, but did you really think you could do it all alone?" Marie asked.

"All I can do is try." Dawn said softly.

"Has Bill called you tonight?" Marie asked.

"The phone rang when I was outside, but by the time I got there, whoever it was had hung up. I thought it might have been him." Dawn said.

"Well, he'll probably be calling back, so if the phone rings I'll let you answer it. Is the spare bedding still in the back bedroom closet?" Marie asked standing up.

"Yes," Dawn said. "But where will you sleep, there's no bed in there."

"Have you forgotten about your hide a bed in the living room?" Marie said smiling.

"Oh, yea." Dawn said smiling up at her friend.

"Now you lie still and try to get rid of that headache, while I go fix myself a bed. I'll see you later." Marie said going back downstairs.

Dawn must have dozed off for a while. When she woke up she could see by the light downstairs that Marie was still awake. She looked at the clock. It was only 10:30pm. Now that she had a nap this late in the evening, she hoped that she would still be

Will Love Conquer All?

able to sleep tonight.

She was just about to go downstairs when the phone rang. Dawn was hoping it would be Bill when she picked up the phone.

"Dawn, where have you been? I've been trying to get a hold of you for ages, but you're never around." Bill said somewhat annoyed. "I even called Marie," Bill said.

"I've been doing things outside and a couple of times you hung up just before I got to the phone." Dawn said. "Marie is here now, she's spending the night."

"Is something wrong then?" Bill asked suddenly.

"No, everything is fine. She's just going to help me with a few things. While she's here it may keep everyone from worrying so much." She said somewhat annoyed that everyone was on her case.

"I'm sorry about what I said the other day." Bill said.

"You mean about Nick? Well you have to get over it Bill. He's just a friend. You must remember, if I wanted him, I would have chose him years ago. I chose you and that hasn't changed. But it is unusual for you to apologize." She said.

"Dawn you sound more like your old self again. Lisa told me that some of your memory is starting to come back." Bill said on a happier note.

"Most of it, but I still don't remember the accident. When will you be back?" Dawn asked.

"It'll probably be 6 more days. I'm sure looking forward to getting home." Bill told her.

"I'll be waiting for you Teddy Bear. I love you and miss you so much." Dawn said.

"I love you too. I better go, but I'll see you soon. You take care of yourself, you hear." Bill said before hanging up the phone.

Dawn felt like a weight had been lifted off of her shoulders. She never liked it when they couldn't reconcile their differences before they went to bed. When it did happen it really bothered her. If something were to happen to one of them before they had an opportunity to fix it, it could never be righted again.

Dawn's headache was almost gone and she felt suddenly like having a cup of tea.

Marie had just finished doing some laundry when Dawn came downstairs.

"Feeling better?" Marie asked, seeing a new glow in Dawn's eyes.

"Yes I am and right now I am going to make us some tea." Dawn said cheerfully.

"Oh, let me make it for you." Marie said.

"No, you're a guest in my house and I'll make it while you sit and visit with me." Dawn said going to the stove to boil some water. She got out some cups and a variety of herbal teas. She placed them on the table, than sat down with her friend, while waiting for the water to boil. They chatted for a while, then after a slight hesitation, Marie looked at Dawn and said.

"Nick told me that you two, knew each other before Bill came along. He told me his side of the story, but I wonder if you would mind telling yours?" Marie said.

Dawn went to get the kettle of hot water. She filled their cups and sat down.

"I suppose you will always wonder if I don't tell you, but it was all a long time ago." She said putting a tea bag into her cup.

"Nick and my parents were friends, as long as I can remember."

"His family would visit my parents occasionally and we would come here. We were just children when we got to know each other. I did like Nick very much and always looked forward to seeing him, but I never knew how he felt. We started to write when we got older, but then I met Bill." Dawn took a sip of her tea. Her thoughts drifting back to her younger years, while Marie sat waiting for Dawn to continue.

"Nick and I still wrote to each other even though Bill and I were dating. Then my parents and I were invited over for Nick's birthday. Bill was upset that I even considered going but---" Dawn hesitated.

"Go on," Marie said.

Will Love Conquer All?

"Well--, we came over for his birthday. After dinner, Nick an I sat outside on the lawn talking, when he asked if I wanted to go for a drive. I have a feeling that our parents thought that someday Nick and I would get married." Dawn said thoughtfully. "But that was not to be. I missed being with Bill, but I had to find out for myself, who was right for me. I thank God to this day, that he made the decision so clear to me." Dawn said.

"I understand you and Nick were sitting outside talking when you began to remember that day." Marie said.

"Yes. It's strange, but from the time Bill brought me here, I felt like I had been here before. The mind is a strange thing," Dawn said.

"So back to your story. What made you decide?" Marie asked.

Dawn looked down at her cup and said. "Just a kiss."

"Was it after that, when you wrote Nick about you and Bill?" Marie asked.

"Something like that, I will always classify Nick as a good friend. After all, we've known each other most of our lives." Dawn said.

"Poor Nick." Marie said.

"Well you know the rest," Dawn said.

"Bill is quite a bit older than you, isn't he?" Marie asked.

"Yes, he's 7 years older, but at a certain age, it doesn't seem to matter any more."

Dawn said smiling as she thought of her beloved husband.

"That does fill in the blanks for me. Now that's all in the past and we can get on with the future." Marie said cheerfully.

Dawn was thankful, that Marie was willing to leave it at that. She really did not want to talk about it any more. Dawn was glad that the following day was Sunday. She needed a day to recuperate and rest her sore tired body. They decided to go to church in the morning, then out for lunch, after which Dawn wanted to rest. She needed all her strength for her task ahead. Dawn was glad that Nick and Marie had plans of their own for the afternoon. Dawn suddenly realized she had not called Joe and it was now too late.

"You can call him tomorrow afternoon." Marie said. On Monday, Marie would see to it, that Dawn would have her breaks and a snack between lunches, which she was quite willing to make. Marie told Dawn, that Nick was planning to come help her on Monday. Even thought Dawn tried to say no, Marie told her it was already arranged.

Dawn turned the topic to Marie and Nick's up coming marriage.

"Have you done much planning yet?" Dawn asked.

"Some," Marie said. "We're planning to have just a small wedding. I have wanted to ask something of you, but I know that with the present situation it may be impossible."

"Just ask, you know I'll do it, if it's at all possible." Dawn said.

"Well--, you see I had hoped to have a garden wedding. You have such a beautiful yard. Well--, I wanted to ask if it was possible to have it here? I know the situation between Nick and Bill isn't good, but I have convinced Nick. I know it maybe a bit more difficult to convince Bill." Marie said.

"Oh, that would be wonderful. I'll have to talk it over with Bill and as you said, it may be some time before I can give you an answer. I'll have to wait for the right time to bring it up." Dawn said

"Nick figured it may not be a good idea with the friction between him and Bill. But it was where he grew up, so he did grudgingly agree. I really don't understand those two." Marie said.

"I don't either, but I do hope they'll at least become civil with each other. "Well," she said thoughtfully. "We'll have to pray that it will all work out. Won't we." Dawn said, and Marie agreed.

"What about Nick's children? How is that going?" Dawn asked.

"Well it is hard, but I think they're starting to come around. They're beginning to realize that their Father deserves some happiness in his life and being alone is not bringing that to him.

I have told them that I want to be their friend, not their Mother. No one can replace her. I also told them that Nick loved their Mother, and that will not change. His love for me will be different, as we are different people. I would never stand between them and their Father." Marie said.

"You are a wonderful person, Marie. They can't do anything but love you for whom you are. I do believe you are the one to make Nick happy and I wish you both all the happiness in the world. I consider Nick and you, very dear friends. I only hope our families will be friends, as we will be neighbours." Dawn said.

It was almost midnight when Dawn and Marie went to bed. Dawn was thankful to have a friend like Marie. She would do her best to see that they could have the wedding of their choice, even though she knew it would not be easy to convince Bill. Dawn knelt down by her bed that evening, asking God to give her wisdom in dealing with Bill and the dislike he had for Nick. She asked for protection over Bill and their children, as well as to give her strength for the following week. The verse *"All things work for good for them that love the Lord"*, popped into her head as she climbed under the covers.

Dawn was grateful to be able to rest Sunday afternoon. Nick came to pick Marie up shortly after they returned home from lunch. Dawn made herself scarce to give Marie her privacy. Dawn didn't want to be around Nick anymore than she had to. Especially with Bill not being at home. Dawn called Joe, who said he would be over in the morning to have a look at her project. He and Bill had talked slightly about the barn before. He knew a bit of what Bill wanted done.

Dawn was resting on her bed, when she suddenly felt guilty for not calling her parents. She suddenly realized it was odd that they had not called. Dawn sat on the side of her bed and dialed the number. She let it ring several times but there was no answer. They must be travelling again Dawn thought as she lay down on her bed. She felt it odd they had not called, but then

Bill had told her that everyone was giving her time to get to know and trust him first.

Oh well, she'd try calling them again in a few days. She lay back down and was soon fast asleep.

Dawn and Marie visited a bit that evening after Nick left. Marie excitedly told Dawn about her day with Nick and his family and how well things seemed to be going. Then before going to bed, Dawn showed Marie what she had in the cupboards and refrigerator for tomorrow's lunch.

* * *

Dawn was up early the next morning. She was thankful to Marie for washing her work clothes, which now lay on a chair in Dawn's bedroom. Dawn made herself some coffee and toast. She was just about to sit down to eat when Marie came into the room. "Come join me, but I didn't expect you to be up so early." Dawn said, letting Pup outside while Marie poured herself a cup of coffee. "I want to try to get the barn cleaned out today. Once that's done it will sure be a relief. I'm sure I have used muscles that I've never used before." Dawn said as they sat down to eat. They both laughed while discussing their latest aches and pains. "Sign of old age." Marie said. "Are you sure you should be doing this hard of work?" Marie asked her friend.

"I'll be fine, I just have to pace myself and rest when I need to. Perhaps a snack between meals would help to keep my strength up." Dawn said. "I won't over do it like the other day, so don't worry."

Marie told Dawn to leave her dishes when she was about to put them into the sink. "After all," Marie said. "That was what I came to help you with."

Dawn put Bill's cap and gloves on, then headed out to work in the barn. She was quite pleased with what she had accomplished in the past two and a half hours. She laid the shovel against the wall of the barn, and then looked at her watch. It was almost 10 o'clock and definitely time for a break. While walking to the house, Dawn saw Nick's truck coming down the hill. She waited by the door, until he got out and walked towards her.

"On your way out to work?" Nick asked.

"No, coming in for a break." She said opening the door. Nick followed Dawn into the house where Marie had coffee and cookies sitting on the table.

Nick went to Marie and kissed her on the cheek, while Dawn went to wash her hands.

"I believe Joe will be out this morning." Nick said to Dawn, when she came back into the kitchen. "I'll give you a hand to clean out the barn today. It's far too much work for you to be doing along," Nick said.

Dawn was not going to argue, for she knew Marie and Nick would not listen to her anyways.

"When will Bill be back?" Nick asked.

"He hope to be back in another 6 days," Dawn said.

"Well I guess that gives you a few days to try to get done what you want," Nick said.

They were just about to go out when Joe drove in. Dawn and Nick thanked Marie, for the snack and headed out the door. The three of them walked over to the barn, where Dawn and Joe discussed what Bill had wanted done. Several shingles also had to be replaced as well as some of the boards on the outside walls. There were several small panes of glass that would have to be replaced, which Dawn said she would get when she went to town. Dawn also talked to Joe about removing the stalls and mangers. Joe then gave Dawn a rough estimate of what it would cost, for painting the entire barn, plus the repairs. "What about the planks inside that need to be replaced?" Joe asked.

"I can do that," Nick said.

"Not unless I can pay you," Dawn said.

"No you won't," Nick replied. "I'll do it for nothing. I said I would help you."

"I can't accept that, you have your own work to do," Dawn said. "I'll only consent if I can pay you."

"No." Nick said, turning to Joe. "I'll look after the inside planks," Nick said.

Joe looked first at Nick, then at Dawn, and wondered what was going on between them. "Ok," Joe said. "If you change your mind about the other, let me know."

Dawn knew she had more than enough money in her bank account to cover the cost of it.

She was thrilled that Joe and his workers were able to start the following morning, which should leave ample time to have it all finished by the time Bill got home.

Dawn went to work, leaving Joe and Nick talking outside. She had half of the barn cleaned out when Nick came in. He stood watching her work for a moment, before going over to help her. He wondered what his life would have been like if she would have married him. For some reason, he had often thought of Dawn, and wondered if she had ever thought of him. Dawn would always have a special place in his heart. If she were free now, he would have probably asked her to marry him, but such was not the case. Nick quickly pushed that idea out of his mind. After all, he did have a wonderful wife who he missed very much. He was now engaged to Marie, who made him happy when she was with him. Why then did Dawn have such an effect on him.

By mid afternoon they had the barn swept clean. Nick went home, only to come back with his tractor and front end loader, pulling a trailer with several planks piled on it. Dawn helped unload the planks, so Nick could load up the straw and haul it out to the field. Nick and Dawn then set to work pulling out the broken planks, and old spikes, which were sticking up where the planks no longer were. They worked together until all the planks were in place. It was a long day, but they continued working even after supper. Dawn stood back and looked over what they had done. She was quite pleased with the results.

"I'll bring my pressure washer over, and add a bit of disinfectant. Then we can wash down the inside, after Joe takes out the stalls and mangers." Nick said turning to face Dawn with a satisfied smile. "I would say we worked together quite well, wouldn't you?"

"Yes, I guess we did, and not even an argument." Dawn said feeling quite content with their accomplishment.

Dawn suddenly noticed that same look in Nick's eyes when he looked at her.

"Why, couldn't it have been you and me," Nick said looking at Dawn. "I had a wonderful wife and love being with Marie, but I still can't help wishing things would have been different."

"Nick, did you ever think the reason you feel that way, is because it was something you couldn't have?" Dawn asked.

Nick hesitated before saying. "I really do care for you Dawn."

"We knew each other most of our lives, but we never saw each other very often."

"I have always liked you too, and still do. But it's different than the feelings I have for Bill." Dawn continued. "If you really think about it, the feelings you had for your wife, and the feelings you have for Marie, are different than what you feel for me. It's more wondering what it would have been like, and the fact that it's not in reach that probably bothers you. What we feel for each other is no more than special friends, because we have known each other almost all our lives. You think about that." Dawn said walking back to the house leaving Nick thinking about what she had said.

Dawn had a long hot shower that evening. She was grateful for all the help she had gotten from Nick and Marie. She wondered how she would explain to Bill, that Nick helped her, but then he didn't have to know right away.

Marie and Dawn had just settled down to a nice steaming cup of tea when the phone rang.

"Hello mom, this is Darcy."

"Hi," Dawn said. "How was your holiday?"

"It was great, but too short. I decided to come home earlier, because it was costing too much money. I heard you've gotten your memory back, which is good to hear," Darcy said.

"Yes little by little it has come back, all except the accident," Dawn added.

"What have you been doing with yourself?" Darcy asked.

Dawn proceeded to tell him of her surprise for Bill. "I want to move Dads saws and tools into the barn on the weekend, before he gets back," Dawn said.

"Dad won't be back until Sunday. What if Lisa and I come and help this weekend. That way we can see your new place, and visit a bit before I have to go back to work." Darcy said.

"That sounds great." Dawn said, before giving Darcy directions of how to find their place.

Marie poured a fresh cup of tea for Dawn then sat down, Dawn looked very tired.

The worst part was now done. Dawn told Marie that her children would be coming to spend the weekend with her and also help move Bill's tools. Joe figured to be done by Thursday afternoon, at the latest Friday, which should work out fine.

"That's great," Marie said. "If you don't need me, I'll go home tomorrow afternoon. I have an appointment that I can't change."

"Oh, I'll be fine. I really do appreciate all the help," Dawn said.

"I can take you home whenever you want to go." Dawn told her.

"Thanks, but Nick said he would come after lunch." Marie said with a twinkle in her eye.

"You do have it bad, girl. Your face lights up every time you talk about him."

Dawn and Marie laughed as Marie answered with. "You haven't seen yourself when you talk about Bill, even after all these years."

"Its love," Dawn said and they both burst out laughing.

They were both tired when they turned in that night. Marie dreamed about her upcoming wedding, while Dawn wondered what Bill would say about the surprise she had for him.

CHAPTER 12

FRIDAY MORNING DAWN SET UP a cot in the back bedroom for Darcy. Marie had already washed and replaced the bedding on the hide-a-bed for Lisa. Dawn made a list of things she needed from town, before going out to talk to Joe.

"Good morning Mrs. Spencer. I see you came out to do a final inspection," he said wiping some paint from his hands.

"I see you have it all finished." Dawn said, walking around to look at the barn, with it's fresh coat of red paint adorned by white trimming around the doors and windows. To the black shingles on the roof, which sported shinny eaves troughs on the sides. No more seen, was the old boards patching holes, or missing shingles on the roof, but now new siding blending into the old and new shingles replacing the lost.

"It does not resemble the old barn at all. It looks great." Dawn said excitedly.

"I must say the same about the inside. I thought you had done a good job when Nick finished washing it down, you have been one busy lady since. This has got to be the cleanest barn in the country. You could live in here," Joe said.

"Well, as I recall when Bill did tinker in his shop before, he practically did. He'll still want to insulate it, so he can heat it in the winter, but I'll leave that for Bill." Dawn said thoughtfully.

"You know," Joe said. "You and Bill are an amazing couple. First he does his best to surprise you with the work in the house. Now you intern do the same for him with the barn.

With all the struggles you two have had in the last while, it just seems to bring you closer together. You two must really care for each other."

"We do. Bill told me not to long ago, that love conquers all, and I believe that. With God's love and the love we have for each other, our troubles have brought us closer together." She said smiling at the thought of the love that her and Bill shared.

Joe shook his head in amazement. "I have seen people, who I thought cared for each other. But when trouble came it was game over."

"Ah, the secret is when going through troubles, it's not just your partners love you rely on, it's God first and then your partner is the added support." Dawn said.

"I guess there might be something to that." Joe said as he turned to help his workers load the remaining equipment.

"Come to the house and I'll write you out a cheque," Dawn said. "I really appreciate you doing this on such short notice."

"No problem, I'm glad to do it for you," he said.

Joe handed Dawn his bill. "I'll be over in a moment, after I check that I have everything put away."

Dawn went to the house to write out the cheque for Joe. After that she would be ready to go to town. She picked up her purse and went out, locking the door behind her. While waiting for Joe, Dawn scratched Pup behind her ear. Pup wagged her tail enjoying the attention she received from her master.

"Thanks again." Dawn said handing Joe the cheque when he arrived at the house.

"Thank you! We'll probably be seeing you around. I hope Bill enjoys his surprise," Joe said.

"I do too." Dawn said waving as he drove off. She patted Pups head "See you later girl. I have to go to town," she said, getting into her car.

The first thing Dawn did was to pick up her mail. She sorted it, throwing away all the junk mail, keeping only a couple of bills and one large brown envelope which came from a layers office, addressed to her. That's strange she thought. Why would she be getting something from a lawyer? Well, she would open it later when she had time. She said to herself while heading for the grocery store. Dawn bought her groceries, and was about to leave, when she met Marie coming in. After talking for a moment, they decided to have a quick lunch. After that, Dawn would have to go home to get ready or her children, who were coming the following day.

"What is your plan for this afternoon?" Marie asked when they were leaving the restaurant.

"Well," Dawn said thoughtfully. "I better see that I get the grass cut before Bill and the kids come home. I've neglected the yard lately. I'm glad that is finished and none too soon either," Dawn said with a sigh.

"I bet you're happy that Bill will be home soon?" Marie said

Dawn's face lit up at the thought Bill's return. "I sure am." She said.

"You know, it's great to see how you two love each other after all these years. I only hope I can have the same in my life." Marie said thoughtfully.

"I'm sure you will." Dawn said laying her hand on Marie's arm. "But right now I better get going so I can get my work done. This evening, my plan is to put my feet up and relax. Lisa and Darcy should be here sometime in the morning, then after moving Bill's things into the barn, it will be ready." Dawn said. "I can't forget to buy some bird seed." Dawn said as if thinking out loud, before going their separate ways.

Dawn was looking forward to a relaxing evening, now that everything was finished. First she put her groceries away. Then not forgetting her animals, she filled Pup's water and food bowl's and also filled the bird feeder. After that Dawn went to work outside in the yard cutting grass and trimming around the house and trees. After finishing that task she made herself some tea and a sandwich. While eating her lunch she sat watching the birds flutter around as the dominant ones ate out of the feeder, while the others picked up the seed that had been scattered on the ground. She was utterly amazed at the amount of seeds little birds could devour.

Dawn sat staring blankly out the window in somewhat of a daze when the phone rang, making her almost jump off her chair.

Dawn was thrilled to hear Bill at the other end. She was hardly able to contain herself from telling Bill of the surprise she had for him.

"How's it going?" Bill asked.

"It's going fine," Dawn said cheerfully.

"How is it on your end?" Dawn asked.

"Better the closer I get to home. I should be home by Sunday night." Bill said. "Will you be there to meet me at the door when I get home?" Bill said jokingly.

"That is still the plan. It seems like months since you left." Dawn said. "Let's never do this again, life is too short to be apart."

"I promise that if I do, I will take you with me." Bill said.

They talked for some time and then decided that the phone bill was going to be a bit expensive.

"I probably won't call you again but I will be home the day after tomorrow, so take care of yourself." Bill said.

"I will." Dawn replied. "You do the same and don't forget I will always love you." Dawn said.

"I know, I love you too," he said.

Dawn held the receiver thoughtfully in her hand. Soon she would feel Bill's strong arms around her. When Bill held her, she felt like they could overcome any problem as long as they were together. Dawn slowly hung up the receiver. She cleared off the table and washed her plate, putting everything back in the cupboard.

Dawn suddenly remembered the brown envelope from the lawyer, which lay near the phone. She slowly picked it up and examined it for a moment. After opening it, she took out the package of papers, and began to read. She had read only a few lines when she gasped in disbelief and the color draining from her face. She quickly sat down as her knees now felt suddenly very weak. She dropped the papers on the table. She was shocked at what she read. She could not believe it was true. She slowly read through the pages. Then put them back into the envelope and placed it in the cupboard.

"It can't be," she cried, tears streaming down her face. "It just can't be. Why God?" She said. "There has to be a mistake!" She cried. Dawn went to her room, where she wept for some time. Slowly she realized what she read had to be true. Bill had probably not wanted to tell her until he felt she was stronger. But then he had to go away, most likely not looking forward to breaking the news to her. She would ask him all about it when he returned. Tears rolled down Dawn's cheeks as she lay there. It must have been hard on her children, so she decided not to say anything to them about the envelope. She wanted them to have a happy reunion, and not relive the past. Dawn wondered how much a person could actually bare, but with Gods help she had to get through this.

Dawn lay there until dark, before going downstairs to let Pup in. Pup wagged her tail, rubbing her head on Dawn's leg, as if sensing something was not right with her master. Dawn knelt down and hugged Pup. She stroked Pups head while saying. "You're a good dog. I'm glad you're here, girl." Pup licked her face as if she understood.

Dawn didn't sleep well that night, but tossed and turned, she was glad when it was time to get up. She got up and let Pup out, then took a long hot bath, to soak her aching heart and muscle. She tried to relax and put everything out of her mind. Her children, who she had not seen in sometime, were coming and that's what she had to concentrate on. Their day would be busy with getting Bill's tools put into the barn, which thankfully would keep her from remembering the letter. Tears began to fill her eyes as she thought of what was in the letter. She quickly got dressed, determined to put it out of her mind. She must get busy doing something, she thought to herself.

Dawn made herself something to eat, trying to think of places to set Bill's saws and tools. She decided to make a banner to hang in the barn, welcoming Bill to his workshop. She found a heavy piece of tan coloured material. It was about 4 feet by 2 feet in size that she decided would be ideal. She was just about to start writing on it, when Pup started barking. Dawn looked out the window to see Darcy and Lisa getting out of the pick up. She dropped everything, and quickly went outside to meet them.

Lisa was nervous when she first saw the dog, but Dawn reassured her that Pup would not harm her. Lisa ran to her Mother hugging her, as tears filler both their eyes."I missed you Mom. You had us all so worried the last while. It's good to see you back to normal again." Lisa said. Dawn reached for Darcy, pulling him toward them. "I love both of you," she said hugging them. "I'm sorry for worrying you."

"You couldn't help it Mom. It was just one of those things" Darcy said, turning to look at the dog while wiping a tear from his eyes. Hoping that no one had noticed.

"Nice dog you have here." He said, kneeling down to play with her. "What's his name, or is it a her?" Darcy asked.

"Her name is Pup." Dawn said putting her arm around her daughter and leading her into the house. Dawn knew that Darcy never felt comfortable to be hugged or kissed. He always said he hated that gushy stuff. In that way he was a bit like his Father used to be. Lisa was different she enjoyed the affection and was also a bit spoilt.

Dawn gave them first a tour of the house, before offering them some juice or pop as neither one drank coffee. She then put out some raisin cookies that Dawn had baked earlier.

She knew they were her children's favourite.

Lisa and Darcy were impressed with what they saw of the house.

"It doesn't feel like home," Lisa said sadly "It isn't like up north."

"That's understandable." Dawn said putting her arm around her. "Just give it time. Let me show you what my surprise is for your Father," Dawn said, leading the way over to the barn.

"It sure looks good from the outside," Darcy said.

"Aren't barns kind of dirty for a workshop." Lisa added.

"Wait and see," Dawn said opening the door. Darcy and Lisa looked in amazement. You would never have known that any animals had ever been inside.

"Dad will be surprised!" Darcy said.

"I'll say," was Lisa's reply as she checked out every corner.

They decided roughly where they should put things, as there was a limited amount of electrical outlets. "Dad will have to add a few more plug-ins, and probably put in a small door, so he doesn't have to open the big door when it's cold," Darcy said looking around.

"I'll leave that for your Father, but let's go get dad's tools. They're still in town at the storage place," Dawn said. "I started to make a banner to hang up, but I didn't get too far on it," Dawn added.

"What if I stay here and work on the banner then." Lisa said. "What were you planning to put on it?"

"How about welcome to Bill's work shop." Dawn said to which they both agreed.

Darcy and Dawn went to town to load everything that was left in the storage room. There were tables, ladders, a variety of different saws, a press drill, several sanders, grinders, and several small toolboxes full of miscellaneous things. There were also numerous other things he had used for building his woodcraft items. They were very careful not to spill anything or they would be sure to hear from Bill about it later. They had to make two trips to get it all, and were due for a rest after unloading everything.

"I'll be glad once we have it all arranged." Dawn said.

"Are you sure that you should be doing all this heavy lifting?" Darcy asked.

"I'm fine. So far it hasn't seemed to be a problem." Dawn said.

They had everything unloaded and arranged, by supper. When they came into the house Lisa showed off the banner, she had just finished. Dawn decided they should all go to town for supper that evening, as she was too tired to make it. There Dawn asked each of them about what was going on in their lives. She then told them of her concern for their spiritual lives as well. Darcy and Lisa both acknowledged that they knew they should start going to church again.

"We never know when our time may be up." Dawn told them.

Darcy and Lisa were up to their usual banter, which made the evening full of laughter and happiness. If only Bill were here to complete the family. *Soon*, she thought to herself. Tomorrow evening they would again be together.

The next morning Darcy and Lisa left to go back to Calgary. Lisa was to catch a ride with some friends back to Edmonton that afternoon. Dawn kissed her children, telling them not to forget that on thanksgiving, they were to come home.

It was already to late to go to church, and upon returning to the house she realized that they had forgotten to put up the banner. But before taking it out she made a little card for Bill that said.

A labour of love
To you from me
I will love you forever
Dawn

Dawn took the card and banner and headed out to the barn, with Pup running ahead of her. She set the card on one of Bill's saws before deciding where to hang the banner. It must be centered. She picked up Bill's hammer and after finding a couple of small nails, she took the ladder and set it where she wanted to attach the first corner. She climbed up and nailed the one corner of the banner on the beam. Dawn then climbed down and stepped back to make sure that it was in the right spot, before moving the ladder to attach the other side. She climbed back up the ladder again and was just stretching to reach the beam, when the ladder slipped. Dawn tried frantically to stop her fall by reaching out to the upright support nearby, but it was too far away.

She went crashing to the floor, hitting her head hard on the cement floor below. Dawn slowly started to get up, but then suddenly collapsed on the floor.

Pup came over to Dawn, whining and licking her face, trying to get her masters attention. She again licked Dawn's hair, where the blood now oozed from under her head. Pup pawed on Dawn's arm wanting her to get up, but Dawn just lay there very still. Pup barked and ran to the door, only to again return to Dawn's side. She stood over Dawn licking her face and whining, but to no avail. Pup again went to the door then with one backward glance and a whimper, she ran off as fast as she possibly could.

* * *

Nick was just about to saddle his horse when he saw Pup running towards him, she was panting heavily. "What are you doing here girl?" He said, stroking her wet fur. Pup pulled away from Nick as if to run back home, but when Nick didn't follow, she ran back to him barking frantically. Then again she would run some distance only to stop and look back and bark at him.

"What's wrong girl, did something happen to Dawn?" Nick asked. Pup just kept barking frantically, trying to get Nick to follow. Nick began to get an uneasy feeling.

Something must have happened, or Pup would not be acting like this. Nick ran to his truck and told Pup to get in, then sped off, with rocks and dust flying from beneath the wheels. Pup was restless. She continued moving around inside the truck, while continuing to whimper. Nick patted her head trying to calm her down, at which time he noticed the blood on Pups paw.

Nick began to panic. He knew Bill would not be home until that evening. He thought perhaps her children would be home, but he decided she was probably alone or Pup would not have come looking for him.

When Nick arrived his first reaction was to go to the house, but Pup knew better.

She barked to get Nick's attention. Then headed for the barn, with Nick in hot pursuit.

Nick's worst fear was realized when he saw Dawn lying lifeless on the cement floor with a pool of blood around her head.

"Dawn!" he shouted running over to her. He kneeled by her side, while Pup stood by watching. Nick quickly felt for her pulse. It was weak and her breathing was shallow but she was still alive.

"Thank-you God," Nick said. But what would another blow to her head do, so soon after her last concussion, he wondered. He took off his jacket and covered her, telling Pup to stay with her while he ran to the house to call for the ambulance. Nick then ran back to the barn where Pup lay with his head on Dawn's waist, waiting for her master to wake up.

Nick knelt down beside Dawn, and began talking to her. "Dawn its Nick. Everything is going to be all right. The ambulance is on the way, and don't forget, Bill is coming home today. You have to be here to show him the work you put into this place, so please keep fighting to come back. You can't leave now, when you just got here. Even if you are married to Bill, at least I can see you once and awhile and talk to you. Please Dawn don't give up." He pleaded. "Think of your children and Bill. They almost lost you once, they need you to come back to them again." Nick's heart went out to Bill, even though he had taken Dawn from him. He knew they loved each other, and also knew only to well, what it was like to lose your wife. Heaven knows Bill had his share of heartaches lately, Nick thought to himself.

It seemed like forever, until the ambulance arrived. They checked her vital signs, then after stabilizing her, they carefully put her on the stretcher. Then after putting her into the ambulance they headed back into town, with lights flashing and siren wailing.

Nick ran into the house and quickly phoned Marie. He told her to meet him at the hospital, leaving her no time to ask questions as to what happened. Nick noticed a small phone directory, near the phone. He shoved into his pocket. He took the keys that hung nearby and locked the door when he left. Nick gave Pup a quick hug saying everything would be ok, but she had to stay here. Nick then sped off after the ambulance.

Luck had it that there was a doctor at the hospital, when Dawn arrived. Nick stood by Dawn's side holding her hand while the doctor checked her.

"Your wife probably has a concussion, but we'll take an x-ray which should tell us more." The doctor said

"She isn't my wife, she's a dear friend and--" just then Marie came in.

She gasped at the sight of Dawn's pale complexion and the blood in her hair. "No!" She shouted as Nick put his arm around her.

Nick and Marie told the Doctor of Dawn's previous accident. They told him about the severe concussion she had received, just a short time ago. They also mentioned which hospital Dawn had been at, so he could possibly find her previous doctor. Two nurses came to wheel Dawn to x-ray, while the doctor went to make his phone call. When he returned, he told Nick and Marie that they would be sending Dawn to Calgary by air ambulance. Tears streamed down Marie's face. Nick too, couldn't help but wipe a tear or two from his eyes, as he held Marie in his arms.

Nick then remembered the phone directory that he had picked up by Dawn's phone and put in his pocket. "I have to try to reach Bill," Nick said sadly. "Stay here with her after she gets back from x-ray and keep talking to her." Nick said going to find a phone.

Nick could not reach Bill on the cell number in the book, or

Darcy at his home.

He then tried Lisa, but there was no answer there either. He paged through the book and found a piece of paper with a trucking companies name and phone number. He dialed the number letting it ring for some time before someone finally answered.

"Hello." Nick said his voice shaking. "Do you know a Bill or Darcy Spencer?" he asked.

"This is Darcy," came the reply.

"Is Bill back yet?" Nick asked.

"No, but I expect him any minute. Why, who is calling?" Darcy asked now very curious.

"I'm your parents neighbour," he said choking back a sob, trying to keep his voice as calm as possible. "It's your Mother." Nick said, then hesitating as he heard a moan on the other end. "They're flying her to Calgary by air ambulance to the hospital that she was in before. You can meet her there."

"How bad is she? What happened?" Darcy asked suddenly.

"I'm sorry, it's not good. I'm really sorry." Nick said again before hanging up the phone.

Nick went back to the room just as they were wheeling Dawn back. He took Dawn's hand in his then leaning over her and said. "Bill and Darcy will meet you in Calgary, Dawn. You have to be strong for them. You have to get better. You did it once you can do it again. Keep fighting Dawn. Your family needs you."

Marie watched Nick as a tear fell on Dawn's hand. Nick kissed her hand then laid her hand gently by her side. Marie knew Nick still had some feelings for Dawn she knew their past and tried her best to understand it. She put her arms around Nick, before continuing to encourage Dawn not to give up.

Soon the paramedics came to take Dawn to the airport. Marie kissed Dawn on the forehead before leaving the room. Nick waited until Marie was gone before he kissed Dawn on her lips. "Dawn I will always love you, no matter what you say. Please fight to come back," Nick said, as they were about to wheel her out to the waiting ambulance.

Chapter 13

Darcy sat on a pail beside the shop. He was in total shock at the news that he had received. He didn't even notice that his Father had parked the truck and was walking towards him.

"Darcy." Bill called, wondering what was wrong with him. Bill found it very strange that Darcy had not come over to greet him when he returned. Usually he would be standing by the truck before it stopped. "Darcy," Bill called again, before laying his hand on his shoulder.

Darcy looked up at his Father his eyes full of tears. Bill's knees felt suddenly weak. He instantly knew something terrible had happened.

"It's Mom. They're flying her to the hospital, here in Calgary. I don't know the details, but it sounds bad." Darcy said, giving his Dad a hug.

Bill quickly leaned against the building for support. "Dear God, no!" He said, closing his eyes.

They both took a moment to let it sink in and to gather their strength before heading to the hospital. They managed to get in touch with Lisa just as she was about to leave for Edmonton. They told her to meet them at the hospital but not the reason, waiting instead to tell her when they got there.

Bill got a hold of Doctor Rogers, who promised to call them the moment Dawn arrived. Bill sat down and hunched over with his head resting in his hands. The toll of everything was catching up with him and he was looking old before his time. Darcy and Lisa were beginning to get very concerned about all the strain it was putting on their Father. They both put their arms around him, offering their support and love.

It seemed like hours before the doctor came into the room and said they could go and see Dawn. It was a shock to see her lying there unconscious. Her face was very pale, with the blood still in her hair, beneath the bandage. "You only have a moment before we take her to surgery," Doctor Rogers said, leaving the family alone.

Bill walked over to Dawn and placed his hand on hers. They were unusually cold. He kissed her and said, "Dawn its Bill, I'm back and you have to get better, so we can go home. I love you." Bill motioned for his children to come closer. "Lisa and Darcy are here and they need you too," Bill told her.

Lisa kissed her Mother on the cheek. "Mom you have to come back to us. We were just getting back to normal. Please keep fighting, we need you."

Darcy also gave his Mother a kiss. "Come on Mom don't give up. Remember the surprise you have for Dad. We love you." He said squeezing her hand.

Bill looked at Darcy, wondering what he was talking about, but then turned his full attention back to his wife. Why had he left her home alone? It's his fault he said to himself. I shouldn't have left her alone. Just then two nurses came into the room to take Dawn to surgery. Bill leaned over kissing Dawn again, saying. "I love you Dawn. I will be here waiting and praying for you. Hang in there, you have done it before you can do it again." One of the nurses then told Bill that he was to sign some papers at the desk. As Bill watched the nurses take Dawn away, he was very afraid of losing her this time.

Bill signed the papers he was asked to before joining his children. Now all they could do was wait for the results. Bill felt extremely tired and weak. He could not bring himself to believe that something this bad was happening again. He had thought that everything would be fine, when Dawn recovered from the last accident. He could even live with the fact that she couldn't remember him and their family, as long as they loved each other. He couldn't begin to imagine what another blow to her head would do, so soon after the last one.

It seemed like an eternity before the doctor came to talk to them. "I am sorry," Doctor Rogers said, soberly. "If she does make it, there will probably be some brain damage." Darcy went to his sister's side, holding her as she wept uncontrollably. Bill stood there in shock, not able to move. "You can go in to see her if you like." Doctor Rogers said, laying his hand on Bill's shoulder in sympathy.

Bill slowly went to Dawn's room, not prepared for what he saw. Dawn was on a life support system, with little chance of survival, but Bill would not give up on her. He hugged Darcy and Lisa as they came into the room. They just held each other and wept. Bill wiped his eyes. "I think it best if you both go back to Darcy's. I'm sure Darcy can find a place for you to sleep tonight," Bill said to Lisa. "Don't forget to say a prayer or two for your Mother."

"I'll stay with Mom. If things don't take a turn for the better, we may have some hard choices to make. But there's nothing you can do here now."

"No Dad! You can't mean that," Lisa cried.

Bill fought back tears as he said. "Lisa you know your Mother would not want this. Her life is now totally in Gods hands. He did give her back to us for a little while and we have to be thankful for that. I won't make the decision without you, but it is something I want you to know may happen. We'll pray for her and encourage her to keep fighting, and see what God has in store for her in the next few days."

Darcy and Lisa talked to their Mother before they left, hoping that some how they could get through to her. Bill sat by Dawn's bedside all night, praying and talking to her about their past, and their dreams for the future. He also begged her, if at all possible, not to leave him. It was hard for Bill to watch the machines, knowing this was the only thing keeping her alive. His only hope was that somehow, these machines would give her enough strength to once again fight on her own. If there would be brain damage would it be severe? He couldn't bring himself to think about that now, but bowed his head and said. "God you created her and you can restore, but your will be done." Bill kissed Dawn on the forehead. "I love you so much. If you can, please fight to come back to me, but I know, it's ultimately in God hands." Bill said, holding Dawn's hand the rest of the night, in silence and in prayer.

Around 10 o'clock the next morning, Lisa and Darcy returned, which was just moments before the Doctor. Doctor Rogers checked Dawn, before looking at her chart. "Bill why don't you go home for awhile. There is still no change and if there is, we'll notify you. You can't help your family if you get sick." Doctor Rogers said laying his hand on Bill shoulder. "If you need something to help you sleep I can prescribe some sleeping pills."

"No, I'm fine." Bill replied.

"Dad, go home for a day. Lisa and I will stay with Mom. You need some rest." Darcy said, looking at his Father. Bill slowly but grudgingly agreed, but first he told Dawn what he was doing. Darcy told Lisa to stay with their Mother while he took his Father to the cafeteria to have something to eat.

"I'll just have coffee." Bill said to Darcy as he sat at a table. But Darcy came back with a full breakfast of sausages and egg, for his Father. "Dad I knew you wouldn't eat if you left. I want you to try to eat this before you get sick, you haven't eaten anything since noon yesterday." Darcy said.

Bill had to admit that he was feeling rather weak. He slowly began to eat. He had no appetite yet he knew he had to keep his strength up for his family. When he finished he thanked Darcy and give him a hug before heading home. Home he thought, where Dawn said she would be waiting for him. There were several times that he had to wipe his eyes, so he could see the road, as he drove home.

**

Bill stopped by the house, before noticing something different about the barn.

He got out and walked slowly towards it, wondering what was going on. Dawn had not mentioned anything to him about this, when he talked to her on the phone. He slowly opened the door, and stood in total amazement at what he saw. This is probably what Darcy meant about a surprise, and it was definitely that. Bill walked over to his saw and picked up the card that Dawn had placed there. His eyes filled with tears when he read.

A labour of love
From me to you
I will love you forever
Dawn

Then he saw the banner hanging by one nail, with the ladder laying some distance away. When he came closer, he saw the blood on the cement. It was then his tears began to flow freely as he wept.

Bill knelt down on the floor where Dawn had fallen, and began to pray out loud.

"Dear God. Please don't take her away from me. I know you can heal her if you want too I need her. You gave her back to me for a while and I have to be thankful for that. The doctor says she will probably have brain damage if she makes it, but I know she wouldn't want to live that way. Lord it is totally in your hands." Bill sobbed.

Bill suddenly felt a hand on his shoulder but he did not look up. He had not heard anyone come in but his heart was very heavy.

Nick kept his hand on Bill's shoulder and prayed. "Lord I am not much of a praying man. I guess I have gotten bitter since you took my wife, but-- I am willing to try it again if you will heal Dawn and bring her back to her family. Amen"

Bill slowly stood up. He wiped the tears from his eyes, before realizing the man behind him was Nick. They looked at each other for a moment, then Bill said. "I hope you'll forgive me for my attitude towards you, the first time you came over Nick. I also want to thank you, for the help you have been to Dawn while I was away. I— I just feel this is all my fault." Bill said slowly. "I should never have left her alone," He said, his eyes again filled with tears.

"It's all right," Nick said. "I guess my attitude towards you wasn't any better. I guess I — I never got over you taking her away from me, but— you were her first choice and I have to accept that. She loves you very much," Nick said thoughtfully before continuing. "This was her way of showing you." He said waving his hand, as he looked around the barn. The two men sat down on the edge of the plank floor. They were silent for a moment before Bill turned to Nick.

"Did you say your wife died?" Bill asked.

"Yes," Nick said sadly. "She died of cancer, a couple of years ago."

"I'm sorry to here that." Bill said. "I can't imagine life without Dawn."

"It is hard to lose you partner." Nick said. "I was angry for a long time. It's just lately, that I am slowly letting it go, and trying to get on with my life."

Nick and Bill talked for some time. Bill asking about the events that happened while he was gone, and Nick tried to then fill him in on everything he felt Bill should know. Nick told Bill how Dawn wanted to do something for him, in return for everything he had done for her. He finished with how Pup had come for Nick, after Dawn had fallen.

They both decided to try to bury the past and get to know each other better.

Nick was hesitant for a moment before saying, "Bill, would you mind if Marie and I went to see Dawn?"

"I don't see why you can't after all, we are all grateful to you for saving her life twice while I was gone." Bill said.

"I'll leave word for the nurse to allow you and Marie in to see her."

"Thanks Bill," Nick said. "I'll keep an eye on your place if you want to stay in the city for awhile. Pup can stay with me until you get back." Nick said.

When Nick got up to leave, Bill stood up and offered his hand in friendship to Nick. As they shook hands, Nick said. "I hope everything turns out ok."

"I do too," Bill said sadly.

For some reason after Nick left, Bill no longer saw him as a threat to his marriage. He felt more at peace. He knew deep down, that he and Dawn had a love for each other that would last a lifetime. What God had joined together, no man could separate, Bill thought to himself.

Bill took one last look, then closed the barn door to walk around the outside and see what all had been done. He then walked slowly to the house, remembering Dawn's note. Bill had been looking forward to the day he got home, and Dawn would greet him at the door, but that was not to be.

Bill went into their bedroom and lay down on their bed. He thought about the short time they had together in this room but then being totally exhaust, he drifted off to sleep. Several hours later Bill woke up in a cold sweat, thinking everything was just a bad dream, only to realize he had not been dreaming. He got up quickly, showered and then headed back to Calgary to be near the woman he loved so much.

***

Five days had passed when the Doctor called Bill and his children into his office.

Bill was sure he knew what the doctor was about to say. He had prayed for God to give him strength to give the answer he knew he must. It would not be easy, as he already knew what Lisa's reaction would be. Darcy would be able to accept it more readily, knowing it was the right thing to do.

"Bill," Doctor Rogers said. "I have called you together to see whether or not you wish to continue with the life support system."

Bill heard Lisa gasp, but he tried to remain calm, even though he felt his heart race.

"What happens if she is taken off? Is there a chance she can continue on her own?" Bill asked.

"There's always a chance." But, he shook his head no and continued. "You must be prepared for it to go the other way too." The doctor said.

"Dad you can't!!" Lisa cried.

Bill turned to Lisa, trying to fight back tears. "Lisa we talked about this at the beginning. You know your Mother would not want to live like this. I want this to be a decision we make together." Bill said. "If God wants her to stay with us he will give her the strength to go on her own. We have to put Mom in Gods hands and believe he will do what is right." Bill wiped a tear from his eye before looking at Darcy. Tears were running down Darcy's cheeks, but he nodded his approval to remove everything.

Bill then looked at Lisa who was now crying uncontrollably. Bill, Darcy and Lisa stood holding each other for sometime before Bill said.

"Lisa you know what I said is right." Lisa slowly nodded as she buried her head in her Father's arms weeping. Bill gave the permission for the doctor to remover her life support. But he wanted to be by Dawn's side all the while, and his children also acknowledged the same.

"I will give you an hour with her, before we do it." Doctor Rogers said. It was all agreed to before Bill and his children returned to Dawn's bedside.

Bill gently took Dawn's hand in his as he kissed her. "Dawn, I have just made the hardest decision of my life. But I feel this is what you would want." Bill said.

"Doctor Rogers has asked us about removing all these machines. We have prayed about it, I know that is what you would want, as we talked about this before. I know that God will do what is right. Dawn, you know that Lisa, Darcy and especially me want you with us forever." Bill hesitated before continuing. "They'll be removing these machines within the hour. I know you are strong and can continue to fight to stay with us, even after that, if you can. I love you more then I can ever tell you. You will always be a part of me. Please if you can hear me and have the strength, keep on fighting. I will be by your side through this and I will not leave you alone."

Darcy went to the other side of the bed. Taking his Mothers hand, he said. "Mom, I know you will fight to stay with us if you can. I love you Mom." A tear fell on his Mothers cheek when he bent over to kiss her.

Darcy stepped back when Lisa came to talk to her Mother. She was doing her best to get control of her emotion when she took her Mothers hand in hers. Lisa laid her head on her Mothers shoulder and wept. Bill sat still, holding Dawn's hand while squeezing it gently. Lisa slowly got up and dried her eyes. "Mom I love you, I don't want you to leave us. Please keep fighting. I know if God wants you, he will take you to a better place, where you don't have to go through all this. But I will miss you." She said before giving her Mother a kiss.

They gathered together as Bill prayed for strength to accept God's will. Whether it was for Dawn's full recovery or whether she was to go to be with her Lord, to join the rest of their family who had gone ahead. Bill again thanked God for the time he and Dawn had together, as well as for the children God had blessed them with. Bill then sat in silence, but continued praying. Soon he felt the Doctors hand on his shoulder. Bill stood up once more to kiss his wife. "I love you very much Dawn," Bill said. Then with the nod of his head, he indicated to the doctor that they were ready. Bill stood there continuing to hold Dawn's hand while squeezing it very gently. Bill heard Lisa crying, but did not take his eyes off of his wife.

Slowly the doctor removed all but the heart monitor, and intravenous, that was in Dawn's arm. Bill held his breath, his eyes locked onto the heart monitor. He watched it go from squiggly lines, down to a strait line. Again he heard Lisa burst out in uncontrollable sobs, but Bill sat calmly, squeezing Dawn's hand a bit harder as he continued to pray. Suddenly Bill noticed a slight movement on the monitor. He began to rub Dawn's arm, then bent over to Dawn, softly saying. "Dawn I know you are trying. I'm here and I will try to help you come back." Bill noticed a very weak heart beat on the monitor then motioned to the doctor, not wanting to get his children's hopes up.

Doctor Rogers said quietly to Bill. "Keep talking to her." He said while feeling for Dawn's pulse. Slowly the monitor began to show that Dawn's heart was beating on it's own. Bill continued talking to her for sometime, before going to the corner where Darcy was trying to calm his sister.

"Lisa, listen to me." Bill said, grabbing her by the shoulders firmly. Lisa calmed down at the firm grip of her Father's hands. Bill looked at Darcy and pointed to the heart monitor. Which now showed that Dawn's heart was very weak, but she was doing it on her own. Darcy looked in amazement while Bill talked to Lisa. "I want to show you something," he said putting his arm around her. He put his hand under Lisa's chin to make her look up at the monitor.

Lisa looked at it for a moment before realizing what it meant. She quickly went over to her Mother and gave her a kiss. "Mom you are going to be ok?"

Darcy held his Mothers hand. "Hang in there, you're doing fine." He said.

Bill told his children they should go get something to eat, but he would stay.

Darcy and Lisa felt that their Father now wanted time alone, with their Mother. They told him they would be back later and would bring him something to eat. They knew their Father would not leave their Mother side for some time and he definitely was not eating properly.

Bill sat talking to Dawn after everyone had left. He now believed that Dawn would again come back to him. She was now fighting on her own, without the machines.

He was beginning to have faith that perhaps God would restore her once again, to full health.

***

It was now two weeks since the life support had been taken off, but Dawn still had not regained consciousness. Darcy had to get back to work and Lisa had grudgingly gone back to school. Bill stayed at Darcy's, but did go home for a couple of nights. Nick and Marie had come to see Dawn when she was on life support, but had not stayed long, because he could not bare to see her like that. One day when Nick came into town on business, he felt he had to see her. At first they wouldn't let him in, saying it was family only. Nick did his best to explained that it was approved by Bill, but it still took several minutes, before they allowed him see Dawn.

Nick walked slowly into Dawn's room. It hurt to see her lying there so pale and thin. It immediately took him back to just before his wife died. Nick wiped a tear from his eye when he walked over and took Dawn's hand in his. He leaned over then kissed her on the forehead.

"Dawn, its Nick. You have to get better. You look better than last time Marie and I were here. You have to come home again. Your family needs you." he said. Nick sat on the chair by the bed, still holding Dawn's hand. "Bill needs you." Nick hesitated before continuing. "I told God I would even try to become a praying man again, if he would bring you back. Bill saw what you did in the barn, and I think he was quite pleased. Surprised too. He and I talked for a while, and you know... I think we could even become friends." Nick wished he knew if anything was getting through to her. "Dawn, can you show me some sign that you can hear me?" he asked. Nick was positive he felt slight movement in her fingers. Nick quickly released Dawn's hand when Bill came into the room. When Bill went over to stand by Dawn's side, Nick told him that he was sure Dawn had acknowledged his presence by moving her fingers.

Bill held Dawn's hand and said. "Dawn, Nick said he was sure you heard him, can you squeeze my hand if you understand?" Bill turned to Nick with a smile on his face.

"Thanks Dawn you're doing great. Soon you will be up and around and I can take you home with me." Bill said. For the first time, in these many days, he believed it could be possible.

The next few days Dawn again had not shown any sign of acknowledging him.

Then once again, Bill was summoned to the Doctors office. Doctor Rogers did not totally believe, that what Bill felt was an acknowledgment from Dawn, but Bill knew in his heart that it was.

"Bill" I called you in, to tell you that Dawn is about 5 weeks pregnant," Doctor

Rogers said. Bill's mouth dropped open in surprise. "You know how weak she is and we don't believe she can carry on with this pregnancy in her present condition."

Bill sat in stunned silence, not knowing what to say. All he knew was that he had to get out of there for some fresh air, as the room suddenly got awful hot.

The doctor put his hand on Bill shoulder. "I am sorry Bill I know this should be a happier occasion. It has be tough for you with everything that's happened," he said.

"I need some air," Bill said getting up quickly to get outside the hospital, where he leaned against the building for support.

God, Bill prayed. *First you took my son, and now you give us another and I don't know if Dawn can handle it now.* Bill closed his eyes feeling totally numb. He had a good idea what the doctor was about to say next, but he didn't want to hear it. Bill slowly went back to Dawn's room. He desperately needs to be able to talk to her and for her to respond. Bill sat down on the chair, beside the bed. Taking Dawn's hand, he laid his head on her arm for some time, before he started talking to her.

"Dawn, I just talked to the doctor and he told me, that we are going to have a baby." Bill said remembering that very special night, when Dawn once again accepted his love. "Oh Dawn, I don't know how much more I can take. I need to have you talk to me again," he said. This time there was no mistaking it, when Dawn squeezed Bill's hand. Bill looked up suddenly at Dawn before saying. "Thank-you God." Bill stood up and kissed Dawn, this time feeling a response in her lips, even if it was a very weak kiss. "Keep fighting Dawn and soon God will bring us back together again. I love you so much," Bill said.

* * *

It was a weak later before Dawn opened her eyes, and still several days after that, that she tried to speak. The Doctor was amazed, and admitted, that it had to be a miracle that she survived at all. He acknowledged too, that seemingly, there was no noticeable sign of brain damage that he could tell. The Doctor was still very concerned about Dawn as she was not getting proper nourishment for her and the baby. One day as Bill sat by her side, Dawn tried to speak, but her voice was very weak.

"Tell me your news again." Dawn said so silent that it was little more then a whisper.

Bill was confused at first, but then realized what she meant. "Yes Dawn, we are going to have another baby, but you have to be very careful and you need some nourishment."

She smiled at him, and for the first time, Bill was thrilled to receive a kiss in return for his.

Just then Doctor Rogers came into the room. He first greeted Bill before going over to talk to Dawn. "How are you doing? It's good to see you awake."

Dawn smiled but everything was still an effort for her. She had a fair amount of pain in her head, but she was alert. The doctor asked Bill if he could talk to him in private, but as Bill was about to go, Dawn's grip tightened on his hand.

"I want to hear what he has to say," Dawn said softly.

Bill and the doctor looked at each other, before Bill nodded, in agreement. He had a good idea what the Doctor was about to say, and the decision was as much Dawn's as his.

Doctor Rogers sat on the edge of Dawn's bed. "As Bill has probably told you, you are about 7 weeks pregnant." He looked at Bill as he continued. "We don't believe Dawn will be able to carry this baby full term, as she is not out of the woods yet," he said. "Her life may depend on whether or not she gives up the baby."

"You mean an abortion?" Bill asked.

"Yes," Doctor Rogers said. "My colleagues and I feel it would be the best for Dawn."

Tears filled Dawn's eyes, as she squeezed Bill hand. *I will never give it up*, Dawn said to herself. *If God wants to take the baby and me then that is the way it will have to be. I will never allow an abortion.*

Dawn looked up at Bill and in a very weak voice said. "No, Bill. I won't allow it."

Doctor Rogers got up to leave. "I'll let you discuss it." He said leaving the room.

Bill gave Dawn a hug, her tears now flowed freely. Bill too could not stop his tears, from running down his face. Bill wiped his eyes, then stroked Dawn's hair, now wet from her tears. "I don't want to lose you Dawn," Bill said.

It was an extreme effort for Dawn to talk, but she had to. "I'm sorry Bill but I cannot kill our child." Dawn hesitated trying to get enough strength to say what she had to.

"If God wants us to have this baby-- he will look after us. If he decides to take this child from us… it's his decision. If.. he takes us both… God will give you strength to go through that too…but I will not consent to an abortion" Dawn said closing her eyes, now very tired from talking. It wasn't long before she went back to sleep.

Bill sat silently holding Dawn's hand. Dawn had made her decision, and he knew she was right, but he was so afraid of losing her. The word, *Oh you of little faith*, came into his mind. He would wait until the next day to be sure Dawn still felt the same. Then he would tell the doctor of their decision. Bill sat watching the slow drip from the bottle that hung on the pole beside Dawn's bed, when Marie and Nick walked into the room.

"How is she?" Marie asked, giving Bill a hug as he choked back a sob. Marie looked at Bill and instantly, knew something else had happened. "Bill, what's wrong? Has Dawn taken a turn for the worse again?" Marie asked afraid of the answer.

Bill slowly explained the situation to her and Nick. Marie's heart went out to both Dawn and Bill, as she realized the difficult time they were having. First losing a son, then Bill almost lost his wife and now he stands the risk of losing both his wife and child.

"Oh Bill. I am so sorry. This should be a time to congratulate the both of you, but it's just too bad this is all happening now. Bill, prayer got her through this once, and if it's God's will he can do it again," Marie said.

"I doubt if you have eaten much lately, by the looks of you. Let's go down to the cafeteria for a bite. Marie will stay with Dawn, in case she wakes up." Nick said to Bill.

"That's a good idea," Marie said. "You can't help Dawn if you don't keep up your own strength."

The two men walked down to the cafeteria in silence. Bill told Nick, he would just have coffee. He then went to sit at a table off to the side, where they would have more privacy. Nick came back with a sandwich, some fruit and two cups of coffee.

"You have to eat something." Nick said.

Bill thanked Nick, before he slowly began to eat his food. He had no appetite lately but did force himself to eat occasionally.

"What have you decided to do?" Nick asked Bill.

"I don't want to lose her," Bill said. The strain was now

taking its toll on him.

"It has to be hard to go through this." Nick said looking into his cup.

"I guess you would know," Bill said. "What would you do?" he asked looking at Nick.

"I would do what ever it took to keep my wife." He said remembering what it was like to lose someone you cared about.

"Would you give up one of your children, to do that, and risk your wife not forgiving you for the rest of your life?" Bill asked.

Nick thought for a moment before answering. "I see your point," Nick said. "I can't answer that."

The two men sat in silence for some time when, Nick said. "I guess praying helped so far, maybe we should pray for guidance, and strength." Nick said as they both bowed their heads and prayed silently.

Marie to sat in silent prayer by Dawn's bedside, until the men returned. Dawn did not wake up, while Nick and Marie were there. The extra effort it took to talk, tired her. She didn't wake up for the rest of the day. Bill told Marie and Nick that he'd decided to go home for the night. Bill gave Dawn a kiss, and told her he loved her. He told her that he would be back the next afternoon, but he doubted if she heard him, as she was now sleeping. Bill walked out of the hospital with Marie and Nick, telling them he would see them another time, also thanking them for their prayers.

***

Bill spent most of the evening sitting in his rocking chair, picturing another small child playing at his feet, or rocking him or her to sleep in the rocking chair. Bill smiled. It might not even be so bad to have a baby now, even if their other children were grown up. He and Dawn would have more time to spend with a child now. They had been both devastated when their son was killed. No one would ever replace Stephen but this child was still a result of the love they have for each other. How could they ever destroy this precious gift God was giving them.

Bill looked up and said. "Lord I give Dawn and the baby to you. Your will be done." Bill was exhausted, but when he gave his burdens over to God, he fell asleep in his chair.

The following morning, Bill set up a kerosene heater in the barn, because the air was beginning to get quite cold. He knew he had to do something, to keep himself occupied. Bill suddenly decided what it was he would do. After spending several weeks either at Darcy's apartment, or at the hospital, it had made him very restless. Bill first off, spent some time looking at all the work Dawn had to have done to clean up the inside of the barn. He and Joe had looked at it slightly, when they were working on the house, but had dreaded the part of cleaning it out. He never imagined getting it this clean. He would have to insulate it, and put a heater in so he could start doing some real work.

But Dawn was part of that plan, and he knew it would be difficult without her.

Bill made the decision to be positive. The cradle he saw in a magazine was what he decided to build for their baby. Bill found some of his wood he had stored away, including part of an old waterbed. He first found a place for his planer and began to take the old finish off the boards. He then selected a couple of large and small dowels as little by little he found almost all the material he needed. He was glad now, that he had kept some of his odds and ends. Otherwise he would have had to go to town, and right now he didn't feel like doing that. There was also some material left from the work that had been done in the house that he had stored in the garden shed, but Dawn had already moved it into the barn. Bill felt guilty for not being here to help Dawn do all this work.

He bent down to pick up a card on the floor, realized it was the note Dawn had left for him. Bill read the words *A labour of love* then he tacked it up near the table where he could see it, as a reminder of what she had done for him. Bill worked on his project losing all track of time. It was 1 o'clock when he looked at his watch, and decided to get cleaned up and go to see Dawn. He would spend the rest of the afternoon and evening, with her. Then in the morning, after checking on her again, he would go home to work on his project.

***

Dawn was awake when Bill arrived. The nurse had told Bill that Dawn had taken some broth and juice for the first time. He was ecstatic, as this was the beginning of her getting some nourishment for herself as well as the baby. Dawn felt better when she was assured that Bill would not go against her wishes. The doctor was none to pleased, as he felt they were making a big mistake. He said that if the baby did survive, it could also have severe problems because of the lack of nourishment. But he had to abide by their decision.

Dawn got tired very easily and once again drifted off to sleep. Bill was starting to feel a bit weak and shaky himself from not eating so he decided to head down to the cafeteria. His clothes were beginning to hang on him, as he had lost a fair amount of weight. For the first time in a long while, he actually was hungry. Bill thought of how good it would be to have Dawn across the table to discuss his new project, like they had done so many times before. He did not want to tell her what he was doing, as it was to be a surprise. He would build it and put it aside, just in case things didn't go well. In which case he would store it for their first grandchild.

After Bill had eaten he went back to Dawn's room. He sat looking at a magazine until a nurse that came in to check Dawn's blood pressure and temperature, which woke her up. "You are a wonder Dawn," the nurse said. "All your vital signs are normal, where as a while back, I would never have believed it possible." She said writing down the numbers on her chart.

"With God nothing is impossible." Dawn said smiling at Bill. Just then a food tray was brought in and the nurse helped Dawn to sit up. She was still very weak, but her voice was beginning to get stronger. Bill helped her as she ate her soup, and a bit of fruit. There was a glass of milk on the tray, which Bill knew she didn't like, but he made her drink it anyway. "Remember it's not just for you." He said, gently placing his hand on her belly. Dawn put her hand on his, as they looked at each other.

"Bill are you sorry that we're having another child, so late in our life? Especially with the other two already grown and on their own." Dawn asked.

Bill kissed Dawn, as he held her in his arm. "What does that tell you?" He said.

Dawn smiled as she lay back in her bed. "I was shocked when the doctor first told me." Bill said. "But now I am actually looking forward to it. What about you Dawn?" Bill asked. "Your the one that has to go through all this."

"After Stephen was killed, I thought it would be nice to have another baby, to take his place. But then I realized no one would ever take his place. Over the years I thought about it, but then as our children got older, I didn't think I wanted anymore." Dawn hesitated, before continuing. "With our love remaining strong even when I could not remember you after the accident, it does seem right to renew our love with a child." Dawn looked at Bill, in sudden shock. "What will Darcy and Lisa say or have you told them?" Dawn asked suddenly.

"No I haven't. I thought we should do it together. I don't suppose they will be all that happy," Bill said.

Dawn reached for Bill's hand. "I feel a bit foolish having a child now, with our other children grown up already." Dawn said sadly.

Bill kissed his wife. "You shouldn't Dawn. It was our love that brought them into this world, and our love for each other has grown stronger with time. It was God who decided to bless us with another one, and they should be happy for us. They'll get used to it, over time. They'll be here on the weekend and we'll tell them then." Bill said.

And as Bill had said, Darcy and Lisa were none to pleased

to hear that they were to have another sibling. But they slowly grew to accept the fact, and Lisa even thought it would be nice to have a little sister. Darcy then informed her that it could be another boy.

They did have one major concern and that was to the state of the baby, with all that had happened. Then there was the concern as to the health of their Mother. Their parents informed them that they were praying that all would be well. God had given them this child, and they would have to except his decision. Lisa and Darcy had to admit they had never prayed so much as they had in the last while.

Dawn lay back resting, as the verse, all *things work for good for them that love the lord*, came into her mind. Perhaps some good had come out of this she thought. If this is what it took to bring her children to God so be it.

***

As Dawn now grew stronger with each passing day, Bill spent a little longer away from the hospital, working on the cradle. He wanted to have the cradle done before Dawn came home and because of the cooler temperature, he would have to do the finishing on it, in the kitchen. When Bill finished the cradle, he covered it and set it in the back corner of the barn, so Dawn would not see it.

It was now two months that Dawn had been in the hospital. Dawn was up and walking around, and look much better now that she was eating again. The next day when Bill talked to the doctor, he told Bill that he could take Dawn home the next day, which was music to Bill's ears. He walked into Dawn's room, watching her as she stood looking out the window. She was deep in thought and hadn't heard Bill come up behind her. Bill wrapped his arms around her waist then kissed her on the side of her neck.

"What are you thinking about?" Bill asked still holding her.

"I was wishing I could go home with you Bill." She said sadly.

"Will you please talk to the doctor, to see when I can go?"

"What about another week." Bill said teasing her.

"Oh Bill." She said turning to face him. "That long yet? Why?" she asked. "I'm doing fine."

"Well, what about tomorrow? Is that soon enough?" He said with a big grin on his face.

"Bill do you mean it?" she said, looking at him anxiously.

"Yes," he said, giving her a big hug. "You're coming home with me tomorrow morning."

Dawn hit him lightly on the shoulder. "You know it's not nice to lie." She said trying to look stern, but the twinkle in her eye did not fool Bill.

"I never lied. I only asked if you wanted to stay another week." He said once again teasing her.

They held each other now knowing, that soon they would be going home together.

Chapter 14

Bill had made arrangements with Marie to stay and help Dawn for the first week.

After that she would come twice a week to help Dawn with cleaning and the laundry.

The doctor had given strict orders that Dawn was to do nothing for a while. Bill also had some concern about the stairs to their bedroom, but decided to wait until Dawn came home to discuss it with her. Nick had offered to help Bill move the furniture down to the back bedroom, but they would now have to find a bed for up stairs.

The day after Dawn got home, they were having tea when Nick drove in. Marie went to the door and was almost knocked over as Pup bolted past her. She went directly to Dawn's side and licked her hand while wagging her tail furiously. Dawn bent down to give her a hug. Then stroking Pups head, Dawn thanked her for saving her life. Nick tried to get Pup to go outside but to no avail. She would not let Dawn out of her site but lay on her mat by the door watching Dawn.

"Leave her," Dawn said. "She'll go out later.

"Thanks Nick for bringing Pup back, and well-- just thanks for every thing."

Dawn said giving Nick a hug. Just then Bill came from the washroom. He went straight to Dawn side and put his arm around her. While holding her firmly he said. "Hands off."

Dawn looked at the stern look on Bill's face, but then just

as quickly it faded into a smile. Bill reached out to shake hands with Nick. "I also want to thank you for saving Dawn's life."

Dawn stood looking at them, wondering what had just happened. She knew Marie and Nick had come to see her, but Bill had never been there at the same time, as far as she could remember.

"What just happened?" She asked Bill, in wonderment.

"It's a long story." "I'll tell you some time." Bill said, offering Nick a chair.

"So you know about the wedding then?" Dawn asked, Bill

"What wedding," Bill asked.

"Nick and Marie are getting married. Isn't that great!" Dawn said, happy she could finally share her friend's happiness with Bill.

Bill looked across the room at Marie. Her face lit up when she looked at Nick, who sat down beside her in contentment with his arm on the back of her chair. "Well congratulations. I guess I should have clued in on it, when I always saw the two of you together," Bill said.

"You had enough on your mind," Nick said.

"When is the big day?" Bill asked.

"Shortly after your baby is born. I want Dawn to stand up for me, so we'll wait until she's stronger." Marie said excitedly. "That will probably be about the beginning of June."

"Bill, would you consider being my best man?" Nick asked looking at Bill.

Bill looked at Dawn first, then after a moment he said. "I guess I could, seeing you got the most beautiful maid of honour for my partner." They all laughed and Dawn realized her hopes had come true. They would now be able to all be friends. Dawn asked Bill if it would be ok to have the wedding in their yard, as Marie and Nick had wanted.

"I guess it would be all right." Bill said turning to Dawn, before continuing.

"As long as you don't over do it and feel fine. I don't see why not."

Nick asked Bill what he'd planned to do, now that he had decided to quite trucking.

"Well, now that Dawn has gone this far to set up my work shop, I plan to go into building different things. I may try the gift show in the city for starters," Bill said.

"This was always our dream, and now it looks like it may actually come true."

Dawn said smiling up at he husband.

"With our new addition on the way, it's time to settle down again," Bill said.

"No more leaving Dawn home alone, for her to pull another stunt like this. I couldn't handle that again," he said looking at Dawn.

* * *

The next day Bill and Dawn discussed moving their bedroom to the lower floor. Dawn reluctantly agreed. She did realize that going up and down the stairs did make her very tired. She also knew it would get more difficult as the months progressed.

"I'm going to miss that room," Dawn said sadly.

"It isn't going anywhere." Bill said with a smile. "When you feel better you can still go up there. The back room is still a fair size, and our bedroom set will fit in there quite nicely," Bill told her.

"What about the roll top desk?" Dawn asked.

Bill thought for a moment. "Well… what about if we rearrange the living room. You can have it either by the west window or the south window. With using the back bedroom, it would be easier when I have to get up at night, when the baby cries." He said teasing her.

Dawn looked at Bill. "You better be careful or I just might take you up on that." She said.

"You know Dawn, I am really looking forward to this baby. It'll be better once he can crawl though," Bill said.

"You were good with all our children, even when they were

tiny," Dawn said looking at her husband lovingly. "God gave me a very loving husband and I am so thankful for that."

Bill never responded to her comment, but said. "There will still be enough room in the back bedroom to put a crib in. Then when he gets older, he will go up stairs and we will have the living room to use just outside of our bedroom. We can also use the back door to go out and sit on our porch in the evenings."

"You know Bill, you may have a point there. I guess it won't be such a bad idea after all." Dawn said.

"Nick said he would give me a hand to move everything down, seeing he needs an excuse to come see Marie. I think Marie and him will make a good couple," Bill said.

"Now don't you see how silly it was to dislike Nick, just because I knew him before you. He was never a threat to you once I made my decision, and that decision will never change." Dawn said laying her hand on Bill's.

"I suppose you're right, but I still don't think I will ever forget it, just as you probably haven't forgotten my old girlfriends." Bill said smiling at her.

"No, we'll never forget, but our love and trust in one another, should never give reason to mistrust each other. Even if we come in contact with some of our old friends." Dawn said.

"I know but it still bothers me. It may get easier once Nick and Marie are married but I am grateful to him for saving your life." Bill said. He then changed the subject. "I was thinking of going to town to get a bed for upstairs. Do you feel up to coming along?" Bill asked.

"It would be nice to go out for a bit. That is if you don't have a lot of other things to do," Dawn said.

"No if you like we'll just pick out a bed and come home." Bill said not wanting to have Dawn over do it. He had some concern because she was not getting her strength back as quick as he had hoped.

Bill hesitated before saying soberly. "Dawn we have to talk about the car accident.

"I don't want to!" Dawn said sharply.

Bill looked at her, wondering about her quick answer. "We have to Dawn. Do you remember any of it?" Bill asked noticing the look on her face.

"No, but I have a good idea what happened." She said, the color draining from her face.

"Why do you say that?" Bill asked.

Dawn got up and went to the cupboard, where she pulled out the large brown envelope. Her eyes began to fill with tears when she handed it to Bill.

Bill looked at the envelope, before going to wrap his arms around Dawn. "I'm sorry you had to find out this way," he said.

"It came just before all this other happened." She said absorbing the comfort of Bill's arms.

"Let's sit down and talk about it." He said escorting her to the chair.

"Who was driving?" Dawn asked fearing it may have been her.

"Your Father was and your Mother was beside him. You were in the back seat." Bill said. "That is probably what saved your life."

"I don't want to hear no more." Dawn said quickly.

"That's fine, but someday if you want to know I will tell you." Bill said. "You have to sign some papers at the lawyer, so that the estate can be settled." Bill continued slowly. "I left it as long as I could, hoping you would remember us first. Then this happened." Now the lawyers are getting anxious to square it away. As the only daughter, everything will probably be left to you." Bill said. "Some day when you're feeling stronger we'll go to your parents house. But right now I have arranged for the neighbours to keep an eye on it. Everything is just as they left it."

Dawn agreed that it should be settled, so Bill made an appointment for the following week. That should give Dawn a bit more time to regain some of her strength back. Bill was still very concerned, and wondered if there was more to her not remembering. Perhaps she didn't want to remember, but either way she refused to listen to the details of the accident.

God said he would not give us more then we could bare, and I figure I have about my limit. It's time to move on. Dawn thought to herself.

Bill told Dawn that whatever money, she received from her parents, she was to put in her own account. He would continue to supply all her needs as long as he lived. He did not want any of her inheritance. Dawn tried to insist, that it be put it in a join account, but Bill would not hear of it.

"Bill," Dawn said. "If we need money later I'm going to insist we put it in joint names." "We have always done things together and made decisions together. I don't like having things separate now. What happens if something happens to me—?"

Bill suddenly interrupted. "Don't you talk like that," he said sharply.

"I'm not out of the woods yet Bill. Once the baby is born, I hope I can get my strength back, but you know it is coming back slower than I had hoped." She said.

"We will talk about it later" Bill said, standing up not wanting to get in an argument with her now. "If you still want to go to town, maybe we should go soon. You must rest this afternoon. You may have to lie down on the couch in the living room if you get to tired. It'll take awhile to get the beds changed around." Bill said.

Once they got to town, they went straight to a furniture store, to look for a bed. They quickly settled on a twin size bed. Bill put his arm around Dawn when he saw her looking at a white and gold day bed. "You know Dawn," he said. "This would look good by the west window up stairs. That way if you wanted to spend some time up there, it could come in handy.

Dawn turn to Bill. "Why do you always refer to our child as a him?" She asked.

"She might be a she." Dawn said smiling up at him.

"He is a he." Bill said casually. "I just know it."

Bill told the salesman, which bed they chose, than said they would also take the day bed, even if Dawn figured they should wait. When they got back home, Nick and Marie were sitting at the table drinking coffee. Dawn went straight to the couch to lay down and rest while the two men moved the furniture down from upstairs. After putting their new purchases in place, they decided to leave the desk where it was, for now. Dawn was not up to rearranging the living room. When Marie had lunch ready, Bill and Dawn insisted that Nick stay, as it was the least they could do for him helping them.

After lunch Dawn told Marie, she would help her put some clean bedding on their bed, while the men sat in the kitchen talking and drinking their coffee.

"I have to try to do something," Dawn said. "I feel so useless, and if I just lay around, I feel I get even weaker."

Marie agreed, but then she insisted that Dawn rest, after that. The trip to town did tire Dawn and she did not want to end up back in the hospital.

* * *

The following week Dawn said she was strong enough to go to the lawyers.

Neither of them knew for sure what was all in her parents will, or what her parents had for money. Bill knew this would not be easy for Dawn. When the lawyer began to read the will, Bill put his arm around Dawn's shoulder for support, at which time she reached over and laid her hand on Bills leg.

Dawn still could not make herself believe that her parents were gone, as she listened to what the lawyer read.

Most of the money was left for both her and Bill. Her parents knew the love and trust that Dawn and Bill had for each other and also knew Bill's pride would not allow him to accept his wife's money. This way there would be no argument. Bill and Dawn looked at each other, both wiping away tears from their eyes. There is also a substantial amount left for each of Bill and Dawn's two children, to be given to them, when they got married or at Bill and Dawn's discretion. The house and property in Red Deer was also in joint names for Bill and Dawn, as well as the small cottage along the coast on Vancouver Island. All other stocks and bonds were to be left for Dawn. Dawn's parents also told both Bill and Dawn how much they cared for them and their children. The request was that they ask Gods wisdom in using their money wisely.

Dawn bit her lip hard, all through the reading of the will. She did her best to fight back her tears.

Bill looked at her several times as he felt her grip tighten on his hand. He was very concerned about her. Dawn was extremely pale and had lost a lot of weight in the past few months. Looking at her, no one would ever suspect that she was going to have a baby. Bill was glad when the reading of the will was over and papers were signed.

He just wanted to take his wife home, as he already knew what to watch for, when she was over doing it. He had dreaded this day. Especially now that Dawn knew her parents would not be there to share in the joy of her fourth child.

They drove all the way home in silence, with Dawn resting her head on Bill's shoulder. She was now more exhausted than she had ever been before. She desperately wanted and needed to lie down. She even felt to tired to tell Bill of how pleased she was that her parents had done things this way. Now Bill had to accept some of the money.

Thankfully it left out any room for arguments.

Marie, who had been doing laundry and cleaning, quickly went to open the door when she saw Bill carry Dawn towards the house.

"What happened?" Marie asked, quickly going to open Bill and Dawn's bed.

"I'm fine." Dawn said quietly. "I have just an over protective husband."

Marie could see for herself why Bill's face was full of

concern. "I'll help Dawn get into bed." Marie told Bill, when he gently sat Dawn on the chair by the bed.

"There's some coffee and cookies on the table." She said fearing Bill was the next one to get sick. Marie got Dawn settled in her bed. She sat holding Dawn's hand for no more than five minutes when Dawn drifted off to sleep. She covered Dawn with another blanket to keep her warm before joining Bill in the kitchen.

"Bill, did everything go ok at the lawyers?" Marie asked. Yes, it went fine but it was just too soon." He said rubbing his head.

"I'm afraid it was just too much for her today." Bill hesitated. "I haven't seen her look this bad for some time. I only hope it doesn't throw her recovery back," he said.

Marie looked at the dark circles around Bill droopy eyes. She could tell that Bill too, had lost weight by the way his clothes hung on him. "Bill, I'm going to open the hide-a-bed for you. That way you can be near Dawn with out disturbing her." Marie said standing up.

"I'll be fine," Bill said.

"You go look at yourself in a mirror, and then tell me that." Marie said firmly.

"You know yourself you're tired. What do you think it would do to Dawn's recovery if you ended up in the hospital with a heart attack? Now I'm going to make up the bed for you then, I will not listen to any more arguments. I'll spend the night to see that you both behave." Marie said, going into the living room.

Bill had never heard Marie talk like that, but he knew she was right. He had to admit that he had not been feeling well and was very tired. The stress of everything was catching up to him. The last thing he needed was for Dawn to worry about him.

It wasn't long before Marie was back, telling Bill to go lie down. She would check on Dawn periodically, so he could get some rest. Marie left the door open between Bill and Dawn's bedroom and the living room. She closed the door between the kitchen and living room, just to the point where it did not latch.

Will Love Conquer All?

She didn't want to disturb Bill by the click of the latch when she went to check on Dawn. Marie was worried about both of them. The last time she seen Dawn look that pale was in the hospital. Bill was now also showing signs of major fatigue, which worried her. Marie went upstairs to use the phone, as not to disturb anyone. Her and Nick had planned to go out that evening, but she wasn't about to leave Bill and Dawn now.

Marie was glad that Nick was in when she called. "Hello, Nick, this is Marie. I just called to tell you that I wouldn't be able to go out tonight."

"Why not?" Nick asked.

"I'm going to spend the night at Bill and Dawn's." Marie said.

"Did something happen at the lawyers?" Nick asked, wondering how things went.

"I think everything went fine, but when Bill carried Dawn into the house, she did not look very well. Bill too is resting. I'm concerned that he is the next one that will end up in the hospital." Marie said. "I think the stress is catching up to him, even if he doesn't admit to it."

Nick was silent for a while. He then told Marie he would come over later to keep her company. Nick sat staring at the wall after he hung up the phone. He'd thought Dawn was well on her way, but he also knew Bill looked very tired lately. If something did happen to Bill, it would kill Dawn now for sure. It was very obvious to see the way Bill and Dawn cared for each other. He was sure that, she would not want to fight to live, if something were to happen too Bill. Even though Nick could never have Dawn for his wife, he did enjoy having Bill and Dawn as neighbours.

Bill had fallen asleep almost immediately and had slept right through the night. The next morning he felt refreshed as well as looking much better when he came in to the kitchen. There he found Marie had prepared a large breakfast for him. He had checked on Dawn before he came out, and was glad to see some color back in her cheeks. Bill and Marie were about to eat went

Dawn joined then.

"Dawn, you should be in bed. I thought you were still sleeping," Bill said.

"I smelled breakfast, and suddenly felt hungry." Dawn said as Bill helped her to the chair.

"That's a good sign," Marie said dishing out some sausage and eggs for Dawn."

"You sure look better this morning." Marie said pouring a glass of milk for her.

"I don't like milk," Dawn said.

"You have to drink it. I will stay here until you do," Bill said.

Dawn remembered Nick saying the same thing to her some time back. "Well, I guess I have to start to get used to it." She said making a face at Bill.

***

Dawn's strength gradually increased every day, but still not to the point where she could do a lot. Bill finally began to relax when he saw she was doing better, but he was still afraid of how she would manage as the months progressed.

Thanksgiving did not turn out as planned. It was changed to a get together for Christmas. Lisa would bring her friend and Nick and Marie agreed to come with Nick's children only if Marie could come and help. Dawn was coming along quite well now, but she did have to still take it easy. Twice her doctor was about to put her in the hospital on total bed rest, but she had refused, promising to rest at home. Bill did lay the law down, and would not let her do anything until Christmas. If she couldn't handle that, Marie and Lisa said they would do it all and she was to only supervise.

As the weather was now getting colder, Bill had Joe come over to do some renovations inside the barn. They cut a large hole in the loft to put up a proper staircase along the side of the wall. Next came the insulating of the entire barn, after which they nailed it out with boards to keep a rustic look. Bill made sure there was a railing put up in the loft around the stair well and on the staircase. The loft for now would be used for storage. He would take all precautions to avoid any more accidents.

A plank floor was added above the cement to level off the floor. Next he divided the barn into two parts. One half would be for displaying his finished product, while the other half would be his workshop. He also put an overhead heater in, to keep the building warm. As well as a small door in the front so he would not have to open the large door unless he needed to. Several florescent lights were also added as well as electrical outlets. Bill then brought in a couch, for Dawn to rest on if she decided to come out to stay for a while.

After they had it completed, Dawn told Bill she wanted to see what he had been spending his days and nights working on. So that evening while they sat eating supper Bill said to Dawn. "How would you like to see what you started in the barn?"

"I would love to. I do hope we can start to spend more time together, instead of you being in the barn all the time." Dawn said.

"I promise to spend more time with you, now that it's finished," Bill said.

"Well, after I help you with dishes, I want to show it to you." Bill said proudly.

Bill made sure Dawn was dressed warm enough as the weather had now turned very cold. When Dawn entered the barn she was utterly amazed at all the changes he had made. He showed her first his workshop, before leading her into the area where he had placed the couch. He told her this area was now to display his finished products. Dawn looked up at the staircase in amazement. "I would never believe this was the same building," Dawn said

"Thanks to you. You actually had the worst part done for me," Bill said holding her close. "I may never have done this for years if it had not been for you."

Taking her hand Bill lead her back to his workbench. He

pointed to the note Dawn had left for him before she fell. "I put it where I can see it to remind me of all you did for me." He said, taking her in his arms, kissing her passionately. Dawn clung to him eagerly returning his kiss.

"I will always love you Bill," she said.

"I love you too. I was so afraid of losing you Dawn. Please don't do that to me again. I really couldn't handle that again." Bill said holding her tight. Slowly he released her. "I think we should go back to the house now. You can come out sometimes when I'm working and tell me what you would like me to make for you. That is if you feel up to it. Then if you want to rest on the couch, it's there for you." Bill said leading her to the door. He switched off the lights and closed the door behind them. Then hand in hand they walked, back to their house.

After taking their coats off, Dawn poured two cups of coffee. They sat counting the days they had left until Christmas. Dawn suggested to Bill, that if possible he should try to make several of the Christmas gifts. He had made several pieces of country furniture for their children in the past, and it may be nice to add a few more items to give to them.

They drank their coffee while leafing through some magazines and marking different items that their children might like or use.

Dawn said she would like to do her part by helping with the finishing, but Bill was reluctant. "We'll see when the time comes." He replied.

Finally after several years, their dream of doing this type of work was now becoming reality.

CHAPTER 15

IT WAS TWO DAYS BEFORE Christmas, and they just gotten a few inches of snow over the night. Dawn was slowly getting back to her old self, but she still had to rest quite often. She told Bill one day, how frustrating it was not to be able to do what she use to do. "I guess I'm not as young as I used to be." She said.

Bill ploughed the driveway that morning, with an older tractor and blade he had bought. His children were coming home today and he didn't want anyone getting stuck in the driveway. Bill then put a cot in the upstairs bedroom, where Darcy and Lisa's friend would sleep. Lisa would have to sleep on the hide-a-bed. Bill told Dawn that when their children got married, they should consider building a small guesthouse, to which Dawn thought might be something for them to consider.

Lisa and her boyfriend arrived just as Dawn was preparing lunch. Pup stood by the door growling as Lisa and her friend walked towards the house. Bill and Dawn glanced at each other, wondering what had gotten into Pup. She had never acted that way before. Bill sternly directed Pup to lie down.

Lisa gave her Mother and Father a hug before introducing her friend, Franklin to them.

"Nice to meet you." Dawn said stretching out her hand to shake his. Franklin stood about six feet and weighed about 150 lb. Dawn's first impression was that he could be a model with his wavy black hair and flawless features.

"Have you ever been called Frank?" Bill asked reaching out to shake his hand.

"Oh." Lisa said rather quickly. "He prefers to go by Franklin."

Dawn caught the quick glance that Bill gave her, as Lisa and Franklin took off their boots and coats. After which Bill showed Franklin where to put his things.

Lisa went to her Mother's side. "Well, what do you think of him?" She asked.

Dawn looked at her daughter. "He's a very nice looking young man, but how can I tell you more, when I just met him. You must use your judgment as to whether or not he is the one for you. You know, your Father and I want the best for you and Darcy. We hope you can both find partners that you will love and respect and they intern will give you the same.

Remember also that it's important to find someone who also knows the Lord and remember your head must rule your heart." Dawn said as she began putting lunch on the table.

Lisa put her bag in her parent's bedroom, for the time being. Then went to wash her hands before going to help her Mother. Bill and Franklin came into the room just as Dawn was about to call them for lunch. They all sat around the table and just as Franklin was about to help himself to the food when Lisa touched his arm. "Dad always gives thanks for the food first," she said. Franklin gave Lisa an odd look before placing his hand on his lap.

Franklin was the only one that did not bowed his head when Bill began to pray.

"Thank-you Lord for the food you have so graciously provided for us. We ask that you bless it to our bodies needs. We also thank-you for bringing Lisa and Franklin safely here, and that you will be with all our families wherever they may be during this Christmas season. And that we do not forget that Christmas is not just a holiday but that it is to celebrate the birth of our Lord Jesus Christ Amen."

Bill glance over at Franklin. He seemed to be nice enough and yet a bit arrogant. He passed him a plate of food, while at the same time asking him what he was majoring in at university.

"I'm going into pharmacy." Franklin said rather proudly. "It'll take me a few years to finish the course, but there is good money to be made in that field."

"Do you work on the side to help put yourself through school?" Dawn asked.

"No, my parents are paying for it. Then if Lisa and I get married, she can work to help pay for it, because she would benefit from it later." Franklin said, looking at Lisa.

Bill and Dawn looked at each other, then at Lisa who sat looking down at her plate.

Pup started to bark, just as they heard someone drive in. Bill got up to see Darcy walking towards the house, his hands full of packages.

"Your just in time for lunch." Bill said, as Darcy handed his Father the packages. Then took off his boots and coat.

Dawn gave her son a hug before setting another plate.

Bill then introduced Darcy to Franklin. "Hi Frank," Darcy said.

"It is Franklin!" Franklin said abruptly.

Darcy looked at his Mother and Father, as if to say. *What's his problem?*

"Franklin is planning to be a pharmacist." Bill told Darcy.

"Good for him." Darcy said, sitting down at the table. "How are you doing, Mom?" Darcy asked.

"I'm almost back to normal." Dawn told him.

Franklin asked Lisa for a glass of water, which she immediately got for him. Then he said. "I understand you're going to have another baby. Don't you think you're a bit old for that? You should know that it's not the best idea to have one at your age."

Darcy looked at him angrily. "Don't you think you should just …" But then he got a look from his Father and finished with. "Never mind." He said grabbing for a slice of bread. He had a feeling that he and Franklin were not about to get along very well.

Bill quickly changed the subject by asking Darcy if he had been busy with the truck. Everyone seemed to join in on the conversation except for Lisa. She sat quietly eating and only spoke when someone directed a question to her.

"Your sure quite for a change." Darcy said to his sister.

"I have her well trained." Franklin said, asking her to get him some coffee, which she did immediately.

That was it. Darcy knew he was not going to like this guy. The only thing this guy had going for him was his looks. Surely Lisa could see that he was pompous, obnoxious and an arrogant idiot. He'd tell her to jump and she would say how high. Somebody had to talk some sense into her. He was more than likely going to ruin their Christmas. He would have some words with him especially if he said another wisecrack like he had said to his Mother.

"Where is your family?" Dawn asked Franklin. Trying her best to break some of the tension.

"My Father is on a cruise with his girlfriend somewhere and my Mother and Sister are in Vancouver with my Mother's family." Franklin said.

It didn't take Dawn long to figure out that Franklin may not be a person that she'd want her the daughter to marry. She was concerned as to what Lisa was getting herself into. After they finished their dessert the men went into the living room, as Dawn and Lisa cleared the table and washed the dishes.

"I'm sorry for what Franklin said to you, Mom." Lisa said.

Dawn said nothing more about it, but she knew that she had to pray, that Lisa did not get herself into a bad situation.

An hour later, Nick and Marie arrived. "This is Nick's daughter, Jackie." Marie said, introducing everyone to a beautiful slim young lady. She looked nothing like her Father. Dawn thought that she must have taken more after her Mother. Only her eyes and the color of her hair seemed to be inherited from her Father.

"Nice to meet you Jackie." Dawn said shaking her hand, before introducing them to each individual family member.

Darcy and Lisa went to shake hands with Nick and Marie. Lisa added a hug and a thank-you for helping her Father and Mother through some bad times, while Franklin stood back staring at Jackie.

"Where's your son?" Dawn asked Nick.

"He'll be along shortly. He decided to try out his cross country skis, in the fresh snow." Nick said.

As the ladies began to get things ready for Christmas day, the men went into the living room, while Franklin sat near the door where he could keep an eye on Lisa and Jackie. He didn't seem a bit interested in visiting with the men. After sometime, he got up and went into the kitchen. He grabbed Lisa's arm and told her that he wanted to go for a walk.

"I can't. I'm busy right now. I promised Mom that I would help her." She said.

"I'm sure she can do without you for a while." He said grabbing her hand, while asking Jackie if she wished to join then. To which she gratefully declined.

Lisa and Franklin put on their coats and boot. Franklin put his arm around her as they walked away from the house and out past the barn. They had walked sometime in silence along the edge of the trees, when Lisa broke the silence.

"That wasn't very nice of you to tell my Mother that she was too old to have a baby." Lisa said.

"Well she is." He said taking his arm away from her shoulder. "She should have had more sense than to have gotten pregnant at her age." He said.

"I won't have you talk about my Mother that way. Besides, why do you always blame the women? You act like the men have no part in it." Lisa said angrily.

"It is their fault. They should be more careful." He said glaring at her.

"If that's the way you feel about women, maybe we should end our relationship right here and now." Lisa snapped back at him as she turned to walk back towards the house.

Franklin grabbed her arm roughly, pulling her back, as he lashed out. "I'm not through with you yet." He said, his eyes dark with anger.

"I think you are." She said, just before Franklin's hand struck her hard on the side of her face, sending her sprawling across a fallen tree. Lisa lay there for a moment in shock, while feeling the sting on her face. Lisa had taken verbal abuse from Franklin before, but she had thought it was her fault for being so aggressive. This was the first time he had laid a hand on her.

Franklin suddenly realized he could be in trouble, as he was not on his turf. He quickly went to Lisa and helped her to her feet while apologizing profusely as he cradled her in his arms. He promised her that he would never do that again and that she was the only one that he ever loved. He brushed the snow off of her clothes before taking her in his arms and kissing her passionately until she began to return his kiss. Then slowly they began to walk back to the house.

When they returned, Dawn immediately saw the bruise on the side of Lisa's face.

She quickly went over to ask what had happened.

"She tripped over a fallen log." Franklin quickly said, giving Lisa a kiss on the forehead.

Dawn looked at him very suspiciously, not truly believing his explanation. "Come into the bathroom and put a cold cloth on it." Dawn said.

"I'm fine Mom." Lisa said. "Just go back to what you were doing. I'll put a cold cloth on it myself. I shouldn't have been so clumsy." Lisa said, now thinking back to how surprisingly quick and natural it was for Franklin to make up an excuse for his actions.

Marie opened the front door, when she saw Nick's son approaching. She first introduced Dawn to Kevin. He looked older then 19 but there was no mistaking whose son he was. Kevin was a bit shorter than Franklin and maybe not the model type, but he was definitely handsome in a rugged way. Which would make any girl turn to take a second look. Nice to meet you Kevin and this is our daughter Lisa's friend, Franklin." Dawn said turning to look at Franklin who was standing by the living room door.

Franklin held out his hand but Kevin just glared at him as he ignored his hand.

"Where are the men?" Kevin asked. Franklin was instantly furious at the rebuff. He did his best to control his anger but he definitely would not forget Kevin for that.

"They're in the living room. Go on in and Bill can introduce you to our son Darcy." Dawn said, going back to her work. She was glad that Franklin had also decided to join the men.

"What's wrong?" Marie asked, noticing the worried look on her friends face.

"I don't think Lisa's bruise is from a fall. I have a feeling that he hit her," Dawn said angrily.

"Perhaps I can talk to her Mrs. Spencer." Jackie said going to the bathroom and knocking on the door. "May I come in?" Jackie asked, before going in and locking the door behind her. Jackie went over to Lisa, who was sitting on the edge of the bathtub holding a cold face cloth on her bruised face. "Here, let me run some cold water on that face cloth for you." Jackie said, taking the cloth from Lisa. Jackie turned to look at Lisa's face, before saying. "I've seen that before. He hit you didn't he Lisa?"

Lisa was silent for a moment before saying. "He loves me though."

"That isn't love Lisa, you should know that. First they call you down then they start hitting. After that they get you to believe that you are the only one that they love. They can be so nice and you actually begin to believe them but it isn't long before it starts all over again. It will only get worse, believe me." Jackie said.

"How do you know so much about it?" Lisa asked.

"I was in the same type of relationship but I finally opened my eyes to what was going on. I knew I wanted a loving relationship like my parents but what I had was far from it. I still have a hard time trusting men." Jackie told her.

"Did your parents know?" Lisa asked.

"I did my best to cover it up. I'm sure they thought I was the clumsiest person in the world, but ...I have a feeling they suspected that something wasn't right." Jackie said thoughtfully. "Now, let me see that. I got pretty good at covering up bruises. Is that your makeup bag?" Jackie asked, pointing to a pouch on the washstand.

Lisa nodded at which time Jackie went to work at the only too familiar pattern.

"Your parent have really improved this place since I was here last." Jackie said.

"I didn't see the house until some time after they moved in, so I wouldn't know." Lisa said, wincing in pain as Jackie tried to gently cover the bruise with a blend of make up.

"It must have been difficult to go through all that, with your Mother. Dad and Marie told us about everything last night." Jackie said. "That's probably why you got yourself into this bad relationship to begin with. You look for someone to show you some love and understanding and so you go into the relationship rather blind. Mine was much the same as my Mother was dying of cancer, when I made a bad choice." Jackie said.

"Oh, I am sorry. That must have been hard to deal with that." Lisa said.

"Did you know that my Dad and your Mother knew each other years ago?" Jackie asked, while putting on the finishing touches of make up.

"No! Did they really?" Lisa asked.

"Yes. Apparently, my Dad was in love with your Mother, but she ended up falling in love with your Father." Marie mentioned it last night so we bugged Dad until he told us part of it. Marie filled us in on the other detail with what your Mother told her." Jackie said.

"Does Dad know?" Lisa asked.

"Yes and apparently he was some upset when he bought this place and then found out who had lived here before. But I believe they have mended the fences, as they seem to have become friends." Jackie said, stepping back to admire her work. "You can hardly notice it." Jackie said, pleased with herself.

Lisa looked in the mirror. "Thanks Jackie. I really appreciate it." Lisa said, giving Jackie a hug.

"No problem. Us girls have to stick together. If you ever want to talk, I'm here." Jackie told her.

"Thanks. I may have to yet. I really don't know what to do next. But right now, tell me the story about our parents." Lisa said curious to know about their parent's romantic past.

The two girls sat on the edge of the tub while Jackie told Lisa the story as it was told to her. Lisa listened intently until someone knocked on the door. The girls stood up and looked at each other, when they heard Franklin's voice.

"Lisa dear, are you all right?" Franklin asked.

Jackie saw Lisa's smile disappear as her jaw dropped open. Jackie made a face and then stuck her tongue out at the door. At which time the both began to laugh.

Jackie took Lisa's arm and opened the door. "Lisa is fine, now go back into the men's domain and leave us ladies alone so we can get to work." Jackie said smiling sweetly at him. Jackie released Lisa's arm and gently pushed Franklin back towards the living room door.

Franklin was taken back by Jackie's light heartedness. He glanced at Lisa before going back into the living room. Still feeling like he had the situation still in his control.

Lisa went to her Mother and gave her a kiss on the cheek.

"What was that for?" Dawn asked.

"Just because I love you!" Lisa said.

"Well if you're all right, would you two girls mind helping Marie and I. You can learn what to do, so that someday we can go to your house for Christmas." Dawn said looking at the side of Lisa's face. If Dawn hadn't of seen it when Lisa first came in, she would not have realized what had happened. Some how the two girls had done a miraculous job of covering it.

A bit later, Dawn and Marie sent the two girls into the living room with some juice and coffee, along with a variety of snacks for the men. They placed it on the games table, at which time Darcy began teasing his sister as seemed to be the practice every time they were in the same room. It wasn't long before Jackie and Kevin joined in on the lighthearted banter. Jackie also got Franklin to join in, as she knew only to well that if he felt left out he would sooner or later take it out on Lisa.

When Dawn began to look very tired, Marie sent Dawn to her room to rest while her and the girls finished doing the clean up. Bill watched as Dawn went to their room. He was so afraid that she might be over doing it. He was grateful to Marie who seemed to know when and just what to say when Dawn was not resting as she was suppose to. He also remembered Marie reading him the riot act when he felt like he was ready to drop.

Shortly after Marie came into the room with more juice and coffee. She laid her hand on both Darcy and shoulder Kevin's. "Would you young men mind if I steal theses two young ladies from you?" She said.

"Well, if they promise to come back later, we may allow them to leave." Darcy said looking up at Jackie.

For a moment Jackie and Darcy's eyes met. Jackie quickly turned and took Lisa's arm while saying. "I guess it is time to get back to work." The look that Darcy gave Jackie made her heart do a flip and she was not prepared for that.

Marie and the girls cleaned up the kitchen when all the baking was completed. Next task was preparing supper, so that Dawn wouldn't have to do it. Lisa had told Marie that she would do it but Marie insisted on having it ready before they left.

Lisa was sorry to see Jackie go. After all, she was the only one who understood her situation. Dawn got up just as Nick and Marie and his family, were about to leave.

"Thanks for the help." Dawn said giving Marie a big hug.

"You are welcome. I'll come by tomorrow afternoon to help you get everything else ready. Then all you have to do, the following morning is put the turkey in the oven." Marie said.

"Really Marie. You have already done so much. Lisa and I can look after the rest." Dawn said.

"All the same." I will pop in for coffee just in case you need another hand." Marie said putting on her coat and boots while, Nick and his family waited for her.

Franklin put his arm around Lisa and pulled her close to him, while everyone was leaving. He wasn't fooling Kevin or Jackie. Everyone shook hands before they left. That is, everyone but Franklin and Kevin. Kevin had totally ignored him all afternoon, which went unnoticed by everyone.

After supper was all done and dishes were washed and put away, in which Franklin had even taken part in, they all went into the living room. Bill brought out the crokinole board. This was a new game for Franklin, but Lisa said she would teach him how to play. Dawn sat quietly watching while crocheting. She hoped she was wrong about Lisa's relationship with Franklin. She didn't know what Lisa and Jackie had talked about, but whatever it was, Lisa was in a better frame of mind.

She looked at Darcy and wondered if he would ever settle down. It had to be a special woman to put up with that kind of lifestyle. Their love and trust in each other would have to be strong, during the long days of separation, as she knew only to well.

Dawn then looked at her dear husband, who had gone through so much in the past while. She smiled as she watched him play his favorite game with his children. It had been some time since she had seen him this relaxed and happy.

Bill turned to Dawn after winning the game he had just played with Darcy. "I still got it Mom." He said to Dawn.

"That's good." Dawn said watching the four of them start a new game.

"We never played games like this in my home when I grew

up." Franklin said.

"I told you that we have fun playing games in my family." Lisa said, looking at him sadly, knowing how much he missed out on, while growing up. He could be so nice and yet there was the dark side of him that probably came from all the fighting and arguing in the home that he grew up in.

When Dawn watched the interaction between Lisa and Franklin, she thought that perhaps she was judging Franklin to quickly. After all, tonight he seemed to be a totally different person.

* * *

Christmas morning was now upon them. Dawn had gotten up early to put the turkey into the oven, before preparing breakfast for her and Bill. They had opened their gifts Christmas Eve, as was the usual practice in their home. During the evening Dawn was sure that Franklin and Lisa did actually care for each other. Even Darcy was beginning to be won over by Franklin's charm.

When Dawn came out of the bathroom, Bill was standing near the door waiting for her. He took her by the hand and motioned for her to follow him. They quietly tip toed through the living room being careful not to wake Lisa, who lay sleeping on the hide-a-bed.

Dawn wondered what Bill was up to, when he lead her into their bedroom and closed the door.

Dawn noticed a large object draped with a blanket, sitting in the corner.

"What is this?" Dawn asked quietly. As she walked over to it, Bill gently pulled her against him. Dawn was taken back by his sudden affection, but she clung to him when he kissed her. Slowly he released her.

"I love you." Bill told her.

Dawn looked into Bill's eyes, which seemed to have that mischievous twinkle in them.

"Now what have you been up to?" Dawn asked softly.

Bill took her hand and led her over to the object in the corner. Then he removed the blanket. Dawn put her hand over her mouth as she gasped.

"Oh Bill! It's beautiful. Where did you get this?" She said, looking at a beautiful baby cradle, with a silk and lace lining covering the tiny mattress.

"I made it." Bill said proudly.

"But When?" She asked running her hand along the edge before giving it a slight push to watch it swing with ease.

"I did it shortly after they told us that we were going to have another baby. When I knew your health was improving, I just had to do something to occupy my mind and this was it. I wasn't going to give it to you until I was sure, you and the baby were going to be all right."

He said rubbing his hand gently on Dawn's belly. Dawn put her hand over his at which time Bill felt the baby move. When their eyes met, Dawn's eyes filled with tears.

"I love you more than I can ever tell you." Dawn said putting her arms around Bill's neck. "What would you have done if we lost the baby?" Dawn asked.

"I figured that I would just put it away." I'm sure that someday we'll have a grandchild." Bill said. "My concern is that you'll get yourself over tired during this holiday season. I was wondering if this may still be too early to give this to you, because if something does go wrong yet... well..." Bill said. The two wrinkles across his forehead becoming more pronounced as he began to worry.

"Bill, I'm glad you did give it to me now. I will do what ever I can to keep your little boy safe." She said. "You felt it yourself that he's doing fine and he even responded to his loving Fathers touch. Thanks again Bill. I will cherish it all my life." She said kissing him lightly. "Now are you ready for breakfast?" Dawn asked.

"Sounds good to me. Maybe we can eat alone while everyone is still sleeping." Bill said, wanting to have his wife to himself for a while. Bill covered the cradle with the blanket, not wanting to show the children just yet.

It was almost noon when the rest of the family woke up, to take their turn at having their showers. Dawn thought that for some reason, Darcy had taken more time to look his best. His hair was neatly combed and he had on his best clothes. The biggest surprise was that he actually had his shirt tucked into his pants.

When everyone began to congregate in the kitchen, Dawn served a light lunch.

After that the men went back into the living room to continue playing their games, while Dawn and Lisa continued on with preparing for the next meal. They were just setting the table when Nick and Marie and his children arrived. Lisa took their coats and laid them all on her parents bed, before joining the ladies in the kitchen. Kevin walked into the living room, making a special point of saying hello to Lisa and asking how her Christmas was so far. All the while looking at her face and arms for the possibility of any new bruises. When Kevin sat down he noticed the white knuckles on Franklin's clinched fist as well as the icy stare to which Kevin just ignored.

When Lisa went into the kitchen, Jackie went over to her and asked how everything was going.

"Great Jackie. He has been a perfect gentlemen." Lisa said happily.

"I'm glad for you, but be careful. Anything can set him off. It can be over the littlest thing that you may never suspect." Jackie said.

"Oh I'm sure that everything will be fine now. He was really sorry for... well you know, the other day and promised that he would never do that again." Lisa said happily.

"Lisa don't..." Jackie said, then suddenly changing her mind. "I hope you're right." She said. Even though deep down, she had a terrible feeling that Lisa was in for a lot more problems.

At the supper table, the younger group sat at one end and Bill and Dawn, Nick and Marie sat at the other end.

It was obvious to Nick, that Bill and Dawn's son Darcy was smitten by his daughter. Nick thought back to years past, when Dawn and her parents came to visit. A smile crossed his face when he thought that there could be a possibility of a marriage between their children.

Dawn looked at Nick before following his gaze. So Jackie was the reason for Darcy's sudden change of appearance. Dawn also began to think back to the years past when in this very house, her and Nick sat talking like that. Suddenly a thought ran through her mind. She glanced over at Nick and when he raised his eyebrows, she was pretty sure that they had both been thinking of the same thing.

Franklin was not happy when he caught Kevin looking at Lisa. When Kevin tried to talk to her, Franklin did his best to divert her attention making it difficult for her to answer any of Kevin's questions. It wasn't long before Jackie saw what Franklin was doing. She was sure that sooner or later he would blow up in a fit of jealous rage. But most of Jackie's attention was taken up by asking Darcy about his travels. She had to admit that she sort of liked Darcy. But she was not to let her guard down and as to let herself get involved in another relationship.

After the meal was done and dishes were cleaned up everyone except Franklin and Lisa, went into the living room.

Franklin told Lisa that he wanted to talk to her in private. He took her by the arm and led her up the stairs. "What was the big secret between you and Kevin when he arrived?" He demanded as his grip tightened on her arm.

"What are you talking about?" She asked, totally confused as to what he meant.

"I saw you talking to him when he first arrived. Then there was the way you looked at each other across the table." He said angrily.

"He only asked how my Christmas was and you were the one going all ga ga over Jackie." She said.

"How dare you?" He said raising his hand, as he was about to strike her.

Lisa closed her eyes as she was sure what was about to happen next. But then she heard Kevin's voice and she opened her eyes to see him grab Franklin's arm.

"If you want to pick on someone, how about you and me go outside to settle this." Kevin said.

"This is none of your business." Franklin snapped, trying to keep his voice down.

"I'm making it my business. Now let go of her arm." Kevin said tightening his grip on Franklin's arm. Franklin may have been three-year Kevin's senior, but there was no doubt to who was the strongest.

Franklin let go of Lisa's arm before jerking loose from Kevin's grip. "So you been tattling to your new boyfriend, have you?" Franklin said his eyes dark with anger.

"She told me nothing. I saw what you did to her the other day. I've met your type before and if you ever lay a hand on her again, you can bet that I will come looking for you." Kevin said, turning to go join the others.

"It was sometime before Lisa and Franklin came down to join the rest of the family. Jackie immediately knew that something had happened when she notice the red mark on Lisa's arm.

* * *

The following morning, Franklin and Lisa said their goodbyes and left for Edmonton, as did Kevin who had to work the following day. Darcy and Jackie decided to hang around for a couple more days after Jackie decided to do some house cleaning for her Father.

Darcy was also pleased that Jackie consented in letting him take her back to Calgary as that was were they were both living.

Kevin had an uneasy feeling about Franklin, so he decided to look up Lisa's address in the phone book before he went home. He knew Franklin wasn't very tough, but in a fit of rage it was amazing the strength they seemed to acquire.

Kevin drove over to Lisa's apartment and rang the buzzer, but there was no answer. He rang it three times without any success. When a young couple came out Kevin told them that he needed to check to see if his girlfriend got home safely. At first they hesitated but then they did consent to allow him access.

Kevin had checked the room number near the buzzer so he knew what floor and the number of her room. When he approached her room, he heard a scream, which sent him running. He had hoped it wasn't Lisa but when he reached the door, he heard the sound of glass breaking as she screamed again.

Kevin heard Lisa pleading with Franklin not to hurt her anymore. Then he heard the fury in Franklin's voice as he told her to shut up and then he heard what he thought sounded like him hitting her. Kevin didn't bother knocking but gave the door two good kicks before if flew open.

Franklin turned and threw a small glass vase at Kevin, which he'd been holding in his hand. He yelled at Kevin to get out and mind his own business. Kevin quickly put his arm up, deflecting the vase, then lunged at Franklin. He grabbed him and threw him out the door before going to Lisa who was huddled in a ball on the floor.

Franklin knew he was no match for Kevin so he quickly left the building.

Kevin closed the door, before he returned to talk calmly to Lisa.

"It's all right. He's gone now. I think I better take you to the hospital, but first I'm going to call the police and have charges laid against that guy." Kevin said just furious at himself for not trying to stop her from going home with that guy. Especially when he had witnessed two separate occasions of his abuse toward Lisa.

"No Please! I don't want to cause any trouble." Lisa said looking up at him.

Kevin placed his hand under her chin to look at her face,

before swearing. "I think I should call your parents." Kevin said helping her to the couch.

"No please! They've gone through enough. Please, promise me that you won't call them." Lisa pleaded before doubling over in pain.

"Where did he all hit you?" Kevin asked.

"My stomach and." She said again moaning in pain.

Kevin quickly called the police to tell them what had happened and told them which hospital he was taking Lisa to. He also knew there was a good chance that they would suspect him but he would deal with that later. Kevin told Lisa that he was calling Jackie and that she should at least notify Darcy, but he promised that for now they would not tell her parents.

As Kevin suspected he got the third degree from the police, but after talking to Lisa, they soon had a warrant out for Franklin's arrest.

* * *

When Darcy answered the phone, he was please to hear Jackie's voice.

"So you missed me already?" He said jokingly.

"You wish, but this is not a social call. We have a bit of an emergency and you can't let on to your parents that anything is wrong. Understand?" She said.

"Yes of course." He said somewhat confused.

"Look, can you come over and I'll tell you about it then." Dad and Marie are not home, thank goodness, but this may be very serious. We have to make a trip to Edmonton tonight. Please hurry, but don't tell your parents what I just told you." Jackie said before giving him directions on how to get to her Father's place.

"Sounds great." Darcy said cheerfully as to not leave any suspicion to his motive of leaving. "I'll see you in a bit then." He said totally confused as he hung up the phone.

"Are you going out tonight son?" Bill asked.

"Yea, that was Jackie and she has some sort of a plan. It's possible that I may not get back until tomorrow afternoon, so don't wait up." Darcy said going upstairs to throw a few things in a bag.

"Darcy, all I have to say is behave yourself and be careful wherever you are going." Dawn said, when he came back into the room. She was very suspicious of his sudden change of plans.

"I will Mom." He said giving her a kiss on the cheek before putting on his boots and coat. "See you both later." He said closing the door behind him.

***

Jackie was waiting with her bag ready. She left a note for her Father, saying that her and Darcy made plans to go to Edmonton and that they would be back before the following evening.

"What's the emergency?" Darcy asked while opening the door to the truck for her. He placed her bag on the back seat of his extended cab then jumped in.

"Please just drive and I will tell you." Jackie said with tears in her eyes as she remembered the terror she went through with her bad relationship. Poor Lisa. It must be real bad if Kevin took her to the hospital. She had taken a lot of abuse but never to the extent of being hospitalized.

Once they were on the way, Darcy turned to Jackie. "Now will you tell me what in blazes is going on?"

"Kevin phoned me. He went to make sure that Lisa was all right when he got back and.." Jackie swallowed hard biting back her tears.

Darcy glances over at her, then asked. "Why did Kevin think that she wouldn't be ok?" He asked.

"Kevin saw Franklin hit her outside the first day he came over. Then after supper he intervened when he was about to do it again." Jackie said.

"You mean this emergency is just because he slapped her a couple of times?" Darcy asked.

"You mean to tell me that you condone that type of behavior?" Jackie snapped back at him.

"Of course not." Darcy said wondering why she got so angry. "Although, there have been a few people I would like to have slapped in my day." Darcy said, teasing her.

"This is no joking matter, Darcy. It's serious and if you can't see that, I don't want to even know you." She said with tears running down her face.

Darcy knew he had over done his teasing. "I'm sorry." He said touching her hand, which she quickly pulled away. "It isn't a joking matter and I do not agree with that type of behavior. Honest. My parents may have their disagreements, but Dad never laid a hand on my Mother or I would have choked him. When I think about it, if they did have a disagreement, it always seemed to be resolve before they went to bed." Darcy said. "That's the way I would want it between my future wife and me. That is if I ever find the right girl." He said smiling at Jackie. "Now, tell me about Lisa and her boyfriend." Darcy said trying to be more serious.

Jackie told him what Kevin had told her. Darcy asked if Lisa was all right and it was then that Jackie told him that Kevin had taken her to the hospital. Jackie saw Darcy's knuckles turn white as he clinched the steering wheel. After that he never said another word until they reached the hospital.

Darcy and Jackie walked over to the information desk and asked to see Lisa. As it was after visiting hours, they didn't want to let them in. Darcy told the receptionist that he was her brother and insisted on seeing her. When they finally consented, Darcy took hold of Jackie's hand. Her first instinct was to pull away but then she realized that he was doing it mainly for her support.

"Kevin met them just outside Lisa's room. "She isn't a pretty sight, so prepare yourself." Kevin said laying his hand on Darcy's shoulder.

"Do you want to go in alone?" Jackie asked.

"No please. You both come in with me." He said looking from Jackie to Kevin.

The light in the room was dim when they walked in. Jackie gasped at the sight of Lisa's swollen face and the bandage she had down the right side of her face. Kevin told them that it took 10 stitches to close the gash on her face. She also had cuts and bruises all over her arms and body.

"Where is Franklin?" Darcy asked.

"The police have a warrant out for his arrest." Kevin told them.

"They better find him before I do, or I will kill him." Darcy said angrily.

Jackie took her other hand and pulled Darcy's arm tightly against her while he still held her hand. "Darcy, two wrongs won't make it right. You have to be here for your sister now." Jackie said. "It won't help your family to hear you are in jail for the same thing Franklin tried to do." She added.

Darcy released Jackie's hand before going to his sister's bedside. "Lisa, are you awake?" Darcy asked.

Lisa tried to open her eyes but they were too swollen. "Yes." She said trying to talk but even her mouth was very swollen which made talking difficult.

"Why didn't you tell me? I would have done something." Darcy said taking her hand in his.

"Please don't tell Dad and Mom. Promise, please." Lisa pleaded.

"Don't you think this will be hard to hide from them?" Darcy asked.

"Darcy, you have to promise." She said trying to sit up, but Darcy gently pushed her back.

"I'll do my best, but if things get worse, I will have to. You know that." He said.

"After a couple of weeks, I should look better and I probably won't see them for a few weeks anyhow." Lisa said.

"It's a good thing that you don't have school for another

week. Lisa if I ever hear he's hanging around you again, I will kill him." Darcy said angrily.

"No Darcy, promise to stay away from him. Dad and Mom have had enough problems. Please." Lisa said.

"Yea, Jackie practically told me the same thing." Darcy added.

"Is Jackie here? If she is let me talk to her. She'll understand, but I doubt if her old boyfriend put her in the hospital. She tried to warn me, but I didn't listen." Lisa said, as a tear began to run down her face.

Darcy released his sister's hand and walked over to Jackie. He studied her face before kissing her on the forehead.

"What was that for?" She asked.

"That's to say, I'm sorry for being a jerk. Now Lisa would like to talk to you." He said.

Jackie sat beside Lisa's bed while holding her hand. While they talked Darcy and Kevin went to see if the doctor was still around. When they did find him, Darcy asked how seriously she had been hurt. He told them that he didn't think there were any serious internal injuries. The swelling in her face would go down in a few days but he wanted to keep her in for a day or two just to be sure that she could see. He definitely recommended that she see a counselor.

When Lisa's sedative began to work, she slowly drifted off to sleep. Darcy said he would stay at Lisa's apartment and it was decided that Jackie would stay a Kevin's. They would see how Lisa was fairing by noon before they would make the decision to return home.

* * *

Darcy did his best to fix Lisa's apartment door, which Kevin kicked open. Then he picked up the broken glass that was spread around the apartment. When Darcy picked up the heavy small glass vase that Franklin had thrown at Kevin, he saw the blood on it and realized that this was probably what he used to hit Lisa with. *If Kevin wouldn't have come when he did, Franklin could have*

Will Love Conquer All?

killed her. Darcy shuddered at the thought. Looking up he said, "Thank-you God." Darcy saw Franklin's jacket draped over a chair. He took it and angrily flung it into the corner, at which moment he heard a knock on the door.

"Lisa honey, are you there? I'm sorry, please open the door. I have to talk to you." Franklin said from the other side of the door.

Darcy stood frozen to the spot as he clenched his fist. He was about to go to the door, but he changed his mind when he remembered what Lisa and Jackie had said.

Franklin continued talking. "Lisa, I love you, please, I know you're home. I heard you in there and the light is on so you can't fool me. Come on baby open the door, I want you to forgive me." He pleaded.

Darcy stood silently wondering what else he might say. Suddenly Franklin's tone of voice changed from calm to now anger. "Lisa open this door now, I know you are in there!"

"Your friend isn't here now to protect you and if you don't let me in I will kick it in. Then I'll really show you that I mean business!" Franklin said now full of fury.

Darcy quickly went to the backside of the door, now prepared for anything.

"Lisa, I'm going to kill you when I get in." Franklin said louder. It was then that Franklin kicked the already partially broken door open. Sending it crashing against the wall. This was what Darcy was waiting for. More charges like breaking and entering along with uttering death threats would be added to Franklin's growing list. That was, if Darcy didn't finish him off first.

"You looking for somebody?" Darcy asked, looking at the surprised look on Franklin's face. Darcy mustered up all his will power to not go for Franklin's throat.

"What are you doing here? Where's Lisa?" Franklin shouted, grabbing the same vase that Darcy had only moments ago picked up and sat on the table nearby the door.

Darcy watched Franklin's every move as he said. "I'm looking for you and it's none of your business. Besides, what do you think you're doing, breaking into my sister's apartment?" Darcy said, surprising himself at his calmness.

"This is non of your business. This is between me and Lisa." Franklin told him.

"Not anymore buddy. You've made it my business and it's just you and me now."

Darcy said, just as Franklin threw the vase. Hitting Darcy on the side of his head.

Darcy dove at Franklin and the fight was on. Just as Darcy pinned Franklin on the floor he grabbed hold of his throat. That's when, he heard Jackie scream.

"No Darcy, don't do it!!" At which time Kevin pulled Darcy off of Franklin.

Darcy released his hold as Kevin grabbed Franklin by the collar and arm and threw him on the couch. He told him to stay put if he knew what was good for him. Darcy stood between Franklin and the door, just waiting for him to try and escape while Kevin called the police.

Jackie watched Darcy wipe the side of his head. It was then that she seen Darcy's hand covered in blood. "What happened? Are you all right?" She said. It was then that seen the gash on the side of his head.

Jackie quickly found the bathroom and returned with a cool damp cloth. "Hold it tight against the wound, I think you're going to need a few stitches." She said.

"I'm fine!" He told her gruffly as he grabbed the cloth from her hand and placed it against the wound. He was so angry with Franklin, that he didn't notice the hurt look on Jackie's face. "I'll be glad to get rid of this scum." Darcy said after hearing the buzzer at the front door.

When Kevin let the police in the building Franklin made a move to get up. Kevin was just as quick and pushed him hard, knocking him back on to the couch.

"I wouldn't try that if you know what's good for you." Kevin said sternly.

It wasn't long before the police arrived at the door. They noticed the broken door and the blood on Darcy's hand and face. They immediately began to question what had happened. Darcy told them about Franklin's death threats against his sister and breaking and entering. Kevin also told them of the earlier incident. After making a quick call they arrested Franklin. Just before they left they asked Darcy what happened to his head.

Darcy pointed to the vase on the floor. "He threw that thing at me after he broke in and I didn't duck fast enough." Darcy said.

Kevin glanced at the vase. "That's what he had in his hand when I found him here beside Lisa." He threw it at me but I managed to deflect it with my arm." Kevin said.

Before leading Franklin out in handcuffs, the police carefully picked up the vase and took it with them after placing it in a bag.

Darcy turned to Kevin and Jackie. "By the way, what brought you back here tonight?" He asked.

"Jackie forgot her bag in your truck and we got in when a couple was leaving. By the looks of things, it was probably a good thing we showed up." Kevin said.

Jackie would not look at Darcy. She was still hurt by his reaction, when all she wanted to do was help him.

Kevin looked at Darcy's head. "Come on, let's get you to the hospital." He said before turning to Jackie. "Are you coming?"

"No. I'll just wait here." She said sitting on the couch.

It was some time before they returned. By that time Jackie was already sleeping on the couch.

"Let her sleep." Darcy said.

"Well, I'll talk to you tomorrow. I have to go to work in the morning. I'll keep looking in on Lisa until she's better. You and Jackie better go home before your parents begin to ask questions." Kevin said.

"Thanks Kevin. I appreciate everything that you've done." Darcy said patting Kevin on the shoulder.

"No problem. I know what it's like to see your sister being slapped around and not being able to do anything about it. But this guy is really nuts. I'm glad that I was able to stop him before he did something even worse. It probably won't do him any good, with you hearing him threaten her and the breaking and entering, along with the assault on Lisa and you." Kevin said.

After Kevin left, Darcy walked over to the couch and covered Jackie with the blanket that he still held in his hand. He carefully brushed a strand of hair out to her face. He felt the softness of her skin. The thought of someone hurting her angered him. How could anyone treat someone so beautiful in that manner? Darcy lightly stroked Jackie's hair before turning in for the night.

By the next afternoon, Lisa looked really bad. The swelling of her eyes had gone down somewhat and thankfully her vision was not impaired. After the doctor gave Lisa some instructions of how to deal with the swelling, he told her that she could go home. Darcy and Jackie got Lisa settled with groceries and whatever she needed until she felt well enough to go out. Kevin assured Darcy that he would continue to check in on her until she felt well enough to go out on her own. Darcy and Jackie were now free to go back to their parent's homes.

Jackie was quiet on their drive home and Darcy didn't pressure her to talk. He thought perhaps she was reliving her bad relationship after what happened to Lisa. He didn't realize that she was hurt by the harsh way he had reacted to her when all she was doing was trying to help him.

Darcy was used to driving in silence. Besides, he had to figure out an excuse for why he had stitches on the side of his head. It would be hard for his parents to miss seeing it, unless he kept his cap on his head.

Chapter 16

All through the month of January Bill and Dawn enjoyed working together in Bill's workshop. In the evening, while sitting in their living room, they would discuss their day's work and what changes if any they should make.

Bill had placed a number of items on consignment, in several stores, and was very pleased with the response. He had also received several specific orders, which he found quite challenging. Dawn did her best to help Bill do the finishing work, but was beginning to find it harder to hide her fatigue. The past few days she was beginning to get pains in her stomach. She knew if she told Bill, he would take her straight to the hospital, which she dreaded. Her next appointment was only two days away. She'd try to wait and talk to the doctor about it then.

Dawn decided to stay in the house the next day to rest. Bill agreed, noticing she had been looking very tired. She did decide to do a bit of laundry and cleaning before she lay down. She put some clothes into the washer, then when going back into the kitchen, Dawn suddenly doubled over with pain. She rubbed her stomach as if to soothe it, then collapsed on the floor, while trying to make her way to a chair. The next thing Dawn knew, Marie was kneeling beside her. Marie helped her to a chair, then ran to the door and called to Nick, who was on his way to talk to Bill. After instructing him to quickly get Bill, Marie went back to check on Dawn.

Book 1 of the **Mountains and Valleys of Life**

* * *

Dawn lay in the hospital bed groggy from the medication she was given. She was thankful the pain had finally subsided. Bill sat by Dawn's side, holding her hand, asking if she was feeling better. He blamed himself for not realizing she was doing more then she should. Dawn looked at Bill's ashen face. "I thought the next time I would be in here, was to have our baby, but it's still too early for that yet. Did you talk to the doctor?" Dawn asked.

"Yes," Bill said. "You're to be on total bed rest for awhile."

"Is everything all right yet? Did he say anything about the baby?" She asked, afraid that something had happened and they weren't telling her.

"So far everything's fine. You just get some rest now." Bill said, brushing her hair away from her eyes.

When Bill assured her that everything was fine, she began to relax.

"Bill I'll be all right, you don't have to stay with me. I think I'll just sleep for awhile," Dawn said. "You have a couple of projects to finish and get some rest. I will see you later."

"I'll go after you fall asleep." He said gently rubbing her arm.

Dawn did not know how long she had been sleeping, but the sun was beginning to set when she looked out the window. She rubbed her eyes then feeling the movement of her baby she placed her hand on her belly. *Thank goodness our baby is still ok,* she thought to herself. She looked out the door of her room, when she heard approaching foot steps. Just as Bill was about to come into Dawn's room, a woman ran up to him and threw her arms around his neck, and hugged him.

"Oh Bill it has been so long since I've seen you, how have you been?" She asked.

Bill stood there in bewilderment. He looked at the woman for a few moments, before saying. "Janice is that you?"

"Yes it is, how about a kiss?" She said kissing him passionately on the lips.

Will Love Conquer All?

"It's been so long. It's good to see you again. I must say you're still looking great." She said, her arms still lingering around his neck. "What have you been up to?" She asked.

Dawn looked at the woman who was clinging to her husband. She tried to remember where she had seen her before, but it was so many years ago. Dawn did not feel comfortable, seeing another woman cling to her husband. She also noticed Bill's hands lingering on this woman's waist. Dawn's heart sank as she looked away, suddenly remembering who it was. She felt like someone had jabbed a knife in her heart, as Bill and Janice stood in the doorway talking.

Bill and Dawn had kept no secrets from each other, not even ones from years before they met. They felt by knowing each other's past, nothing could ruin their future.

But things from the past always have away of catching up to you. Dawn had seen Janice a time or two when she was dating Bill. He had pointed her out to Dawn one day. She remembered the look on Bill's face, when he saw her in the arms of another man in a restaurant. Bill had asked Janice to marry him, but she had turned him down, which had hurt Bill deeply. When they talked about it years later, Bill said he knew he would have made the biggest mistake of his life, if he had married her. Janice was the type of person that always flirted with other men, even when she was with him. He had heard later that Janice had been with other men, even though they were supposed to be steady. It was sometime before Bill entered Dawn's room. When he reached for Dawn's hand she slowly pulled it away. "Dawn," Bill said. "What's wrong? I know you well enough to know something's bothering you, so tell me," he demanded.

When Dawn turned her head to look at Bill, her eyes were full of tears. "I just find it hard to see my husband hugging and kissing another woman in the hall way, for everyone to see," she said.

"Dawn you're being silly. She's just an old friend," Bill said. "Besides, she kissed me."

"I didn't see you make any attempt to reject her advance. It took awhile, but I finally remembered where I had seen her before." Dawn said turning away. Another pain ripped through her heart, when she thought of Bill's hands lingering on Janice's waist.

"Dawn, I believe you are actually jealous." Bill said teasing her.

"You have a lot to talk about." Dawn snapped back at him, after turning to face him. "Look how you reacted to Nick and I didn't even know who he was at the time."

"You didn't see me greet him the way she did to you. Did you?" Dawn said.

"How would I know how you greeted him? I wasn't home when you remembered who he was." Bill threw back at her.

Dawn gasped in shock. Tears streaming down her face, as Bill's remark cut deep.

"Bill do you have that little trust in me after all these years?" she said.

"Well I could say the same to you." He said looking away.

"Bill it is not you I don't trust. As you remember, you told me several things about her. From her actions today, I would say she hasn't changed." Dawn said.

"Let's drop it." Bill said going to look out the window.

The rest of the time was spent in a strained silence. It wasn't long before Bill decided to leave, as visiting hours were almost over anyway.

"Bill," Dawn said, holding out her hand to him. She did not want them to be angry at each other, when they were about to be separated. Bill was hesitant, but then took her hand.

"I love you Bill. I would never be unfaithful to you. You know that." Dawn said, looking into his eyes.

"I know." He said, giving her a quick kiss.

"Be careful." Dawn said warning him, but feeling a fear inside her that she had never felt before. Bill looked down at his wife. Then squeezing her hand gently, he left without saying another word.

Dawn lay there a moment, before getting up to look out the window. She watched Bill walk over to his truck. Her heart was filled with love for her husband, but then she saw Janice run over to him. Dawn watched as they stood there talking for a moment, but her heart sank when Bill went around to the other side of the truck. He opened the door and Janice got in. She saw Janice slide over to sit very close to Bill. Then after Bill got in, he drove off. Dawn felt suddenly very weak. Her knees almost buckling under her, as she stood holding onto the windowsill.

"Mrs. Spencer, what are you doing out of bed?" The nurse said. "You know the doctor told you total bed rest, and he meant it. By the looks of you, I can see why, you need the rest." She said helping Dawn into her bed. Little did the nurse know that Dawn's problem now had nothing to do with her physical health it was her heart that was breaking.

* * *

Bill ordered two coffees after he and Janice found a secluded corner in the restaurant to talk. Bill looked at Janice. She was still as beautiful as ever, but her actions and mannerism had not changed. He often thought she could have been an actress for all the roles she played. She also looked the part, with her slim figure and raven black hair, which would turn any mans head.

She could be as sweet as pie one moment then flip to uncaring and nasty. He remembered how she told him that there was no way she would marry him, because he was too poor. She said she was only using him until she could find someone better, which she said she already had. She was the total opposite of Dawn, who was loving and kind. Always doing her best to treat everyone equal, which was why he was so surprised by her actions tonight. He already regretted saying what he had to Dawn, about her and Nick. He was upset with Dawn's accusation and it just came out. Yes he would have been upset too if roles were reversed.

"What brings you to town and what is so important that you

wanted to talk about?" Bill asked, while looking at Janice.

"I was looking for you. Someone said your wife was in the hospital and that you would probably be around to see her in the evening." She said sweetly. "By the way how is your wife?" Janice said looking at Bill, in a way that could melt any mans heart.

Bill knew that look only to well, and quickly looked away. "She's better now." Bill said.

"What is her problem?" Janice asked laying her hand on his.

"She's having some problems with her pregnancy." He said, remembering Dawn's words. *Be careful.*

Janice quickly removed her hand from his, then in that pouting voice that got many men to feel sorry for her said. "My aren't you the stud."

Bill looked at her with annoyance. "I asked you before what you wanted to talk about that was so important? I don't have all night," Bill said curtly.

"Well." She started slowly taking hold if his arm, as she leaned on his shoulder.

Bill smelled the aroma of that old familiar perfume, which he used to like, as she continued. "You remember that night we spent together by the lake." She said looking deep into his eyes, before continuing. "Well…I thought I should tell you." she trailed off, leaving Bill in suspense.

"Go on," Bill said.

"Well Bill, we have a son." Janice said giving him that same sweet look.

Bill's mouth dropped open. He looked into Janice's eyes, which always had a spell binding effect on him.

Slowly he gathered his thoughts, and looked down at his coffee cup. "Why are you telling me now after what, 24 years?"

"I wasn't going to tell you at all, but Larry insisted on knowing who his real Father was. So I told him. He wants to meet you." Janice said. "I told him I would stay with him, until he got to know you. He felt uncomfortable to come alone. Oh, Bill I made a big mistake turning you down. I didn't realize how

Will Love Conquer All?

much I loved you until you left. I still love you and would do anything for you to love me again." She said kissing his cheek.

"It's a little to late for that, don't you think." Bill said angrily.

"Please Bill, I have changed. I'm sorry for hurting you." She said, putting her hand under his chin, turning his head to make him look at her. "Bill, tell me you still feel the same way about me." She said kissing him full on the mouth with a long passionate kiss. Bill began to respond from an old habit, but quickly caught himself, and pushed her away. "What do you think you are trying to prove by this?" He said harshly.

"I think I have already proven my point." She said wiping lipstick from his face.

"When can we get together for you to met our son?" Janice said, feeling she already had a good start on what she came for.

Bill hesitated. He did not want to be seen in public with Janice again, so he told her to bring Larry to the farm the next day. Then after giving her directions on how to get there, Janice told him she would walk back to the motel. That was fine with Bill. He didn't, want to be seen at a motel with another woman. His mind was working overtime while on his drive home.

How could he tell Dawn this, especially now with her and the baby? He was thankful he had told Dawn everything about Janice and their relationship, so he had nothing more to hide. He loved Dawn very much and did not want to hurt her. Janice always held a spell over him, which he found he still had not been able to break. He wondered why Janice was telling him this now, after all these years. He wondered if she was married, but then what difference did that make. If she hadn't changed, she would still be flirting with other men.

Bill did not sleep well that night, but walked the floor for hours before going into the bedroom. He went to the corner of the room and took off the blanket that covered the cradle. He gives it a push and watched as it swung back and forth. He remembered the look on Dawn's face when he gave it to her. He also remembered how he felt when he felt the baby move.

Closing his eyes, he could almost feel Dawn's gentle touch and her sweet kisses. He needed to hold her close now. Oh how could he hurt her with this news and yet he knew this was something he could not hide from her. Why had he been so stupid? *Be sure your sins will find you out,* he thought, as he covered the cradle with the blanket. Then a thought hit him. Was Janice actually telling him the truth? Was Larry really his son? After all, he had heard that she was with other men during and immediately after him. But then why would she tell her son, if it weren't true?

Bill lay on the couch, not able to bring himself to lay in Dawn and his bed tonight as he reflected on his past.

The next day Bill had made coffee and sat waiting for Janice and Larry to arrive.

He was extremely nervous and for once, he was actually glad Dawn was not home. He heard them drive in, but did not move until they knocked on the door. Bill slowly got up and opened the door to find a tall handsome man standing in front of him, with Janice by his side.

"Bill this is our son Larry. Larry I would like you to meet your Father, Bill Spencer." Janice said.

Larry stuck out his hand. "I'm glad to finally meet you Sir. Mother has told me a lot about you." He said respectfully.

"I wish I could say the same." Bill said shaking his hand. Bill caught the look that passed from Larry to Janice. Almost like a wink but then he dismissed it. "Have a seat and I'll get the coffee." Bill said.

"No you sit down, I'll get it. You just visit with your son." Janice said.

They talked for several hours getting to know each other. Bill asked how long they were staying and Janice informed Bill she was divorcing her husband, who had been unfaithful to her for most of their marriage. Larry patted his Mother's hand in sympathy.

Larry informed Bill, they had no set time limit on how long

they would stay.

However Larry would like to spend some time to get to know his Father. Janice asked if it would be possible for them to stay with Bill for a few days, as it would make it much easier for Bill and Larry to get to know each other better. Janice also offered to help in the house. After all Dawn was not home and someone would have to cook for them. Bill said he would first discuss it with Dawn before making a decision like that. After talking a bit longer, Janice told Bill she had a few things to do in town.

When Janice and Larry left, Bill sat by the kitchen table, worrying about how he would tell Dawn what he had just been told.

* * *

The instant Bill walked through the door, Dawn's heart sank. She could tell something was seriously wrong by the look on Bill's face.

"Bill what's wrong, has something happened to Darcy or Lisa?" She asked reaching for his hand. Bill did not kiss her as he usually did, but assured her the kids were fine. "Something's wrong I can see it in your face. Please tell me." She pleaded.

Bill sat by her bed still holding her hand, as he gently fondled it in his. "Dawn I would do anything in this world, if I didn't have to tell you this," he said.

Dawn sat still and quiet, bracing herself for the worst. Bill slowly continued. "As you already know Janice is in town." Bill felt Dawn's grip tighten on his hand, as he continued. "She sort of dropped a bomb shell on me last night." Bill said, sitting in silence, wondering how he could tell her the rest.

"Oh no!" Dawn said laying her head back on the pillow, as if totally exhausted.

Bill looked at her, as she lay there with her eyes closed tightly. "You and her have a child." Don't you?" She said pulling her hand out of his. She turned her head, not able to stop her tears from running down her cheeks.

"How did you know?" Bill asked Dawn.

"As you remember, you told me about the two of you. I always feared that someday this would happen. But after all this time, I had totally put the idea out of my mind."

"I must say, she has timed it just right for her," Dawn said looking at Bill. "Do you believe her?" Dawn asked.

"I don't know." Bill said looking down at the floor. "She asked if her and Larry could stay at the farm for a while. That way Larry and I can get to know each other better. It would only be for a few days," Bill said.

Dawn sat up quickly. "She will stay in my house over my dead body!" Dawn said furiously. When again a pain gripped at her stomach, she winced and slowly lay back down.

"It's my house to." Bill said getting defensive, seemingly not noticing the pain Dawn was in. "They will be gone before you get home. She can cook and see that the house is kept clean until you got back." Bill said.

"She would probably do more than that," Dawn said.

"What do you mean by that?" Bill snapped.

"I'm sorry." Dawn said. "Maybe you better go before I say something else I shouldn't." She said turning away.

Bill stood up. He looked down at Dawn then left without saying another word.

Bill drove home a very unhappy man. He would tell Janice, that Larry could stay, but it was best that Janice went back home. To Bill's surprise, Janice and Larry were waiting for him at home. They insisted on staying there to help him, until his wife was well enough to come home. They would not take no for an answer either.

Bill gave in. He told Larry to take the couch while Janice could have the upstairs room but Janice insisted that she would take the couch. That way she would have Bill's breakfast ready in the morning without disturbing Larry, who liked to sleep late. Bill felt very uncomfortable. It was out of character for him to let someone take control of his life.

Bill let them get settled in, while he went to work in his shop.

He was not happy about Dawn's insinuations and decided not to go back to the hospital that evening. He was thankful for the work he had to do which helped take his mind off of his problems. For some reason he did not feel comfortable around Larry. He thought if he was his son there should have been a different feeling when they met, but there wasn't. Perhaps it would just take time.

Janice had a delicious supper prepared for him, when he came into the house.

Bill bowed his head giving thanks silently for the food, while Janice and Larry started to eat. They were half ways through their meal when a car drove up. Larry quickly offered to answer the door. His eyes widened when he saw Jackie there, holding a basket.

"Is Mr. Spencer in?" Jackie asked

"Yes, come on in Jackie." Bill said standing up.

"I'm sorry to disturb you. I didn't know you had company." Jackie said, wondering who these people were. "Marie and I baked some Muffins and pie and thought we would bring some over for you." She said handing the basket to Bill.

"Thanks Jackie I appreciate that." Bill said setting it on the counter. "Oh, I'm sorry. I should introduce you. Jackie this is an old friend of mine Janice and a-a her son Larry." Bill said turning to Janice and Larry. "This is our neighbours daughter Jackie."

"Nice to meet you," Jackie said. "How is Mrs. Spencer doing?" She asked.

"She is better today." Bill said wishing it that it was actually true.

"Well I'm sorry to disturb your supper. I better go," Jackie said.

But as she was about to leave, Larry quickly stepped in. "No stay for coffee. Then after you can show me what there is to do around this part of the world."

"That's a great idea." Janice said pouring Jackie a cup

Book 1 of the *Mountains and Valleys of Life*

of coffee.

Jackie reluctantly was persuaded and waited while they finished their meal.

"Thanks Janice," Bill said. "That was very good."

"Yea Mom, you out did yourself. It was delicious and now if you'll excuse us. I believe this beautiful young lady and I have something to do. So don't wait up," Larry said.

"Behave yourself Larry." Bill said, warning him.

"I will be as good as you Dad." Larry said, at which Jackie turned in utter surprise to look at Bill, before being escorted out to Larry's car.

Bill sat in silence. He felt uncomfortable with Larry calling him Dad. Not only that, Jackie was a nice girl, and he hoped Larry would not do something foolish.

"Come on Bill, he's a grown man and she's a young lady. Don't worry about them. They'll be fine. Besides this way we have the evening for ourselves." Janice said leaning over his shoulder to rub up against him as she began to clear the table.

Bill sat drinking his coffee watching Janice as she began to wash the dishes.

"Come help dry, so we can go sit in the living room." Janice said throwing the towel at Bill.

Dishes were something Bill hated and it was very seldom he ever helped Dawn with them. After dishes, Bill sat in his rocking chair looking at a magazine until Janice came into the room. "Come sit beside me." Janice said taking Bill by the hand at which he reluctantly obeyed. "I want to remember what it was like to be with you again." She said snuggling up to him. Bill put his arm around her shoulder. They sat reminiscing over old times. They laughed together at some of the funny things in their past. "It's almost like old times again. Isn't it Bill?" Janice said. Then their eyes locked. Bill sat staring once again into those deep blue eyes. Janice suddenly got up and excused herself, only to return wearing a flimsy see through nightgown.

"What do you think you are doing?" Bill said angrily as he

stood up.

Janice came over to him and put her arms around his neck. Their eyes locked once again. The smell of Janice's perfume took Bill back to his younger year. He took her in his arms and began kissing her. She eagerly returned his affections while clinging to him like nothing had changed.

Bill suddenly pushed her away angrily. "If you ever try that again you will have to leave." He said going into his bedroom, closing the door behind him. What had he done? Bill began to feel he had betrayed his wife.

Janice grabbed her housecoat and put it on, before knocking on Bill's door. He did not answer. "I'm sorry Bill. I know I shouldn't have done that, but you are the one who kissed me. I wasn't the only one at fault," she said. "It's hard to forget your first love." She said beginning to cry.

Bill felt very guilty. She was right. He had kissed her even if she did entice him.

Bill opened the door. "I'm sorry Janice it was my fault as much as it was yours. But don't ever try that again. I mean it or I will ask you to leave. Now if you don't mind, I'm going to call it a night." Bill said.

Janice agreed wiping away her tears. She wished him a good night before Bill closed his door.

Bill had a very troubled night. He had been unfaithful to Dawn. Bill finally got down on his knees and asked God for forgiveness and wisdom to deal with his new problem.

***

Dawn was not very unhappy with Bill for allowing Janice to move into their home. She was even more upset when two weeks past and she was able to go home only to find them still there.

"She's moving into a new house and it'll only be another couple of days," Bill had said. Darcy came home that weekend, and was not too happy to hear about the half brother he was supposed to have. He definitely, did not like him or trust him.

Darcy was outside when Larry drove in with Jackie. He couldn't believe it. Darcy stood there waiting for them to come to the house. "Will you occupy my girlfriend while I get something from my room." He said to Darcy.

For the first time Darcy had to admit he cared a lot for Jackie. They had spent a lot of time together after they had gone to help Lisa. He was beginning to feel she also care for him, even if they had never told each other. Darcy now suspected Larry was the reason why she had become very distant, and had been coming home more lately. He took Jackie's arm and led her around the corner. "Jackie why are you hanging around that guy? He's nothing but a Jerk. You deserve better than him," Darcy said.

"He is fun to be with," Jackie told him.

"Be careful. He'll only hurt you and if he does..." Darcy said angrily but he couldn't finish. Larry came out and asked Darcy if he could talk to him in private.

"What do you want?" Darcy snapped at him.

"How about a friendly competition bro." Larry said putting his arm around Darcy's shoulder, which Darcy quickly pushed off.

"You will never be my brother. So don't ever call me that. Darcy snapped.

"Come on. I can see you are interested in Jackie. Let's see who can win her hand in marriage first. You or me." Larry said casually. "Just like your Mom and mine," he added.

"What are you talking about?" Darcy asked.

"Never mind, it's Jackie we'll be competing for and bro I do have a head start," he said.

Darcy was angry now. "Don't you care, how you could hurt Jackie? She's a person with feelings, not an object to toy with."

"Well bro if you feel that strongly about her, you better plan your strategy. Right now she is my toy to play with, if you get my drift." Larry said, walking away.

It was all Darcy could do, to hold himself back from beating the tar out of Larry.

Will Love Conquer All?

He took his fist and hit the side of the house hard only to hurt his hand.

Darcy found his Dad was different now. He was distant, and his parents hardly talked to each other, which concerned him. He had never seen them like this. He found Janice, cold and callus until his Father came around. At those times she would be sweet to everyone.

Darcy suddenly realized what Larry had meant when he said, like you're Mom and mine. There was some sort of plan here to break up his parent's marriage. He was not going to allow it. Darcy tried to talk to his Father that afternoon, but Bill did not agree with what Darcy suspected.

"It's natural for your Mom and Janice to not like each other. Janice will be gone in a couple of days, but you will have to get used to Larry, as you are brothers," Bill said.

"Dad, I don't understand, if he is really your son, why has he none of your features or your nature?" Darcy asked.

"Well son, sometimes it just works that way." Bill said putting his arm around Darcy. "Darcy don't do as I did you can see how my mistake has hurt our family, especially your Mother. I would do anything to change it, but I can't."

"Dad you have to get rid of Janice and Larry or you will lose Mom. I have never seen you and Mom like this before, please Dad, you have to listen," Darcy pleaded.

"They will be gone soon." Bill said, turning back to his work.

Darcy was angry that he was allowing Janice to ruin everyone's life. Not only that, Larry was now about to ruin Jackie's. Darcy also noticed Nick and Marie did not come over anymore, so Darcy decided to go talk to Nick.

***

Nick, who was working out in the yard, walked over to Darcy when he drove in.

"Hi Darcy, how are you?" He said shaking his hand.

"Can I talk to you for a moment?" Darcy asked.

"Sure, let's go into the house." Nick said leading the way. "Jackie isn't home right now, if that is who you are looking for." Nick said

"I know." Darcy said in a tone that made Nick glance at him.

"Now, have a seat and tell me what the problem is." Nick said, after taking off his boots.

Darcy told Nick of what he feared was happening, with his parents. He also included Larry's offer of competing for Jackie.

"Mr. Helmsley, can you talk some sense into Dad, and Jackie," Darcy said.

"I will definitely talk to Jackie, but I can't make the decisions for her. I had hoped things would work out between you and Jackie." Nick said.

"Me too." Darcy said quietly, looking down at the floor.

Nick looked at him. He believed there was more than just concern that Darcy felt for his daughter. "As for your Father and Mother, I would only make things worse."

"Why is that?" Darcy asked looking at him.

"It's a long story. Your Mother and I were friends year ago." Nick said.

"I have nothing but time today. I would like to hear it," Darcy said

Nick began to tell him the whole story.

After he was finished, Darcy asked. "How come you and Dad can still be friends, and it's so different with Mom and Janice?"

"Your Mother loves your Father very much. I respect that even if I still care for her. I want the best for her. She once told me that I only thought I still loved her, and that it was not love, but wanting something I could not have."

Nick continued. "Janice and Larry's situation is sort of the same, only their love and feelings are shallow. It's just trying to get what they can't have and they don't care whose life they ruin. It's a game for them, then they move on to their next victim."

Darcy was silent and then said. "You know Dad feels so guilty about his new so called son, and yet somehow I don't believe he is his son, and I told Dad that."

"There are tests to find out." Nick said. "By the way, how is your Mother?"

"She's hanging in there but I don't know for how long. Janice has her doing all kinds of things for her. Then when Dad walks in, Janice makes it look like she has been doing thing for Mom. I can't do anything about it." Darcy said sadly.

"I will have Marie go talk to your Mother, but you can see why it's not good for me to intervene." Nick said. Darcy nodded in agreement. "Before you go Darcy, let's pray about it," Nick said. Bowing their heads they prayed for God's help and guidance.

***

A week had past since Bill said that Janice and Larry would leave, but there was always some excuse. Dawn could not take it any longer. She had confided in Marie the day she came over to visit. If Janice and Larry did not leave by Monday, she would go to her parent's house in Red Deer. She was to way exhausted to put up with Janice and Larry any longer. Besides Bill would have to take a stand sometime. He was the one that had to fix this. Marie had encouraged her not to leave, but she understood the situation. Things were not good here and it was harming Dawn's health as well as Bill's. Dawn needed to get more rest. Not only for her health, but it was putting the life of her unborn child at risk also.

Monday morning after Bill left their room, Dawn packed her bags. She knew Janice would have Bill's breakfast ready. Janice took credit for every meal Dawn made, but breakfast was the only meal Janice did make. That was because she had not yet figured out, how to have Dawn make it and still take credit for it.

Dawn could tell that Bill was getting really run down. It hurt Dawn terribly to see him like that, but there was nothing she could do. For the sake of their baby, she couldn't stay any longer.

Bill was about to go outside when Dawn told him she wanted to talk to him in their room. Bill was shocked to see the packed bags on the bed. "What's this?" He asked.

"I'm sorry Bill I just can't take it any more. You have to make the decision whether you want us." She said, placing his hand on her belly. "Or them," she added.

"I have given it time and I can't handle it anymore. You seem to want to believe her over me. We never mistrusted each other before she came. The strain is just too much Bill. I'm just exhausted. I can't fight her any more." She said laying her head on his broad chest. Bill slowly put his arms around her. He held her like he hadn't in sometime.

What have I done to my family he thought? "Please don't leave me. I love you and I'm so sorry," Bill said.

"I can't stay here, I'm going to my parents house in Red Deer and if things change let me know. I won't be calling because she would answer. If you want to talk to me you know the number." Dawn said holding him. "Oh Bill. It feels so good to be in your arms. I love you so much and it will almost kill me to leave. But I have been given no other choice." Dawn said quickly breaking loose from him. She went to pick up her bags, before Bill could convince her to stay. Bill took the suitcases from Dawn, and carried them to the car. He knew she had made up her mind and he was not going to be able to change it, unless Janice left. He also knew Dawn must have agonized over this for some time, to have made such a difficult decision. But Larry was his son and he didn't want to cause problems, when he was just beginning to know him. Bill had not noticed the terrible toll it had taken on Dawn until now, and he felt very guilty.

Bill helped her in the car and kissed her. "Drive safely and take my love with you. I will get this all straightened out, I promise." Bill said.

"Bill promise me one more thing. Have a blood test done, because I don't believe Larry is your son. I'm also afraid Larry will ruin Jackie's life. Please, she is a nice girl. Keep an eye on them." Dawn said putting her hand out to touching the side of Bill's face. "I will miss my teddy bear so much. I'll be praying for you every moment of the day." Dawn said taking her hand away from the side of Bill's face, then driving away without looking back.

Her leaving hit Bill hard. He went straight to his workshop and the first thing he saw, was Dawn's note. The words labour of love seemed to be embedded into his brain.

Bill went up into the hayloft where he wept and prayed. What had he done to his family?

Chapter 17

Dawn fought back tears. She had to concentrate on her driving and was glad the weather and roads were good for this time of year. She was relieved when she finally reached her destination. Tears filled her eyes. Her Parents were not going to be there to meet her. A terrible loneliness seems to engulf her, when she stepped through the door. The realization of everything struck her hard and the tears now flowed freely. She was alone. How would she ever make it without Bill? Had she lost her husband to another woman? "No!!" she cried. She would not give up on him. She loved him too much and she knew he loved her too. She would continue to pray that their love would conquer even this. *"Lord look after him and protect him from the evil around him. Please give him strength to fight it."* She prayed. Dawn took her suitcase to the room, her and Bill stayed in when they came to visit her parents. The house felt so empty. Everything was exactly as her parents had left it.

Dawn didn't know how long she sat there on the bed crying, and asking God to help her. She couldn't do this alone. She finally was so exhausted and sure there were no tears left to cry. She sat there for a while calming down. Softly she whispered " God I give it to you, I can do nothing."

She slowly hung up her clothes, placing some of her things in the dresser drawers. Then lying on the couch she stared out at the trees in the front yard. She couldn't believe this was happening to her. Bill and her had never been so far apart as they were now. *Why lord? Why have you allowed this to happen to us? Bill and I have always been faithful to each other and loved each other. Why did you allow this woman to come between us? Lord I have lost one son, my parents, and now perhaps my husband, how much can one person bare, Lord? Protect our other children, as well as the little one inside me. For if I lose this one, and my husband I wouldn't want to go on.*

Dawn looked around the room it was as if her parents had gone away for the day. She decided that if she felt up to it, she would go through her parent's room. But as she was extremely tired both mentally and physically she would first take a well, deserved rest.

* * *

Bill was busy working when Larry came into the workshop. He asked Larry if he would mind holding the end of the board when, it came through the saw. Larry hated working with wood, actually he did not like to work at all. But he did hold the two pieces that came through, while Bill guided it in on the other end. Larry hated the smell of sawdust and did not appreciate, having it on his clean clothes.

"Was there something you wanted?" Bill asked, switching off the saw. He took the two strips of board that Larry was holding and laid them aside. He had never came into Bill's workshop before so Bill knew there was something he wanted.

"I was wondering if I could borrow 100 dollars from you." Larry said picking up a small piece of wood, and sticking it against the saw blade, which had not yet fully stopped.

"Don't!" Bill yelled, as the blade caught the stick, flipping it out of Larry's hand, only to jerk his hand toward the blade.

Bill quickly grabbed a clean rag from a bag he had nearby. When Larry saw the blood, dripping from his hand, he almost passed out. Bill giving it a quick glance, wrapped it tightly with the rag, then lead Larry to the house. Bill said somewhat annoyed at Larry's stupidity.

"Your lucky it's only a little cut. Didn't you ever learn to keep your hands away from saw blades?" Bill said.

When Janice seen the blood, she got hysterical, but Bill told her to calm down. "It's nothing a few stitches wouldn't fix." He said as he drove Larry to the hospital.

While Bill sat waiting, Dawn's words came back to him. It sent him quickly going in search of his doctor. After explaining his situation, he asked if it was possible to have a test done, to find out if Larry was actually his son. First they told him, they would need a sample of each of their blood. After taking a sample of Bill's they told him it would be a few days before they would get the results back. Bill asked if it would be possible to take a sample of Larry's before they stitched up his hand.

Larry did not question, why they had to take a sample of his blood, for he and his Mother were to busy complaining about the service in the hospital. When they got back to the house, Larry went upstairs.

Bill took the opportunity to tell Janice to sit down because he wanted to talk to her.

"Janice, I want you to leave. I am a married man and I don't feel right with you staying here while Dawn is away." Bill said.

"Why did she leave? Did you find out that she wasn't having your child, after all?" Janice asked.

"What kind of stupid talk is that?" Bill said angrily.

"Come on Bill. You know her and Nick had plenty of time together when you were gone. You must have had some doubt. After all, Nick was in love with her years ago and still is." Janice said. She had to work fast if she wanted to keep Bill for herself.

"How did you know that?" Bill asked.

"I have my ways." Janice said. "You poor dear. You know I love you, and will help you through this." She said, taking his hand while looking into his eyes.

"That won't work again. I want you to leave, now!" Bill said pulling his hand away from hers.

"All right then." Janice said doing her pouting act. "I will leave the day after tomorrow. By then my house should be finished." Janice said.

"Be sure you do, or you will find your bags packed and sitting outside." Bill said getting up to go out to his workshop. He was no longer taken in by Janice's childish pouting. Instead it now irritated him.

Janice was angry for not being able to sway Bill her way, so she decided to try another tactic. She quickly went to the phone and dialed a number. She didn't care whose life she had to ruin next to get her way. "Hi, Marie this is Janice. How are you?"

"I'm fine. What can I do for you, Janice?" Marie asked, wondering why Janice was calling her.

"I just thought you should know the terrible news that Bill just told me. It's so sad." Janice said pitifully.

"Did something happen to Dawn?" Marie asked quickly.

"No it's -- well. It's just that Bill found out that Dawn isn't having his child after all. Nick is the Father." Janice said.

"I don't believe you." Marie said angrily.

"Why would Bill say it, if it wasn't true. Dawn told him herself. That is why she actually left." Janice said knowing the seed of deception was now sown.

Marie hung up the phone without another word, while Janice stood there smiling, at the lie she had planted in Marie's mind. Now how could she get Nick to go to see Dawn? She wondered. That would prove to be bit harder, but she was determined to try.

Darcy and Jackie drove into the yard just when Janice hung up the phone. Jackie had come home with Darcy, wanting to spend sometime with Nick and Marie. It also allowed her to spend time with Darcy, which she thoroughly enjoyed.

When they entered the house Jackie took off her boots, and went to the bathroom.

"Where is my Mother?" Darcy asked Janice.

"Oh, didn't you know? Your Mother doesn't live here anymore. She left your Father." Janice said revealing in her victory.

"What!!" Darcy said in utter shock. "It can't be!" Darcy said.

Just then Larry came downstairs. "Hi bro. How's our competition doing?" He asked.

"I told you, I will not play you and your Mother's stupid games." He said angrily.

"Come on Darcy you know I can get Jackie before you can. It won't be long before I will have another trophy under my belt." Larry said laughing at Darcy.

Darcy clinched his fist as he lashed out saying. "You touch her or hurt her in anyway, you will be answerable to me, and don't you forget it." At that Darcy turned and went outside, slamming the door behind him. Darcy now full of rage headed to the barn to confront his Father. He knew if he had spent a moment longer around Larry, he would have decked him right there.

Larry was stunned when he turned and saw Jackie standing in the bathroom door way. "Hi honey, I didn't know you were here."

"Obviously." Jackie said going to slip her on boots.

"Come on honey. You know I was only teasing Darcy. Just a bit of brotherly love." He said.

"It looks like your family doesn't know the meaning of love." Jackie said looking directly at Janice before following Darcy outside.

***

When Darcy came in, Bill was staring at Dawn's note. He turned when he heard the door slam. Bill knew by the look on his sons face, that he was angry.

"Dad what has gotten into you? You still have that woman living with you, even after the way she treated Mom? You never could see how she used Mom, but the instant you walked into the room, she would act like the big hero. I don't know and understand you anymore. Is she better in bed than Mom or…"

"That's enough Darcy." His Father said abruptly.

"What's enough? You and Mom were so close. Man, she is

Will Love Conquer All?

having your baby and you treat her this way, by getting rid of her and keeping this woman." Darcy said, picking up a piece of wood and threw it across the room in anger.

"Darcy I said that's enough." Bill demanded turning away, to again stare at Dawn's note.

Jackie took hold of Darcy's arm asking him to calm down.

"Dad explain it to me. What is going on? Are you and Mom split up?" Darcy asked.

Bill did not look at his son, but kept his eyes transfixed on Dawn's note.

"Your Mother went to rest at your grandparents house in Red Deer, for awhile." Bill said.

"She went there alone? Dad don't you care how she will feel there alone."

Bill was silent.

"Is this woman and her son staying here for good now?" Darcy asked.

"He is my son too, Darcy." Bill said sadly.

"Dad he is not your son, I am. At least I thought I was. Those two are just using you and wrecking your marriage, if you can't see that, then you can have them as your family. I won't be part of it." Darcy said slamming the door behind him, when he left.

"Darcy!!" Bill called.

Jackie stood there a moment looking at Bill's ashen face. The strain of the past few weeks were definitely showing on up Bill. "I will talk to him, Mr. Spencer. I do hope you and Mrs. Spencer can work things out. She's a very sweet person and I know you both care for each other very much," Jackie said.

"Thanks Jackie." Bill said sitting down on a stool.

Darcy opened the truck door for Jackie. After getting in he looked at Jackie, asking if she wanted him to take her to her Father's or Marie's.

"I think I'll go to Dad's, but what have you planned now? It's obvious that you won't be staying here," Jackie said.

"I don't know Jackie. I would never have believed this would ever happen in my family. I actually don't feel too good right now." He said driving out of the yard.

When they arrived at Nick's farm, Jackie knocked on her Father's door. They both stood waiting for Nick to answer. Jackie opened the door and called, "Dad are you home?" They then stepped into the house. Darcy was taking off his boots when he heard Jackie cry out. "Dad what's wrong?"

Darcy quickly went to see what the problem was. It was then he saw Nick sitting on a chair with his hand resting on the telephone. He seemingly did not notice that Jackie was there talking to him.

"Dad let me know what's wrong? Did something happen to Marie? Is she all right?" Jackie asked.

Quietly and slowly Nick said. "No, she is not all right. Janice called her. She said that Dawn told Bill, that she was having my child, but I was never with her. I don't believe Dawn would say that when it isn't true. Marie apparently believed Janice, because she just called off our wedding." He said holding his head with his hands.

"That witch is not only ruining my parents lives, now she's working on other people." Darcy said clinching his fist.

"Why would she do this Dad?" Jackie asked.

"I think she figures if I go to talk to Dawn, it would prove to Bill that I was involved."

"That way she can have Bill to herself. She doesn't care how many people she hurts on the way." Nick said.

"What can we do?" Jackie asked as tears filled her eyes.

"I don't know Jackie. Pray I guess." Nick said, now very depressed.

"What about you two, how is that going?" Nick asked teasing his daughter, trying to lighten the mood. He did not want to talk about Marie right now.

"What are you talking about?" Jackie asked.

"I can tell the way you two look at each other, that you're in love with each other. Whether you have said it to each other or not, I don't know. I'm telling you that if you do love each other, don't leave it too long or it may happen like Dawn and Me. You can never go back." Nick said.

Darcy was watching Jackie all the while. When she looked at him, he smiled and said. "I'll see that it won't happen to us, Sir."

"Good boy." Nick said giving Jackie and Darcy a hug. "I would be proud to have you as my son-in-law."

"Don't I have any say in this?" Jackie said as her Father left the room.

"Only when you say, I do." Darcy said winking at her. He pulled Jackie to him and wrapped his arms around her. He then asked the most important question of his life.

"Will you marry me, Jackie Hemsley?"

"Isn't this a bit sudden?" she asked.

"No, your Dad is right. I don't want to lose you. I definitely don't want to take the chance he did. Do you?" Darcy asked.

"Oh Darcy, I do love you too." She said, putting her arms around his neck.

"More than Larry?" He asked.

"I never loved him. It was just... well a spell he kind of has over you," she said. "But you broke that spell today." Jackie told him.

"Well in that case, I will tell you that I have loved you from the second time I saw you." Darcy said.

"Not the first day?" She asked, smiling up at him enjoying the warmth of his body near hers.

"No the first day I was just smitten, but after I talked to you the second time, I was in love. Then heart broken when you went with Larry." Darcy said as he cringed at the thought of Larry holding Jackie. "Now do I get an answer?" Darcy asked, pulling her tighter against him. "I won't let you go until you say yes."

"Well in that case maybe I won't answer." She said, teasing him.

Darcy bent over and kissed her gently on the lips, then as

she returned his kiss he became more passionate. Soon Jackie pushed him gently away and said softly. "Not now with Dad being depressed. I don't want him to see our joy, when his world came crashing down. We'll tell him later. By the way the answer is yes, so you can release me now," Jackie said.

Darcy found Nick and asked if he would be all right if they left him alone. Nick said he was fine, and they should go and enjoy themselves. There was nothing they could do anyhow.

"Get your coat Jackie, and let's go." Darcy said giving Nick a hug when they were about to leave. "Thank-you Mr. Helmsely," Darcy said

"Your welcome but I don't know for what. Just drive carefully." he said.

Jackie and Darcy got into the truck, and drove up the road. After finding a secluded place, Darcy stopped the truck and looked at Jackie. "Jackie I don't want to risk losing you. I love you too much."

"You won't lose me." She said taking his hand.

"I thought that of my parents too, but... Will you marry me tomorrow, please?" Darcy asked, looking into Jackie's eyes. "We can keep it quiet for awhile until things settle down around here. But as your Dad said, he waited too long and I don't want to take that chance." Darcy told her.

"I don't either Darcy but..," Jackie sat there thinking for several minute while Darcy sat patiently waiting for her answer. It was all so sudden.

"Ok, I will marry you today if you like." Jackie said touching the side of Darcy's face.

Darcy took her in his arms. They kissed each other passionately, but slowly he released her. "I guess one more night won't kill me to wait. Then you will be mine for ever."

"I do want us to be honest with each other about our past, as it has a way of ruining the future. One thing I can tell you is that I have never done what my Father did." Darcy said starting the truck.

Will Love Conquer All?

"By the way where are we going, to get married?" Jackie asked.

"In Edmonton, at the church of your choice. But first you have to go shopping for your wedding dress." Darcy said.

"I don't need a fancy dress." Jackie said.

"No, I want my bride to look like a bride. We also need family, so I figured Kevin could give you away and be my best man and Lisa could be your maid of honour. I'm sure we can bribe them to keep it quiet for a while." Darcy said.

"Oh Darcy, you are a romantic. I love you." Jackie said.

"That isn't all. Then the four of us will go out for supper, before we check into a honeymoon suite. I want us to remember our wedding night." Darcy said

* * *

Lisa was watching television when Jackie and Darcy arrived. She was surprised to see them. Darcy never came to see her before, other than the time Franklin had beaten her.

"We have something to ask you Lisa and then we want your promise to keep it a secret for a while." Darcy said.

Lisa looked at them, knowing something was different, but not knowing what.

"Ok, I promise to keep your secret. What is it?" Lisa asked.

Darcy and Jackie looked at each other, then putting his arm around Jackie, Darcy said. "We are getting married."

"Oh! That's great." Lisa said giving them each a hug. "When?" She asked.

"That's the secret, tomorrow." Darcy said.

"What! You mean you are eloping?" Lisa said in surprise.

"No not really. I want Jackie to buy the wedding dress of her choice and I want you to go help her. Then you can be our bridesmaid, and Kevin can give Jackie away, as well as be my best man. But we haven't told him yet." Darcy said, continuing on telling her the rest of their plans.

Jackie called Kevin and asked him to meet her at Lisa's. He assured him that everything was fine.

"What about Dad and Mom, aren't you going to tell them?" Lisa asked.

"In the right time, but not now with what's happened there." Darcy said, his face showing the anger he felt, when he thought about it.

"What happened, is the baby ok, or is it Mom again?" Lisa asked.

Darcy told Lisa what had happened with their parents, and the trouble Janice was causing everyone. Then he told her about their so-called new brother.

Jackie tried to console Lisa as she began to cry. After the buzzer sounded and Kevin told Darcy who it was, he was let in. When Kevin entered the room, he saw the anger in Darcy's face and Lisa crying on the couch. He wondered what was happening, because everything looked far from fine to him.

"What is going on here? I thought everything was ok." Kevin said.

Kevin and Darcy sat on the chairs by the table, where Darcy proceeded to tell him about Janice and the trouble she had caused between his parents. He went on informing him that now, she was involving Kevin's Father, and Marie in her wicked scheme. Kevin sat there quietly contemplating what he had just heard. He felt bad for his Father, who had gone through difficult times when he lost his wife, and now Marie. Kevin liked Marie and thought she would be the right person to put some joy back into his Father's life.

Darcy then went on to tell him about Jackie and his marriage plans. Kevin was not too sure he liked their plans, but if they loved each other, who was he to stand in their way. He agreed to keep it a secret under the present circumstances.

When every one got over the initial shock of everything, Darcy and Jackie decided on a church. After talking to the minister on the telephone, they went to meet with him in person, leaving Kevin and Lisa alone.

"How have you been?" Kevin asked Lisa. "I see the scar has

healed nicely." He said gently stroking the side of her face.

"I'm fine and yes, the bruises have healed on the outside." She said moving away from him.

"Thanks, for all your help. I don't know how I can ever repay you."

She said, trying to avoid eye contact.

"Don't let that incident ruin your life Lisa. Look at Jackie. I'm glad she has found someone that will not mistreat her. Darcy and you grew up with loving parents, and you have learned what it means to love each other." Kevin said.

"Until now." She said going into her room crying, at the thought of her parent's separation.

Kevin followed her and sat down on the side of her bed. "Lisa, they love each other and true love always finds its way," he said.

"What about your Father and my Mother that didn't work out." Lisa said, looking at him with tear filled eyes.

"That was different. Dad loved your Mother, but she only liked him as a friend. Your parents love each other, and have gone through a lot over the years. Neither one will forget. Their love has always stood through it all. It's like a bump in the road." Kevin said.

"More like a mountain." Lisa said. "I don't know if I would ever forgive Dad if something happened to Mom."

"Your Mother probably needed to get away for a rest, and that may be all it was. Talk to her, she probably needs that now." Kevin said.

Lisa sat up beside Kevin on the bed. "What will happen to your Dad?" Lisa asked.

"I don't know, but maybe you and me should go talk to your Mother someday. Perhaps we can help straighten some of this out." Kevin said thoughtfully.

"I would do anything." Lisa said as tears ran down her cheeks. "I like your Dad and Marie. I thought they made such a nice couple." Lisa said

"I was beginning to think that too." Kevin added.

Book 1 of the ***Mountains and Valleys of Life***

***

The pastor Darcy and Jackie had chosen, preferred several weeks of counselling before marriage, but in this situation he agreed. However, he did want to talk to them for at least a couple of hours.

The next morning, Darcy picked Jackie up from Kevin's apartment. Kevin had already gone to work, but he had made arrangements to get off early. Lisa had class only in the morning, which would work out just about right.

After lunch, Darcy took Jackie and Lisa to the bridal shop, where they began looking at dresses. Darcy still had a few arrangements of his own to make. Jackie offered to pay for her own dress, but Darcy refused to allow her to do that. This was what he wanted to do for her.

The two girls first chose a beautiful forest green dress for Lisa. It was a slim ankle length dress with a slit to the knee. The front had a modest neckline, but the back was open down to her waist. Lisa looked at the price. "It's far too expensive." She told Jackie.

The sales ladies informed them, if Jackie bought her bridal gown there, they would receive 15% off both dresses. Jackie insisted on paying half of Lisa's dress. After all it was her wedding and Darcy was paying for her gown. It would be her gift to Lisa, for being her bridesmaid. Lisa finally consented.

Jackie's dress was a modest slim fitting gown, with a detachable train. It had a much lower neckline than she was comfortable with. For her headpiece she chose a white hat, with an attached veil. She could wear it either covering her eyes or her entire face, of which she chose the later. Jackie was pleased that the gown she liked was not that expensive. She didn't want Darcy over spending. The girls then decided to see about flowers.

Jackie's pick was two white roses with a hint of green on the edges of the petals, mingled with a touch of baby's breath that lay on a small white Bible. Lisa's would carry a single rose of the same color with one also placed in her blonde hair.

They had finished earlier than they first thought, so decided to quickly have their hair done. Darcy had just arrived at the Bridal shop when the girls returned. He paid for Jackie's dress, while the girls picked up their flowers. Darcy then drove the girls back to Lisa's apartment, where Kevin, after getting ready himself, would pick them up. Darcy would get dressed at his apartment then would meet everyone at the church at 7 p.m.

Kevin stood breathless, looking at the two girls when he entered the door to Lisa's apartment.

He knew his sister was beautiful, but not until now did he realize how beautiful Lisa actually was. He went first to his sister. "Jackie you look great. I do hope this is really the right thing you are doing?" he said.

"It is. I have never been so sure of anything in my life." Jackie said excitedly.

"In that case, I wish you both the best of everything." He said giving her a hug.

Kevin then turned to Lisa. He looked her up and down. "You are beautiful. I will be the luckiest man tonight, to have someone like you on my arm." He said, watching Lisa blush.

"I'm sure you say that to all your girlfriends." She told him, still avoiding eye contact.

He leaned over her shoulder, to whisper in her ear. "Ah, but this time I actually mean it."

Lisa could smell his cologne as she felt him slightly brush against her. Kevin stirred something within her that she had never felt before. She had never paid much attention to him, but she did realize there was gentleness about him. He looked very handsome, standing there in his rented tuxedo. Why had she not noticed it before? Their drive to the church was in silence. Jackie was very nervous yet excited about her wedding. Lisa's nervousness was caused by the nearness of Kevin.

Darcy was standing at the front of the church with the minister while someone played the organ. It was when Lisa began walking down the isle, that Jackie noticed baby's breath had been place on the outside of every pew. There were about 15 people there. When the wedding march was played, Kevin offered his sister his arm, and they slowly began to walk down the isle. Jackie's eyes were fixed on Darcy, standing in the front, wearing a black tuxedo with a white carnation on his lapel. Her heart made a flip when Darcy smiled at her. If she ever entertained, doubt about what she was doing, it now all vanished. She never realized, until this exact moment, how much she actually did love him. She would be only too happy to spend the rest of her life with him. She knew it would be hard, having him on the road so much of the time, but he definitely was the one for her.

After they said their vows to each other, a young lady got up to sing a beautiful song while they signed some papers.

Jackie looked at Darcy wondering how this all came about, but he only smiled and gave her hand a squeeze. It felt strange when the minister introduced them to their unknown guests as Mr. and Mrs. Darcy Spencer.

Lisa had a hard time keeping here eyes off of Kevin, as they followed Darcy and Jackie to the back of the church.

While Darcy and Jackie stood in the foyer, the people that sat in the pews came back to congratulated them. Darcy introduced Jackie to the minister's wife, who told her that they were having music practice that night and decided to add a few finishing touches to their wedding. Darcy and Jackie thanked everyone for making it a memorable day for them. They promised to visit this church again, the next time they were back in Edmonton.

Lisa unhooked Jackie's train before she got into the car that Darcy had rented for the evening. He said that he didn't think it was appropriate to use his truck. Lisa went with Kevin, to the restaurant where Darcy arranged a private place, to have their meal. They laughed and talked, as siblings told stories about each other. By the end of the evening they felt they had gotten to know one another quite well. Darcy and Jackie excused themselves, but Kevin and Lisa sat talking for a few more moments.

Kevin suddenly became very quiet, then quickly ushered Lisa out to his car.

"Is something wrong? Are you feeling all right?" Lisa asked, at his sudden change of behaviour.

Darcy looked at his watch. "Do you think your Mother would mind if we went to visit her this evening?" He asked.

"She would probably enjoy the company, but wouldn't it be after 11, by the time we got there? We would have to change our clothes first." Lisa said. "Don't you have to work this week end?" Lisa asked.

"No, and perhaps you could ask if she would mind if I spent the night there too. Then in the morning, we could talk a few things over." Lisa noticed Kevin was always looking in the mirror, on their drive home.

"We'll go to my place first, where I'll change my clothes. Then I'll take you to your place, but you should phone your Mother from my apartment." Darcy said.

"Why does it have to be tonight? Can't we go in the morning?" Lisa asked.

"I think it's best we go tonight. I will tell you why later." Kevin said.

They drove in silence, and upon arriving at his apartment, she told him she would wait for him in the car. She would call her Mother from her place but Kevin said he would not allow that.

Lisa called her Mother when Kevin went across the hall to his friend's apartment. Her Mother said she would be only too happy to have company, no matter when they got there. Kevin left his television and lights on, which Lisa found strange, but accepted his reasoning. He said there was less chance of someone breaking in, when you make it look like someone is home. He told her they would be taking his friends truck, as they headed out the back of the building to where it was parked. Kevin then drove out the opposite direction from where they had came in.

Kevin went in with Lisa when they arrived at her apartment.

When she was about to go change, Kevin grabbed her arm. "Let me have one more look at you before you change." He said stepping back to admiring her. Kevin came very near to her and their eyes met. For a brief moment Lisa thought Kevin was about to kiss her. He leaned close enough that she could almost feel his lips on hers, but abruptly he stepped back. "I guess you better change so we won't get there too late." He said turning away, leaving Lisa shaking and a bit disappointed.

When they left the apartment, Lisa thought she would leave a light on too, but Kevin switched it off and closed the door. Then making sure it was locked, Kevin quickly ushered Lisa into the truck, all the while scanning the area with his eyes.

They drove some distance in silence, before Lisa turned to Kevin.

"What is going on? I see you looking in the mirror, as if you expect someone to be following us. Then this idea of going to Mom's tonight, I don't buy your excuse one bit." Lisa said looking at Kevin.

"You're watching too many movies." Kevin said teasing her.

"I want to know." Lisa said getting annoyed with him. "What is going on?" She demanded.

"Well - - if you must know." He said hesitating again.

"Spill it!" she demanded.

"Feisty aren't we. You are beginning to get me interested." He said teasing her.

"Flattery won't get you off the hook. Now please." she said laying her hand on his arm. "I know something happened at the restaurant, because you haven't been the same since."

"I'm sorry. I guess you'll have to know, sooner or later. I saw Franklin watching you just before we left." he said.

Lisa gasped. "I thought he was in jail." She said gripping Kevin's arm.

"So did I, but apparently not. I didn't want you to be alone tonight. I was hoping if he was following us that he'll believe we are still at my place."

Will Love Conquer All?

"So that was the reason for switching vehicles." Lisa said.

"I don't think he'll find us at your Mothers and in the mean time, I will find out why he is out of jail." Kevin said.

Lisa was silent the rest of the way. She had hoped she was finished with Franklin. She knew it was best for her to move out of town, when her schooling was done, but that wouldn't be for another month and a half. Lisa gave Kevin the address of her grandparent's house, then when they got closer, Lisa guided him the rest of the way.

"Now remember Lisa. Try not to spill the beans about Darcy and Jackie." Kevin said.

"That won't be easy," she told him. "It's to bad because I'm sure Mom would be happy for them." Hesitating Lisa added. "She would be disappointed that she couldn't have been there for them. But with everything else, it would only bring back memories of her and Dad. That would make her even more unhappy," she said.

"Well Lisa, your wedding will have to be the one that will cheer her up. "I'm sure she will participate in yours." Kevin said, driving into the driveway.

"I don't think I will ever get married. I don't trust men anymore," she said angrily.

"Do you trust me?" Kevin asked.

"Yes, but your different." she said to him.

Kevin looked at her after stopping the truck. "In what way am I different?"

He asked, with a twinkle in his eye.

Lisa felt that same feeling, when once again their eyes met. "I... we better go in."

She said quickly opening the door, then walked toward the house. Kevin got their bags before following her.

Dawn met her daughter at the door with a big hug. Then giving Kevin a hug she told them to come in. She was glad to have company, to break the loneliness.

"You two are an answer to prayers tonight. I was going crazy here by myself. What made you come tonight?" Dawn asked.

"We both had the weekend off and decided we would come to see you." Lisa said, glancing over at Kevin.

"How did you know I was here?" Dawn asked.

"Darcy and Jackie told us." Lisa said hearing Kevin clear his throat, as a reminder to Lisa. She quickly went on to add. "After Darcy talked to Dad."

The color drained from Dawn's face and both Kevin and Lisa knew instantly how deep her hurt went.

"How is your Father did he say?" Dawn asked, fidgeting with her wedding band.

"They said he looks old and has lost a lot of weight." Lisa said slowly.

"Mom what is going on? The story is going around that this is not Dad's baby and that you told Dad Mr. Helmsley was the Father." Lisa blurted out.

Dawn gasped in shock as she stood up suddenly, only to double over with a pain that seemed to rip through her body. Kevin and Lisa both rushed to her side, to help her back onto her chair.

"That is not true, you know that Lisa. I would never be unfaithful to your Father. Who would say such a thing? I know your Father would never lie like that. Janice!!" Dawn said, as tears filled her eyes. Dawn looked at Kevin. "Has she told Marie that story, too?" Dawn asked Kevin.

"Yes, and apparently Marie must have believed her. She called off the wedding." Kevin said.

"Oh no!!" Dawn said in despair.

"I am sorry Mom, this isn't what I wanted us to talk about tonight. Can we change to some other topic?" Lisa asked.

"I'm sorry Lisa. I came here to rest, and get away from..." She stopped short of mentioning Janice's name. "I do miss talking to your Father, but I told him I would not call him. He would have to call me. But now, if she is trying to poison his mind, it may get to the point that... I'm sorry but do you mind if I go to bed?

Will Love Conquer All?

I am very tired." Dawn said suddenly standing up, with the aid of Kevin and Lisa. "Your beds are ready, and Lisa, you can show Kevin where his is." Dawn said feeling like she was carrying the weight of the world on her, when she slowly left the room.

"I wish you wouldn't have brought it up tonight Lisa." Kevin scolded her. "Your Mother was hoping for a nice visit. You could have waited until at least tomorrow and gradually worked it in." Kevin said, now upset with her.

Lisa looked at him. "I know. I wish I would have waited now too." she said.

"Well, what's done is done." He said giving her a hug.

Lisa's first reaction was to pull away. She stood there at first very tense, then slowly relaxed and laid her head on his shoulder. She put her arms around him holding him close to her, while tears ran down her face. She lost track of time, enjoying the comfort and support of his arms. When he released her, he wiped the tears from her face. "Do you feel better now?" he asked.

"Yes, I'm sorry. I'll show you to your room." She said quickly turning away.

Before Lisa showed Kevin his room, he made sure the doors were locked, while Lisa shut off the lights. "Goodnight then." Kevin said brushing lightly up against her when he walked past her, after she directed him to his room.

"Goodnight." She said quietly watching him go downstairs.

***

The next morning Kevin was awakened, by someone arguing the living room. He quickly got dressed and reached the living room the same time as Dawn. There to Kevin's amazement, stood Franklin in the middle of the living room with Lisa.

"What are you doing here?" Kevin said angrily.

"I came to talk to Lisa, as if it's any of your business." he snapped.

"How did you know where I was?" Lisa asked.

"I'm no fool. You figured you could trick me into believing that you were staying at Kevin's. I phoned your parents place, and some lady said you could be with your Mother, and gave me the address. I see you have your new boyfriend with you again." Franklin said.

Dawn stood there in bewilderment as to what was going on. "I think you better leave Franklin." Dawn said, taking Franklin by the arm, trying to lead him to the door. Franklin now became even angrier at being told to leave. He gave Dawn a shove sending her sprawling across the coffee table. Lisa quickly went to her Mother, when she moaned in pain, but Franklin roughly grabbed Lisa's arm. "You're coming with me," he demanded.

"No she is not!!" Kevin said angrily, wrestling with Franklin, until he pinned him to the floor. Lisa quickly called 911, and told them to send the police to the address she gave them. Then after going to her Mother, who was now in obvious distress, Lisa again dialled 911 this time asking for an ambulance. She had a terrible feeling something was seriously wrong.

"I will get you for this Lisa." Franklin said before the police arrived.

The police arrived only seconds before the ambulance. They assessed the situation and then allowed Lisa to accompany her Mother to the hospital. Kevin said he would meet Lisa there, after giving a statement to the police.

After the doctor arrived, Lisa quickly found a phone to call her Father. When she heard a lady answer her parents phone, she began to feel a renewed anger at her Father.

But right now, it was imperative that she got a message through to him.

"Hello this is Lisa, Bill's daughter. Is Dad there?" Lisa asked.

"He's out in his shop right now. Can I help you?" Janice asked

"This is an emergency. Mom is in the hospital and it's urgent that he get here as soon as possible." Lisa said.

"Of course dear. I will be sure to tell him." Janice said sweetly.

Lisa went back to wait for the doctor. On his return he asked

Lisa where her Father was.

"I just called him and left a message. How is she?" Lisa said nervously just as Kevin approached her.

Kevin put his arm around Lisa, while the doctor began to explain the situation.

"We have to take the baby by C section. It's a very critical situation, as your Mother appears very weak. The problem is the baby will be premature, so we can only hope for the best. I think it would be wise if your Father got here as soon as possible." He said leaving, Lisa with tears streaming down her face. Kevin guided her to the waiting room, where Lisa sat blaming herself for getting involved with someone like Franklin. If only they wouldn't have came to see her Mother last night, this wouldn't have happened.

"Lisa, I'm going to try to reach Jackie and Darcy. Are you going to be all right?" Kevin asked. Lisa only nodded her head. She felt numb all over.

Chapter 18

Bill spent very little time in the house, after Dawn left, which angered Janice.

Larry was also getting very restless and bored, especially since he could not find out where Jackie was.

Bill was going into town for some supplies one morning and refused to take Janice along with him. He told her that he had some important business to take care of and all her tricks did not work on Bill this time.

Bill's specific reason was because he wanted to check with his doctor, to find out whether the test results were back. When Bill entered the hospital he saw his doctor in the hall and quickly went to catch up to him.

"Excuse me Doctor, but did you ever get those test results back?" Bill asked.

"That was to see if that young man was your son as I recall." The doctor said slowly recalling what test Bill was referring to. The doctor rummaged through the bundle of papers he held in his hand. "No it doesn't appear so," he said.

Bill turned to walk away when the doctor called to him back.

"Mr. Spencer, just one moment. I think it is here." The doctor briefly glanced at the letter, while Bill stood nervously by. His doctor handed the letter to him and said.

"I'm sorry Mr. Spencer, but he is definitely not your son."

Bill read through the letter. "May I have a copy of this?" Bill asked.

Will Love Conquer All?

At that, his doctor gave instruction for the lady at the front desk to make a copy for Bill before walking away. Bill's anger toward Janice burned inside of him. Why was he so gullible to be taken in by her again? She had intentionally ruined his life. Would Dawn ever forgive him? After the receptionist gave Bill a copy of the report, he tried to call Dawn. That's strange, Bill thought to himself. Where would she be this early in the morning? He had an uneasy feeling about it, but right now his anger toward Janice, and her deceit was foremost on his mind.

Bill drove straight home without getting his supplies. Upon entering the house, he looked around. Since Dawn left the house was never the same. Janice did very little housework now and Larry left his things lying wherever he dropped them.

Janice and Larry were in the living room when Bill entered the house. "Janice, I want you and Larry out of my house now and no more excuses!" Bill said angrily.

"Oh Bill you can't mean that. You know how I feel about you." She said somewhat surprised at his sudden return. Janice began to pout as she squeezed out a tear that ran down her cheek.

"Don't try that, it won't work on me any more." he snapped.

Janice, now angry at not getting her way, said. "If that's the case. I will go to court and you'll pay child support for all the years Larry was growing up." Janice shouted her true colors now beginning to erupt.

"You can try to do that, but I know the truth. I don't think you'll want to try that now. I don't know what your game was, but I want you two out of here with in the hour or I will throw everything outside including you." Bill said angrily.

"Come on Mom let's get out of this dump. Darcy is no competition and it's no fun now that I can't find Jackie anywhere." Larry said.

Bill gave him an angry look, then turned and headed out to his workshop.

Janice was furious. She immediately began hatching out another scheme. She would have to turn Dawn against Bill and she knew exactly how she would do it.

*　*　*

The next morning, Bill sat at the kitchen table drinking his coffee. He was finally alone as his unwanted guests had left. He heard a vehicle drive in, but he didn't get up until he heard the knock on the door.

"Bill!" Nick said angrily. "Why haven't you returned the calls? Don't you care at all for your family or what is wrong with you? I truly believed you once loved your wife, but now I'm not sure any more." Nick said angrily.

"What calls?" Bill asked.

"Don't act stupid to me. If I were a fighting man I would hit you. Then to top it all off, you have a lot of nerve telling that woman that Dawn's baby was mine. That is as low as you can get. If it were mine, I would be with Dawn and the baby now, praying it would live." Nick said his face full of furry.

"Nick, shut up!! Where is Dawn? What happened?" Bill demanded.

"Are you trying to tell me you really don't know?" Nick said surprised.

When Nick told Bill what had happened, he instantly knew that Janice had deliberately not given him the message.

Bill never bothered to change clothes, but ran to his truck and drove directly to the hospital in Red Deer. What a fool he had been. He was not there for Dawn when their son was born, because he had stupidly let himself be deceived by the one woman he had thought he would never trust in his life again. He had already lost precious time and if things were was as bad as Nick said, he may not get to see his son at all.

Bill arrived at the hospital to be greeted by a very angry daughter. Kevin intervened by quickly pushing Lisa aside before telling Bill where he could find Dawn.

Dawn was pale and very weak. Bill was astounded at how frail she was. "Dawn!"

Will Love Conquer All?

He said taking her hand in his. Dawn slowly turned to look at him. A tear ran down her face, but she said nothing.

"I'm sorry Dawn, can you ever forgive me? I have been such a fool." Bill said pleading with her.

Dawn just lay there studying his face. How he had changed in just a short while.

"I didn't know until Nick came over. I tried to call you the other morning, but you must have been in here. I'm so sorry that I wasn't here for you." He said, bending over to kiss her. Dawn did not return his kiss. He had hurt her deeply, by not calling her once since she left.

Dawn turned away as tears ran down her face. He had not told her if Janice had left.

She could not face him until then.

"I am going to see our son but I will be back shortly." Bill said.

Bill found a nurse and asked if he could see his son. She pointed to the tiny infant lying in the incubator. It hurt to see his child lying there with tubes all over. He stood there for sometime amazed at how small he was compared to his other children. "May I touch him?" He asked the nurse. "You will have to discuss that with your doctor. But - -" She said looking at his not so clean work clothes, which he understood.

When Bill went in search of the doctor, he was told that he wouldn't be in again until that evening.

Bill slowly walked back to Dawn's room. He sat quietly on the chair beside Dawn's bed. Bill thought Dawn was sleeping, and did not want to disturb her. He didn't realize that Dawn just did not want to acknowledge that he was there. Someone touched Bill on the shoulder and by the smell of the perfume, he knew instantly who it was. Bill turned and pushed Janice out of the room and closed the door.

"What are you doing here?" He said furious with Janice for showing up here, after what she had done. "How dare you not tell me Dawn was in the hospital?"

Dawn lay there staining to hear what was being said.

Book 1 of the *Mountains and Valleys of Life*

"I'm sorry Bill it just slipped my mind. I was upset when you asked me to leave. Please don't be angry." Janice said in her sweetest voice.

"Don't bother trying to butter me up. I want you out of here and I don't want to see you or your son around my family ever again. Do you hear me?" He said grabbing her arm.

"Your hurting me, I just wanted to apologize to Dawn." She said trying to make a move towards the door.

"Don't bother. I don't want you spreading any more of your lies. Haven't you caused enough trouble yet?" He said blocking her way.

"Maybe you should have a blood test done to see whose baby this really is. What makes you think it isn't Nick's?" Janice said angrily.

"I don't need to, because I know he is my son. I trust Dawn. No one can trust you. That's the difference between you and Dawn. I wouldn't blame her if she never forgave me for letting you ruin our lives. Now I suggest very strongly that you leave. I would say if your husband didn't divorce you, he would be an idiot. I'm sure he can't wait until your gone. Maybe I should call him and let him know what your up to." Bill said absolutely furious for being such a fool as to fall for her lies again.

"You wouldn't dare?" She snapped before storming off.

Bill stood there shaking with anger. He tried to calm down before going back into Dawn's room. Bill quietly went over and sat down on the chair beside Dawn's bed, then cupping his head in his hands. *Please God let Dawn forgive me, and give strength to our son that we may bring him home soon.* Bill prayed.

"Bill." Dawn said softly. Bill looked up to see Dawn's outstretched hand. He took her hand in his and gently wiped away a tear that rolled down Dawn's cheek.

"I love you Dawn. Will you please forgive me?" Bill asked

Dawn squeezed his hand. "I have never doubted that, and yes Bill, you know I will forgive you. I love you and have missed you more than you know." Dawn said.

Will Love Conquer All?

Bill bent over and kissed her. "I don't think our children are going to forgive me as easy as you did." Bill said sadly.

"Don't worry about Darcy and Lisa. I will talk to them and they'll get over it in time." Dawn said touching the side of her husbands face. "Have they let you hold our son?" She asked.

"No" Bill replied. "I talked to the nurse and she said I would have to talk to the doctor. I know by the look she gave me, they wouldn't let me near him with these clothes on." Bill said. "I left immediately after Nick told me and I didn't take anything with me. I think I will have to buy some new clothes, and have a shower. After that we will see about holding our son." Bill said.

"Do you have a key for the house?" Dawn asked

"Yes, and I'll be back as soon as I get cleaned up." Bill said kissing Dawn on the forehead.

Lisa looked at her Father when he came into the waiting room. Kevin had held her back, telling her to wait, until her parents had a chance to talk. She was now wondering what had happened.

"I'm going to get some clean clothes and have a shower. I'll be back later."

Bill said going to his daughter who stood by the door. "I am sorry Lisa." He said giving her a hug. I love you, and I hope you can forgive me, as your Mother has." With that he left.

Lisa looked at Kevin. "How could she forgive him so quickly after what he did?" Lisa asked.

Kevin got off his chair and stood in front of her. He placed his hands on her shoulders and said. "Lisa, think for a moment. Just put your self in your parents place. Say I was your Dad and you were your Mom, and we loved each other more than anything." He said looking into her eyes.

Lisa felt uncomfortable and tried not to look at him, but she couldn't bring herself to look away.

"Then one of my old friends showed up, telling me I had a son. Would you want me to get to know him? Or would you tell me to not have anything to do with him, and have me possibly become bitter and eventually have it ruin our marriage." Kevin asked.

"You wouldn't have to let his Mother move in." Lisa snapped back.

"No, but what if she pushed her way in, making him feel guilty because of the past. Perhaps it actually made sense that she would help when your Mother wasn't feeling well." Kevin said.

"He still should have known better. He must have seen through her years ago, or he would have married her then." She said their eyes still locked on each other.

"Think Lisa. We all have a weakness in us. We may know better but then we let someone over power us. In the long run, we get hurt and so do others, but it isn't intentional. And don't forget Men think differently than women do." Kevin said.

Lisa looked at him for a moment and then pushed his arms away from her.

She was now very angry with him. "You don't have to throw it in my face. You think I haven't blamed myself for putting Mom in here." Lisa said turning away with tears running down her checks.

Kevin grabbed her and swung her around to face him. "That wasn't what I meant." he said sharply. "It's not your fault that this happened. Do you hear me? I'm trying to tell you that no one is perfect. We all have our faults and if two people love each other as your parents do, how can you stand in their way because of a momentary weakness that we all have. If your Mother forgave him, and God has forgiven him, why can't you?"

"Leave me alone." Lisa said going to sit on the corner chair.

"I wish I could." Kevin said quietly to himself.

Lisa heard what he said and wondered what he meant by that.

Darcy and Jackie arrived, walking in hand in hand looking very happy. But the moment Jackie looked at Lisa and Kevin she knew something was wrong.

"Did something happen to the baby?" She asked looking

Will Love Conquer All?

at Kevin.

"No, everything's still the same." Kevin said sitting as far from Lisa as possible.

"What happened?" Darcy asked. "By the looks of you two something is going on."

"Dad was just here." Lisa said. "Of course Kevin is sticking up for him now."

"Lisa! That is not what I said and by talking like that, is what starts problems. I said, if your Mother forgave him, you could too." Kevin said as their eyes met again.

He knew right now, he was not Lisa's favourite person.

"Lisa, Kevin's right. Jackie made me understand both sides, and I am happy that Mom and Dad are back together. Would you rather Mom stay mad at him and they get a divorce?" Darcy asked Lisa.

"Don't talk so stupid. You know that isn't what I would want." Lisa said sulking in her corner.

"We're going to see Mom now, but we will have to get back to Calgary today. We both have to work tomorrow, so we can't stay long." Darcy said.

"Where are you going to live and still keep your secret?" Lisa asked.

"Well." Jackie said. "Both of us have to give a months notice anyway, so we'll keep both places until then. Darcy will be on the road most of the time and when he gets back, we'll have our calls forwarded to where ever we are. We will then move into our new place, which we hope to find." Jackie said looking at Darcy with a twinkle in her eye. "Now that things are slowly coming together here again, we hope they soon will with Dad and Marie too. Then we can tell everyone. But until then we want secrecy from you two." Jackie said

Darcy and Jackie left the room, leaving a strained atmosphere behind them.

Darcy knocked on his Mothers door before they walked in, hand in hand.

"Hi, Mrs. Spencer. You are looking much better today." Jackie said noticing a much more relax Dawn.

"Yea Mom, you do look different." Darcy said.

"I'm somewhat better. Your Father was here a bit ago. You've just missed him." Dawn said with a slight smile.

"Darcy, I don't want you and Lisa to turn against your Father. He did what he felt he had to do, and now it's over."

"He loves his children very much and has been deceived which has also bruised his ego. Please don't make it worse." Dawn said.

"You mean Larry was not his son?" Darcy asked.

"No, from what I understand, he isn't but he hasn't told me directly. He will in his own time. Your Father is a wonderful person and don't ever forget that." Dawn said looking at her son.

"Yes Mom I know. Jackie made me understand that we all have our weaknesses, but Lisa may be harder to convince." Darcy told her.

Dawn looked at Darcy then Jackie, studying their faces. "Do you two have something to tell me?" Dawn asked.

"Why do you say that?" Darcy asked.

"You two look too happy, something is going on." Dawn said very curious.

"We just decided we liked to be with each other." Darcy said looking at his beautiful wife.

"What Darcy is saying Mrs. Spencer is, we have fallen in love with each other."

Jackie said, as Darcy put his arm around her.

"Oh that is wonderful news, but Darcy is very head strong." Dawn said.

"I have noticed that, but I think we will work on that. How is the baby today?" Jackie asked.

"There is still no change, but he is a fighter like the rest of them. All we can do is pray." Dawn said as tears filled her eyes.

"You better get your strength back too Mom. Because if he's like the rest of us you will need it when you take him home." Darcy said trying to cheer her up. "We really would like to stay longer, but we both have to work tomorrow. Now that Dad is here I feel better." Darcy said kissing his Mother on the forehead.

"We will be praying too." Jackie said, kissing her now Mother-in-law. "We'll keep in touch." Jackie said and at that they left Dawn, with a renewed happiness.

Bill had come back to her and Darcy had fallen in love with a sweet girl. Her thoughts went to the look Nick had given her at Christmas. She knew he would be pleased, but that was soon over shadowed at the thought of Nick and Marie. If only she could talk to Marie.

But she may not believe her because Janice told Marie that it was Dawn who had told Bill, that ugly lie. So the only logical person to talk to Marie would be, Bill. She may listen to him.

It hurt Dawn very much to be mistrusted by her friend. Dawn was sure Marie was feeling terribly betrayed right now. She just had to persuade Bill to call her as soon as possible, to straighten this all out.

When Kevin and Lisa came into the room, Dawn instantly could feel the tension that was between them. Kevin was the first to speak. "Mrs. Spencer, I would like to thank you for letting me stay over, but I must be getting back home. I have to work in the morning. I'm really sorry for what happened, it was my fault for not stepping in sooner." Kevin said.

"It wasn't your fault. It was mine." She said as tears filled her eyes.

"Lisa, it was no ones fault, but I do want to sit down sometime soon and find out what has been going on in your life. I'm a bit concerned to what has been happening." Dawn said, taking her daughters hand.

"Darcy mentioned that you would be harder to convince, when it came to forgiving your Father. I'm telling you now, that I will not stand for any disrespect towards your Father. He loves us all very much, and you better know that. He has gone through enough, and I don't want something happening to him because he is fretting over you not forgiving him." Dawn said.

"None of us are perfect. We all have our weaknesses, but if we can't forgive each other how can we expect God to forgive us."

Lisa listened to her Mother's stern lecture somewhat embarrassed at Kevin's being there to hear it. "I'm sorry Mom. I promise I will try." Lisa said.

"Now are you staying longer, or do you have to go back too?" Dawn asked Lisa.

"I should be getting back. I guess I'll take the bus." Lisa said not wanting to go back with Kevin.

"I'm sure Kevin would take you back. You will both have to go to the house to pick up your things." Dawn said wondering why her daughter was so bitter.

"Yes she is welcome to come with me. That is if she wants to?" Kevin said glancing at Lisa from the corner of his eye.

"All right. I suppose it is cheaper than taking a bus." Lisa said.

"That is if I don't expect you to pay your share." Kevin said teasing her.

"Then I will take the bus." Lisa snapped back only to have him wink at her.

"Lisa, what has come over you?" Dawn said sternly. "You know he was only teasing you."

"He's being a pain." Lisa said.

"We really have to be going." Kevin told them. "Will you be all right now Mrs.Spencer?" He asked.

"I am fine. Bill will be back shortly, so you two run along, and try to be friends." Dawn said.

"Don't worry, she can't stay mad at me for long, because she actually likes me." Kevin said teasing her.

"In your dreams. Lisa said before kissing her Mother goodbye.

Dawn was worried about her daughter. She wondered if Lisa was falling in love with Kevin but for some reason, she was fighting it for fear of getting hurt again. Dawn was worried that Lisa could miss out on the best thing in life and that is love.

***

Will Love Conquer All?

Dawn woke up to a gentle kiss. She opened her eyes realizing that she was not dreaming, but Bill was actually with her again. Dawn put her arms around his neck, pulling him down to her as he wrapped his arms around her.

"Oh Bill, you don't know how I have missed you holding me." Dawn said.

"I've missed you too. Don't ever leave me again." Bill said.

"You know I didn't leave you because I wanted to Bill. I just didn't have the strength to keep ahead of Janice. I felt our baby deserved a chance, but maybe I was wrong and should have been there for you." Dawn said. Bill moved the chair closer to the side of the bed.

"No, I don't blame you. You did what you felt you had to. I should have known Janice was not to be trusted. You we're right, Larry was not my son. Do you understand that if he was, I couldn't have turned my back on him?" Bill said.

"I wouldn't want you to, but with what I saw, I couldn't believe a son of yours would be so cruel and callous." Dawn told him. "Why did she do this?" Dawn asked.

"Why does Janice do anything, but what I don't understand is how she can ruin her sons life by playing her stupid games." Bill said. "Well, they are out of our lives forever. We have another son and if you're up to it, I would like you to come with me to see him?" Bill said.

"Oh Bill, do you think they will let me hold him?" Dawn asked.

"Just for a very short time." Bill said, helping Dawn out of bed.

When Dawn slipped on her housecoat and slippers, she was still feeling weak.

She walked very slowly. Bill offered to get her a wheel chair, which she declined.

"I have to get some of my strength back and lying in bed or being wheeled around won't do it for me."

Bill and Dawn stood looking in the window, when the nurse waved them in. "You can sit on the chair beside him." The nurse told Dawn upon entering the room.

Carefully the nurse took their baby out of the incubator and placed him in Dawn's arms. Dawn's heart ached, as she looked at all the tubes he was hooked up to. She held him close while Bill wiped tears from his eyes. He gently stroked his son's head with his finger. Bill put his finger in his son's tiny hand, only to have him instantly grip it. It was then, Bill knew God would not take this child from them. Dawn sat rocking him, wishing she could hold him longer, but the nurse said it was time to put him back into the incubator. Bill and Dawn kissed their son, before handing him back to the nurse.

When Dawn returned to her room, she decided to sit in a chair. "Bill I have a favour to ask of you." She said.

"If I can, you know I will do it." Bill said.

"I don't know if you know what Janice has all done. Apparently she told Marie, that I told you, this was not our son, but that Nick was the Father. You know that isn't true." Dawn said looking at him.

"Yes I know." Bill said.

"That is when Marie called off the wedding. She apparently believed her." Dawn said sadly. "Bill, you are the only one she may listen to. I hate for her to be deceived like that."

"I'm sure her and Nick cared for each other and this could ruin both their lives." Dawn told him.

"I'll call her when I get back to the house. It isn't just her I have to apologize to, but Nick also. Because of what I did in the past, it has caused problems in our life as well as others." Bill said sadly.

"It could have been worse Bill. We were truthful with each other from the beginning, and I knew there could be a possibility of that happening. But now it's over and we can get on with the rest of our lives." Dawn said.

"Where did Darcy and Lisa go?" Bill asked.

"They all had to go home." Darcy had to work tomorrow, and Lisa has school, but I'm very concerned about Lisa. Something must have happened and I have a feeling it has to do with Franklin. He has a violent temper." Dawn said.

"What happened that they rushed you into the hospital?" Bill asked.

Dawn told him what happened the morning Franklin showed up. Bill was not happy with Franklin, when Dawn told him what she suspected. Bill made up his mind to call the police and find out what they had done with him.

"Bill," Dawn said, "Have you thought of a name for our son?"

"No I don't suppose I have. Anything but the same name, as his Father. What would you like to call him?" Bill asked looking at his wife. How he longed to take her and his little son home.

"Oh Bill I think it would be nice to call him Billy." Dawn said.

"No!" Bill said. Dawn knew he would not go for that idea. She had tried it with the other boys, but in her heart she wished he would allow it.

"Well then, what about Jeffrey William Spencer?" Dawn said.

Bill sat silent running the name over in his mind. "That I agree to." Bill said.

"Ok, so we will agree to call him Jeffrey then." She said.

Dawn then asked Bill what he had been doing in his shop. He told her that his production hadn't been going to well since she left.

This was what they both missed. It was being together and discussing things, but soon visiting hours would be up. Bill told Dawn to get some rest and he assured her, that he would call Marie when he got back to the house.

***

Bill sat in what was now their house. An inheritance that Dawn's parents had given them. He wondered what they would have said and done, if they were still here. Especially with what had just gone on in his life. Would they have still trusted him or would they have changed their will. He remembered how they had mentioned the love and trust that was between him and Dawn. Bill began to realize that Dawn was actually the most trusting. She had to be strong to have left as she had. He would always respect and listen to her opinion more, from now on. If they disagreed, they would have to sit down and talk it over. Why had he allowed Janice to move in without considering Dawn's feelings? After all, he thought suddenly, how would he have liked it if Nick just moved in and took over as Janice had? What a fool he had been. Bill thought of how Marie had helped Dawn, and became a dear friend to both of them. He had to admit that Nick wasn't such a bad person after all. He must work on overcoming his jealousy. After all Dawn had picked him over Nick and he knew only to well what it felt like when someone rejects you. Bill was thankful that Janice had turned him down years ago. He was sure his life would have been sheer hell married to her. As for Nick's rejection it was by a very special person, who had to hurt deeply. It couldn't have been easy for Nick to have her move into his old home. The least Bill could do was to help him regain his new love Marie, Bill thought while picking up the phone and dialing her number.

"Hello Marie, this is Bill." He said when she answered the phone. "I called to apologize for everything that has happened in the last while."

"Bill it isn't your fault. I'm just sorry things turned out bad for you too." Marie said, sounding very distant.

"No, Marie you don't understand, everything is wonderful between me and Dawn. I have never loved her more and we have a baby boy." Bill said proudly.

Marie was silent not knowing what to say.

"Marie are you still there?" Bill asked.

"Yes, I'm still here." Marie answered not able to figure out why he would be happy about Dawn's baby and why did he call it his son.

"Marie I understand that Janice told you that Dawn was having Nick's baby. That was a lie. Dawn never told me that and I sure never told such a thing to Janice. I'm sorry for letting her

Will Love Conquer All?

move in and ruin everyone's lives. Especially when she also lied about Larry being my son." Bill said now feeling foolish.

"You mean that wasn't true either?" Marie said sounding more like her old self.

"No, I had a test done in the hospital when he cut himself, and we are definitely not a match." Bill said.

"Oh I am so sorry. How are Dawn and the baby? Isn't it a bit early for her to have had him?" Marie said.

Bill told Marie the whole story and then finishing with, "Dawn really misses you. She hopes you and Nick can clear this up, and still go on with your wedding plans."

"Oh I don't think he'll forgive me for what I said to him, and especially for not believing him." Marie said with a quiver in her voice.

"I'll talk to him. After all, I too need to ask both you and Nick to forgive me for everything." Bill said apologetically.

"Bill it wasn't you. Janice is a wicked woman, but if it makes you feel better, I forgive you. That is if you still let Nick and I get married in your backyard, if he still wants me."

Marie said trailing off the last few words.

"It's a deal now I have to give Nick a call, I'm truly sorry." He said hanging up the phone.

Bill called and talked to Nick for some time apologizing and asking forgiveness for letting Janice ruin everyone's life. He told Nick of his promise to Marie about still allowing them to have their wedding in their backyard and hoped it would still take place. He said Dawn would love to have Nick and Marie visit. After all, they would be proud to show off their new son. He especially thanked Nick for coming over to tell him about Marie.

He really didn't know. Nick also apologized for threatening to hit Bill, but Bill's reply was that he didn't blame him. He would have actually done it, if the role were reversed.

Bill was relieved knowing things were getting back to normal. It hit him hard to think what he could have lost.

The next afternoon Bill walked into Dawn's room with a

large bouquet of red roses, mingling with white baby breath.

"Oh! Bill they are beautiful." Dawn said.

"How are you feeling today?" Bill asked, watching as Dawn set the flowers on the windowsill.

"I'm fine. Just a bit tired, otherwise I can't wait to go home." Dawn said.

"Have you talked to the doctor today?" Bill asked.

"Yes." Dawn said, going to give Bill a hug. "He was in this morning. He is quite surprised, and please at how well Jeffrey is doing, but we probably won't be able to take him home for at least two weeks, or until he gains enough weight. That is, hoping no complications creep up." Dawn said, still very worried. Dawn laid her head against Bill's chest while he held her in his arms.

"How long before you can go?" Bill asked.

"I told the doctor that we would be staying in Red Deer for a while, so he may allow me to go out tomorrow or the next day." Dawn said. "We can come visit our son anytime we want."

"It will be good to take you both home." Bill said.

"What will you do with yourself, while you are here?" Dawn asked.

"I thought it might be a good time to go through some of your Father's things downstairs, as well as the things in the garage. It has to be done sometime." Bill said.

"Yes, I also thought of going through some things while I was here, but I haven't yet. Perhaps this is the right time to do it." Dawn said agreeing with him.

"Yes, we have left everything the way it was, but I believe this would be a good time to start. We have to decide what to do with the house, because we can't leave it empty forever. The insurance companies may give us a problem if something happens to it." Bill said.

"You mean sell it?" Dawn asked. "I can't do that." She said.

"No, I don't mean that. Not right now anyways. Perhaps we could rent it out or have someone house sit for awhile until we decide what to do. Either way, we have to clear out what ever is important, as well as the non essential things like clothes and other miscellaneous things." Bill said.

"We can slowly work at it together." he told her. Bill covered Dawn with a blanket when she went to lie down on her bed.

"I know your right, but it won't be easy." Dawn sadly.

"Why don't you ask Lisa to come down on a weekend? She may be able to help you go through your Mother's things." Bill said.

"That's probably what I should do, because I can't do it alone. That way I can give her some things. Dawn said, somewhat more at ease at the thought of not doing it alone.

***

Dawn went home two days later, and for the next week all she did was rest or go to the hospital to see Jeffrey. She slowly began to feel like her old self, as her strength began to return. She called Lisa one evening and asked if she would come and help her, which she did. Between the three of them, they managed to sort through a fair amount of things. Lisa told her Mother she would prefer to leave her items here for now, because she hoped to be leaving Edmonton in about a month. So after packing them, they stored her things in a corner of the basement. During the course of the day, Dawn tried to bring up the subject of Franklin, but Lisa avoided it so Dawn did not pursue it.

Bill went through Dawn's Father's things. He packed up several items to give to Darcy. Then in the later part of the afternoon, which was now part of their schedule, they went to be with their son.

When Jeffrey was ten days old, the doctors finally told Bill and Dawn that he was doing very well. He told them that if Jeffery continued to improve as he had, they should be able to take him home the following week. The doctor did tell them it was best that they stayed in town for a few days after his release, just to be safe. Dawn and Bill were at least able to feed him, and hold him for longer periods of time each day, but they looked forward to the day they could take him home.

Bill had asked Nick if he would check on their place and Pup occasionally, while they were gone. He also made arrangements for Marie to clean up the house so it would be clean when Dawn got home.

He asked Marie if she would make sure that there would not be a trace of anything that would indicate that Janice and Larry had ever been in the house.

The day finally arrived that they could go back to their own home. Dawn was looking forward to placing Jeffrey into the cradle that his Father had made for him. They had accomplished the sorting out of her parent's things, but the furniture would stay as it was for now. They were bringing home their newborn son, who was doing fine and gaining weight. But most importantly Bill and Dawn were together again. Love does conquer all, she thought remembering what Bill had once told her.

Chapter 19

Kevin had spent the past several days in Red Deer, trying to find a proper place to rent, yet still with in his means. He would be starting his new job tomorrow, which meant today was his last day to find a place to live. Kevin was beginning to get desperate.

He began to wonder if Bill and Dawn would let him stay in their house until he could find a place. It had been a month since the incident with Franklin that almost caused Dawn to lose her child. He did hear that Mother and baby were doing fine and were now back home.

Kevin found a phone and dialed their number. He would be ever so grateful if they would allow him to stay there for now.

"Hello Mrs. Spencer. This is Kevin Helmsley. How are you and the baby doing?"

"Hi Kevin. I'm doing fine, and the baby has grown since you saw him last. How have things been for you? Are you still in Edmonton?"

"I'm fine, thank you." Kevin said.

"Marie said you may be getting a better job, is that right?" Dawn asked.

"Yes, that's what I am calling about. I'm moving to Red Deer, and I haven't had a lot of time to find a place to live. I was wondering if I could stay in the basement of your house here in Red Deer?" Then he quickly added. "Only temporarily, until I can find something."

Dawn hesitated. "If you can wait a moment, I will discuss it with Bill. He just came in from outside."

Kevin waited, nervously. He hesitated to ask, but he was getting desperate to find somewhere to stay.

"Kevin, we'll agree, if you promise not to have any parties and keep the house clean." "We aren't saying you can't have a few friends visit, but you understand what we mean." Dawn said.

"Yes, Mrs. Spencer, and I will pay you for the time I am there. I don't expect to stay there for nothing." Kevin told her.

"We'll discuss that later. I will notify the neighbours that you will be staying there and you can get a key from them." Dawn said.

"Thanks Mrs. Spencer. This really gets me out of a jam." Kevin said.

"Have you talked to Lisa lately?" Dawn asked.

"No, I think she's still mad at me because of something I said to her at the hospital, a few weeks back." Kevin replied.

"Kevin, I have to go. The baby is crying." Dawn said.

"Sounds like he has a good set of lungs." Kevin said hearing the baby in the background. "Thanks a lot for letting me stay there. I will look after it." Kevin said hanging up the phone.

Kevin had already put his furniture in storage until he found a place. This would now give him time to find the appropriate apartment so he would not have to move twice.

He disliked moving. It was just that a week had past and he was still no farther in finding a place he could afford.

Kevin went to pick up the key. He had met the people next door briefly, when he was there a month ago. They seemed to be very nice people.

* * *

Later that evening, Kevin came from the bathroom, glad to finally have a place to relax. It was then he heard on the television, that someone had escaped from custody. Whoever it was, had been charged with assault, and was considered dangerous, but Kevin had missed the name. His mind flashed back to Franklin and what he had done to Lisa. It was because of Franklin that the Spencer's almost lost their infant son. It made his blood boil when he thought of it, but thankfully Franklin would be locked up for some time. He suddenly had a terrible thought, and wished he had heard the name of the man who had escaped. But then there were a lot of guys like Franklin in the country. Kevin said to himself. He picked up the phone to call Lisa, but put it back not wanting to worry her unnecessarily.

Kevin turned off the television and tried to sleep, but he could not get Lisa out of his mind. He could still see her standing beside Jackie, when he entered her apartment, the day of the wedding.

He was reminded of how beautiful she looked, with that dark green dress and her blond hair swept of to one side. Lisa was not as tall as Jackie, and did have a temper, but she was all in all a very nice person. She distrusted men, even losing faith in her Father, but he remembered how long it took Jackie to even talk to a man after she had gotten out of her bad relationship. Kevin was afraid for Lisa. Franklin was dangerous and there was no telling what he would try when he got out of jail.

Kevin had just fallen asleep, when he was abruptly awakened by a noise. He presumed that it was a firecracker, or the backfire of a car. He had just rolled over and was about to go back to sleep, when he heard something upstairs.

Kevin slowly and quietly got out of bed. He crept softly up the stairs, but not before grabbing a 2" dowel that had been standing in the corner of his room. He slowly crept quietly through the kitchen. Then carefully he looked around the corner into the living room. He could now see the front door, but quickly ducked back when he saw someone walk past the front window. The drapes were mostly closed except for three feet of shear, which allowed some light in. The Patio door curtains, on the opposite end of the room were thankfully closed. He heard someone moaning, and realized that someone actually was in the house.

Kevin bent down low. Slowly and carefully he took another peak around the corner. This time he saw someone lying on the floor. He raised the dowel he held in his hand then he saw the blond hair as this person got to her knees. It was Lisa.

He was about to go to her, when he saw someone by the window. He quickly in a loud whisper said. "Get down Lisa!!"

Lisa was shocked, to hear someone was in the house. Fear gripped her heart as she instantly dropped to the floor at his command. Had Franklin gotten in the house? She wondered. But it couldn't have been him. Who was in here? She said to herself while lying there frozen to the floor. She heard someone trying to get in the door behind her, but was glad she had quickly locked it, before she fell to the floor. She began to wonder what had hit her, when she opened the door. She did remember hearing a noise and at the same time feeling like someone had hit her shoulder, but she was too afraid, to check what it was. Her only thought had been to get safely into the house and lock the door.

But who was in here with her? Because she was confident that Franklin was still outside.

"Lisa is that you? This is Kevin"

"Kevin!!" She called in surprise.

"Quiet! Someone's outside by the window." Kevin said.

"It's Franklin." Lisa said, rubbing her shoulder, which now began to ache.

Something felt wet under her jacket, but she just wiped her hand on her sleeve not thinking any more about it. Kevin crawled along the floor, on his belly until he got to her side. "Are you all right?" he asked.

"I think so," she said beginning to feel very strange.

Stay low, and lets get to an area where there are no windows." Kevin said helping her along, as they crept into the hallway. They could not be seen there. "Stay here." He said, crawling into the kitchen. Kevin cautiously reached up and grabbed the phone to dial 911. He quietly told the person at the other end of their situation, as well as telling them who he suspected was outside and why. After a moment he was told the police would be there shortly.

Kevin crept back to Lisa's side, still holding the 2' dowel in his hand. He was ready to use it if he had to.

"Kevin, I don't feel very good. I feel like I may past out." Lisa said leaning heavily against him.

"Hang in there sweetheart, I'll keep you safe." He said, putting his arm around her. His first thought was that she was really scared, but then he felt something wet on her back.

It was then he saw a dark substance on his hand and the moment he smelled it, he instantly knew what it was. He gently laid Lisa on the floor, kissing her forehead and wishing the police would hurry and get there. "Lisa honey, hang in there I will be right back." Kevin said.

Lisa grabbed his arm. "Please, don't leave me." she pleaded.

"Baby I will never leave you again. But I have one more phone call to make. Then I promise to stay by your side." He said gently wiping her hair from her eyes.

Kevin crept quickly back to the phone to again dial 911. This time telling them he was also requesting an ambulance. He said that he was sure his friend had been shot and she had already lost a lot of blood. He said he didn't want to risk putting the light on yet to see how bad she was hurt.

It was then he heard the breaking of glass. Kevin dropped the phone and dove to the hallway, where Lisa lay now unconscious. "I will kill him if you die." Kevin said quietly. Then he heard the police yelling outside for Franklin to give up. Then he heard someone run along the side of the house, followed by the sound of squealing tires and police sirens. Franklin had obviously gotten away, but the police were in hot pursuit.

Kevin sat stroking Lisa's hair, telling her to hang in there. He would never let anyone harm her again. Then there was a knock at the door and he heard. "Police!"

Kevin quickly got up and switching on a light when he

went to open the door. The officer saw the blood on Kevin and instantly asked if he was all right.

"It's not me it's my friend." He said rushing back to Lisa, who's coat was now soaked in blood. The officer bent down to check Lisa's pulse as the paramedics came through the front door.

Kevin kneeling by Lisa's side said. "I want to go with her. Son, they have to go immediately, and look at yourself. You have to get dressed first." The police officer told him. "You go get cleaned up and dressed. Then I'll take you to the hospital myself. You can give me your statement there." The officer said.

Kevin knew he was right, but he had promised not to leave Lisa. He already felt like he was letting her down.

"Son she won't know you aren't with her right now." The officer said putting his arm on Kevin's shoulder. "Go get cleaned up." He ordered yet sympathetic to Kevin's plight.

Kevin scrubbed the blood from his hands, and quickly got dressed. He wanted to get to the hospital as soon as possible, and was thankful the police officer was true to his word. Lisa was already in surgery when they arrived, so Kevin sat in a small room telling the officer what had happened at the house.

"Where are her parents?" The police officer asked. Kevin groaned and grabbed his head. "I think you better notify them, she is in critical condition. I'm sure they would want to be here with her now," he added.

Kevin agreed to call immediately, after the police officer left. Kevin thought for a moment before going to a phone and dialing his Father's number. Kevin was beginning to think his Dad would never answer, but when he finally heard the sleepy voice of his Father, Kevin said. "Dad this is Kevin wake up this in an emergency."

At that Nick was wide-awake. "What's wrong, are you hurt?"

"No, but I want you to go get Marie and get over to the Spencer's fast. Lisa has been shot and is in surgery. I think it's bad. They should get here as soon as possible. Be sure to tell them she's in the Red Deer hospital. You and Marie will have to babysit, because I don't think they will want to bring the baby." Kevin said before hanging up the phone.

Nick quickly dialed Marie telling her to get dressed fast and meet him at Bill and Dawn's. He told her Lisa had been hurt and Dawn would need someone to look after the baby while they went to the hospital.

Nick was shaking as he drove into Bill and Dawn's yard. He hated being the bearer of bad news once again and wasn't sure how to brake this to them. He quickly knocked on their door. He heard Pups growl coming from inside, but when he called her name, she was silent. He knocked again then finally a sleepy Bill opened the door.

"What are you doing here this time of night?" Bill said looking at his watch. It was almost 3 a.m. Dawn, tying the belt of her housecoat, came into the kitchen to see what all the commotion was about.

"Nick is something wrong?" Dawn asked.

"Both of you sit down." He said, nervously. He saw the worried glance that passed from Dawn to Bill.

"It's Lisa." Nick started slowly not knowing how much to say. "Kevin just phoned, she is in the Red Deer hospital." Nick said.

"Red Deer?" Dawn asked in surprise.

"Yes, Red Deer, and she's hurt quite bad. Kevin said he thought you should get there as soon as possible." Nick added.

"But how can I go with the baby." She said looking at Bill.

"That's where I come in." Marie said after entering the house unnoticed. "Nick will help me. You just get ready and go and give her our best." Marie said giving Dawn a hug.

Bill and Dawn got ready as quick as possible. Then after giving some brief instructions they were gone, leaving Nick and Marie standing there looking at each other.

Marie went to the cupboard and asked if Nick would like a cup of coffee. A month had past since Bill called to apologize and told her the lies Janice was spreading.

But neither her or Nick had make a move to rekindle their

relationship.

Marie sat across from Nick while waiting for the coffee. "Nick I'm sorry for saying what I did about you and Dawn. Can you ever forgive me?" Marie asked.

Nick sat looking at her in silence. "I guess I was really always jealous of you and Dawn's friendship. I know you still have feelings for her." Marie said, looking away from his gaze.

Nick sat there in silence, which began to make Marie feel very uncomfortable. She wondered why he didn't answer her. When the coffee was ready, Marie filled their cups, not knowing what to do or say next.

"You know." Nick said, when their eyes met. "Dawn once told me it wasn't really the same love I felt for her as what I felt for my wife and you. But it was wanting something I couldn't have, or something like that." he said. "I'm beginning to understand what she meant. I really do like Dawn. She will always be a special friend of mine, but after you said what you did, and called off the wedding it cut deep. It was then I realized how much I really did care for you." Nick said.

"I'm sorry Nick." Marie said, tears filling her eyes. "I love you very much and after Janice told me those lies I went to pieces. I guess I wasn't thinking straight. I should have known Dawn would never betray Bill and - -"

"You should have known I would never hurt you that way." Nick said. "We have to trust each other, if we want to make a life together." Then the baby began to cry.

They both got up and went to check on Jeffery. When Marie picked him up and held him in her arms, she instantly had an uneasy feeling. "Oh Nick I haven't had a lot of experience with babies."

"There is nothing to it, you feed them and burp them and change them. You'll do fine, I'll help you." Nick said.

They took the baby into the kitchen, where Marie handed Jeffery to Nick while she warmed up the bottle. She watched Nick play with Jeffery. It came natural to him, but she had never had a lot to do with babies. She had often wondered what it would be like to have one.

Nick handed Marie the baby, then took the bottle and dropped a few drops on his wrist. "You have to check to be sure it isn't too warm." Nick said to Marie.

"This is all so new to me." Marie said.

"You're doing fine. After all, you will have to learn sometime." Nick told her.

Marie looked up at him wondering what he had meant by that.

"Well," he said. Wouldn't you like to have a child of your own someday?"

Marie looked at the baby in her arms. She had never felt this way before. She gently rocked him, while he drank his bottle. "It does feel good." She said.

"It's even better when it's your own." Nick said as their eyes met.

"We never talked about it, but would you like to have a baby?" Nick asked.

Marie blushed, and looked down at Jeffrey's tiny hands. He gripped her finger, when she put hers in his tiny hand. A smile lit up her face. After Jeffery drank part of his bottle, Nick showed Marie how to burp him. After the bottle was empty, then came the diaper change. "Not my favourite part." Nick had to admit.

Marie was a natural, and soon Jeffery was back in his cradle. They stood side by side watching Jeffery while Marie rocked him to sleep.

Marie turned and went into the living room and sat on the couch. Nick stood a moment longer looking at the baby before joining Marie.

"Marie." Nick said taking her hand. "Will you marry me?"

Marie's eyes lit up when she looked at his face. "Yes Nick, I will marry you."

"This time will you trust me that I will never do anything that will intentionally hurt you?" Nick said.

"Oh Nick," she said. "I am so sorry for not trusting you."

"Now will you answer my other question that you didn't before?" Nick asked.

"What was that?" she asked

"The one about the baby." Nick said.

Marie looked deep into his eyes. "Yes Nick, I think it would be the best gift we could give to each other. I would be proud to have your baby." Marie said.

"Will you kiss me to seal that?" He said teasing her, before taking her in his arms, kissing her like he had never done before.

They began discussing their wedding plans with the same time frame as before. Bill and Dawn now had their baby and Dawn was beginning to regain her strength. Suddenly their plans were over shadowed when Marie asked Nick what Kevin had told him about Lisa. They both sat their silently praying for her recovery before Marie dozed off. Nick slowly slid off the couch and let her lay down. He picked up a blanket and covered her. He then sat in the rocking chair where he too dozed off.

***

Kevin met Bill and Dawn the instant they entered the waiting room. "I'm glad you are both here." He said, now somewhat relieved.

"Kevin what's going on? Nick said Lisa was hurt bad? What happened and why is she in Red Deer?" Bill asked, demanding some answers.

"She has been shot." Kevin said, looking at his hands, which were a few hours ago covered with Lisa's blood.

"Shot!!" Bill and Dawn said in unison.

"By who?" Bill asked.

"Please sit down, it's a long story. I think it's time you knew everything."

Kevin said. He proceeded to tell them of the beating Lisa got at the hands of Franklin, and how she asked everyone to promise not to tell her parents. She had said they had enough problems without hers. Kevin saw Bill's clinched fist and knew exactly how he felt. He told how they were together when he saw Franklin watching them. This is where Kevin had to be careful, not to give away Jackie and Darcy's secret. He did wonder when they would finally tell their parents they were married.

"So that is why you came to Red Deer together." Dawn said.

"I thought I could throw him off track, but I'm sorry I shouldn't have led him here. It was because of that you almost lost your baby." Kevin said.

"What happened tonight?" Bill asked.

Kevin told them what had happened at the house, but he did not know how Lisa got there or anything prior to that. He only knew that Franklin left in his car, with the police in hot pursuit.

"Have you heard anything from the doctors?" Dawn asked.

"No they haven't told me anything." Kevin said beginning to pace the floor.

Bill got up to find a nurse. He was hoping to get some news about his daughter's condition.

"The doctor will be in to talk to you shortly." She told him.

Bill went back to join Kevin in pacing the floor, both stopping when the doctor entered the room.

"Are you Mr. and Mrs. Spencer?" He asked.

"Yes." Bill said. Dawn quickly went over to Bill then took his hand in hers.

"Your daughter is out of surgery. She is a very lucky girl. The bullet wasn't that far from her heart and she has lost a lot of blood. It did a fair amount of damage inside and will take some time to heal. She is stable, but in very critical condition. She will have to take it easy for awhile." The doctor told them. Bill took Dawn in his arms when she began to cry.

"Can we go see her?" Bill asked.

"Only for a few minutes." the doctor said.

Kevin decided to stay back and let her parents go in alone. But Bill put his arm around Kevin, telling him to join them, as they walked to the room where Lisa lay so very still and pale.

Dawn went quickly to her daughter's side and began stroking

Book 1 of the ***Mountains and Valleys of Life***

her blonde hair.

"Lisa its Mom. Everything is going to be ok now. You are safe and everything is going to be all right. Dad and Kevin are here too." Bill went to the opposite side of the bed, while Kevin stood at the bottom of the bed, rubbing the top of Lisa's feet.

Bill bent over and kissed his daughter on her forehead. He took his daughter's hand in his and said. "Lisa, no one will hurt you again. We love you and want to take you home. Everything is going to be all right, from now on."

Kevin kept rubbing her feet and for a moment he thought he felt her move them, but wasn't sure. The nurse soon came in, saying it was best if they let her rest. She told them to go home and get some rest, as there wasn't much they could do now. There was a good chance she would be awake by morning.

Bill went and placed his strong but gentle hands on Dawn's shoulder. "Come Dawn, you need your rest. We'll come back in the morning." Bill said.

Dawn hesitated, but then kissed her daughter telling her she would be back to see her, in the morning.

"Kevin do you have your car here? No I came with the police, but if you don't mind I would like to stay for a while. I made a promise to Lisa, before they took her away, that I wouldn't leave her. If you don't mind, I would like to keep that promise." Kevin said looking at Lisa.

Bill and Dawn smiled at each other. They began to wonder if Kevin was beginning to fall in love with their daughter. "Ok son." Bill said placing his hand on Kevin's shoulder. "If anything comes up give us a call."

"I will Mr. Spencer and - -" he took Bill's arm, leading him away from Dawn.

"There's blood on the floor in the hall. I didn't take time to clean it up. I don't think there is any on the rug, but I'm not sure." Kevin said. "Oh and there is a broken window somewhere. I heard it break just before the police came." Kevin added.

"Thanks Kevin, I'll check into that. I don't know if I can hide the blood from Dawn, but I'll see what I can do. Thanks for warning me." Bill said, going back to Dawn side.

"Is everything all right?" Dawn asked, when they left the hospital.

"Yes, Kevin said there is a broken window somewhere, because he heard glass breaking, and there is a few things to clean up." Bill said.

* * *

Kevin asked the nurse, if he could sit quietly on the chair beside Lisa's bed. The nurse hesitated for a moment. "If you don't disturber her too much." she said.

Kevin went over and stroked Lisa brow. "Sweetheart its Kevin. I promised I wouldn't leave you. I will be sitting here in the chair when you wake up. I love you Lisa, and I want to be with you and protect you, so no one will ever hurt you again." Kevin sat on the chair watching her. Her face was pale and there were two intravenous bags hanging on the pole. Just then the police officer came to the door. He motioned for Kevin to come out of the room.

"Have you called her parents?" He asked.

"Yes they just left to go to the house, but I wanted to stay here." Kevin told him.

"Where is Franklin?" Kevin asked suddenly. "Is there any chance he may show up here?" Kevin asked nervously.

"No, he won't bother her anymore." The officer said.

"How can you be so sure?" Kevin said angrily.

"Calm down son, it's all over. He had a fatal accident, when we went after him." The officer said.

"You mean he's dead?" Kevin asked.

"I'm afraid so, but how is your girlfriend." The officer asked.

"She's stable and all I can do is Pray." Kevin said sadly.

"Just keep doing that." The officer said laying his hand on Kevin's shoulder.

After he left, Kevin sat in the chair for several hours. It wasn't long before he realized it was morning and Lisa had not stirred. He left for a moment to make a phone call. He had to tell his new boss why he would not make it in for work. Being a new job, he was afraid what might be said, but after explaining to his boss the whole story, he was told it was all right for today. Kevin was glad to have gotten an understanding boss, but Kevin did promised to be at work the following morning. He went back to Lisa's room and took her hand. "Hey Lisa I'm still here. I haven't left you as I promised." Kevin said. It was then Lisa opened her eyes slightly to look at him. He saw the flicker of a smile then she drifted off to sleep again. When Dawn and Bill arrived, Kevin was holding Lisa's hand with his head lying on the bed. He was fast asleep. Kevin jumped when Bill touched his shoulder.

"Has she woken up yet?" Dawn asked

"She did for just a moment, but then went back to sleep." Kevin said.

"Kevin, why don't you go to the cafeteria and have your breakfast." Bill said.

"I might do that." Kevin said getting up to moved his chair against the wall.

"I'll walk with you." Dawn said. "Bill I'm going to call home to check on how Marie is making out with Jeffrey."

"That might be a good idea." Bill said, watching them walk out of the room.

Lisa began to slowly move her head. Bill went quickly to her side. "Lisa." He called stroking her forehead.

Lisa slowly opened her eyes, letting them focus slowly on her Father. "Dad?" She said softly.

"Yes Lisa, it's me, you're going to be all right." Bill said.

"Where is Kevin? Is he all right?" Lisa suddenly asked, trying to get up, but the pain that shot through her upper body made her moan and quickly layback.

Bill gently laid his hand on her right shoulder saying. "Kevin is fine. I just sent him to go get something to eat. He has been by your side all night." Bill told her.

Lisa closed her eyes letting the pain ease before looking at her Father. "Dad why do we let people, who we think care for us, hurt us?" Lisa asked.

"I don't know Lisa." Maybe we are too trusting, and rely on our poor judgments instead of asking God. We seem to jump in with both feet and then pride won't let us admit we made a bad mistake." Bill said.

Lisa lay there a moment. "You know Dad, you asked if I would forgive you, and I thought I never would but I am to blame for bringing Franklin into the family. I blamed you for Mom being here, instead of at home with you, we both let someone almost ruin our lives and in so doing …I …almost made you and Mom lose the baby." She said, tears running down her face. "Will you forgive me?" Lisa said, looking at her Father.

"Lisa that was not your fault and I don't want you blaming yourself for that." Bill said.

"You have nothing to be forgiven for, you are a beautiful young lady and don't let guys like Franklin put you down, and make you feel worthless and tell you everything is your fault. Mind you, don't think your perfect either." He said tapping the end of her nose in the way he did when he teased her as a child.

"I forgive you Dad. Your still a great Dad and I love you." Lisa said.

Bill kissed her on the forehead. "I don't think I deserve that, but thank-you. I love you too Lisa." Bill said as Dawn entered the room. "How is the baby?" Bill asked.

"He's fine, but it's taking Marie a bit of getting used to, but Nick is helping her."

Dawn said. "I think I should get back by evening though. Lisa it's good to see you awake. How are you feeling?" Dawn asked.

"I feel so tired. It hurts a lot, but otherwise, fine I guess. Us Spencer women are tough. We keep on fighting no matter what happens." Lisa said taking her Mothers hand.

"I guess that's what us men like about you." Came Kevin's

voice from the door.

Lisa looked at him and blushed, then quickly looking away.

"How you doing?" Kevin asked going to the foot of the bed, rubbing her feet as he had before.

"That's what I felt." Lisa said looking at him. "Keep doing that it feels good."

"Thanks for saving my life, again." Lisa said.

"Well he won't try that again, so you don't have to worry." Kevin told her.

"How can you be so sure of that?" Bill asked.

Kevin looked at Lisa then back at Bill. "He's dead." Kevin told them.

"Oh!" Lisa gasped. "I didn't want him dead. I just wanted him to go away."

"What happened?" Dawn asked softly.

"The police were chasing him and somehow he crashed his car and was killed."

Kevin told them. It was then he saw tears stream down Lisa's face. How could she care for someone like that? After all he had tried twice to kill her.

Dawn stroked her Daughter's forehead. "Lisa it's ok, it's all over. Just remember God is in control, and has a reason for allowing these things to happen."

It was obvious that Lisa was getting very tired. Dawn told her they would all leave so she could rest.

Lisa looked at Kevin standing at the end of the bed. He was about 5' 10" which was a couple inches taller then her. He was about 150 pounds, and she had realized he was very strong for his size. She watched him run his fingers through his black hair, but she could not see the color of his eyes, but she was sure they were brown like hers. It was then he looked at her. The smile that crossed his face, even showed in his eyes. Lisa tried to look away but for some reason she couldn't. Lisa's parents left the room, but Kevin lingered behind. He stopped rubbing her feet, and came up beside her. He reached out to stroke her cheek gently with his finger. Then bending over he kissed her gently on the forehead, before following her parents. When he left Lisa's heart pounded wildly at the thought of his gentle kiss but tiredness took over and she drifted off to sleep.

By evening Lisa was no longer on the critical list, but was upgraded to stable.

Even though her parents did not feel good about leaving her, they had to get home to their infant son. Kevin promised to look after Lisa. Then the moment she was released from the hospital, he would bring her home, where her parents could nurse her back to health.

Chapter 20

It was evening when Bill and Dawn arrived back home, Nick was watching tv and Marie was rocking the baby while feeding him his bottle. Dawn quickly went to Marie.

"How has he been?" Dawn asked.

"He was fine and we quite enjoyed looking after him." Marie said, looking at Nick with a twinkle in her eye.

Dawn looked at the two of them. There was no doubt that they had made up.

Dawn took her son from Marie. "All right you two, what else happened here?" Dawn asked.

Nick sat drinking his coffee, and casually said. "Marie has once again accepted my proposal."

Bill went over and shook Nick's hand, congratulating them once again. He was glad everything seemed to be working out in spite of everything.

"How is Lisa?" Marie asked on a somber note.

"She's coming along slowly. She lost a lot of blood and is very weak yet, but she is in fairly good spirits," Dawn said.

"I have a feeling that has something to do with your son." Bill said looking at Nick. "I'm very grateful to him for saving Lisa's life. You can be proud of him." Bill added.

Nick and Marie didn't want to ask to many question, but knew both Bill and Dawn looked as if they could use a good nights rest.

"Thanks for everything." Dawn said.

Will Love Conquer All?

"I will talk to you tomorrow. Now you both try to get some sleep." Marie said.

Bill and Dawn watched out the window as Nick and Marie drove off, each in their own vehicles.

Bill stroked his sons head then put his arm around Dawn, as they went to their bedroom. Bill sat on the bed watching Dawn change Jeffrey's diaper. She was about to place him in the cradle when Bill interrupted. "Let me hold." Bill said. Dawn turned to hand their son to his Father. She sat beside, watching Bill talk to his son, while Jeffrey griped Bill's finger and hung on. Bill said proudly. "He has quite a grip for a little guy."

"Well, Father like son." Dawn said, placing her arm around Bill.

"Now aren't you glad we didn't listen to the doctor, when he wanted to destroy our sons life?" Dawn asked.

Bill got very quiet for several moments while looking at his little son. "I was so afraid of losing you Dawn. As I sit here holding our son, I can't even imagine how I would have felt if I would have consented to destroying his life." Bill said.

"It's all over now, and we have each other and a healthy baby boy." Dawn said.

Bill looked at Dawn. "Lately I'm getting a glimpse of what Job in the Bible, must have felt like. Between the deaths and the near deaths in our family, plus people trying to pull our family apart and what have you. I feel almost like we're being tested, like him." Bill said.

"Maybe we are." Dawn said. "Maybe the worst is over and things will turn around for us now. God has been faithful, even though sometimes I felt like he was far away. At times I felt like I couldn't handle any more," Dawn said

"I felt the same way," Bill added. He kissed his son, then handed him back to Dawn. Dawn lovingly looked at her son then kissed him, before laying him gently in his cradle. Both Bill and Dawn stood hand in hand rocking their son to sleep, in the cradle that was made by a Father's loving hands. Bill turned to Dawn. Taking her in his arms he held her tight as she laid her head on his chest. Dawn had always felt so comfortable in Bill's arms and with time that never changed. She clung to him for several moments in silence as they just enjoyed being there together.

"I will always love you Bill," Dawn said.

"I love you too and now we better get some rest." Bill said kissing his wife tenderly, before releasing her.

* * *

Dawn was up early the next morning with the baby. "Good morning." Dawn said when Bill entered the kitchen. "Did you have a good sleep?" Dawn asked.

"Not really." Bill said on his way to the bathroom.

Dawn had Bill's breakfast waiting on the table when he sat down. "Why didn't you sleep good last night?" Dawn asked.

"I kept thinking of how Lisa was treated by Franklin, and we never knew about it." Bill said.

"I had a feeling something was wrong at Christmas, when they came in from their walk, she had a bruise on her face and Franklin had said she had fallen on a log but it didn't look that way to me." Dawn said.

"Why didn't you tell me?" Bill said.

"What could we do? I asked Lisa about it, then Jackie talked to her. He seemed to be so nice after that. I thought perhaps I was wrong." Dawn said.

"Well, it is sad his life had to end that way, but on the other hand he can't hurt her any more. I have a feeling there's something happening between Kevin and Lisa though." Bill said.

"Would that bother you, seeing he is Nick's son?" Dawn asked.

"At first it may have, but not anymore." Bill said. "I have actually gotten to like his kids. They seem very sensible and were brought up to go to church. They're much like ours in not going very often, but I guess we did that at first too." Bill said.

"Are you going to work in your shop today?" Dawn asked.

"Yes, I have a few things I just have to finish. I got behind in a few orders the past while, and I'm just beginning to get caught up." Bill said.

"I wish I could help you, but until Jeffrey is bigger, I don't want to take him out too much yet." Dawn said, putting some dishes in the sink.

"No you just do your things in here. I'm fine, just knowing your near." Bill said smiling at her.

When Bill had gone out to work, Dawn did her laundry, and house cleaning. She had just given Jeffrey a bath, when Marie knocked on the door.

"Hi Marie. Come on in." Dawn said.

Marie went straight to Jeffrey who was lying in his bouncer. "I never knew until the other day what it would be like to have a baby around." Marie said.

"Well, how did it feel?" Dawn said studying her.

"It felt good. A lot of work, but good." Marie said thoughtfully.

"Do you think Nick and you will have a little one some day? Have you talked about it?" Dawn asked.

"Not until the other day. Nick asked me if I wanted a baby and I said yes."

Marie said gleaming. "Well, not until after we are married." She added.

"Oh Marie I am so happy everything turned out for you." Dawn said.

Marie's smile disappeared when she looked at Dawn. "Dawn I'm so sorry for ever believing Janice. I feel like a total jerk. Will you forgive me?" Marie asked.

"Of course I will. It did hurt to see how Janice had turned everyone against me." Dawn said. "Bill and I talked the other night about Job's life in the Bible. It seems to us that our lives, the past while, has been one test after another. But I have a feeling things are going to get better now." Dawn said. "Jeffrey is healthy and growing, and Lisa is on her way to recovery, and I have been feeling better and getting my strength back. Darcy is fine as far as I know, but it is funny that we haven't talked to him much lately." Dawn said thoughtfully.

"That's strange. Nick told me the similar thing about Jackie." Marie said, as they looked at each other. "You don't suppose those two have been up to something, do you?" Marie asked.

"That wouldn't surprise me, especially the way Darcy looked at her, the last time I saw them together." Dawn added. "Enough talking about my children, how about your wedding plans?"

"Well, we decided to have it the same time as before. That is if it's all right with you and Bill?" Marie said, looking questionably at Dawn.

"Oh of course. Lisa will be recuperating at home when she gets out of the hospital and I'm sure she would be only too happy to help. Otherwise she would go nuts at home, with us old folks." Dawn said.

"Oh Dawn it's so close and I am getting nervous and excited all at the same time." Marie said

"That's natural, but there is nothing that can compare to being with someone you love and that love you in return." Dawn said, going over to Jeffrey as he began to fuss.

"Jeffrey reminds me of Bill sometimes. Bill likes to fuss for attention once and a while to, you will find that out." Dawn said.

"I'll remember that." Marie said.

Dawn and Marie spent most of the day discussing Nick and Marie's upcoming wedding. When Dawn asked Marie to stay for supper, she declined, because she said Nick had already made other arrangements for the evening.

Bill came up to the house, just as Marie was leaving. "What have you two been up to all afternoon?" Bill asked casually.

"Discussing men." Marie said cheerfully.

"Well, was it good or bad?" Bill asked, teasing her.

"We decided they could act like children, sometimes." Marie's replied.

"Well, that can be good or bad." Bill added. "Maybe us men feel the same way about you women, but we love you anyhow."

Will Love Conquer All?

Bill said still teasing Marie.

"Oh, you men." Marie said blushing, as she walked to her car.

"Behave yourself." Bill said shaking his finger at Marie, who just smiled and waved as she drove off.

Bill got cleaned up for supper, and as they began to eat Bill said. "I was thinking about building a couple of arches for the backyard, for the wedding. What do you think?" Bill asked Dawn.

"Bill, I think that would be a great idea. Marie would love that." Dawn said.

"Well then, after I finish the project I'm on, I'll build them. Have you called to see how Lisa is today?" Bill asked.

"No, I was going to do that after supper. She has a phone by her bed, so we can both talk to her." Dawn said.

After Dawn cleaned up the dishes, she dialed the hospital and asked for Lisa's room. "Hi, Lisa. How are you doing today?" Dawn asked.

"Better I guess. I got rid if all the intravenous, so that makes me feel better. They got me up today and I walked around my room but I still feel weak." Lisa added.

"It will take time, so don't over do it, I will let you talk to your Dad." Dawn said. Bill took the phone from Dawn and asked Lisa how things were going. He asked her if this was going to interfere with her last bit of school.

To which Lisa replied that Kevin was checking into it for her. Bill said that he would talk to her later seeing Kevin had just arrived.

***

Kevin stood staring out the window.

"Is something wrong?" Lisa asked Kevin.

"No." Kevin said turning to look at her.

He was beginning to make her nervous and by not talking and it was also annoying. "By the way." Lisa said. "Why were you at the house the other night?"

"I've been staying there." Kevin said.

"Why?" Lisa asked curiously.

"Because I have to have a place to stay." He said teasing her.

Lisa was getting upset, for having to drag every word out of him. "What about your job and place in Edmonton?" she asked.

"I quit and have a new job here. I'm still looking for a place, and until then your parents allowed me to stay downstairs." Kevin said.

"Oh!!" Lisa said, surprised that he had left without her hearing about it.

"You haven't said why you suddenly appeared at the house and how you got there." Kevin said.

"I don't really know why I came." Lisa said with a far away look in her eyes. "I just had a very strong feeling that I had to leave Edmonton," she said.

"How did you get to Red Deer?" Kevin asked.

"I took a bus and then a cab to the house. I had just unlocked the door when the cab driver drove off. Then for some reason I looked back and that was when I saw Franklin walking across the street towards me. It was as if he had been sitting there waiting for me." Lisa said with a terrifying look in her eyes. "I quickly unlocked the door and went into the house, but before I turned to lock the door, it felt like someone hit me hard on the shoulder. Thankfully I got the door locked before I fell to the floor, well, you know the rest." Lisa said. "Do you think it was God that lead me here?" Lisa asked looking up at Kevin.

"If I had stayed in Edmonton, maybe he would have shot me while I was alone with no one to help me." Lisa said as chills ran through her body and tears began to steam down her face.

"I think you might be right, it's all over and you are safe now." Kevin told her.

"What are your plans when you finish school?" Kevin asked, still watching at her.

"I don't know for sure." Lisa said, pulling the covers around her, as she began to feel cold.

Kevin took the blanket from the foot end of the bed, and

began to cover her with it. When their hands touched, he gently took her hand. Kevin stood there staring into her eyes. Then slowly he bent over to kiss her lightly on the lips.

Lisa heart felt like it was beating loud enough for him to hear. She had never been with anyone who could make her feel this way. Their eyes locked as he once again stood studying her face, as if waiting for her permission to do it again. Kevin touched her cheek gently with his finger, then bent over and kissed her again, but this time she eagerly returned his kiss. Kevin took her gently in his arm, careful not to hurt her wounded shoulder.

"I love you Lisa, I can only hope that you feel the same. I promise no one will every hurt you again." He said looking into her eyes.

"As I recall you made another promise too." Lisa said studying his brown eyes.

"What was that?" Kevin asked.

Lisa hesitated, letting everything sink in, before telling him. "You promised you would never leave me."

Kevin smiled. "Is that what you really want?" He asked.

Lisa put her arms around his neck. "Kiss me again and see if you can guess what my answer is?" she said. Kevin bent over and kissed her gently. Lisa wrapped her arms around him and eagerly returned his kiss. He held her tighter while thinking that he had almost lost her.

Lisa felt the sharp pain in her shoulder, but her love for Kevin over weighed the pain. Kevin suddenly released his grip on her. "Oh sweetheart, I am sorry I forgot about your shoulder."

"That's ok, so did I." Lisa said.

"Well?" Kevin asked. "Do I get your answer?"

"You mean after that, you still need one." Lisa said holding his hand as she smiled up at him.

"No, but I still want to hear you tell me." Kevin said studying her facial expression.

"Lisa brought Kevin's hand to her lips and kissed it. Looking deep into his eyes. "Yes Kevin, I would like for you to keep that promise. I love you and I want to be with you."

Kevin kissed her hand. "In that case Lisa Spencer, will you marry me?" He put his fingers on her lips to stop her from answering and added. "It may be next fall before I'll make enough to support us, so you have to be willing to wait." Kevin said.

"That sounds fine with me as long as I know we will be together and you won't leave me. I will gladly wait until then." Lisa said squeezing his hand.

Kevin pulled out a small ring box, and opened it. He took out the ring and placed it on Lisa's finger. "With this ring, we are officially engaged. I promise you, from this time on, I belong to you and you alone." Kevin said.

"Oh Kevin it is beautiful. I promise to you that I will be true to you, until death." They kissed each other for some time as a seal of their promises.

"When do you think we should tell your parents?" Kevin asked.

"Well, I will tell you one thing. I won't keep it a secret like Darcy and Jackie," Lisa said. "I will never take this ring off, but it must have cost you a fortune." Lisa said looking at her ring.

"Nothing is to expensive for a once in a life time commitment." Kevin said.

Kevin looked at Lisa for a moment. "Could you really tell by my kiss that you wanted me?"

Lisa smiled back at him with a gleam in her eye. "Definitely. All us Spencer women can tell by a kiss, remember." she said.

"Poor Dad, It must have been hard to lose the one you love, just because of a kiss." Kevin said.

They both started to laugh. "Yes but he met someone else he loves and I'm glad he did or I, wouldn't have you now."

"That works both ways." Kevin replied.

* * *

It was several days later and the weather was beginning to

turning warm again. Spring was here. Lisa was released from the hospital and Kevin took her home to her parents, where she was to recuperate. Kevin and Lisa were surprised to see Darcy and Jackie there when they drove in.

The four of them had a moment alone, before Lisa and Darcy's parents came out. Jackie said nervously. "We told Dad and Marie to come over this evening, and we are going to finally tell them we are married."

"Everything seems to have settled down now and we felt we should tell them before Nick and Marie's wedding next month." Darcy said putting his arm around Jackie, looking at her in a moon struck fashion.

Kevin looked at Lisa, when Darcy and Jackie turned their attention to each other. He leaned over to Lisa, and said. "Do you think you can take your ring off just long enough for them to tell our parents first?"

Lisa made a face at him, but slipped off her ring giving it to Kevin to put in his pocket until later.

"Don't worry, I'll see you get it back as soon as possible." He said putting his arm around her, giving her a squeeze as he pulled her close to him. Kevin released Lisa when he saw her Mother coming out to give Lisa a hug. She led Lisa into the house with the rest trailing behind. Soon they all sat around the table talking, and playing with their baby brother.

Dawn and Bill decided to call Nick and Marie and ask them to join them for supper, not knowing Darcy and Jackie had told them to come over later.

When Nick and Marie arrived, Nick scolded Jackie for not keeping in contact, to which she gave the excuse that she had been rather busy the past while. Nick never replied, but caught the look that passed from Darcy to Jackie. Nick frowned at the thought that perhaps they had already moved in together, which he did not agree with.

Marie and Jackie began to pitch in and help with supper. Lisa said she still had an excuse, and would sit and keep Jeffrey occupied, while the men went into the living room, to wait until supper was ready.

"I'm sorry we didn't come to see you when you were in the hospital, Lisa, but Kevin did keep us updated on all that was going on." Jackie said.

"I wouldn't want to go through that again. Ever!" Lisa said.

"What have you and Darcy been up to? Neither Darcy or you have been keeping in touch as much lately." Dawn said to Jackie.

Jackie was nervous. She was not sure what to say, when Lisa looked at her Mother and said. "Mom you know Darcy's always on the road, and Jackie didn't want to interfere with Nick and Marie life. Especially not with everything that had been going on."

Jackie gave Lisa a thankful glance. Dawn left it at that, but had a feeling there was something more that was not being said. Soon it was time to call the men to come for supper. Bill gave thanks for the food then everyone began to eat, and talk. Jackie and Darcy were somewhat quieter than usual and kept glancing at one another nervously. Nick noticed their unusual behaviour, and could stand it no longer.

"What is it with you two? Something is going on and I think you should tell us." Nick demanded. The room became very quite and all eyes except Kevin and Lisa's, were on Darcy and Jackie. They looked at each other wondering what would happen next.

Darcy stood up, and looked at Jackie. "We were going to wait until later to tell you, but I guess now is as good a time as any. Jackie and I are married." he said.

Everyone gasped and then you could have heard a pin drop.

"Come on you guys. You should be happy for them. I know we are." Lisa said looking at Kevin.

"You mean you knew?" Dawn asked, looking at Kevin and Lisa.

Lisa nudged Kevin, and he knowingly handed her the ring, which she slipped on under the table. Darcy saw how pale Jackie looked, so he sat down and took her hand.

They had hoped for a happier reaction, but instead they feared what would be said next.

"If I may at the same time, announce that Lisa and I too are engaged." Kevin said, putting his hand up to stop his Father from say something. "Lisa and I are planning to first get married next fall, so I hope none of you have anything against a long engagement. Now I want to be the first to once again congratulate my sister and my brother in law." Kevin said getting up to give his sister a hug. "They will come around, it's just the initial shock. Give it a few moments." Kevin said whispering to her, before going over to shake Darcy's hand.

Dawn was the next to get up and congratulate Jackie and welcoming her into their family with a hug. "It isn't that I don't approve, it's just that I always thought weddings should have family around. I wanted all my children to have a memorable wedding."

Dawn said.

"Oh but ours was." Jackie said.

"Well." Nick said. "Let's hear about it then."

Darcy started by telling them about the night they had come home to find Janice here and his Mother gone.

Bill sat quietly listening, once again ashamed of being made a fool of by Janice.

He was the cause of his son and Jackie's eloping.

Darcy went on to tell them of how they had gone to Nick's to find him upset over Marie's phone call and how he had told them he felt that Darcy and Jackie loved each other. Darcy reminded Nick that he said if they did love each other they should be sure to tell each other before it was too late. Dawn and Nick glanced at each other briefly before turning their attention to what Darcy was saying. "That was when I knew I wanted.

Jackie to marry me as I wasn't going to risk losing her." Darcy said. "She was hesitant at first, but then she did consent. That is when we told Kevin and Lisa we wanted them to be part of our wedding?" he said.

"Tell them about your wedding Jackie." Lisa said. "It was actually very special."

Jackie looked at Darcy and smiled, as she relived her wedding day. She told them of the dress Darcy had bought her and how even some people in the church got involved. "We had a private supper, then went to the honeymoon suite Darcy had booked for us."

"It was really very romantic." Jackie said, looking into her husband's eyes. "We couldn't be happier and are sorry we didn't tell you sooner. We hope you won't hold it against us just because we wanted to be with each other." Jackie said.

Nick got up and hugged his daughter. "I am happy for you. It's just that I had hoped to be there to give you away," he said.

"I'm sorry Dad, but with everything that happened we just couldn't take the chance of losing each other, as you know only to well." Jackie said.

Nick then went to welcome Darcy, into his family as well. Then going to Kevin and Lisa he congratulated them, but warned them not to try the same thing.

Bill was the last to congratulate his son. He told him to always love and respect his wife, and then going to Jackie, he welcomed her into their family. He told her that he was proud to have her as his daughter in law.

"I am not a bit surprised to hear you two are engaged. After Kevin had said he promised Lisa that he would never leave her, I knew it would be happening sooner or later. Congratulations and I do wish the best for you two." Bill said congratulating Kevin and Lisa. But he also told them not to do the same as Darcy and Jackie.

"Thanks, Dad. Now that is enough of this, I'm hungry and my food is getting cold." Lisa said

Everyone sat down and began eating. "Marie, I want to hear all about your wedding plans." Lisa said noticing she was obviously feeling left out.

"Oh it's coming together slowly." She said casually.

Dawn then realized what Lisa was doing. She was proud of her daughter for thinking of someone else, even with her exciting news. Marie was definitely feeling like someone had stolen her thunder. Dawn joined in with Lisa and Jackie, as they talked about Nick and Marie's up coming wedding.

"Do you mind if I help in even some small way?" Lisa asked Marie, who now was beginning to feel better.

"I think we could use all the help we can get, especially as the day comes closer. If you and Jackie wouldn't mind, you could help do the decorating. It would be appreciated." Marie said. Nick winked at her, sending her heart racing.

"Oh of course." both girls said.

"I think us men will just stay out of your way." Bill said, when everyone was done eating. "What do you say us men go into the other room and let the ladies do their planning?" To which they all agreed as all four men left the room.

Marie congratulated both Jackie and Lisa. "I'm really happy for both of you."

Marie said hugging the girls.

As the girls went to start washing the dishes Marie turned to Dawn. "You know Dawn I believe you were right. Things are beginning to turn around for the better."

After dishes everyone went to sit in the living room, but Dawn stepped outside to feed Pup the scraps. She took in a deep breath of fresh air, then stood staring up at the trees, not really seeing them but thinking of how fast her children had grown up. She jumped when see felt someone touched her arm.

"I'm sorry," Nick said. "I didn't mean to startle you. I hoped I could talk to you in private for a moment." He said looking at her. "You know it's funny. Our parents had hoped we would someday get married, which never happened. But tonight we are told that our families were brought together through both of our children. I just wanted to also tell you that you might be right." Nick added.

"About what?" Dawn asked.

"You told me once that I loved you differently then I loved my wife and Marie and something about wanting something I couldn't have." Nick said. "I guess I realized that, when I almost lost Marie. When she told me that she wouldn't marry me, it really hurt. I will never forget you and I hope we can always be friends." Nick said.

"That we always will be, and I hope I can be there for you and Marie just as you were there for Bill and I." Dawn said.

Nick leaned over and kissed Dawn on the cheek. It was that lingering look and the same gleam in his eyes, before he went back in to join the others that left her a bit unnerved.

Just then Bill came from around the corner and took Dawn in his arms. "I love you." Bill said.

"Were you listening to us?" Dawn asked.

"Marie and I both were. We came out to see where you were, but then we didn't want to interfere. We both heard what was said, which just confirmed our love for each other. I'm sorry, I guess we shouldn't have been listening." Bill said apologizing.

"There is nothing to hide," Dawn said. "You told me a long time ago that our love for each other would conquer all and Bill, after tonight I believe that even more."

"Our children have seen how with Gods help, our love for each other has withstood the good and the bad. I believed theirs will too if they turn their lives over to him."

Dawn laid her head on Bill's chest, as they stood there holding each other. She never wanted to see the day that Bill would no longer hold her in his arms. "I will always Love you Bill." Dawn said. They kissed each other, knowing their love was definitely until death do us part.

Printed in Canada